His compassion,
his vision captivated her....

Would it open the door
to her heart?

BLIND FAITH

Portraits

Blind Faith
Masquerade
Stillpoint

BLIND FAITH

JUDITH PELLA

BETHANY HOUSE PUBLISHERS
MINNEAPOLIS, MINNESOTA 55438

Blind Faith
Copyright © 1996
Judith Pella

Cover illustration by William Graf

The characters and events in this book are fictitious. Any similarity to real persons, living or dead, or to events is purely coincidental.

Scripture quotations are taken from the HOLY BIBLE, NEW INTERNATIONAL VERSION®. Copyright © 1973, 1978, 1984 by International Bible Society. Used by permission of Zondervan Publishing House. All rights reserved. The "NIV" and "New International Version" trademarks are registered in the United States Patent and Trademark Office by International Bible Society. Use of either trademark requires the permission of International Bible Society.

Verses marked KJV are from the King James Version of the Bible.

Published by Bethany House Publishers
A Ministry of Bethany Fellowship, Inc.
11300 Hampshire Avenue South
Minneapolis, Minnesota 55438

Printed in the United States of America.

Library of Congress Cataloging-in-Publication Data

Pella, Judith

    p. cm. — (Portraits)
    ISBN 1–55661–880–8

CIP applied for

CIP

To Janet Thurston,

whose friendship and support are so special to me.

In God, "may you live long and prosper."

JUDITH PELLA is the bestselling author/coauthor of six major fiction series, including the powerful and poignant LONE STAR LEGACY series and THE RUSSIANS. She and her family make their home in northern California.

"For now we see through a glass, darkly; but then face to face . . ."

1 Corinthians 13:12, KJV

Prologue

*T*he old man shuffled along with the gait of one who had no real concept of time. Indeed, he even looked like someone who belonged to a different time—an epoch long past when men wore felt fedoras and overcoats, suspenders to hold up trousers, and wing-tipped shoes. But this man's fedora was time-worn like his overcoat, and the shoes were scuffed. He'd purchased them secondhand to replace the stiff, new, and uncomfortable clothes given him by the State of California. He had hoped the secondhand clothes would help him feel more like himself—or at least more a part of the world he'd been isolated from for thirty-seven years.

But, of course, they didn't.

He should have tried to dress as he'd seen men on television dress. Jeans, T-shirts, baseball hats. But he had never worn a pair of blue jeans in his life. Back in nineteen fifty-nine, only kids and farmers wore jeans. And only baseball players wore billed caps. He'd feel too ridiculous in such duds.

It didn't matter much, though, if he never fit in to this new world. He wouldn't be in it much longer. And because of that he gave no more than a passing thought to his appearance. He had larger things to consider.

He paused at his destination at the end of a long hospital corridor. A sign on a door read "radiology." Grimacing, he opened the door and went in.

"Hello, Mr. Sullivan," said the receptionist. "Have a seat and we'll be with you in a minute."

There were two others in the waiting room, both with noses buried in magazines. Not wanting to appear sociable, he grabbed his own magazine, the only one left in the rack—a well-used copy of *Sunset*.

A slight smile flickered across his face that did nothing for his ashen, unshaven countenance nor his bloodshot, dull gray eyes. He had about as much in common with the idyllic, picturesque scenes in the magazine as he did with jeans, baseball caps, and the modern men who wore them. And as depressing as it was, he couldn't help but contrast his pitiful life with the photos before him.

He'd never had a real home. He spent his childhood in a Chicago slum. Even after he married and moved to San Francisco, he and his little family had bounced from one run-down dwelling to another, never staying longer than a few weeks in one place, always looking for something better. He'd had dreams back then. He wanted to be a big shot who could give his wife a fancy house with a decent kitchen and nice furniture.

Instead, all he ever gave her was grief.

But he wasn't entirely to blame. He'd been betrayed, double-crossed by someone he thought he could trust. He was left to take the fall for things he hadn't done. And as a result he had lost every-thing—his wife, his family, his freedom, his dreams. And the betrayer would pay as Charlie Sullivan himself had been paying for these past thirty-seven years and as he knew he would continue to pay until he died. He had long ago given up hope that he'd ever taste the sweet savor of revenge. Now, he knew it was fated to be so. His unexpected release from prison was proof.

It also gave him hope that perhaps he could make up for some other things as well. He had believed that some mistakes a guy made could never be fixed. Now he wasn't so certain.

It was too late to do anything for Betsy, who had died so young. But, was it possible he might have a chance to leave this lousy world with at least one good deed on his record? He doubted it would get him into heaven—he'd given up on that long ago—but maybe he could make up for some of his mistakes. And just maybe in the process he might be able to pass away with the assurance he'd be remembered by someone.

Aw, Charlie, you're an old fool.

Anyone who might have once cared had done without him all these years. They wouldn't appreciate him showing up. In fact, they'd probably just tell him to go to blazes. And he would deserve no less. It was pure selfishness for him to want to be part of their lives now.

Yet . . . it was so hard to leave knowing he was of less consequence than a speck of dust.

It would have been better if he'd been left to die in prison. But he was told it would be the humane thing to let him out so he could spend his final days a free man, perhaps making right the things he had botched before.

Could he do that without a few risks? His old enemy was now an important man. Surely Charlie couldn't get near him without danger to himself—though he didn't expect to survive his final deed on earth. But, until then, maybe one of his offspring would take pity on him. Not that he wanted pity. He just didn't want to be alone anymore.

"Mr. Sullivan, the doctor will see you now," said the receptionist.

Slowly, Charlie Sullivan rose, dreading what was coming. Maybe he ought to save everyone a lot of trouble and simply shoot himself. But he knew, however tempting it sometimes was, that he would never do it. His freedom was too dear to him to squander even a moment of it.

One

When the sun broke through the fog, it was bright and warm despite the cool breeze off the ocean. The intriguing display of light and shadow accompanying the sun combined to make for interesting images. Irene Lorenzo tried to make the most of it. On this northern California coast good weather was too fickle to waste.

The children seemed to know that, too. Adam and Mark were busy building a city in the sand for their Matchbox cars. They were barefooted and had insisted on wearing shorts and T-shirts in spite of the fact that it was the middle of October. Irene couldn't very well argue with the sun. But she carried their jeans and sweat shirts in a tote bag, just in case. Irene, not as hardy as the ten- and six-year-old boys, was garbed in Levi's and a flannel shirt. She'd been fooled too many times by the autumn sun.

Irene looked over her sketch. The two boys in the foreground, digging in the sand, were too "blah," not giving off the kind of vibrant motion Adam and Mark were displaying. As she tried to determine what was missing, one of her models rose and ran toward her.

"I'm hungry, Mom," said Mark.

"I've got some apples."

"No chips?"

"That'll just make you thirsty."

"I'm thirsty, too."

"Have an apple; it'll solve everything." She reached into her tote bag and withdrew a Golden Delicious. Mark extended a sandy paw. "Why don't you wash off in the water first?" Irene suggested.

"Aw!" the boy groused, then jogged off to the water's edge.

Irene smiled, her hazel eyes full of the affection she felt for her children. Mark hated baths—despised cleanliness of any sort. His half of the boys' bedroom would be a shambles if Irene didn't make him clean it. Adam, the exact opposite, seemed to thrive on order and neatness. Not for the first time, Irene wondered how much the past years had affected them. The smile on her face faded.

Their life had been so unsettled, and being the eldest, Adam had taken the brunt of that fact. Irene had fought hard against the divorce, but since it had become fact, even she had to admit the children's lives—and her own—had improved greatly. There had been room for nothing but improvement. Irene could hardly remember a time when her marriage had been good. Maybe in the beginning . . . for a short time. After all, she had fallen in love with Greg.

Irene met him in a Bible study group for singles. She had been attending the Bread of Life Baptist Church for years, nearly all her life. Greg had become a Christian at a concert and was new to the church—any church. Even with the touch of mischief in his eyes, his ready grin, and just as ready passion over spiritual matters, had immediately charmed not only her but just about everyone in the church. Everyone, that is, except Irene's mother. For some reason even Millie Lorenzo couldn't explain, she had never warmed up to the man. But Irene had paid little attention to the woman already known for being a bit critical.

Even now, however, Irene couldn't say Greg was purposely deceptive. He probably had been sincere in his new faith and no doubt did believe he loved Irene when they married a mere month after meeting. It was as much Irene's fault as anyone's for rushing into things, not getting to know Greg better before taking the matrimonial plunge. Millie always contended that Greg had pushed Irene. But Irene wasn't so sure. Or maybe she had been just as naive as her mother claimed.

At the time, Irene thought that as long as the man was a Christian, nothing else really mattered. Her first mistake.

What followed was a life that now, eleven years later, Irene wanted desperately to forget. Just a few months into marriage the roller coaster had begun. They changed homes almost as often as Greg changed jobs. She later learned that Greg had always been a drifter, wandering mostly around California, but also up and down the West Coast—even as far as Alaska. When his job in San Francisco fizzled out a few months after they were married, he said he wanted to leave the city where Irene had grown up. Hindsight told her that Greg had merely wanted to get her away from the influence of her family and friends. After that, they lived in Santa Rosa for a while, then farther north in Eureka, then in Oregon—Eugene, Portland, Medford . . . Irene couldn't remember all the towns.

She had hoped children would help settle him down, but it only made things worse by heaping more responsibility on a man who had a decided aversion to that very thing. Whether the drinking was a result of all this, or the cause, was irrelevant. It had begun slowly, building over the years until it became an issue in itself. But Greg was one of those *functional* alcoholics. He never lost a job because of drinking—he usually quit long before that could happen. In public he carried himself surprisingly well when drunk; at home he didn't bother. He wasn't physically abusive—but the yelling, the depression, the disinterest, was an abuse of an entirely different sort.

Irene had also hoped their faith would help, but that, too, seemed to do no good. She regularly prayed, attended support groups, and sought counseling. Greg would repent, then fall away just as regularly. Eventually she gave up on Greg, the church, even God.

What a life for two innocent children! In retrospect Irene knew it had been wrong to cling to the marriage because of them. But that hadn't been her only reason. Well-meaning church members kept telling her that if she just remained faithful God would reward her. Divorce was a horrible thing, they said, and if she left him she could never marry again. Forgive Greg as God forgave His children. So Irene stuck with the form of marriage long after it had ended in her heart.

The real irony, however, was that it had been Greg—not Irene—who had finally put an end to the sham.

"Irene, you're just no fun anymore," he had whined.

She had nearly laughed in his face. And when the divorce papers came, she had signed them with a dizzying sense of relief, as if she had just stepped off a long carnival ride. That had been a year ago. Since then she had moved back to the Bay Area, landed a job at a graphic design firm, and had even resumed her maiden name. The past was growing dimmer each day.

A shadow creeping over her sketchbook made Irene glance up at the sky. After less than a half hour, the fog was inching back over the sun. Well, it was time they got going anyway. They were expected at her parents' for a family dinner party.

She put the apple back in the tote bag; Mark had gotten side-tracked looking for shells and seemed to have lost interest in his growling stomach.

"Hey, guys! Let's start thinking about leaving," she called.

There were protests, especially from Adam, who had put a great deal of effort into his "city" and wasn't ready to leave it to the whim of the waves. She let them linger for another fifteen minutes, then coaxed them into the car. It was her grandmother's eighty-first birthday, and she didn't want the old girl to think she didn't care enough to be on time.

~~~

Irene had grown up in the Twin Peaks area of San Francisco, in a cozy, middle-class neighborhood, set on some of the hills that made the city famous. They had always been cramped in the four bedroom house, where parents, grandparents, and four children competed for space.

Now that Grandpa had died and the kids had all moved away, only Irene's parents and grandmother lived there. The place should have an empty feel to it. But it didn't seem any different. It was still cramped with lots of heavy old furniture, none of it fine enough to be considered antique. The floral upholstery, carpets, and drapes dated back to the 1970s, along with the slightly garish color scheme. Bric-a-brac and lace doilies were everywhere, and the walls were a veritable showcase of cheap prints—Blue Boy and Pink Lady, Whistler's Mother and a couple Norman Rockwells. But Irene loved every mismatched, tasteless nuance of the place, even the mingled smells of garlic and Pine Sol.

The house was on a steep, quiet street, and all the houses were so close they were practically attached. There was no front yard to speak of, and only a little more in the back. But Irene's father had made the most of his little plot of earth. Ray Lorenzo was in the landscaping business and had always considered their house to be the best advertisement for his business. Thus, he had introduced some very creative landscaping to their skimpy yard and even had a small vegetable garden in the back. His dahlias were in bloom now, their showy heads still bright in the ebbing sun.

Grandma was the first to greet them. She planted a moist, slightly scratchy kiss on each of their cheeks.

"Hi, Grandma! How are you doing?" said Irene.

"Not too bad for an old lady." At eighty-one, Theresa Sellese was a bit bent and definitely wrinkled, but she had almost as much energy as young Mark. A little woman, and shrinking, it seemed, by the inch every year. Her black hair, pulled into a matronly bun, was streaked with gray, but not enough to account for her age, and her sharp brown eyes were filled with wry amusement.

The boys dashed off into the living room where the sounds of a televised baseball game could be heard.

"Well, what strange voice am I hearing!" came Millie Lorenzo's voice from the kitchen. In a moment she appeared, drying her hands on a dish towel.

Irene cleared her throat and smiled weakly. She was well aware that it had been over a week since she had last seen her family. "Give me a break, Mom. I've worked overtime every day this week. And then art class—"

"So, you don't have a phone?"

"Oh, Millie, lighten up," said Theresa with a wink at Irene. "The girl does have a life, you know." Theresa prided herself on staying abreast of current slang.

"Work and school. What kind of life is that? When are you gonna meet a man?"

Irene groaned. How was it, even now that Irene was thirty-two, her mother still had the power to reduce her to an intimidated ten-year-old? But a new voice called from the adjacent living room, sparing Irene from having to respond to her mother's oft-repeated query.

"Hey, can you keep it down out there? This is the World Series, you know." Ray Lorenzo's passion for gardening was surpassed only by baseball—a passion he had passed on to his grandsons.

Irene poked her head into the room. Her father, sitting in his big, worn easy chair, was a small, compactly built man with gray hair and a balding pate, whom Irene had almost never seen wear anything but khaki pants and plaid flannel shirts. The kids were both sprawled on the couch, and all three had eyes glued to the Giants-Mariners game. Irene smiled a silent hello to her father, who replied with a wave.

The fragrance of spaghetti sauce, heavily laced with garlic and oregano, filled the air and enticed her into the kitchen. That smell could easily send Irene on a delightful trip down memory lane. Spaghetti on Sunday was more than a tradition in her family, and, she mused, if no one fixed it, the pots and pans would climb out of the cupboard and do it themselves. Irene's childhood had been a good one, very normal and for the most part pleasant, in spite of her mom's sometimes contentious nature.

"You look pale," said Millie. "Are you eating all right?"

"Yes. I just don't have time to get out in the sun—when it chooses to show itself."

"You work too much, and they can't be paying you decently. I mean, how much money can such a shoestring operation have? It's my grandchildren I worry about. They are growing boys and need good food."

"We're hardly starving," said Irene defensively. Her mother had wanted Irene to move in with them after the divorce, but she had instinctively known that would never work. Irene had yearned for independence, longed to be able to make it on her own, and knew it would never happen if she succumbed to such an arrangement with her parents.

Millie Lorenzo never was reticent about expressing her opinion. She was a strong woman, perhaps even domineering—especially when contrasted with the quiet, laid-back nature of her husband. But anyone who knew them well understood that Ray was very content with his marriage and seemed to have a good perspective on when to let his wife have her way and when to stand up to her. And though Millie could argue a point to the bitter end just because she was always so dead sure of herself, she also realized when her husband had reached his limit. She was far more deferring to him than she was to others.

Though as energetic as Theresa, Millie lacked her mother's cultivated sense of humor. Not that she didn't laugh and joke—she just could not laugh at herself. She had an intense pride in herself and her family; these things were simply not joking matters. And that pride was evident in her appearance. Her graying hair was colored—though she'd never admit it—to an auburn brown and beauty-shop styled every week. Her clothes were meticulous, and she tried to follow the fashions. Her one nemesis was her weight—thirty pounds more than it should have been. It eluded even her obstinate attentions.

"So, what do you hear from that no-good ex of yours?" asked Millie.

"Mom . . ."

"What? Are you gonna defend him?"

"No, I just don't want him spoken of like that when the kids might hear."

"They're gonna find out sooner or later what a jerk he is."

"Maybe she would rather it be later," offered Theresa.

Millie shrugged, obviously not willing to argue with her mother. "No child support or anything, I suppose?"

"It's just as well," said Irene. "I'd rather be completely independent of him."

"He does have an obligation," said Theresa.

"When did that matter to him, even when he was around?" said Millie.

"Can we talk about something else?" sighed Irene. "Will Connie and Norm be here soon?"

"They're late as usual," said Millie.

"Who can blame them with four kids to get ready?" said Theresa.

"I had four kids and was never late for anything."

Theresa chuckled. "My old memory must be better than yours, Millie."

With an irritated "Harrumph," Millie turned to her daughter and changed the subject. "Irene, would you start a salad?"

In another ten minutes a burst of activity at the front door, obviously the arrival of Irene's sister and family, drew them from their labors.

Two

Irene and Connie were only a year apart in age and just as close in relationship. The most difficult part of Irene's enforced exile from her home during her marriage had been the separation from her sister. There was an older sister who now lived on the East Coast and an older brother who lived in Los Angeles, but they had never been as much a part of Irene's life as Connie.

The younger of the two, Connie's petite frame was smaller by three inches and more pounds than Irene wanted to acknowledge. She also had naturally curly hair—something Irene, with her straight auburn tresses, had always envied. Connie's eyes were hazel, like her sister's, prompting some to believe they were twins, though neither could see much resemblance. In many respects the two were very different; Connie was athletic, outgoing, less introspective. But Irene's more serious, sensitive nature had always played well against their contrasts. Their dad called them two peas in the same pod.

After dinner that evening the two women, wanting some exercise after the heavy meal, went for a walk around the neighborhood. They talked for a while about their everyday lives—even though Irene lived only a couple blocks away from Connie in San Bruno and they saw each other almost daily, there were always many things to catch up on. The children, their homes and jobs, their friends. Sometimes the talk was trivial and seemingly frivolous, sometimes very deep, attesting to the many different levels of their relationship.

"Did I ever mention to you that we had a new fifth-grade teacher at school?" Connie said after the conversation drifted to their jobs.

"Yes," said Irene, slightly wary. The man was thirty-six, single, and not bad-looking, at least according to Connie's report a few weeks after school had started in September.

"Well, I've had a chance to get to know him better. His class is tutoring my first-graders in our cross-tutoring program."

"Uh-huh."

"He's a real nice guy."

"Too bad you're married."

"Come on, Irene."

"What do you want me to say? 'Oh, please, Connie, get me a date with him quick!'"

"Yes—exactly!"

"Well, I'm just not there yet."

"I could believe that, if it's true. I mean"—Connie added quickly when Irene opened her mouth defensively—"you must be enjoying your independence. That is perfectly understandable. But I just don't like to think you may be steering clear of relationships out of fear."

"Who would blame me if I were?"

"The point is, Reenie, you have to get over it sometime."

"Why? Maybe I'll stay single forever."

"Fine, if that's what you *want* to do. But is it?"

Irene sighed and absently brushed a strand of her shoulder-length hair out of her eyes. "I don't know. Sometimes single sounds just fine. But then, at times, I really envy what you and Norm have. I think how nice it would be to share my life with someone. But that person would have to be practically perfect to make me take the risk again."

"Or at least God's perfect choice for you."

"Oh, please, Connie! I'd rather he be an axe murderer than a Christian."

Connie nodded, looking smug.

"What's that look supposed to mean?" said Irene, irritated.

"You know what I think about all that."

"Right. My faith goes too deep for me to abandon it so easily."

"You've been a Christian all your life, Reenie. Remember, we walked together down the aisle at church. I was nine; you were ten. You held my hand—in fact, I think you were *dragging* me along with you."

"A lot has happened since then."

"I've never yet heard you deny the existence of God."

"No, but I'm working on it."

"Don't be glib, Reenie."

"I won't as long as you don't tell me you're praying for me."

Connie smiled, but said nothing.

They walked for a short while in silence, down a hill, turning a corner at the bottom. Irene wondered how, as kids, they had been able to ride their bikes up and down these hills as if they were flat. She was out of breath just at the thought of walking back up that hill to get home. Irene was suddenly struck with a yearning for those carefree younger years. What fun she and Connie used to have! They had even attended college together, until Irene quit in her third year to marry Greg. It seemed all the fun had stopped then.

"So, what about Don?" Connie was asking.

"Don who?"

"The teacher."

"It's not as if I haven't dated a few times since Greg left. Just never seriously enough to suit you or Mom."

"Yeah, the minute it starts to get serious, you stop seeing the man."

"Who says that's my fault?"

"No comment," Connie replied.

They were silent again as they ascended a hill on their way back home. It was steep enough to leave them panting as they crowned the top. When they reached their parents' doorstep, Irene paused before going back in.

"I'll think about it, okay?"

Connie's only response was a sly grin.

Irene didn't know if she'd do more than think about it. Those few dates she was so quick to mention had meant nothing to her. She had probably just agreed to go out in order to keep her family quiet.

Was she afraid?

Probably. How would she ever be sure of a man again? How would she know if he was being honest? And even if he was honest, how could she guard against it all falling apart later? What about the upheaval to her children?

Then there was the simple fact that she found the whole dating ritual to be a horrible ordeal, an agony to her shy nature. If God really did want to get her attention, he'd provide her with a man she could get to know without having to date, who also had impeccable moral and social credentials—totally risk-free.

Of course, no such man existed. There would always be an element of risk in any relationship. The real consideration was if she was

willing to take such a risk. Connie would say that with God supporting her she could. But Connie sometimes had a rather simplistic view
of spiritual matters. Her answers were hardly adequate when Irene
would probe, *"Wasn't God supporting me in the mess with Greg? Where
was God then? I felt like I was out there alone, deserted. Hung out to
dry, and forgotten when the rain came."*

*Sorry, Connie. God is going to have to go to some lengths to win me
back.*

As much as any man would have to do to win her love again.

Three

The noontime traffic was relentless, especially for the man standing on the corner of Montgomery and Market in downtown San Francisco—the financial district. He was six one with light, sandy hair and features sculpted into a firm but pleasing specimen. He stood with an air of assurance in his expensive tan cashmere suit. Only the tilt of his head, ear inclined toward the traffic noise, indicated the slightest concern about the glut of vehicles. The screeching brakes, blaring horns, and revving engines were far from welcoming, but the man was not one to waver long in indecision or to greet challenge with fear.

And for Joel Costain crossing the street was indeed a challenge. A small one, to be sure—one he had conquered many, many years ago—but even a sighted person would find the city's midday rush hour daunting. For a blind man, it always involved an element of nerve. But having been blind all his life, Joel was used to taking risks. Sight was a concept he understood only by listening to the experiences of others, its absence was a handicap only because he happened to dwell in a world made to accommodate the sighted. If he were to suddenly lose his hearing or his sense of touch, *that* would be a handicap.

All at once there was a break in the traffic. Joel gripped the harness in his left hand with slightly more firmness, then said, "Forward, Ebony."

The guide dog stepped off the curb in obedience to the command, but Joel had complete faith that his dog had also been assessing the flow of traffic and was using her well-developed canine judgment. The two—man and dog—had been a team for seven years now and knew each other intimately. Sometimes Joel wondered if Ebony could read his mind.

Three minutes later, walking briskly as was his habit, Joel reached the towering structure of the TransAmerica pyramid. The dog knew the building well and by pure habit began nosing toward it. Joel entered through the handicap door—Ebony was not fond of the revolving doors at the main entrance. As he crossed the small lobby and approached the elevator, he was met with a friendly greeting.

"Hello, Mr. Costain. Have a nice lunch?"

"Hi, Wanda. Kept it simple today. Ebony needed some exercise, so I just grabbed a hot dog from a street vendor."

Wanda was one of the building's security guards, a petite but sturdily built Hispanic woman—a description Joel had gleaned over the years by listening to others, but also by his own methods of observation. She was well-suited to her job and held her post with the all the haughty authority of a marine. She was especially intimidating to curious tourists.

"Let me get that for you, Mr. Costain," Wanda said as Joel neared the elevator.

Joel conceded to the offer because he knew it wasn't her intention to patronize his handicap. Wanda did this for all building "residents" whom she respected enough to deem worthy of her attentions. There were CEOs who had to press their own elevator button, but there were also a list of sighted executives and professionals who received the perk.

The elevator glided almost soundlessly up to the sixteenth floor, and Joel stepped out into his law office, encompassing the entire sixteenth floor as well as the one above. He greeted several people—mostly by name because he recognized the voices. He crossed the spacious reception area, turned down a broad corridor, finally pausing at the third door to the right where he entered. Inside was an office decorated in warm burgundy florals and cool blue carpet—all very tasteful, Joel was certain, since one of the most sought-after decorators in the city had designed it.

"Hello, Linda," Joel said to his secretary, seated behind an antique mahogany desk. "What does the afternoon look like?"

"You've got that new client in fifteen minutes."

"I forgot about that." Joel felt his Braille watch. "I met Andrew Donavan earlier and he wanted to come in. I told him I might be free now." Donavan was president of a computer software firm started five years ago. Already grossing half a billion dollars, he was a client to be catered to.

"You should know better than to make your own appointments, Mr. Costain," Linda said in a half-joking, half-chiding manner—which only a superb secretary, as she was, could get away with.

Joel smiled. "When will I learn? Well, give him a call and schedule something for him. Anything else?"

She handed him a sheet, typed on a Braille writer. "You have appointments until five, then a staff meeting. This"—she gave the paper a shake to indicate it—"is the agenda for the meeting."

"Okay. I guess I have ten minutes to catch my breath." Gripping his dog's harness, he walked to a door leading to the inner office and stepped inside.

He removed Ebony's harness, and the dog went to lie in her favorite spot behind Joel's desk where the afternoon sunlight often cast a nice warm beam. Sitting at his desk, Joel quickly scanned with his fingertips the sheet Linda had given him. Nothing earth shattering there; it would be a routine monthly meeting. His new client, on the other hand, was a bit of a mystery. Normally he would review whatever information he had about the person so he could be somewhat informed, but this man had divulged little about himself. Joel was prepared for the possibility that the client would not be able to afford the firm's fees. Believing that everyone was entitled to the best, Joel had gained the reputation for bending over backward to accommodate the less fortunate. As a tax lawyer, it was naturally the more affluent who gravitated toward him. But Joel felt strongly that the middle class also deserved to have some clout with the IRS and so was in the habit of taking on a handful of worthy *pro bono* cases each year, usually in addition to his general workload.

He had no idea if this new client would turn out to be such a case.

⚬⚭⚬

Greg Mitchell gave a low whistle as he stepped off the elevator into a world that couldn't be further removed from his own. The sixteenth floor of the TransAmerica Building in downtown San Francisco housed the law offices of Eberhard, Wilson, Petri, and Costain. Quite swanky, too. Plush carpets, expensive furniture, stylishly dressed women, and men in silk neckties and eight hundred dollar suits.

He tried not to feel self-conscious about his cheap, off-the-rack sport coat and trousers. He should have worn a white shirt and tie instead of the polo shirt. But his good looks—thick, dark hair, dancing blue eyes, and broad, well-formed shoulders—made up for, at least in his mind, his lack of style. In fact, when he entered the office with the brass plate on the door reading "Joel Costain," he really thought he had a chance with the pretty secretary seated behind the fancy desk.

Flashing a charming grin, he said, "I've got an appointment with Mr. Costain. Name's Greg Mitchell."

The secretary glanced at an appointment book then nodded, "Yes, Mr. Mitchell. Please have a seat. He's on the phone, so it'll be just a minute."

"This is some office," Greg said.

"Eberhard, Wilson, Petri, and Costain is one of the best law firms in the city."

"I don't doubt it." He smiled again. "But I couldn't get much work done with secretaries like you around." He gave her a wink.

"Please, Mr. Mitchell, have a seat."

He sat down and took up a magazine, the current issue of the *New Yorker*. Boring. But he flipped through the pages, hoping to find something he might use to rekindle a conversation with the secretary. He hadn't taken her statement as a complete rebuff. She was here to work, not get picked up by handsome men. But the unmistakable glint in her lovely green eyes made him certain she'd be disappointed if he didn't try again.

He was about to launch a new offensive when she spoke. "You may go in, Mr. Mitchell."

"Thanks." Greg winked again as he brushed past the pretty woman. He didn't have to push his interest. If all went well with the lawyer, he'd be returning and could continue to pursue the secretary.

Costain's office continued the rich ambiance of the reception area with book-lined walls, a Persian carpet, soft leather furniture. Costain rose from his chair and extended his hand across the desk. It was only as Greg stepped forward to grasp the proffered hand that he caught a glimpse of a dog lying on the floor next to the desk. Greg remembered then that Charlie had mentioned that Costain was blind. Greg took Costain's hand, scanning the lawyer's face carefully to see if the man could possibly be faking. He appeared pretty normal and even seemed to look Greg directly in the eye, making him wonder even more.

Costain was tall, with blond hair, blue eyes, an Armani cashmere suit, and soft hands with a firm grip.

"Have a seat, Mr. Mitchell." Costain indicated one of the leather chairs in front of the desk. Resuming his own seat, he continued, "What can I do for you? You were vague on the phone as to your business."

"Yeah—I mean, yes, I'm afraid I had to be. What I have to discuss is kind of delicate."

"As are most matters requiring the services of an attorney."

"This is personal."

Costain nodded.

Greg continued, "This is harder than I thought it would be."

"I would recommend just saying it straight out."

"Kind of like ripping off a bandage, huh?" Greg paused. Then, "Okay, here goes. This might be a shock to you—it about knocked me off my feet when I heard—but, well . . . you see, I just learned that you and I are brothers."

"Brothers?"

"Yeah, you know, long lost brothers, separated at birth, all that stuff."

Costain maintained a cool expression. If he was surprised, he sure wasn't showing it.

"Have you any evidence of this?" asked Costain.

"I've got some paperwork—not with me, of course. I wanted to speak to you first."

"Can you at least verbally describe some of this evidence and tell me how you came to this conclusion?"

"It wasn't easy, that's for sure. I've got some hospital records, adoption agency papers, that kind of stuff. And the most obvious piece of proof is that my brother was born blind thirty-seven years ago—your age, I believe."

"Please explain how such records were released to you without a court order or at the very least authorization from my adoptive parents or myself."

"Your parents declined to give authorization."

"That still doesn't answer my question."

"There are ways. . . ."

"What ways, Mr. Mitchell?"

And for the next ten minutes Costain questioned Greg with as much intensity as if he were on trial. Greg started to squirm, even perspire. And sometimes the man would pin such an incisive gaze on Greg that it seemed his every detail was being closely scrutinized. But how could that be if the lawyer was blind? Greg made a couple of discreet hand motions in Costain's face to see if it elicited a response, but there was nothing.

Finally, Greg had had enough of the cross-examination.

"Listen, you don't have to believe me if you don't want to. I just thought you'd want to know."

"Your good deed for the day?"

"Hey, man, that's out of line! If you don't believe me, that's one thing. But I don't have to take your implication that I got some other motive."

Costain immediately recanted. "I'm sorry, Mr. Mitchell." He rubbed his clean-shaven chin with his long, patrician fingers. "This is just quite a surprise. It's not every day a brother materializes out of thin air."

"But you agree it could be possible?"

"Yes . . . I suppose so. But I think my adoptive parents would have said something if they knew about you."

"Sure, but stuff like this was kept pretty hush-hush back when we were kids."

"True." Costain was silent for a long while. When he spoke again it was with a heavy sigh. Was he going to make this hard on Greg? "You can understand that the story you've related about a mother dying in childbirth and a father in prison is rather farfetched—"

"You calling me a liar?" challenged Greg sharply.

Costain shifted in his chair. "This is just going to take time to sink in. And, of course, I will need to make my own inquiries."

"That's fine." Greg made a pointed effort to calm down. "But time isn't exactly on our side. The old man is dying of cancer. Who knows how long he's got."

"How come he didn't come with you?"

"He just wanted me to pave the way, that's all."

"I'd like a couple days to mull all this over."

"I'll call you back in two days."

"Where can I reach you in case I have further questions?"

Greg hesitated, trying to consider the possible ramifications of Costain knowing where he was staying. Nothing major occurred to him, and deciding it might encourage further suspicion if he hedged, Greg answered, "I'm at the Super 8 Motel on Lombard. Just remember, we don't have a lot of time. And believe me, it'll be to your advantage to act on this sooner than later."

"What do you mean by that?" Skepticism—or was it outright hostility?—colored Costain's voice once again.

"I—I can't explain it all right now, especially not until you are with us one hundred percent."

"I won't make another move until you explain everything."

"You better watch it, Costain. 'Cause if you screw it up for me—"

"You're not helping yourself with statements like that, Mr. Mitchell. I could take them as threats."

"Yeah? Well, they *are* threats! You think just because you sit in this cushy office you can push me around? If you are my brother, it's me who should be hostile. Look at you! Raised by some ritzy Sausalito socialites with the best schools, clothes, trips, cars. You know where I was raised? In an East L.A. barrio. I was one of the only white kids in my school, and I had to fight every minute just to stay alive. I quit school when I was in tenth grade, ran away from home, and have been living on my own ever since. Lucky me, I didn't get adopted out; I was raised by family—an aunt whose drunken husband beat me up every day."

"So, I'm the fortunate one?"

"Yeah, but I suppose you're gonna whine about being blind. Man, that's nothing—be thankful you were blind or you would have ended up like me."

"I guess I can't argue with that."

Greg jumped up and leaned across the desk, shoving a finger in Costain's face. He backed off a bit when the dog stirred, making a low growl.

"You just hear this, Costain. One way or another, I'm gonna get something out of all this. And if you're in my way, I'll get it out of you. What would all your rich society crowd think if they heard about your sordid family?"

"Threats aren't going to help you, Mr. Mitchell."

"Threats are all people like you understand."

"I think you better leave."

"You ain't heard the last of me, Costain."

Greg stalked out of the office, passing the pretty secretary without even giving her a second glance.

Four

In a far different part of San Francisco, Charlie Sullivan paced impatiently across the threadbare carpet of his room in a cheap motel on Filmore Street. Pausing a moment by the window, he glanced out. The din of traffic, occasionally interrupted by sirens, came through the thin glass almost as clearly as if the window was open. But the pane was so dirty, sounds were all that penetrated. Charlie swiped a hand across the glass, though most of the dirt was outside.

Where was Greg? He was over an hour late. The call earlier that morning had indicated he was after something big.

"I'll meet you at your place at noon and we can celebrate," Greg had said.

It was now one o'clock and no Greg. Maybe he had overestimated his news. That wouldn't surprise Charlie, who had immediately sized up Greg Mitchell as a blowhard who liked to make everything he did seem more important than it was.

Too much like his old man.

Charlie lit a cigarette and sat on the edge of the bed, trying to stay calm.

Could something have happened to Greg? If only Charlie knew whether he was safe from his enemies. After so long, could there possibly be a danger? Charlie had tried to be careful in all his inquiries, still it was possible Sandy had found out. It would be ironic if Sandy got to him before Charlie got to Sandy. The other day he had suspected he was being followed. Were they on to Greg—?

A sharp knock on the door sent a jarring start through Charlie's body. At the door, he leaned his head close and said, "Who is it?"

"Me. Greg."

Charlie released the chain lock and opened the door. Greg slipped in quickly.

"How come you're late?" asked Charlie.

"Gee, were you worried, Dad?"

"Stop being sarcastic. I went to a lot of trouble to find you. I'd hate to have my efforts wasted, that's all." It was hard for Charlie to admit his real feelings. Here was the son he'd been separated from for more than three decades, yet, since their reunion, they hadn't embraced once, much less exchanged words of affection. It didn't help that Greg was just as hard-boiled as his father.

"Well, I hit the jackpot today, myself."

"You found him?"

"Yep, I did. Talked to him and everything—"

"I thought I told you to leave that to me?"

"I had to make sure."

"I specifically instructed you not to approach him. After all I've gone through to keep a low profile—"

"I'm no idiot, Charlie. I was careful."

"You better have been. If anyone gets on to him . . ."

"Sounds like you're more concerned about him being in danger than me. Who knows how many killers you've led to my door!"

"You weren't that hard to find, Greg—anyone could have done it. But I want to keep Costain under wraps until I've got everything sorted out."

"What'd you mean?"

"Never mind. I'll deal with Costain from now on, do you hear?" Charlie paused as he snubbed out his cigarette and lit another one— the things were killing him, but he still couldn't stop. "So, how did it go with him?"

"I'm gonna get in touch with him in a couple days. He's gotta let it all sink in, you know."

"What'd you tell him?"

"Just the bare minimum."

"How did he respond?"

"Disbelief. Then he kicked me out of his fancy office."

"Kicked you out? Why?" Charlie puffed hard on his cigarette.

" 'Cause he's a—"

"What'd you do to him? What'd you say?"

"Oh, sure, it's all my fault!" Greg turned his mouth into a chilling sneer.

"It is your fault for going in half-cocked. What's he supposed to think? You had nothing to prove your claims.''

"We can show him the stuff when we meet again.''

"No, I want him to have it ahead of time so he can verify it if he wants—''

"The documents were stolen, Charlie. He can really open a can of worms if he pokes around the agency.''

"I want him to be sure.'' Charlie paused in order to breathe in a couple long drags of smoke. "You tell him about the money?''

"Heck, no! Listen, Charlie, if he snubs us, you aren't gonna let him in on it, are you?''

"You don't have to worry about that.''

"Why should I share with someone who thinks he's too good for us? Anyway, he's got plenty of money already. I don't like that this whole deal depends on him.''

"Don't you get greedy, Greg.''

"What about the notebook? When are we gonna use it? I think we ought to put some feelers out just to make sure your man even cares.''

"Oh, he'll care.''

"How do I know that? At least let me see those copies again.''

"Why?''

"I didn't get a good look last time. I just want to be sure they're as incriminating as you implied. Better yet, let me see the original.''

"No one sees that until I'm ready.'' Charlie shook his head impatiently, but he got the copies from a drawer because he saw no reason not to. He puffed his cigarette as he handed them to Greg, then immediately started coughing.

Even as he was bent over, hacking away, Charlie wondered if he could trust Greg. From the moment he met his eldest son, he'd sensed Greg was a self-seeking con artist. Knowing that Greg's help would have a price, Charlie had let him believe there was a great deal of money involved in his plans and that Greg's share would hinge on Joel Costain accepting the proposition. Charlie wouldn't put it past Greg to misrepresent the deal to Joel or even go so far as to prevent Costain from receiving his share. Charlie wasn't going to take any chances— it was better to keep Greg in the dark as much as possible. If all went well they *could* score a large sum of money. Charlie just wanted to make sure both his sons benefited equally.

Greg rose and put the papers back in the drawer, and a sour, dank silence descended on the two men. They eyed each other like cocks in a ring, distrusting the other's every move. Charlie puffed on another cigarette, inhaling the smoke deeply as if willing it to speed along the job the cancer had started.

Finally, rubbing the gray stubble on his chin, Charlie asked softly, "What's he like, Greg?" Joel was the child he never knew, and yet, maybe because Betsy had died giving him life, he meant something special to Charlie.

"An arrogant, snob lawyer. It is kind of ironic though that the son of a no-account convict and the brother of a reprobate like me should be a lawyer."

"What's he look like? Is he . . . disfigured?"

"Naw. He's almost as good-looking as me. I think we have the same eyes," Greg smirked, "except for the obvious difference that mine work."

"Blue, like his mother's."

"Hey, Charlie, you ain't gonna get sentimental on me, are you?"

"Shut up, Greg."

"I tested him and he's blind as a bat . . . I guess."

"You guess?"

"I don't know . . . it's hard to explain. Sometimes I wasn't so sure, that's all. Once or twice it seemed he was looking right at me."

"It might mean he's been trained very well. Probably smart, too. I mean, it couldn't have been easy for a blind fellow to finish law school."

"Yeah, big deal. So, what about the money, Charlie? Now that I've found your long lost son, how much longer—"

"You don't have any class, Greg."

"Hey, I wasn't raised in Sausalito with a silver spoon in my mouth."

Charlie shrugged. Maybe he ought to go easier on Greg, but Charlie had been around too many like Greg in prison—so abrasive at times he made it that much harder on himself. And Charlie couldn't swallow Greg's assertions that he'd never been arrested. Still, Greg was his son, and if he hadn't botched up being a father, Greg might have turned out better. Then again, it was possible, if things had been different, Charlie might have ended up with two no-account sons instead of one.

Charlie glanced over at Greg and tried to be more congenial.

"Well, looks like we have a couple days' wait ahead of us. Let's try to lay low until then. Since you already made contact with Costain, it'll be best if you contact him again. How about Wednesday night, nine o'clock at—"

"A strip joint in North Beach?" Greg grinned mockingly.

"There's a coffee shop on Fisherman's Wharf called Michael's. I think Joel would feel more comfortable meeting there. In the meantime, I'll make copies of those adoption documents and get them in the mail."

"Whatever you say, Dad. I am only the bad son, after all."

⌒ɷɷɷᕲ

Greg left the cheap motel the moment Charlie stretched out on his bed to rest.

The old man would soon be asleep because, just before, he had taken a couple of his pain pills. They usually knocked him out for several hours. And that should give Greg enough time to start setting into motion the plan that had begun to form in his mind after he left Costain's office. He was going to insure that he didn't get left out in the cold.

When the old man had found him several weeks ago, Greg couldn't have been more shocked. He had known his father was in prison but had never cared much. The brother was a surprise, though. But, again, he didn't really care. He was a loner and family ties were more stifling than desired. Marriage, for instance, had been a monumental mistake. The first time, he had been into Christianity, so marriage was the thing to do. Greg had thought it might be nice to be respectable for a change. He was wrong.

He felt imprisoned. And when the kids started coming, it only got worse. He loved those boys, but he just wasn't cut out to be a father. He needed his independence. Besides, the kids were better off without him—so was Irene, for that matter. And he was definitely better off without them.

So, when Charlie hit him with an instant family, Greg's natural instinct was to say, "Nice to meet you," then take off. That is, until Charlie had mentioned the money angle. Financially, Greg was hurting. His short-lived second marriage had broken up three months ago, and his ex had taken everything. Of course she had been all but supporting him for years—they had lived together before his divorce from Irene was final—but the only thing she had left him with were his clothes.

He had drifted down to Los Angeles, and that's where Charlie found him. Apparently he had some old scores to settle, and if Greg helped him, he could count on a sizable payback. Gradually, Charlie had revealed he had a notebook full of evidence that would link a well-known San Franciscan and political hopeful to the Mafia. The man, Charlie claimed, was wealthy and would pay dearly to get that notebook. The copies had impressed Greg that this was indeed a viable deal, not the ramblings of a bitter ex-con.

But it seemed that lately Charlie had lost interest in the blackmailing scheme, if indeed he had been interested in it in the first place. Greg suspected it had merely been a ploy to insure Greg's help in locating Charlie's other son. Charlie could never have burglarized that adoption agency without Greg's expertise. Charlie's waning interest, however, didn't mean the plan was bogus. Greg had done some homework and found that the man Charlie wanted to blackmail was real—in fact, he was a candidate for mayor of San Francisco. The contents of the notebook were nearly forty years old and probably couldn't get anyone thrown into jail, but even a hint of a Mafia connection could destroy a person's political ambitions.

And since this afternoon, Costain had started to worry Greg. As far as he could learn, Costain was something of a Boy Scout, especially for a lawyer. Even worse, the man appeared to be an idealist. He would never throw in with blackmail, and the way Charlie was talking, the old man would probably side with Costain. So, if indeed Charlie was going to abandon the blackmail scheme, Greg wanted to be prepared to launch it on his own.

Thus, he walked a couple blocks to Van Ness, found a place with a public copy machine, and made his own copies of Charlie's duplicates. He'd have to get the real thing before he could get too far, but it couldn't hurt to test the waters. He'd contact the politician, and if it fell flat, then so be it. But if he got a bite, then he'd know to pressure Charlie for the originals.

Greg was confident that, either way, he couldn't lose. But the enticement of striking out on his own meant he'd keep the booty for himself. The lawyer didn't need more money, and Charlie was practically dead anyway.

A half hour later Greg returned to the hotel, slipped into the room with the key he'd lifted from Charlie's jacket, and replaced the papers. Charlie would never be the wiser. This deal promised to be a piece of cake.

Five

Joel Costain waited for Greg to leave the office, then rose from his seat and walked to the window. He felt the warmth of the sun penetrating the pane and heard distant traffic sounds far below. Lacing a hand through his hair, he sighed, then turned and strode quickly to the door.

"Linda," he said, stepping out into the waiting area. "Mr. Mitchell isn't still here, is he?"

"No, he's gone. I'll look in the outer reception area if you like. It's only been a couple minutes so I might be able to call down to the lobby and catch him."

"Never mind."

"Is everything all right, Mr. Costain?"

"Yeah. Would you call Jim Kincaid and ask if he is free to see me sometime this afternoon?"

"Yes, sir. What about your afternoon appointments?"

"Cancel what you need to in order to fit Jim in."

Joel started toward his office, then paused and turned back to his secretary. "Linda, would you describe Mr. Mitchell to me?"

"Sure. He was about your height—"

"A little shorter, I think," corrected Joel.

"Now that you mention it, I think he was. Are you really sure you need me, boss?" There was a touch of friendly sarcasm in her tone.

Joel smiled. "Judging heights is a snap. I could even tell by his big hand and strong grip that he was probably a bit husky."

"Muscular, not fat—as if he works out."

"Go on. . . ."

"He was nice-looking, I guess. Dark hair, blue eyes. A slightly crooked nose, as though it had once been broken. Clean shaven. Full lips—" she faltered over this, perhaps embarrassed by that particular observation. "I only noticed because of his friendly smile—a winning smile, I suppose you'd call it. I'd say he was late thirties, early forties." She had been Costain's secretary for three years and had learned well the knack of visual observation—one of the few things Joel had difficulty doing himself.

"Thanks. If you think of anything else, let me know." He paused, then added, "Linda, was there . . . that is, do you think there was any resemblance between us?"

"That's hard to say. I wasn't looking for it, but . . . maybe around the eyes. I really don't know."

"It's not important," said Joel. "You've been a big help. Thanks."

An hour later, Joel was seated at a table in the penthouse restaurant atop the TransAmerica Building. The dining room was elegantly decorated, well suiting the upscale image of the businesses located in the building. There was a spectacular view of San Francisco from the large windows circling the room.

So Joel had been told. Views, of course, had little meaning to him, but he took a table by a window because he knew Jim Kincaid, the firm's investigator, had always seemed to enjoy it. It was Jim who had suggested they meet here since he hadn't yet had time for lunch. While he waited for Jim, Joel sipped a cup of coffee and tried to make some sense of the shocking events of the day—without success. Anyway, it seemed useless to mull over his meeting with Greg Mitchell until he verified the legitimacy of the man's claim.

But a big part of him wanted to forget the whole thing. He was not a man who welcomed change of any kind. If he were, he wouldn't still be with Eberhard, doing work he found uninteresting, at best— downright meaningless, at worst. The leather furnishings, the authentic Persian rugs, the Armani suits, rubbing shoulders with the rich and powerful . . . all that glitter had drawn him at one time. He once believed that being a partner in a prestigious firm was the ultimate proof that he was just as good as anyone else, sighted or otherwise. Joel had never been satisfied with being successful "for a blind man." He made himself compete with the sighted—by their rules, on their level. And that part of his competitive nature hadn't changed significantly. Mainly the focus had changed. Perhaps he was just becoming mature enough to realize the achievements in and of themselves were not satisfying.

Yet it was difficult to break away from this life he had made for himself. Order was quite important to him . . . probably because of his handicap. On a practical level, if things were out of place he could become lost and helpless. It was a good feeling to move about your daily life with confidence, and for him, maybe it was even a necessity. He didn't like to admit it, and often didn't, but he *needed* a certain amount of security—in a physical sense.

But it was impossible for this not to carry over into his emotional life as well, though he fought it tenaciously. For that reason the appearance of Greg Mitchell felt like a threat.

A voice interrupted Joel's thoughts. "Hi, Joel. Wow! Look at that view! The sky's so clear today I can see Coit Tower, even the Golden Gate Bridge."

"Afternoon, Jim." Joel rose and shook the investigator's hand.

When he was settled, Jim asked, "So, what can I do for you?"

"You want to order first?"

Jim ordered a big meal, while Joel, whose hot dog on the run had been enough, kept to coffee. They talked while they waited for Jim's lunch to arrive.

"This is a personal matter, Jim," said Joel, "so you can bill me for your work . . . that is, if you want to take on what I have for you. I know you're swamped just with the firm's—"

"Say no more, Joel! I owe you for taking care of that tax matter last year. Don't even think of paying me. Now, what is it?"

Joel recounted his visit from Greg Mitchell.

"Wow!" said Jim. "Talk about something out of left field. I guess you want me to see if the guy is legit?"

"Yeah. And anything else you can find out about him . . . and that Charlie Sullivan, too."

"No problem."

"Hopefully it will turn out to be nothing—a big mistake."

"Too bad you couldn't get copies of those records he said he had."

"It was pretty convenient that he didn't happen to have them with him."

"If he even had such records. I have a friend who tried to find her birth parents, and it wasn't easy. Adoptions occurring when we were born were securely closed."

"If they exist at all, I have a feeling he might have come by the records illegally. But why would he lie? What's in it for him?" Joel mused.

"You said it yourself. He threatened you."

"Even so, I never had the feeling that was his intention. It would be pretty lame grounds for blackmail anyway. I mean, who really cares about a man's family background these days?"

"I don't even think Eberhard would mind, and he's as old school as they come."

"But, if blackmail isn't his game. . . ?"

Joel didn't complete his question because at that moment Jim's meal arrived. There seemed only one possibility, anyway—if Greg Mitchell wasn't trying to swindle Joel, then he might honestly be Joel's brother.

Six

━━━━━━━━━━━━━━━━━━━━

*B*alancing a bag of groceries in one arm and the mail in the other, Irene wasn't surprised the lock refused to cooperate with her key. When the phone inside started to ring, she groaned in frustration. Finally, she let go of the key, dropping the mail in the process and sliding the grocery bag down to the porch. Turning the key again, the door opened smoothly.

"Excuse me," came a voice from behind.

She gasped, having been so intent on what she was doing.

"Sorry," the male voice responded.

Irene turned to find a rather good-looking man in his mid-thirties, with blond hair and blue eyes. He was dressed in expensive casuals—khaki chinos, bulky fisherman's knit sweater, and loafers.

"That's okay," Irene said. "As you can see, everything's happening at once."

"May I give you a hand?"

"I guess it's under control. Can I help you?" She bent to gather up the mail and noticed for the first time the dog at the man's side—a black lab wearing a guide-dog harness. She straightened up quickly. "Oh! I'm so sorry, I didn't realize—I wouldn't . . ."

"Ebony always gives away my secret."

"What?" With the phone ringing and the unexpected intrusion of the stranger, Irene hardly noticed the amusement in the man's eyes.

A smiled played at the corners of the handsome stranger's mouth. "A blind man's joke. Maybe I should just tell you my business."

"Please do—but first, let me try to get the phone." She ran into the house and unloaded her burdens on the kitchen counter, grabbing the phone just as it stopped its incessant ringing. Her hand still on the receiver, Irene stole a moment to gather her churning thoughts.

"Now, what can I do for you?" she said, returning to the porch.

"My name is Joel Costain," he said, holding out his business card. "I'm looking for Irene Mitchell."

"I'm Irene Mitchell, only it's Lorenzo now—Irene Lorenzo." She glanced at the card, arching an eyebrow in puzzlement. "You're a lawyer."

"Yes, do you have a few minutes?"

She had gotten off work a little early and had hoped to squeeze in a nice, luxurious bath before the boys came home from school. Against her better judgment, she had succumbed to her sister's pressure and had accepted a date with Ron—or was it Don?—the fifth-grade teacher, for that evening. However, curiosity about this lawyer's business won out.

"Yes, I do." She hesitated about inviting a stranger in—after all, this was the big city and she was alone. Then again, if she couldn't fend off a blind man, she needed to spend more time at the gym. "Come in, Mr. Costain."

He started forward with the dog in the lead. Irene quickly added, "Can . . . I help you?" Uncertainty laced her question. Would her offer be construed as an insult?

Joel smiled, a nice smile that made Irene feel silly for being so suspicious. But there was something vaguely disturbing about that smile, too, which she couldn't quite identify. Still, sensing no danger, she shook away the feeling.

"We can manage," he said, nodding toward the dog. "It is okay if the dog comes in, isn't it?"

"No problem."

"Be a good girl, Ebony," Joel murmured to the dog before following Irene into the house.

Irene was immediately greeted by the mess that had been left during the morning rush out the door. Her home was usually tidy, though not meticulously so. The front room was cozily furnished in a blue-and-brown plaid couch she'd borrowed from her sister and some old end tables and lamps from her grandmother. Her father had built the beautiful oak kitchen table and chairs, the only furniture in the place she could claim as her own. The kitchen, dining room, and living room flowed together so nothing was hidden—the table covered with dirty breakfast dishes and cereal boxes, the counter with yesterday's junk mail, three of Mark's rejected shirts strewn down the hall toward his room, and a couple of newspapers scattered on the coffee table along with more dirty dishes.

Instinctively she regretted letting in the stranger. Then she remembered he was blind, and with guilty relief offered him a seat.

"I could use some directing for that," he said, another smile turning up at the corner of his mouth.

Irene showed him to the couch but noticed a football right where he was about to plant himself. Deftly, she swiped it away, and Joel sat without mishap. She also snatched up the newspaper and a handful of the dirty dishes.

"I've been kind of busy lately," she said in a half-hearted attempt to explain the mess. As she deposited the dishes in the kitchen she asked, "You're not here to sell me something, are you?"

"No, I'm here to make some inquiries about your ex-husband, Greg Mitchell."

"Is he in trouble?" Irene cringed inwardly at her natural assumption.

"Not that I know of. It's kind of a complicated matter."

Irene took a seat in a faded upholstered chair adjacent to the couch, suddenly uneasy. "Go on."

"Would you know where I might locate him?"

"I haven't seen Greg in over a year." A year spent putting her life back together, she thought grimly.

"Oh." Mr. Costain was obviously deflated. "I don't know if you want to be bothered with all the details. You're no longer married to him, and I hesitate to involve you—but he seems to have disappeared."

"What do you mean, 'disappeared'?" Irene heard the old concern creeping into her voice and hated herself for it. She shouldn't care anymore. But she did.

"He came to my office in San Francisco with some claims that I needed a few days to pursue. He gave me the name of a motel where he could be reached, but when I tried him there, he was gone. He hadn't checked out, but the clerk hadn't seen him for nearly three days."

"I didn't even know he was in the city. I doubt I can be much help."

"Yes, I see that."

"I'm sorry." She tried hard to sound matter-of-fact, but it was difficult to ignore the growing knot in her stomach. Did she feel sorry for this blind man or merely for her inability to shake the bonds of the past?

"It is important that I locate him, if you can think of anything that might help."

"I know it's none of my business; I'm not even sure I *want* it to be my business, but are you sure he's not in trouble?" It wouldn't have been the first time Greg had run afoul of the law. He'd spent a couple short terms in jail for his drinking and had been arrested twice for check fraud, though both times he had been released for insufficient evidence. She didn't, however, offer this information to Mr. Costain.

"I really don't know," said Joel. "In fact, I know very little about him, except . . ." He lifted his eyes in Irene's direction, startling her with their animation. They were not the dull and dead eyes of a blind man, as she had expected; in fact, she felt compelled to meet his gaze.

"He came to me a little less than a week ago, claiming to be, as he put it, my long lost brother. Do you want to hear more?"

"You have made me curious." She managed to keep her tone steady even as her uneasiness increased.

"It seems, Miss—it is Miss, isn't it?"

"Yes."

"Well, Miss Lorenzo, thirty-seven years ago our father was imprisoned for life, and the stress of all that sent our mother, who was pregnant with me, into premature labor. She died in childbirth. An aunt agreed to take four-year-old Greg but, perhaps understandably, didn't want to be saddled with a blind infant. So, I was put up for adoption."

"Quite an incredible story. And you believed Greg—? Because I must tell you, Mr. Costain, that Greg can be a consummate liar." Memories of broken promises and elaborate excuses littered Irene's thoughts, pulling her back to a time she didn't care to revisit.

"I haven't decided whether to believe him or not. I did some research, and the part about the father and prison—even the wife's premature labor—check out. The old newspapers, however, didn't elaborate on what became of the . . . children."

Until his final words, he had spoken evenly, almost dispassionately. Professional, businesslike, as a lawyer should. But at his hesitation, Irene realized his emotions were being very carefully controlled—

though not easily. He wasn't about to reveal his feelings to her—a stranger—but she guessed this was a difficult struggle for him. For some reason, he wasn't dismissing Greg's story out-of-hand.

"Mr. Costain, I am really sorry, but I've no idea how to help you."

"Do you perhaps have a current address for him?"

"Greg was never in one place long enough to have an address that meant anything. Occasionally he sends things to the boys—our sons—and telephones once in a while. But I've heard nothing from him for at least six months, and as I said, I haven't seen him since our divorce was final a year ago. We were separated for several years before that. In all that time, I've spoken to him no more than six times. So, Mr. Costain, if you're expecting to be reunited with a brother with whom you can share your life, don't count on it, at least if he treats brotherhood in the same way he treats fatherhood." She paused, both surprised and embarrassed at the bitterness betrayed in her tone. Her life had gone on, in many ways better for Greg's absence, yet Adam and Mark deserved so much more than a father who was merely a voice on the phone. She chuckled nervously to diffuse her unwelcome anger. "I don't usually pour out my life to perfect strangers."

"Neither do I, but there is a certain safety in talking to someone you will probably never see again." He stood and sighed, the friendly smile gone from his features, replaced instead with discouragement. "Thank you for your time, Miss Lorenzo. Could you call me if you think of anything that might help?"

"Yes, I will, Mr. Costain."

She walked with him to the front door, Ebony padding alongside. Pausing as she opened the door, she said, "I have thought of something, though I don't know how much use it will be. . . ." She went back to the coffee table, jotted down two items on a scrap of paper, then handed it to Joel. It wasn't until he didn't immediately respond that she recalled he couldn't possibly perceive her gesture. "Here's a paper with a couple of names," she explained, waiting until he held out his hand before placing the paper in it. "These two guys were Greg's friends. They drank together and . . . I don't know what else. I didn't like them. But I think they are still around. Steve Ardel and Jack Rizzo. I'm not sure about current addresses, but I did see Jack a couple weeks ago at the market."

Joel took the paper. "Thanks again. I do appreciate your time."

"Well, good luck," she said, unable to think of anything else.

Irene watched him stride down the walkway with such a confident gait that she wondered if the dog was there just for show. Or maybe he had such confidence in his dog that he had not a worry in the world. Then again, if Greg Mitchell was really his brother, Mr. Costain's worries were only just beginning. . . .

⚭

Irene's art things were set up by a big window in her bedroom. It wasn't much of a studio. Besides her easel and art supply cabinet, there was also a desk and sewing machine jammed into what might have been a spacious bedroom. But all seven hundred square feet of her San Bruno duplex was a mansion compared to some of the places she had lived in during her marriage. And situated not far from Connie's house, it couldn't have been more ideal.

When the sun chose to shine, the bedroom's southern exposure was perfect for working at her easel in the late afternoons when she got home from work. She studied the painting now occupying her easel. It was a seascape, her favorite subject. For this, she had gone south to Half Moon Bay, a craggy and picturesque place on the coast. That day the sea had been calm and the water almost glassy. She liked the Impressionistic style and had attempted it in this painting, but it was far from the level of Monet or Van Gogh. She knew she had a lot to learn.

Irene had always possessed a talent for art, though it had only been since her divorce that she had done anything serious about it. She had majored in art during her short time in college but had strayed completely away from that interest in the turbulent years that followed. Deciding she needed a diversion outside of work and family after she and Greg split up, her interest in art had resurfaced. And in that time she had found much fulfillment through canvas, brush, pen, and pastels. She was taking a night school art class again, and maybe she'd even finish a painting someday—a feat she had yet to accomplish. At times she even entertained ideas of somehow making a living from her art.

It was a romantic notion, of course, and it would probably lose some of its enjoyment, anyway, if she *had* to do it.

She wished she had time now to do something about the glaring flaws in the Half Moon Bay painting. The water was too phoney looking—too much like a mirror, not enough like the real sea that constantly changed, even on calm days, rippling and swelling. It needed a sparse dabbing of color here and there to capture the effect in her mind's eye. But it was not always easy to translate what was in her head to the stark reality of the canvas.

Wandering to the bathroom, she turned on the tub water. Maybe there was still time for that bath.

A few minutes later she eased herself into the lilac-scented water.

She laid her head back, closed her eyes, and let herself relax. Her mind wandered to the conversation a few minutes ago with Joel Costain. Greg had always led her to believe he was an orphan. During his infrequent introspective moments he'd tell Irene, "Is it any wonder I'm such a mess, never having a real family to steer me straight?"

He told her he had lived in several foster homes, but no one ever chose to take the plunge and adopt him permanently. She had felt sorry for him, being shuttled from home to home, always nursing a sense of rejection. And there was no reason to believe this wasn't the truth. Greg might have only recently learned he had a brother. It really didn't matter one way or another. And it certainly didn't involve her. It was odd, though, that Greg should make such an announcement as he had to Costain, then disappear. Or was it? Greg had never been the reliable sort. Maybe a new deal turned up that required him to leave town; maybe he was in trouble with the law. With Greg, it could be anything.

Irene did feel a bit sorry for Mr. Costain. He might be putting a lot of effort into chasing a phantasm. She hadn't wanted to come down too hard on Greg—after all, Costain was a stranger—yet Irene doubted Greg could have completely altruistic motives in seeking out this lost brother. Greg didn't care about his own children; it didn't fit that he'd go to all the trouble of finding a brother—unless there was something in it for him.

But how far did her responsibility go toward warning Costain? Irene had never known or heard of a gullible lawyer, thus it seemed Costain ought to be able to take care of himself. Even if he was blind.

It was none of her business.

Fifteen minutes later, the front door opened and then slammed shut, followed by the energetic sounds of Adam and Mark.

"Mom, we're home!"

"I'll be out in a minute!" she called back.

Reluctantly she exited the soothing bath, toweled herself dry, donned her big, thick terry cloth robe, and went to the kitchen to greet her kids.

"Mom! Guess what? Willie Martin is on my soccer team!" Adam announced loudly over the competition of a television cartoon.

"Me, too! Me, too!" Mark parroted as he ran up to his mother, giving her a brief hug before returning to the floor in front of the TV.

"Mom," said Adam, "would you get it through Mark's thick skull that he isn't gonna be on my team?"

Irene plopped down on the sofa. "Come here, Mark," Irene said. When the six-year-old sidled up to her, she put an arm around him. "Remember when you signed up, I explained you'd be with your own age group, like it was with tee ball?"

"Yeah . . . but tee ball is for little kids, soccer isn't," said Mark.

"That's true, of course." Irene searched her mind for a good explanation. "But Adam has been playing soccer for three years, so it wouldn't be fair to put someone who hasn't played at all on his team."

"Willie has never played at all either."

"Oh . . ." Irene smiled weakly, momentarily defeated. "Well—"

"That doesn't matter," said Adam rather arrogantly. "No matter how long you've been playing, my team would cremate you twerpy six-year-olds."

"You would not!"

"Would too!"

"All right, enough of that," said Irene, trying to regain her parental authority. "Mark, there are many reasons why they divide the kids up by age. But isn't it exciting that you're going to get to play this year? And, Adam, isn't it great you'll get to play soccer with your best friend!"

Her diversionary tactic worked well, and the boys began to chatter about the upcoming practices and uniforms. After a few minutes, Irene returned to the kitchen to see about after-school snacks.

While Irene was passing out bananas, a peculiar thought popped into her mind. If what Joel Costain had said about Greg was true, then it meant Costain was her children's uncle. When Costain had left an hour ago, she'd had no reason to believe she would ever see him again. Should this new wrinkle change that?

Irene certainly had no intention of informing Adam and Mark about Costain—at least not right away. There was no reason to do so, because if the uncle was anything like the father then her sons did not need the man.

Seven

*A*fter leaving Irene, Joel placed a quick phone call to Jim Kincaid and asked him to locate Rizzo and Ardel. He wasn't ready to return to the office himself. Though he had no appointments that afternoon, he did have a stack of paper work that had been steadily growing since Greg Mitchell had entered his life. But he knew he'd get no work done today. His mind was in too much of a turmoil.

It had been five days since Greg had come to his office. He'd told Joel he would contact him in two days and had seemed pretty adamant about it. When nothing had happened after three days, Joel discovered, as he had told Irene, Greg was missing. As much as part of him wanted to, Joel couldn't just drop the matter. But the more he was learning about Greg Mitchell, the more Joel thought he should have his own head examined for continuing the search.

Feeling the need for some fresh air and exercise, Joel had the taxi driver take him to Golden Gate Park where he could have a good walk. He and Ebony had wandered through the park often and knew well its paths and obstacles. The day was warm, and Joel felt a hint of moisture in the air, indicative of impending rain. November was fast approaching, so it was about time for a fall storm. Joel just hoped it would hold off while he was in the park.

The beauty of nature was not lost on Joel, and he benefited as anyone might from a walk in the park. The peaceful sounds of birds chirping and the wind rustling leaves in the trees were wonderfully soothing to Joel's troubled thoughts. And he hoped the fresh air and exercise would help him figure out what to do next.

What if he never found Greg again? Why had he disappeared in the first place? Greg had seemed pretty determined to make contact again and hardly seemed the type to be easily intimidated—even by Joel's less-than-warm reception.

Joel felt bad about that. Maybe that's why he was going to such lengths to locate Greg now. He wasn't normally so hard. But, as he had tried to explain to both Greg and Jim Kincaid, Greg's claims had been so shocking they had left him completely unsettled. What made it worse was a gnawing sense that they were true. Kincaid's investigation had quickly affirmed the story about Charlie Sullivan. Kincaid had only to research back newspapers to verify that. San Francisco had followed the story of Sullivan's arrest and trial closely. Even if it had only involved a minor criminal, such events were far more spectacular forty years ago. A trucking company had been burglarized, and though it had not been mentioned in the papers, the money stolen couldn't have been a huge sum considering the place. Whether it was recovered was never mentioned. However, apparently during the commission of the crime, a police detective had been killed. Because Charlie Sullivan was already a two-time loser, he was, when convicted, punished to the full extent of the law—life in prison.

Kincaid had called San Quentin and learned that Sullivan had been paroled six months ago. He had terminal cancer, and apparently the parole board decided he was no longer a threat to society. Why he hadn't qualified for parole before this, Joel could only wonder.

Greg Mitchell's background provided no significant surprises. A few minor arrests, a couple short stays in jail, a drinking problem that dated back ten or more years. As Irene had confirmed, Greg was a rolling stone. He had no permanent address, no stable relationships. Another ex-wife had been totally hostile, refusing to speak to Joel. There were no children by that second marriage.

Jim was trying to follow the adoption angle, hoping the loose ends would meld from that direction. But what Joel was feeling inside had little to do with the burden of proof. He had sensed the truth of Greg Mitchell's announcement almost from the beginning. Why else had he reacted so unpleasantly toward Greg? The whole affair simply stirred up too many emotions.

Joel was very close to his family. His adoptive parents meant a lot to him. But if what Greg Mitchell said was true, then hadn't his parents essentially lied to him all his life? There had been many opportunities, especially when he became an adult, for them to inform him he had a living blood parent and sibling. How could they not have known? Charlie Sullivan had made the front page of the newspaper thirty-seven years ago, and there had been clear mention of the birth of the blind child no one wanted.

Walt and Adrianne Costain had to have known. But if so, where did that place all their talk about the godly virtues of honesty and forthrightness? They had been dishonest about a matter of huge proportion.

Or had they?

Joel wished he could talk to them. But they were on vacation, and he wasn't ready to call them—at least not until he had something substantial to tell them, perhaps even to be able to introduce them to Greg. He recalled what Greg had said about them refusing to authorize release of information. The adoption agency must have contacted them recently. Why hadn't they informed him? He was thirty-seven years old—were they still trying to protect him? Now, he had to wonder if their sudden decision to go to Hawaii had been purely coincidental.

Regardless, would it do any good to heap recriminations on his parents? They must have believed they were doing the right thing. And maybe they were. What difference would it have made in his life to know about this other family? If what Greg said was true, Joel's father was a convicted murderer and thief. Would Joel have visited him in prison? Tried to make his life more pleasant? What had the man done for Joel? Forsaken his newborn son to an uncertain fate. Sullivan had a family, yet he had acted selfishly and irresponsibly. Would Joel really have sought a relationship with such a man? Why would he have any interest in the kind of people who would abandon a poor blind baby? His parents might well have felt they were doing the best thing for him.

His adoptive parents had always worked hard to make Joel as autonomous as possible, but they weren't perfect. There had been times when they tried to shield him from the harshness of life. And even if he had often rebelled against that, he could not deny that they had always supported him, loved him. *They* were his real parents.

He paused in his path. Was that the scent of honeysuckle? He inhaled deeply. And his thoughts, triggered by scent as the sighted's are stirred by old photos, wandered back to the camp in Oregon where wild honeysuckle grew almost as thick as grass. He had been twelve years old, and it had not been his first experience at camps for blind children. He had been to special schools and camps for years—his parents had seen to it that their son was provided with every opportunity available to the handicapped. But at twelve, with typical adolescent angst, Joel had come to hate the idea, the stigma, of being handicapped. He wanted only to be *normal*. His parents had driven him up to the camp, but Joel had sulked the entire way and upon arrival had dug in his heels, refusing to go in.

Now Joel had to smile as he walked with his dog down the fragrant path, remembering how his father had dealt with the situation in a most unexpected way. Walter Costain had headed a short way into the woods surrounding the camp. Joel joined him willingly, figuring they would have one of their father-son talks in which Joel—even at twelve a convincing debater—would talk his father into taking him back home. After walking for a couple minutes they paused, and Joel quickly took the opportunity to present his argument.

"Dad, haven't I always been cooperative in the past? So, why can't you give me a break this time? I can take care of myself; I don't need these schools anymore. I know more than the teachers—half the time they have *me* teach some of the kids who've just lost their sight. All I want is to hang out with my friends this summer. You've never forced me to do stuff before. Why now?"

His comment had been met by silence.

"Dad? You're not gonna make me do this, are you?"

More silence.

"Dad? Come on, say something."

Silence.

Joel had spun around, his arms outstretched. His hands hadn't made contact with his father's body. Joel had been so intent on his problem, he hadn't paid any attention to the sound of his father's retreating footsteps; he'd just thought his father was walking around a bit, not leaving altogether. In frustration both with himself and his situation, he grew angry.

"This isn't funny, Dad!" he yelled.

But he didn't panic. He *could* take care of himself—well, to some extent, at least. But in his anger and frustration he became cocky and careless.

"Okay, I'll show him!"

He started walking with the same confidence as if he had his white cane, which he had been refusing to use. After only two steps, he tripped and fell sprawling to the ground. Yelling and close to tears—

tears of anger—he pounded his fist against the ground. Tenaciously, he pulled himself up and started off in, he thought, a new direction. But he tripped again, probably over the same whatever-it-was. Spitting out bits of grass and dirt and moss, he clawed his way to his feet again, but not before he felt around on the ground and located the obstacle. This time he headed away from it, took four strides, then an urgent voice called out, "Joel, stop!"

He obeyed instantly.

His father spoke again, "Lift up your hands, Joel."

Joel did so and brushed into a low tree branch that was as thick as a man's leg. He had been a mere two inches from cracking his head against it. He should have been able to sense the tree's presence and his distance from it by gauging the echo of his footsteps as they bounced off the mass of the tree trunk. Of course, the method didn't always work perfectly—and it took concentration and attention Joel had been rather short on just then.

However, Joel was in no way grateful to his father for sparing him. "Are you having a good laugh, Dad? Go ahead, I don't care! Nothing you do now will make me go to that camp. You just want to get rid of me. Okay, fine with me. I'm gone!"

He spun away from the branch, but after only one big stride, met another obstacle—his father. Walter Costain put his arms around his son.

"I'm sorry, Joel." His voice shook slightly with emotion.

"You made your point," Joel said bitterly.

"What's that?"

"That I'm a helpless, stupid blind kid!"

Walter had sighed, then put his arm around Joel and led him to a big log where they sat. He continued, "My point is, son, that you aren't normal. You'll always be different, Joel, do you understand that? Always. For some reason, God allowed this to happen to you. And it's something you have to accept. But I've always believed that God intends good to come out of this."

"Like maybe He'll heal me?" There was a certain belligerence in Joel's tone. He attended church with his family regularly, and every time the subject of miracles was mentioned, he always wondered. Medically, he knew nothing could be done about his impairment. He had been born prematurely, and at that time the technology for such problems was not very advanced. While in an incubator, he had received too much oxygen, permanently blinding him. But God could heal it if He chose. Jesus had healed many blind men in the Bible, hadn't He? The fact that Joel's prayers for healing had gone unheeded had dampened his young faith.

"Healing isn't the only miracle that can come out of this," replied Joel's father. "We've talked about this many times before, son."

"Yeah, well tell me again—what else?"

"You know I can't do that. I can't predict God's plan for you. But I can say that any guess I would make would be far inferior to the real thing. You are God's child, and He has only *good* intended for you."

"So, being blind is good?"

"Do you think it's bad? As in biblical times when they thought it was a result of sin? That couldn't be further from the truth. God is simply not that way."

Joel knew in his heart his father was right. He'd had a personal, life changing experience with God. And the God he had met, the God of his own father, was indeed the giver of good things. "Okay, Dad, but you're getting away from the point. Why should I go to camp? You say I should accept this as God's plan for me—well, then, why not just let things happen as they will? You're right, I'm not normal, so why fight it?"

"God allowed you to be blind, Joel, not helpless. You can accept what God has done without relinquishing power—albeit God-given power—over your situation. Joel, what happened here in the woods today doesn't have to be your lot in life because you are blind. But it will be if you refuse to accept your handicap."

"Dad . . ." Joel's tone now was plaintive, the belligerence and anger dissolved, "I still wish I could see like everyone else."

"I know . . . I wish it could be, too. Remember the first Braille Scripture you learned?"

Joel nodded. "Isaiah 42:16. 'I will lead the blind by ways they have not known, along unfamiliar paths I will guide them; I will turn the darkness into light before them and make the rough places smooth.' "

"When I think," said Walter, "of those unfamiliar paths, I get kind of excited for you. I believe there is more adventure awaiting you, Joel, than most so-called normal fellows will ever experience in their lives."

Ruefully, Joel rubbed his scraped elbow from the fall a few minutes earlier. "I guess that's one way of looking at it."

Joel went to camp that summer, and though the moments of rebellion and doubt were hardly over, he had taken a big step that day toward not only becoming the independent, fairly self-sufficient man he now was, but he had also moved closer to becoming a true man of God. And his parents had always been an important part of his achievements. In fact, he wondered if he would have achieved anything without them.

Joel pondered what it would have been like to be the blind child of a hapless, petty crook, or raised by an unstable, alcoholic aunt and uncle. He saw more clearly than ever what his father meant by God's good and perfect plan for him. So, in that case, wasn't it logical that what was happening now was also God's plan? For some reason, at this particular stage in his life, God had sent Greg Mitchell into his life. On the surface, it seemed a huge disruption, an unnecessary intrusion. Yet Joel knew better than to accept surface appearances, especially where spiritual matters were concerned.

Joel bent down and rubbed Ebony's sleek black coat. "But where do we go from here, girl? If I can't find Greg, it looks like everything's at a dead end, anyway."

He often carried on conversations with his dog who, of course, was far more than a faithful pet. He figured there was nothing wrong with talking to the animal as long as he didn't begin to hear answers. But Joel suddenly realized he needed to be directing his question elsewhere. He often felt that his one-sided discussions with Ebony were simply another form of prayer, yet this was a time, he was certain, when the more formal variety was due.

"Come on, Ebony, let's find a place to sit down for a minute."

In ten minutes, Joel returned to his taxi. He had offered his questions and confusion to God. He still was not sure of the answers, but he did know that God would be there to smooth the rough places.

Eight

*I*rene sat curled up on the sofa. Mark cuddled up next to her while Adam sprawled on the floor sorting through his baseball cards. It was nine o'clock, and Irene had just returned from her dinner with Don the teacher. The baby-sitter hadn't put the boys to bed, despite Irene's parting admonition to get them to bed by eight. But Irene needed to unwind for a few minutes and didn't need going-to-bed tension just yet, even if it was a school night. So when she said good-bye to Don, who volunteered to take the sitter home, the first thing Irene did was to sink onto the sofa. The boys were, for the moment, content and quiet, and Irene's thoughts drifted back to her date.

Don was a good-looking man, about her age. But dinner had been painfully quiet. They were both too shy for the result of their date to be anything but dull. Or maybe it was more the fact that what he had to say just didn't interest her. He probably felt the same about her. The only thing they had in common was school—she had kids, he was a teacher. But even that had quickly fallen flat.

Flat. A good word for the evening.

Was it Don? Or was it her? She didn't know. Maybe it didn't matter. One thing she did know was that she should feel *something* in order to generate a relationship, even a friendship with a man. She hated to use the word, but it seemed there ought to be *chemistry* of some kind between two people.

Maybe she was being too romantic. Too picky. Too—

Well, she couldn't help it. She'd had one disastrous marriage, and if she ever did it again, she wanted it to be right. She wanted a deep, meaningful relationship with a man. She wanted to feel as if he completed her in some way and that she completed him.

Was that really expecting too much?

"Hey! I've got two Barry Bonds!" Adam's exuberance pierced the silence along with Irene's thoughts.

"Can I have one?" asked Mark.

To which Adam surprisingly replied, "Sure." And he slid the card across the coffee table to his brother.

"Thanks!" Mark lifted the card with a grateful grin.

A smile managed to penetrate Irene's intense thoughts. Why did she want to change the way things were, anyway? She had a nice little family, a cozy home. As her grandma often said, maybe it was best to "leave well enough alone."

The ringing telephone was not a welcome intrusion. For a fleeting moment she debated ignoring it, but she couldn't think of who would call at this hour unless it was important. Then Adam jumped up, jogged to the kitchen, and answered it before she could follow her instinct.

"Mom!" he yelled. "It's for you. Some man."

"Adam, you're going to break his eardrums," Irene said, uncoiling herself and rising.

"Oops, sorry," Adam said as he handed his mother the receiver and returned to his baseball cards.

"Hello?" said Irene.

"Ms. Lorenzo? Irene Lorenzo?"

"Yes."

"This is officer Robert Dunagan of the San Francisco Police Department. I'm afraid I have some bad news for you."

"What . . . is it?"

"It's your ex-husband—Gregory Mitchell. He's been involved in a car accident."

"Oh no! Is he . . . is he all right?"

"I'm afraid not, Ms. Lorenzo. He's been killed."

Irene's knees went weak and she stumbled backward. A nearby chair caught her wavering frame.

"You okay, Ms. Lorenzo? You are the nearest next-of-kin we were able to reach. Ms. Lorenzo?"

"I'm . . . okay, I think." But her voice had to find its way past a suddenly tight throat. "Are you sure?"

"As certain as we can be. However, if you could come down here and identify the body, we'd appreciate it."

"How did it happen?"

"We would prefer to give you those details in person. Could you come tomorrow morning? And can we expect you to take care of funeral arrangements?"

"Yes, of course. Is nine or ten okay?"

"That would be fine. Would you write down my name and the phone number of the department? You can contact me when you get here. Okay?"

"Yes. . . ."

ᏀᎷᏀ

"Mark, Adam," Irene said as she rose on shaky legs, following the phone call. "Let's run over to Aunt Connie's."

It wasn't an unusual request; they often went to Connie's in the evenings—though usually earlier than this—to share dessert or play games. The cousins liked playing together—Connie's six-year-old, Pete, was Mark's best friend. And the adults enjoyed each other's company, too. So Mark and Adam wasted no time dashing out the door. To them it was a real treat to do something this late on a school night. They piled into Irene's old Toyota and arrived in three minutes.

Connie greeted them at the door. "What's this? The midnight marauders?" She let them in, and soon the kids were sharing a bowl of popcorn with their cousins.

Connie, immediately sensing something amiss, sent her eldest daughter, Jennifer, into the kitchen to make more popcorn.

"What's going on, Reenie?" asked Connie.

"Connie, can I talk to you alone?" said Irene.

"Sure."

"Where's Norm?"

"Out in the garage."

"Let's go out there."

"What's wrong?"

"Let's find Norm," said Irene. "I'm going to need both of you for this one."

When they were all gathered in the garage, Irene told them about the phone call.

"They had no details?" said Norm.

"I guess they didn't want to get into that on the phone. A car accident."

"Alcohol related?"

"I don't know. I guess I should have asked. I wouldn't be surprised, would you?"

Norm shook his head. He'd had to drive a drunk Greg home more times than he cared to remember.

"I just can't believe it," said Connie. "It doesn't look like you've told the boys."

"Not yet," said Irene. "I couldn't do it alone. I'm a real coward."

"How do you think they'll react?"

"It's going to affect Adam hardest. Mark was only three when Greg left for the last time. I think he's seen him twice since then." Irene ran a hand through her hair. Tears welled up in her eyes.

"Reenie, how are *you* taking it?" asked Connie.

Irene blinked hard. "You both know I no longer loved him. I didn't even *like* him much anymore. But"—a tear ran down her cheek and she swiped it away—"I keep thinking of how his life was so wasted. He could have had so much." Irene gestured to indicate Norm and Connie's comfortable home, the pleasant sounds of children, even the fragrance of popcorn wafting in through the partially opened garage door. "We could have had a life like this, but he just threw it away. How do I feel? Cheated. Angry. And . . . very, very sad."

They stood silently in the garage for several minutes. Irene's mind was like a video machine replaying the scenes of her life with Greg. She wanted desperately to make the mental machine stop, but she couldn't. It seemed the silence only fed the monster of her memories. So she started talking again.

"What am I going to tell the boys—? Oh, that's a dumb question. I know what I have to tell them, but how? That's dumb, too. I just have to tell them straight out. You know what I think I fear most? That it won't matter to them at all. I wouldn't blame them—but how awful for them to have had such a father. I think those little scars on Adam and Mark's hearts are what I resent most about Greg—Oh, I shouldn't talk this way about the dead—"

Connie put an arm around Irene. "Let's sit in the dining room, and I'll make some decaf."

"I'm babbling, aren't I?"

"Come on," said Norm, taking Irene in hand and leading her through the kitchen and into the dining room.

In a few minutes Connie joined them at the table with the coffee. It was a formal dining room, separated from the other rooms and allowing some privacy away from the children.

"I better get this over with. . . ." said Irene.

"Let them finish their popcorn," said Connie. "There are going to be lots of questions."

"And I don't have any answers."

"Irene, is it okay if we take a couple minutes to pray before we call in the boys?" asked Norm.

Irene shrugged. She may have had her doubts about God, but she wasn't so arrogant to think there was nothing outside herself that could provide strength and hope. She supposed that made her some kind of twisted, ambivalent Christian, after all. Maybe Connie was right. It was just too hard to shake a lifetime of belief.

Norm did all the praying, keeping it simple and to the point.

Irene remembered the long, complex prayers Greg used to pray—when he was "being" a Christian. He knew all the proper jargon and had a knack for putting on just the right tone to make it sound as if he was truly reaching God. Irene knew now that Norm's few simple words held more power and sincerity than a score of Greg's ornate, "proper" prayers. If God did care at all, He'd listen to words uttered by a man like Norm.

And telling Adam and Mark turned out to be quite easy, too. Maybe God was listening. . . .

But the telling hadn't gone perfectly. There was one difficult moment when Mark asked, "Mom, is Dad in heaven now?"

Irene had hesitated over a reply. In a way, she resented that "heaven" had to be an issue. She should never have let Connie take her kids to church. It now boxed her into an untenable position. If she still put stock in such things, she would have had to say, "No, your father was a reprobate sinner." Of course, she wouldn't have been so blunt. But why did she have to deal with it at all?

A quick glance at her sister didn't help. Connie avoided her eyes. Why did her sister have to choose now to be silent about her faith?

Lamely, Irene answered her son, "I don't know, Mark."

Adam had another difficult question. "Will there be a funeral, Mom?"

"I suppose that's up to us," she answered slowly. "We're his only family, the only people who cared about him. We can't afford anything fancy, but we could have a service or something." But again came the awkwardness. A service, where? In church? She hadn't been to church in a long time.

"When?" Adam persisted, completely unaware of the turmoil his questions were causing.

"I have to go into the city tomorrow. We'll plan something when I get back." She looked at Connie. "The police want me to make an identification. Also, I should arrange to do something about the . . . well, you know, arrangements." Then to her sons, "How would you guys like to have a day off from school? You can go to grandma's in the morning, and when I'm done in the city we can spend the rest of the day together."

"Can we go to McDonald's?" asked Mark.

"Of course."

Taking everything into account, it had gone fairly well. The boys seemed to react with just the right balance of grief and stoicism. But later that night as she was putting them to bed, Adam gave an indication of his deeper conflicts.

"I don't feel like crying, Mom. Is that bad?"

"No, Adam. There isn't a right or wrong way to react. At times you may miss your dad a lot, times when you think about him. And there will be times when you don't, because that's how it was when he was alive. Whatever you're feeling, Adam, is okay. I only hope that you will feel free to talk to me about it. You might even feel angry at your dad—I know I sometimes do. But it's okay. We're human, not saints."

"What I think about most," said Adam, "are the things I wish we would have done together. Dad never saw me play soccer or Little League. He never took me camping, or—" Tears brimmed in his eyes and he attempted to blot them away with his fists. "We'll never do any of that stuff, now, Mom."

"I know, honey." Irene wrapped her arms around her son, tears falling from her eyes also.

Mark wiggled into the embrace. And it was another half hour before the two children were back in their beds. Irene switched off their light, but stood in the doorway for several minutes until she heard their steady breathing.

"God, give them good dreams," she murmured, not even realizing what she was saying.

It was not until she slipped into her bed, exhausted, that she remembered the lawyer, Joel Costain. No one but Irene would know to tell him about Greg's death.

Nine

*I*rene made the call before she left for the police station. She didn't like delivering such news by telephone. Even if Joel Costain and Greg were all but strangers, it wouldn't be pleasant for the lawyer to learn that any hopes he had of a reunion with his brother were forever ended.

"Well, Miss Lorenzo, I didn't think I'd hear from you again."

"I wish this call wasn't necessary . . . that is, I don't mean . . ." she fumbled, upset that she was coming off so unpolished before this big-time lawyer. It didn't help to hear a familiar and unnerving timbre in his tone.

"So, what can I do for you?" prompted Joel.

Irene gathered her wits and said in a more poised manner, "Mr. Costain, I'm afraid I have some shocking news. . . . The police called last night. It seems Greg has been killed in an automobile accident."

"No . . ." Joel breathed, his soft tone containing more than mere shock.

"I couldn't believe it myself. He did have a drinking problem, so it's not all that surprising. . . ." Irene shook her head. "What am I saying? I still can't believe it."

"How did it happen?"

"I don't have any details. I'm on my way to the police station now to make an identification. And I guess I have to do something about his . . . remains." Her voice began to fray with poorly disguised emotion.

"I'm sorry, Miss Lorenzo. This must be terribly hard for you. It makes me appreciate all the more your taking the time to call."

"I thought you'd want to know."

There was a long moment of silence, and Irene sensed the conversation wasn't over yet, but she could think of nothing to fill the void.

Finally, Joel said, "Would you mind if I met you at the police station? I'd like to bring my secretary so she can make an identification also. I just want to be certain that the man who came to my office is the same man."

"I understand. I'll meet you there in about an hour, then."

She arrived at the station after dropping the boys off at their grandmother's house. She had been to this very place once before— bailing Greg out of jail on one of his drunk-driving arrests. It still completely intimidated her. A human zoo, with people of every kind roaming the corridors, some at a frantic pace, some, like herself, quite bewildered. She asked at the front desk for Officer Dunagan and was given directions to his department. As she was proceeding there, she saw Joel ahead of her, walking with his guide dog. Next to him was an attractive young woman she assumed to be his secretary.

"Mr. Costain," she called, not too loudly for fear of drawing too much attention.

He heard and turned. His smile of greeting sent an electriclike charge through her body. There was an unsettling moment of recognition—then in a flash it was gone. Perhaps she had imagined it. Yet . . . his smile had momentarily seemed so like Greg's. She tried hard to ignore her sudden agitation, but her hands were trembling.

"I'm glad I found you so easily," said Irene. "I wasn't certain if I was heading in the right direction."

"We're a bit lost, too. Linda was about to ask someone for further directions," said Joel.

"Oh, I assumed that as an attorney you'd be familiar with the police department."

"I'm a tax lawyer, not a criminal lawyer—though at times there seems to be very little difference." A wry smile flashed across his face, making him look even more like Greg. He then introduced Irene to his secretary, Linda.

"Anyway, we found each other," Irene said. "I think it's just around that corner."

"Lead the way," Joel said.

They finally found Dunagan, who took them immediately to the morgue. Irene thought of all the times she had viewed dead bodies in the movies and on television. She had actually believed that if she ever really saw one, it would have little effect because of such exposure. But the truth was, nothing could have prepared her for the horror of reality as they made their way through the cold chrome morgue. Maybe it was affecting her more because of her relationship to Greg. Linda, though she grew a bit pale, was more stoic.

No doubt Dunagan had done this countless times. When they reached their destination, he unceremoniously yanked out the slab from the refrigeration unit, checked the toe tag, then reached for the sheet. As he grabbed a corner of the cover, Irene took a sharp breath. The sound must have stirred Dunagan's numb humanity because he stopped suddenly, inclining his head toward her.

"You ladies up to this? You aren't gonna faint or anything?"

Linda nodded that she was ready.

Irene took another steadying breath. "Do I have a choice?"

"We all want to know for certain."

"Yes . . ." Irene swallowed with determination. "Go on, Officer Dunagan."

Dunagan pulled back the sheet.

"Dear God . . ." Irene breathed. Was it an unconscious prayer? Or a meaningless oath? God had been so wrapped up in the mess with her and Greg and was perhaps even part of his death. It seemed right that in this awful moment God should have a part—that He should be present. But whether that presence was a comfort or a torment, Irene didn't know.

And that dilemma quickly faded in the face of the many stronger emotions tearing at Irene's senses. Beneath the facial bruises and lacerations was indeed Greg Mitchell. And he was . . . so very dead. Gone forever. Sudden images of the living Greg flashed through her mind—the laughing, charming Greg with whom she had fallen in love; the spirit-filled Greg raising his hands in praise to God; the angry Greg blaming her for his failures; the repentant Greg, so sorry—so very sorry—for his mistakes. But this man before her was neither laughing nor angry nor sorrowful. He was cold, empty, lifeless. An almost staggering sense of waste accosted Irene. It made her feel weak in the knees.

Her head began to swim. She stumbled back until she felt something solid behind her, strong arms reaching up to hold her. She leaned against Joel Costain without apology. She couldn't have continued standing otherwise.

"It's okay, Irene." And there was something in Joel's tone that made her believe it would be okay, if not now, then soon.

"Is that a positive ID, Miss Lorenzo?" asked Dunagan.

She nodded, unable to make her trembling lips function.

Joel said to his secretary, "Is it the same man who came to my office, Linda?"

"Yes, Mr. Costain." Her voice was shaky, too.

Dunagan then shoved at the slab, and it slid back into place with a clank. Another snap, and the refrigerator door was closed. A shudder rippled through Irene as she realized that the door in her heart representing Greg might not be closed so easily. His death bared her old wounds, making her feel as vulnerable to him as when he had been alive, manipulating her.

"There are a few more questions we'd like to ask you upstairs," said Dunagan to Irene.

"Can't it wait, officer?" said Joel. "As you can see, this has been difficult."

"I wish we could, but I've got a ton of paper work to get through—"

"It's all right," said Irene, finding her voice, though it sounded like a thin echo. "Let's get it over with."

"Could my secretary leave?" asked Joel.

"Yeah," answered Dunagan.

Irene never envied anyone more than she did the secretary as she walked away from that place.

⁂

They were taken to a large room where very busy-looking police officers and detectives occupied about a dozen desks. Seated across from a few desks were also civilians. Irene wondered if they were criminals being booked or people like her—innocent, ignorant, naive.

Dunagan took them to a desk occupied by a middle-aged man wearing a rumpled dress shirt, opened at the collar, with a soiled necktie hanging loosely around his neck. His light brown hair, balding at the top, and the five o'clock shadow on his face were liberally sprinkled with gray. He scowled up at them by lifting only his eyes, keeping his head and shoulders hunched over the paper work he was doing.

"This is Detective Reiley, of homicide—"

"Homicide?" Irene asked.

"New evidence has come to light," explained Dunagan. "Mitchell's death may not have been an accident."

"What do you mean?"

It was Reiley who answered in a brusque tone, "Until we can substantiate suicide—"

"Are you saying Greg committed suicide?"

"Until the facts are conclusive, Mrs.—uh—" Reiley shuffled through the papers on his desk, then shook his head in defeat. "What's the wife's name?" he asked Dunagan.

Irene wondered why he didn't just ask her, but Dunagan was answering before she could say anything.

"Irene Lorenzo."

"Different last name," said Reiley meaningfully, though Irene could not guess what his meaning might be.

"I'm Greg Mitchell's ex-wife."

Reiley looked at her as if seeing her for the first time. "Okay." Then his eyes shifted to Joel. "Who are you?"

"Joel Costain. I'm . . . at least there is a possibility Greg Mitchell was my brother."

"That's very interesting. Hey, Dunagan, grab some chairs." Dunagan quickly obeyed, and when the chairs were in place in front of Reiley's desk, Irene and Joel seated themselves. Dunagan, after wishing them the best, headed across the room. Reiley then continued, "Now that we're all comfy, why don't you enlighten me about your involvement in this, Mr. Costain."

Joel explained about Greg's visit, concluding with, "Of course, I may never know for certain. But I do have my firm's investigator working on it."

"Your firm. . . ?" Joel handed Reiley his card. "A lawyer," said Reiley, then adding, his tone loaded with sarcasm, "I just love lawyers."

"Perhaps now you can answer a few of our questions?" asked Joel.

"That's what I love about lawyers," Reiley smirked. Then he yelled across the room, "Dunagan, where's your report?"

"I gave it to you, Phil."

The detective riffled through the several disorganized stacks of papers on his desk. Finally, with a satisfied grunt, he pulled something out of the mess. There were a few sheets stapled together. He flipped through these quickly then looked up at Irene and Joel. "Okay, here's as much as I can tell you at this time. Mitchell's blood-alcohol level was sky-high at the time of the accident. His car was driven over a cliff near China Beach. You know where that is?"

"Just west of the Presidio army base," said Irene.

"That's right. The car blew up before it hit the bay, though. Also, there were no skid marks at the scene, leading us to conclude that no effort was made to prevent the vehicle from taking its fatal dive off the cliff. Either he was too drunk to make the attempt, or he didn't want to, or—which I doubt is the case—someone else sent the car over the edge. My job is to rule out the final scenario."

"That's why homicide is involved?" asked Irene.

"Yeah. Just routine."

"But suicide . . ." Irene was still trying to grasp this shocking revelation. "I . . . I can't believe he'd do something like that."

"You're saying he was happy and content, without a single reason in the world to take his own life?" asked Reiley.

"No, I suppose not. I haven't seen him in a long time. Maybe he'd changed. But, when we were together, he was too arrogant for despondency. He had a great ability to blame others for his problems."

"So, you're saying you don't think he could have killed himself?"

"After all he went through when we were together, he never once spoke of suicide. There were some pretty low moments. I don't know . . . maybe he finally reached his limit, maybe something happened to send him over the edge—"

"Oh no . . ." Joel breathed dismally.

All eyes shifted to him.

"What is it, Costain?" said Reiley.

"When he came to me, I pretty much sent him packing," said Joel.

"You mean it was a less than congenial meeting?"

Joel nodded. His face was pale, his brow creased and troubled. "When I didn't immediately accept his news, he became a bit belligerent and even threatened me."

"What kind of threats?"

"Idle threats about blackmail. He said he'd tell my society friends about my disreputable family roots."

"That was disturbing to you?"

"It made me a lot less favorably disposed to his claims."

"Also, I'm sure you didn't welcome the idea of it getting around that you had such a shady character for a brother, not to mention a jailbird for a father."

"Why should that bother me?"

"I've heard of your law firm. Pretty ritzy outfit."

"Mr. Reiley," Irene cut in, "aren't we getting off the subject? Exactly what information do you need to close your investigation?"

Reiley cocked one of his graying, bushy eyebrows, letting his eyes rest momentarily on Joel. Then he focused his gaze on Irene. "I'm getting what I need, Miz—uh—Lorenzo. A suicide note would be nice, but apparently one doesn't seem to exist, so we have to go at our investigation the hard way."

"Surely this is all just a formality. I mean, if Greg was drunk, it couldn't be anything else but an accident."

"Naturally . . . naturally. Just a formality."

"I'd like to make funeral arrangements."

"Of course, we can release the body as soon as the final autopsy report is in."

"So, what do I do next?"

"I'm sure I'll want to contact you again—and you, too, Costain. I've got your addresses and phone numbers. I'll be in touch."

Ten

Somehow Irene maneuvered her little Toyota through the mid-morning city traffic. Actually, concentrating on the crazy San Francisco streets helped steady her a bit. She had offered to give Joel a ride back to his office. He seemed disturbed about the events of the morning also; however, since Irene hardly knew him, she could only guess it was the cause of his withdrawn demeanor.

For a brief instant Irene's attention wandered from the street and she glanced at Joel. When her eyes flicked back to the road, a Cadillac was pulling away from the curb, right in her path. She slammed on her brakes, and with a heart-stopping screech, the Toyota lurched to a stop—a handful of inches from the Cadillac.

The driver poked his head out his window. "Hey, watch where you're going!"

Irene was shaking all over. "Oh, my . . . my . . ."

The Cadillac pulled away, but Irene had stalled out the Toyota's engine. She tried several times to get it to start, knowing it was the wrong thing to do. She could only think of getting out of there, going someplace quiet and safe. In the meantime, cars were piling up behind her, horns blaring, drivers yelling out their windows.

"Don't worry about them," assured Joel after the engine gave a hopelessly flooded sound.

"I feel so stupid." She hit her hand against the steering wheel. "This crummy car! It was a worthless piece of junk when Greg bought it. He said, 'Why put money into a car when they only depreciate?' What he really wanted to do was buy booze or gamble or party with our money. Now, I'm stuck with it because he left me with nothing but debt. He never cared about anyone, not me, not his kids—just himself, and whether he was happy. Why couldn't he—" She stopped, startled, bringing a hand to her mouth. Then she dropped her head into her hands with a frustrated sigh.

Joel reached over and gently patted her shoulder, a thoughtful gesture Greg would never have done.

She inhaled a ragged breath. "I didn't realize that was still there."

"It's good to get it out."

"No, it's not. I've got to spend the day with my kids, who are grieving the death of their father. How can I do it? How. . . ?"

"Look, Irene, maybe a cup of coffee and a couple minutes to relax will help you get through the rest of the day."

"That sounds good."

"There's a quiet espresso bar not far from here. I need some time to regroup, too, before I have to face my office, if you don't mind company."

"The last thing I want is to be alone right now."

They left Irene's car, which had finally started, at the Trans-America Building where a man who worked for Joel's firm took care of parking it. Irene was glad to relinquish the keys, though she was self-conscious about someone used to parking limos driving her beat-up old heap. She immediately forgot about it as they walked to the coffee shop, a block away from Joel's building.

"I appreciate you suggesting coming here. I'm already feeling better," she said as they seated themselves at a little wrought iron table in the back of the shop. "It's odd," she went on, "how things change perspective so suddenly. Until yesterday I thought I didn't care anymore about Greg. Now, he's dead and I have all these emotions. . . ."

"I think I know how you feel. Maybe that's a bit presumptuous of me. But I, too, didn't know what to think about Greg yesterday. It probably would have been very easy to forget all about him. Now. . ." he paused, a flicker of uncertainty crossing his brow. "I'll never know what might have been. I'll never know him. And this is the crazy part—deep down, I think I really wanted to. You know, Irene—you don't mind if I call you Irene, do you? I feel like we've progressed to first names."

"Please do. I feel much more comfortable with that . . . Joel."

"Well, what was I saying. . . ? I suppose I was rambling."

"I've done a lot of that lately myself. I guess there are volumes inside that we need to get out. Feel free to go on."

"I was going to say how I'd always wanted a brother. Of course, my parents couldn't have children, and adopting a blind child was challenge enough for them. But it would have been fun to have a sighted brother to pal around with. I guess I got into enough trouble with friends, but there's something about a brother, isn't there?"

"I'm close to my younger sister in that way." It occurred to Irene how easily she could talk to this complete stranger. "I've always thought that the nice thing about having my sister also be my best friend is that she is stuck with me. She can't dump me for someone else. I suppose a psychiatrist would have a field day with that statement—it's blatant insecurity." Irene shrugged. "Well, Joel, I'm not sure if this'll make you feel any better, but I doubt Greg would have been that kind of brother. He was pretty self-centered—" she caught herself. "You must think me terrible for speaking so of the dead."

"I don't think you're terrible, at all. I appreciate your honesty. From the little I've learned about Greg in the last week, I realize he was a troubled man. Yet, I can't help wondering how things might have been had I been raised where he was raised, and vice versa."

A waiter came and took their order. Just coffee. The fragrance of fresh baked goods was not tempting at all.

"So, you believe his claim, then, about being brothers?" Irene asked.

"I don't know. I'm going to find out, though. I have to. I see no reason why he would fabricate such a tale."

"It's entirely possible he'd use a family relationship in order to borrow money from you. Not even large amounts—just a little here and there. He was good at that."

"Yeah, I guess so."

"How will you find out?"

"As I mentioned to the police, I have my firm's investigator working on it. I hope I can find Charlie Sullivan."

"Who's that?"

"I thought I mentioned him. He's my . . . that is, Greg said he was our . . . father." Rubbing his chin, he gave a bemused shake of his head. "That's even harder than accepting a brother. If you knew my father—Walt Costain—you'd know why. A truly great man, in every way. It was from him I learned to accept myself and my handicap—not only accept it, but to actually thank God for it. He'd say,

'If God let it happen, then there is going to be something awesome to come out of it.' "

Irene wanted to ask if he really believed that, but wanting to avoid a spiritual discussion, she deftly changed the subject. "You have no idea what happened to this Charlie Sullivan?"

Joel didn't answer immediately, as if taking a moment to recover from the shift in the conversation.

Then he said, "He was released from prison six months ago—San Quentin. He began out-patient cancer treatment at the UC Medical Center. The address he gave the hospital turned out to be bogus. That's as far as we got. All I was able to find out at the hospital was that they discovered his colon cancer had metastasized to his lungs, contraindicating further radiation treatments. He had his last treatment a few weeks ago and they released him. And now, he, too, seems to have disappeared. Or he doesn't want to be found."

"Did the hospital indicate how far along his illness was?"

"They couldn't release that kind of information to a complete stranger. According to Greg, the man was dying. It's quite ironic, isn't it? No sooner do I get this new family than they are suddenly gone."

"Maybe you shouldn't pursue this any further," Irene said as their coffee arrived.

"You don't know me very well, Irene. One of my flaws is stubbornness and tenacity. I've considered forgetting about it, but I know I won't. Not yet, at least."

"I guess you've come by those traits the hard way. I mean, it must not have been easy for you to become an attorney."

"When it came time for me to decide on my future occupation," Joel said after spooning two teaspoons of sugar and cream into his coffee, "I looked around—figuratively, of course!—and chose the most difficult career that would allow me in. Actually, I had considered medicine—"

"Oh, come on!"

He chuckled. "It's not as impossible as it seems. I have a blind friend who graduated from medical school. He was given a few special considerations—I think they let him forego the brain surgery class. He's a practicing psychiatrist now. What my friend did was a fantastic achievement. Yet, I wanted to compete on a more level playing field. My dad's an architect, but you can see the obvious drawbacks in that profession for a blind person. Law seemed to offer all the challenge I was seeking, without the limitations."

"None?"

A shadow momentarily invaded his expression. "I sound pretty arrogant, don't I?"

"Aren't all lawyers?" Irene smiled, then realized he couldn't see her smile and might not have perceived her jest. "That was a joke," she added.

"I know. You were smiling."

"How could you possibly know?"

"Heard it in your voice."

"I'm impressed. And even though I can see, I know I could never make it through law school. So maybe you have a right to be arrogant."

He shrugged. "No, I don't." His tone grew more earnest. "I realize now more than ever that only God's intervention could have made my life turn out how it has. You know what they say, 'There but for grace . . .'"

"Yes . . . of course." Irene glanced at her watch, again avoiding the spiritual turn of the conversation. "I'd better get going. My children are accepting Greg's death pretty well, but I still want to be there for them."

"I understand."

"So, I guess life goes on. Will you be all right, Joel?"

He nodded, but she saw something in his eyes, in the crease of his brow, that made her wonder if he was in reality as stoic and cool as he tried to appear.

When they walked up to the TransAmerica Building, Joel hesitated, as if gathering his resolve before facing the work day. Maybe that was why Irene suggested what she did; maybe she sensed in Joel, as well as in herself, that everything inside them was not fully aired. And maybe it was because she felt a strange kinship with Joel and the kind of emotions bombarding them.

"Joel, would you like to join my kids and me for lunch? I told them we'd go to McDonald's."

Joel's features brightened, but he said quickly, "I wouldn't want to interfere. They may expect your undivided attention."

"It's not usually like that. Half the time we spend 'together' they are off playing. I'm just available to them. I'd appreciate having adult company around. There's nothing worse than eating a Big Mac all alone."

Eleven

Irene first drove to her parents' house to pick up Adam and Mark. Joel waited in the car while Irene ran up to the house. She hoped it would be a quick stop.

Millie appraised her daughter carefully after she opened the front door. "You look a little better than when you dropped off the kids this morning." Irene sensed her mother's veiled concern.

"I feel better, I guess." Irene tried to be reassuring.

"You gotta go on with your life, Irene," Millie advised with a rare tenderness.

"I know, Mom."

"Good, because I won't stand for anything else." Millie gave Irene a quick embrace and peck on the cheek.

"Who's that?" Millie asked, staring pointedly at Joel in the car.

"That. . . ? Well, it's a long story."

"You been seeing someone we don't know about?" Millie put on the glasses hanging by a chain around her neck. "Good-looking." She smiled and waved since his head was turned slightly toward the house. When he didn't respond, she said, "Kind of stuck up, though, isn't he?"

"Mom, he's blind. And I'm not dating him." She really didn't want to get into Joel's story right then. "Where are the boys? I don't want to keep Joel waiting."

"Listen here, Miss-always-in-a-hurry," scolded Millie. "You don't come waltzing to my door with some handsome blind man in tow and then brush off my questions. Now, what gives?"

"He's a lawyer from San Francisco—"

"A lawyer? That makes up a little for being blind. You could do worse, I guess—what am I saying? You *did* do worse—"

"Can we at least go inside and talk about this—while we get the boys?"

Irene now had no choice but to tell her mother everything; it was the only way to diffuse Millie's illusions.

Millie yelled out to the backyard where Adam and Mark were playing, and while they were gathering up their jackets and the few toys they had brought, Irene very briefly explained to her mother about Joel.

When she finished, she added quickly, "And, Mom, I don't want the boys to know any of this right now."

"Why not? That man may be their uncle."

"And he may not be. I just want to be certain." And because Millie had a tendency to do whatever she pleased, especially if she felt she was right—which was most of the time—Irene reiterated her request, "Just don't say anything, Mom. Please?"

With a roll of her eyes and a shrug of her shoulders, Millie agreed, then proceeded to follow Irene and her grandsons out to the car.

"Mr. Costain," said Millie, and she thrust a hand through the opened car window, "I'm Irene's mother, Millie Lorenzo."

Joel took the hand—it was hard even for him not to know it was there. He shook it gently. "Glad to meet you, Mrs. Lorenzo."

"Irene told me about"—Millie gave a side-glance toward the boys who were piling onto the backseat, but Joel's dog, also sitting in the back, absorbed their attention—"about you and Greg. It's a sad, sad thing, what happened to Greg. There was never any love lost between us, but he is—or, was—the father of my precious grandchildren, so he did at least one thing right. But Irene is the one who is most responsible for how well they're turning out."

Irene hated to interrupt a rare compliment from her mother, yet she was, as usual, uncomfortable with the way the woman always managed to find a way to insult Greg, even now that he was dead.

"We ought to get going, Mom. Thanks for watching the kids," said Irene.

"Have you decided what you're going to do about a funeral?" asked Millie.

"Not yet," said Irene impatiently.

"Just remember, you don't have to go into debt over it. Heaven knows he wouldn't have done as much for you."

"I've been thinking," said Joel, "that I'd like to help with the expense."

"I wouldn't think of it," said Irene.

"Irene," Millie scolded as if her daughter were a child, "Mr. Costain just wants to do you a favor."

"Mom," came Mark's voice from the backseat, "aren't we ever going to McDonald's?"

Bless you, Mark! Irene thought. Then she said, "The kids are restless. I'll see you later, Mom." She started the engine, and as the final good-byes were said, pulled away from the curb.

They were quiet, even the boys, as they drove to the McDonald's by the mall. Irene wondered if she had offended Joel. But how could she accept such an offer from someone she hardly knew? Her mother often faulted her for her pride and independence, in spite of the obvious fact that Irene had inherited those traits directly from Millie. Irene tried very hard never to ask anyone, especially her family, for money. For a time she had even been too proud to ask for other kinds of help. It had to be a real emergency, like the time she had a flat tire and no spare, before she called her dad or Norm. She paid for after-school daycare for her children before she called on her mother to sit for them on such a regular basis.

Lately though, Irene was improving in this area. She was calling her dad or Norm more often for fix-it jobs, and she had felt free to ask her mother to care for Adam and Mark while she was in San Francisco. She still couldn't ask for money. Her family had offered, and she knew she was going to have to break down and at least accept a *loan* for funeral expenses from one of them, preferably Connie. She had some money saved and would borrow only what that didn't cover. Even in death, Greg was draining what little money she had managed to save.

They reached McDonald's. The kids bounded in, followed by Irene, Joel, and his dog. They spent the next ten minutes ordering and finding a table.

"I hate to admit this," said Joel when they were seated, "but it's been years since I've been to a McD's."

"Don't you have any kids?" asked Adam.

"No, I don't," said Joel.

Irene realized she knew nothing personal about Joel. "You're not married?" she asked, though she had already guessed the answer from the fact that he wore no wedding ring and had yet to mention a wife.

"My wife died six years ago. I never remarried."

"I'm sorry," said Irene.

"It took me a while, but I've finally managed to get on with my life."

"How long were you married?"

"I proposed right after I found out I passed the Bar. We were married six years. But we had dated off and on through most of college, so we went through a lot together."

Adam and Mark finished their Happy Meals and dashed off for Playland—Adam, of course, saying that he was only going to keep an eye on his little brother.

"See what I meant?" said Irene. "If you weren't here, I'd be spending most of my time alone."

Joel smiled. "You've got a couple of nice kids. Ellen and I wanted children, but a law associate's life is practically owned by his firm. I would have been an absentee father during those years. We decided to start a family when I made junior partner. Then Ellen got cancer—Hodgkin's disease. We fought that for three years. She was at advanced stage three when she first saw a doctor—she kept putting it off because she was very athletic and couldn't accept the fact that she might be sick. I was too busy with my work to notice anything. Ironically, I made partner shortly before she died, but by then it was too late."

"I've never had anyone close to me die," said Irene. "Except Greg."

They were silent a moment, then Joel looked directly at Irene, his eyes seeming to peer directly into Irene's. She had to remind herself that he was a blind man. "Do you believe in God, Irene?"

"Well, I . . . I . . . sure, I believe."

"That's the only way I was able to make it through Ellen's illness and death."

Irene thought about brushing off his statement, changing the subject as she had in the past. But there was something in his intensity that made her certain he would only nudge her back one way or another. Perhaps it was best to confront the issue head on and have done with it.

"That surprises me, Joel," she began. "I would think someone like you would be far more apt than anyone to shy away from such a crutch."

"I would, if I thought of God as a crutch—but that's a pretty limiting view of the God of the universe, Creator of all things. It's like saying water is a crutch because I need it. God is such an integral part of my world, such an elemental necessity, that it's rather silly to think I could get along without Him if I just tossed Him aside, showed some grit, pulled myself up by my bootstraps, and did it on my own. I just can't separate Him out as easily as I can my white cane."

"I used to have a deep faith, Joel; in fact, I had been a Christian most of my life, but my marriage to Greg pretty much killed it. There were simply too many times when I felt all alone, as if my prayers were being ignored—or worse, that God was saying no to the cries of my heart."

"I'm sorry, Irene."

"My sister is a Christian. She keeps telling me I'm going to come back. I don't know."

"Do you want to talk about something else?"

She gaped in shock. Since when did a Christian pass on such a prime opportunity to *witness* to someone like her?

"Does my question surprise you, Irene?"

"Yeah, a bit."

"I've never been one to push my faith down other people's throats. Besides, it sounds like you've probably heard all the pat arguments."

"What an understatement!" She paused. This was as good a time as any to move on to another topic. "I've been thinking about funeral arrangements for Greg, and though I meant what I said at my mother's, it has occurred to me that you might want to have some input as to how he should be buried—the kind of service, whatever."

"No, not at all, it isn't my place. You would be the best judge. But I still do want to take care of expenses—"

"That doesn't seem right either, Joel. You don't owe Greg or me anything."

"My place is rather confusing, but I feel like I do owe Greg, especially if it's true about him being my brother. Maybe *owe* is the wrong word. Or maybe it's not owing him, but rather owing *myself*. I want to do *something*. It might be the only connection I'll ever have to him."

"It could get expensive."

An ironic smile slipped across his lips. "Irene, money is nothing to me. But I can tell you haven't got it to throw around. So let me take care of things. I won't even notice the expense, and it will make me feel great."

"I don't know. I have some money saved up—"

"You're the stubborn type, aren't you?"

She gave a sheepish nod.

"Was that slight movement of your head a nod or a shake?" He paused, then answered his own question. "I think it was a nod, because even if you are stubborn, you are honest—with yourself and with others. Right?" His tone was good-natured, not challenging.

And Irene smiled in spite of herself. "Okay, okay! You're right. I'm stubborn. But don't take it personally. It's hard for me to accept help from anyone."

"I'm the last person who ought to judge you for that. As I mentioned before, I've been called stubborn a time or two also."

"Well, about the money," said Irene, "let's just take it one step at a time. I have no idea what these things cost."

"No funeral is cheap."

"I was thinking of having Greg cremated. I think that would be cheaper. Also, I told Mark and Adam we'd have a service of some kind."

"Those sound like good plans."

"They're for the boys' sake. I'm not sure what I'd do if they weren't around."

"You'd do the same, Irene. You're too good a person to let Greg die completely uncared for."

"Some would say I was being co-dependent."

Joel chuckled. "I'm sorry. I don't mean to make light of what you're saying. But that word is so overused these days. I don't see how you can be truly 'co-dependent' if you follow your heart."

"Well, my heart tells me no human being deserves to pass from this world as though he never existed."

Twelve

*F*og curled up from the sidewalk like the aftermath of a fire. It gave the black night the feeling of charred remains. Not even a passing automobile penetrated the silence. The heavy, clodding footsteps broke through it without any sense of respect for the blanketed quiet. How had he ended up in such a deserted part of the city?

But Charlie Sullivan had bigger things to worry about now—like where his next breath was going to come from or if it would come at all. He had to stop. His diseased lungs were screaming in pain, and he was gulping air so loudly that he might as well stand in the middle of the street and wave down his pursuers, saving them a lot of trouble.

Finally, he found a place, a recessed alcove in the big building that formed Pier 15, where he could rest his tortured lungs. Hugging close to the wall, he stopped. But his noisy wheezing kept on, seeming even louder now without the camouflaging sounds of his pounding footsteps.

He was on the Embarcadero. The pungent odor of seawater and fish stung his nostrils. The wail of a foghorn was the only comfort he had on that damp, cold night. He tried hard to still his breathing so he could listen for his pursuers, the sound of leather-soled shoes banging the cement, or an engine slowing while dark figures inside a vehicle peered through the darkness.

Nothing.

Maybe he was safe. But wasn't that an impossibility? Sure, he might have eluded them this time, but for how much longer? Whoever was after him must be determined, to have tracked him after all these years. But the question was, who could it be? Was Sandy on to him? It seemed the only possibility. But why then was the man being so restrained? If Sandy suspected he was in danger from Charlie, why not act? A man in Sandy's position must have the resources to eliminate a two-bit ex-con like Charlie. Was he holding back because of uncertainty, because he feared Charlie could destroy him even if dead? Good thing Sandy didn't realize Charlie would find no fulfillment in that. After thirty-seven years of suffering and loss, Charlie would only be satisfied by *seeing* his old nemesis fall.

Greg's death only deepened Charlie's thirst for revenge. Unlike the police, Charlie wasn't completely certain his son's death was an accident. It was all just too coincidental. He kept asking himself if his elusive pursuers, his old enemy, had gotten to Greg. Would they also eventually get to Joel Costain?

Charlie had tried to be careful, especially where Greg and Joel were concerned. But Greg had been acting pretty cocky. He had questioned Charlie several times about the proposed blackmail scheme, suggesting each time that they ought to move ahead with the plan, even before they found Joel. It was best to catch Sandy by surprise, at least off guard, Greg had advised. But because Charlie had other things in mind for Sandy, he had wanted to find Joel first, maybe even get to know him a little. Charlie's time was short because of his cancer—it would be a lot shorter once he contacted Sandy.

Greg's death put a whole new wrinkle in Charlie's plans. If Sandy was involved, as Charlie suspected, then it meant Sandy had somehow been alerted to his danger. Perhaps he even knew about the notebook. If that was the case, no one related to Charlie was safe.

If Sandy, through killing Greg, was sending some sort of message to Charlie, maybe he should heed that message. Wasn't it crazy to keep going, to keep hoping to fulfill the plan that had been driving him for years? How much was he willing to risk for revenge? Yet, wasn't the loss of Greg just another reason to keep going? And, if Sandy was still dangerous enough to eliminate an enemy as he most likely had with Greg, then was there any other choice but to bring him down, bring him to his knees, utterly destroy him? Charlie had only one thing left dear to him, and he *could not* let Sandy get to Joel, too.

Charlie had thought—hoped—that his release from prison would go unnoticed. After all, Charlie's old partner was a respected member of the community now—a man worth millions, a political hopeful. Why should he care any more about that business years ago? Charlie was certain Sandy hadn't known anything about the notebook, or he would have done something about it long before this.

But someone knew. Someone was on Charlie's tail.

An hour ago Charlie had been sitting in a bar on Mission having a last drink before the place closed. The doctors had given him pain medicine, but there was still nothing like a shot or two of Jack Daniels to soothe away his gnawing torment. A couple of thugs had come in; one ordered a Bloody Mary, and the other, a beer. They took their drinks to a booth, sat down, and were quiet as they drank. Charlie was sitting at the bar, talking with the friendly bartender, but the moment the thugs were seated, he had felt uncomfortable. It seemed their eyes were burning into his back.

It wasn't the first time since Greg's death that Charlie had suspected he was being followed. But either he was crazy or whoever was watching him was very good, because each time Charlie had failed to identify a single suspect. In fact, this was the first time he had actually seen anyone. Were they getting careless? Or were they ready to show their intentions? Or—and this was appearing more and more likely—was Charlie just a paranoid fool?

Charlie tossed back the last of his drink and said, "I gotta hit the john before you close."

He slid off the barstool and headed to the back where the rest rooms were located. He stood in the men's room for a few minutes, then quietly opened the door and slipped out. He crept down a short corridor where he knew a back door was located. He tried the door, but it was locked. His heart began to pound as he frantically cast about for what to do next. There was only one choice—the front door. He returned to the bar. Relief flooded over him when he saw that the thugs were gone.

"I'm about ready to close, Charlie," said the bartender.

"What happened to those two guys?"

"Finished their drinks and left—and I was glad they didn't order more. I'll tell you, I had my eye on the .38 I keep under the counter the whole time they were here."

"Ever see 'em before?"

"Strangers. There something wrong, Charlie?"

"Naw. I guess I didn't like the look of 'em either."

"You wanta wait until I close up? We can leave together. Even if they are building yuppie museums and espresso shops here, it's still the Mission District."

"Thanks, but I'll be okay."

Now, of course, he could almost laugh at his false bravado. He had left the bar alone and walked less than a block when he sensed he was being followed. He had turned a couple corners then stopped suddenly, hearing shoes scrape against the cement behind him. Turning sharply, he saw no one. But it couldn't be his imagination. Moving once more, he'd heard the echo of steps again. Panic set in at the thought of those big goons from the bar. Weaving through the nearly deserted streets, cutting through back alleys, he spent the next half hour trying to shake the ghosts at his heels. Jogging as fast as his failing lungs would allow, he had ended up on the Embarcadero. It would have been smarter to have headed to a more populated part of town, north of Market street. But as much as he had wanted to escape his pursuers, he also wanted to find out just who they were or *if* they even existed.

He was tired of living like a fugitive. Tired, period. Since his release from prison, he had kept a low profile; since Greg's death he had taken even more precautions. Was it worth his trouble?

But was he ready to give up? What if all these things were just a product of his imagination? What if there were no pursuers, no enemies? He had given thirty-seven years of his life already. He had never stopped dreaming of getting out and taking care of his enemy, even when hope of parole had seemed truly lost. It was too hard now to throw it all away—at least until he had something substantial to go on. Until then, he'd continue to be careful and definitely stay far away from Joel. He would lay low, too, as he had been doing for the last couple of days, moving from one cheap hotel to another, never the same one twice in a row. And he could never go to the same bar or restaurant either. It had been dumb to go back to that bar, but he had hit it off with the bartender and . . . well, a man couldn't live entirely in a vacuum. He was hungry for companionship, even a friendly conversation once in a while would suffice. He was actually beginning to miss the relationships he'd made in prison. But if he ever wanted to enjoy even a dollar of the money he felt was due him, and if he wanted to live long enough to taste revenge, he'd have to make a few more sacrifices.

For now.

Someday, though, he hoped he would be able to experience a hint of a normal life, perhaps even enjoy a relationship with the son he had never known.

Thirteen

*I*rene returned to work the next day, and her children returned to
school. Life did indeed go on. But that night she was plagued with
nightmares about morgues and ghoulish bodies. Once even her body
was on a slab. Mostly, however, it was Greg she saw—nothing specific,
but vague images that left her disturbed and out of sorts.

When Joel called her the next day, it surprised her how glad she
was to hear from him again. There had been something so warm and
real about him that she could almost forget he might well be Greg's
brother. Joel asked her to dinner, saying he wanted to hear more
about Greg. That sounded like a valid enough reason to Irene. She
accepted.

Irene drove to his house to pick him up. He lived in a row house
on Greenwich, one of the nicer areas in downtown San Francisco. It
was at the top of one of San Francisco's steep hills, and it looked out
on Coit Tower, up yet another hill. Joel's place was white stucco, with
a Spanish-style tile roof and pots of geraniums and fuchsias coloring
the front stoop. All very quaint, in keeping with the rest of the upscale
neighborhood. The house was two stories and rather narrow from the
front but surprisingly spacious inside. Furnished simply but elegantly,
it gave the impression of a decorator's touch. The colors were light—
a pale café au lait sofa and matching chair, pale blue-and-brown-
striped chintz armchairs, and white carpet. Tables and cabinets in the
living room were a dark mahogany but were of such a delicate design
that they in no way overpowered the lightness of the room. The artwork on the walls seemed chosen to specifically complement the decor. It made her wonder about a blind man with such lovely surroundings he could hardly appreciate.

For that same reason, Irene was surprised to see a television. Less unexpected was a very nice stereo system. A few CDs were scattered about on the floor in front of the stereo. While Joel got his coat, Irene bent over and picked up one of the CDs. Les Paul. Another on the floor was of Josh Redmond.

"You like jazz?" she asked.

"Yeah," he answered, slipping into his leather jacket. "Especially the Blues."

She glanced at him. She tried not to think about the fact that Greg had liked the Blues, too.

"Kind of depressing music, isn't it?"

"In a way, but it has so much feeling and passion it makes up for everything else. I don't like it all. But as a lawyer, I've had impassion and logic so drilled into me, I need a release like that once in a while. What music do you like?"

She laid down the disc. "I'm embarrassed to admit it."

"Come on, it can't be worse than a Christian admitting he likes something in addition to hymns and choruses."

She smiled. "That could get you excommunicated from some churches."

"Now, let me guess . . . you're a Country Western girl."

"That's spooky. What gave me away?"

"Blind man's sixth sense."

"I don't believe that for a minute."

"Okay, just a lucky guess. You don't seem like a rock and roll type; so what's left? Logic. You know?"

"Well, you're right. And I guess, now that I think of it, I like Country for the same reason you like the Blues. It has heart, feeling. Maybe I'm a glutton for a sad story. Maybe . . ."

Her voice trailed away as a sudden image, as if from her nightmares, invaded her mind with her own sad story. And its unhappy ending of a body on a slab in a morgue. Before she realized it a sob escaped her lips.

"You okay, Irene?"

"I'm afraid my emotions are awfully close to the surface lately." Her voice quaked as she spoke.

"Would you like to sit for a minute and talk? Our reservations aren't for another half hour, and the way you drive, we'll get there in five minutes." An encouraging and understanding smile accompanied his jest.

A smile twitched her lips also, but the heaviness remained. They sat down on the sofa, where Irene kicked off her pumps and curled her feet up under her.

"Joel, you were lucky you couldn't see him," she said suddenly. "I'm afraid I'll never be able to wipe that image from my mind. I had nightmares about it last night. Still, I had to confront it—that's the only way I could be certain he was really dead."

"I don't feel so lucky. I was spared another ugly chapter in Greg Mitchell's life, and it only makes me feel worse."

"Do you think it would be better had you been dragged down with him?" She was a bit relieved the focus of the conversation had shifted from her.

"No, of course not. But, like you will always see his dead image, I fear I will always hear his bitterness, his resentment, that day in my office. And I keep hearing myself telling him to leave. I'll always wonder if I didn't drive him to do what he did. Why couldn't I embrace him?" He shook his head. "That cool, hard logic in me. I play that part so much I forget to let myself *feel*."

"Not completely, Joel. I've seen your pain."

"It didn't come soon enough."

"I've never before realized how powerful Greg was. Even dead he's still manipulating us. In my darkest moments, when we were married, I used to wish he'd drop dead. It wouldn't have helped. I think it's only worse in death. It's harder to hate poor, dead Greg."

"Did you hate him, Irene? I can't imagine you hating anyone."

"Insomuch as hate is the other side of love, yes, I did. It was all mixed up together."

"And love?"

"No." But her response was too quick, too defensive to be convincing.

"I don't mean to pry."

"You're so easy to talk to, Joel. I don't understand it, but I think it's no coincidence we're together here and now."

"Like maybe God had a hand in it?" Amusement played about his eyes as he spoke.

"Heavens no!" she said lightly. Then serious again, "You and I have a lot in common where Greg is concerned. Though neither of us loved him, he's touched both our lives in ways we will never be able to escape. Maybe he'll haunt us for the rest of our lives."

"That's pretty profound—and scary."

"Sadder than a Willie Nelson song."

She smiled, anxious to lighten the moment.

He chuckled softly.

Irene studied him frankly, realizing she was taking advantage of his handicap, but unable to stop herself. She couldn't see much of Greg in him now. Nor could she see the cold, hard lawyer. But she couldn't identify exactly what she did see. Already she could tell there were many different facets to him. He fit no stereotype—not of the lawyer, not of the Christian, not of the obviously affluent. She sensed it would take a long time to discover him, but that it would no doubt be an interesting journey. Not that it was a journey she planned on taking. Her only interest sprang purely out of curiosity. She'd never known anyone who was blind, and she had to admit the whole realm was fascinating. She couldn't prevent herself from wondering what made such a man tick. How did he "view" life? What kind of perceptions did a man have who had never seen *anything*?

Curiosity, that's all. Morbid curiosity perhaps, but nothing more.

Ebony had been lying in a corner but now stood, stretched languidly, and ambled to the sofa. She nuzzled her nose against Joel's leg.

"You need some attention, girl?" said Joel, running his hand over the dog's sleek black coat. "I have to apologize, Irene."

"For what?" His statement caught her off guard.

"It's pretty easy for me to shut people out, to get so wrapped up in my thoughts I forget I'm not alone."

"I was afraid I was doing that to you."

"Really?"

"I guess you don't have to be blind to shut people out."

"I suppose not. . . ."

He continued petting his dog.

"She's a beautiful dog," Irene said absently, probably because she was suddenly uncomfortable with the silence.

"Yes, she is. I've had her seven years. Ellen helped me pick her out. I know dogs are supposed to be man's best friends, but in this case it's really true. Aside from the enormous amount of trust I must place in her every day, she also provided me with a lot of comfort and support during the time of Ellen's illness and death. It's a perfect relationship, really. Her love and loyalty are totally unconditional. . . .

Well, she does insist on the most expensive dog food, and she gets cranky if she doesn't get fed right on time."

"Does she have a brother?" Irene asked wryly.

Joel burst out laughing. Then he said, "Irene, it feels good to laugh—really laugh. Thanks."

"Glad to oblige." She smiled, needing a break also from the doldrums she was slipping into.

"I'll bet you have an awfully nice smile," he said.

"What makes you think I'm smiling?"

"I can hear it in your voice."

"I'm really impressed, Joel. Have I said that before? Well, I mean it. There are times when you look at me and I can't tell at all that something is—" She stopped because she had been about to say "wrong." It must certainly be politically incorrect to refer to a handicap in such a negative way. For that matter, it was probably bad form to refer to it as a handicap at all.

"Irene, you don't have to worry about offending me. I've probably heard it all, over the years. In my mind, the worst thing you can do is ignore a person's . . . differences so much that it makes everyone feel awkward. You don't have to do that. I'm tough. Do you have questions? Maybe just some weird curiosity? Go ahead, ask me anything."

"Some of the things I'm curious about seem like things my kids would ask. I feel silly."

"I don't want to make *you* feel awkward. But it's always better to have things out in the open, don't you think?"

"Well . . . okay. I was wondering how you do that with your eyes. You rarely turn your ear toward voices like I've seen other blind people do."

"I have my father to thank for that. He drummed into me at an early age, 'Joel, always look a man in the eyes.' He was pretty relentless about it. He believed strongly that I had to accept my differences, but that there was no reason why I couldn't function like anyone else. There have been times when I've looked a person in the nose instead of the eyes, but I've gotten pretty good at the trick. Both my parents spent countless hours working with me. Years of special schools helped, too."

"It paid off." Irene paused, wondering if he had really meant she

could ask him anything. She forged ahead, "Do you ever feel inade-
quate?"

"Doesn't everyone?" A slight smile tugged at his lips. "If you
think I'm arrogant now, you should have seen me years ago. When I
started college, I thought I was invincible. Accepted at Stanford, living on my own for the first time, on my way to fulfilling my life goals.
Despite all that, though, I was still constantly trying to prove myself.
I did some crazy things in order to be accepted by my college peers."

"You?"

"I wasn't always the conservative, three-piece-suit lawyer. I was a
regular wild child. Gave my parents fits. I got four concussions in two
years. Driving, sky diving—"

"Sky diving? I don't believe you."

He nodded sheepishly. "But my coup de force—or should I say,
coup de *farce*?—was playing on the Stanford football team. I was beef-
ier in those days and worked out all the time. I had a couple friends
on the team, and I used to needle them terribly every time they lost
a game, telling them even I could do better. Finally, they called me
out—and I never, ever backed down from a challenge in those days.
So, I suited up in my friend's spare uniform for a game against UCLA.
We decided ahead of time that I'd go in on a short yardage play at
the goal line. All I'd have to do when I got the ball was run straight
ahead a few feet. My friend whose uniform I had on was a running
back. With the helmet and all the gear, the coach never noticed the
switch. So, completely ignorant, he put me in near the end of the second quarter; we were down by two touchdowns, and on the one yard
line. Most of the team was in on the scam so it was no problem getting
to the huddle. I followed their voices. We broke the huddle, the quar-
terback took a snap, handed the ball off to me, and I started running."

"Did you make the touchdown?"

"Yes, and immediately afterward I was hit by UCLA's defensive
line—and I mean literally hit. I ended up in the hospital."

"Your poor mother. 'Fits' is probably a mild description of what
she went through."

They talked for a bit more and soon they both felt like getting out.
Joel put his coat on again while Irene gathered up her purse and
jacket. She allowed Joel to lightly take her elbow with his fingertips,

as he had instructed her was the proper way to walk with a visually impaired person. She marveled at how comfortable she felt. Maybe too much so.

But she felt too good to worry about it just then.

Fourteen

Charlie's eyes snapped open. The pain. Never had it been worse. He was drenched in sweat. He gulped for air, despite the fact that every breath sliced painfully through his body.

He groped in the dark on the night table for the bottle of pills. His trembling hand bumped something—crash! A glass of water hit the floor, shattering on the bare boards. He didn't care. He'd take the pills dry if he had to. But where were they? In his panic he didn't think to turn on the light. All that mattered was relief.

In the daytime he was able to cope by regularly popping his pills, usually washing them down with a shot of whiskey. But at night, especially on those rare nights when he could sleep, the time easily got away from him until it was the pain itself that reminded him to take his medicine. By then it was too late. He had fallen into a dead sleep tonight, no doubt aided by his lengthy visit to a bar earlier. The pain came on suddenly. No warning, unmercifully wrenching him from his sleep.

Finally his hand fumbled upon the plastic prescription bottle. It rolled to the edge of the table, but he caught it before it fell onto the floor with the broken glass. Quickly he popped off the lid, thankful it wasn't one of those unmanageable child-proof lids. He took two pills, swallowing them without water. Then he dropped his head back onto his sweat-soaked pillow. Desperately, he willed the medicine to work, but experience told him it could be twenty minutes to a half hour before it did. He decided then to go out as soon as it was light and buy an alarm clock so he could take the pills before it got this bad.

When he first found out about his colon cancer, he had been determined to take his symptoms stoically. He feared getting hooked on drugs. But as the months progressed and the pain worsened, he slowly changed his views on the matter. When the doctors told him they could do no more for him, he figured becoming a drug addict was the least of his problems.

That last doctor's appointment had been over a month ago. He was told then that he had six months to live, give or take a week or two. By then he had already been out of prison long enough to locate Greg, though he had not yet approached him. The doctor's grim pronouncement had spurred Charlie into setting up that first meeting. Feeling more urgency, Charlie decided he'd be able to find Joel faster with Greg's help. The agency that had handled Joel's adoption had gone out of business but had transferred all its records to another agency. They, however, refused to divulge their records to Charlie. Greg had proved invaluable in greasing the proper wheels, charming the right secretary, or whatever else he had to do to finally get ahold of the documents.

He felt bad about using Greg as he had, placing him on the front lines, so to speak, risking him while sheltering Joel. But there hadn't been a choice. Charlie needed a confidant, someone to do the footwork, someone to carry on should he drop dead earlier than expected. Only after he had already confided in Greg did he realize his eldest son was less than trustworthy. Luckily he hadn't revealed everything to Greg—keeping back enough to keep Greg in line and to prevent him from spilling out his guts under pressure. That may have been what got Greg killed.

And Charlie was sorry.

All he had ever wanted was to do something for his kids, make up for being such a lousy father.

Who was he kidding? His motives weren't completely altruistic. He was doing this as much for himself as for them. He had wanted his sons to give him a sense of immortality. Greg had mentioned that he had a couple of kids—Charlie's grandchildren. That's what he wanted—to know part of him would live on. Not merely to know, but to *glimpse* his posterity. Every step on that path had only made Charlie hunger for more. It hadn't been enough to know his sons were "out there," he had to see them; and now that he knew about Greg's kids, Charlie longed to see them, too. But seeing wouldn't be enough, would it? He'd want to talk to them, play with them, maybe be a grandpa who would tuck them in at night and read them a bedtime story.

But such a dream was as farfetched as a child's bedtime fairy tale. He was never going to meet his grandkids. He doubted he would even meet Joel. The horrible pain was a true reality check. His body was telling him the doctors were wrong. He had far less than six months. He could die any day.

Without even laying eyes on the only son he had left. That hurt worse than his physical pain.

But he had already decided it was too risky. Greg's death was proof of that.

Or was it?

Maybe Greg had been killed in an accident. Maybe Charlie was paranoid. Since that incident a couple days ago on the Embarcadero, he had not had any sense of being followed or watched. Wouldn't he be the most pathetic of fools if his stupid suspicions were just bunk? Keeping him from a beautiful reunion with his long lost family.

Besides, he was going to have to make his move eventually. If he was dying sooner than expected, he couldn't keep up this cat-and-mouse game much longer. Maybe it was time to take the next step. Time to contact Joel.

The thought made him nearly forget his pain. To actually see his son! To talk to the child Betsy had died giving life to!

Charlie had already made a few subtle inquiries about Joel Costain, and, contrary to Greg's less-than-complimentary report, Charlie had heard that Joel was a good man, respected and well-liked by his associates. He was the kind of man Charlie would be proud to call his son—not that Charlie had anything to do with how Joel had turned out. Still, Charlie would like to know him. And he believed such a man would accept Charlie—that's what he wanted more than anything.

Fifteen

*I*rene was jarred awake by the blaring phone next to her bed. She had no idea what time it was. The closed drapes let in little light. She grabbed the phone on the third ring.

"Hello," she said thickly.

"Miz Lorenzo?"

"Yes . . ."

"This is Detective Reiley. I was wondering if we could get together to talk."

"Now?"

"The earlier the better. This is important."

Irene glanced at her bedside clock. It was seven o'clock. Detective Reiley was certainly an early bird. "I could get there by eight-thirty." Irene rubbed the sleep from her eyes. "What's it about?" she asked, her head starting to clear.

"I'll let you know when I see you. Eight-thirty, then?"

"Yes . . . right."

The phone clicked on the other end, and still bemused, Irene hung up her receiver. She swung her feet out of bed, rubbed her face a couple more times, then stood and stretched.

She had gotten to bed last night around midnight. She still couldn't believe she and Joel had spent so much time together. They had gone to dinner at a seafood restaurant on Fisherman's Wharf. She'd made the mistake of having a cappuccino after dinner, so Joel suggested they walk around the wharf since she was certain she wouldn't be able to sleep. They had a nice time. Talked about everything from politics to their childhoods, to trivial chitchat. They had even broached the subject of religion. Before she realized it, Irene had told Joel all about her discouragement with church and God. He understood and made no attempt to defend God.

It had been a clear night. The moonlight shimmered on the dark waters of the bay. The autumn air was crisp and chilly. It touched her senses, made her feel alive and, for the first time in days, that she was truly free of the bondage of the past. Maybe that's why she had begun spilling out the anguish of those years with Greg.

"Haven't you ever doubted God, Joel? Haven't you ever wondered if Christianity wasn't just a huge deception? What's that saying—'If God didn't exist, it would be necessary to invent Him.' "

"I guess we only have our experiences to give evidence of His existence."

"What about when there are no experiences? When you are dry and dead and cold inside? What then?"

"Is that how it was with you, Irene?"

"The fire was dead, not even a warm coal to fan back to life."

"Not a single ember?"

"The fire had been kicked out, Joel. Then sand and water was thrown on it, and it had been kicked again . . . and again. You don't know how many times I tried to come back. Greg's faith would revive, and I'd start to hope again, praise God, and tell my friends of God's faithfulness. We'd go along for a while, and I'd start to believe it was real. Then Greg would fall away again. I'd keep hanging on, though— praying, trusting. But each time a little more died inside me. One day, in a small prayer group I attended, I was praying out loud for Greg and suddenly realized I hadn't heard a thing I said. The words had been completely rote—from my lips, not my heart. It was scary. I'd been a Christian most of my life, and it was always my choice. My parents hardly ever go to church. *I* sought God out; I gave my life to Him. I trusted Him, Joel. I loved Him. And suddenly He was gone. I felt nothing. Oh, I know you shouldn't base your faith on feelings. But you can't base it on *nothing* either, can you?" She looked up at Joel. "Can you, Joel?" she implored.

"I wouldn't want to." Was he hedging her entreaty? But, no, his tone was sincere, as if he truly understood how awful it would be to find the God you loved and served to be suddenly gone.

"I still don't know who deserted whom. . . ." she continued. "Maybe it was all my fault. I guess if what I believed all my life was true, then I had to be to blame. Didn't He say, 'I will never leave you nor forsake you'? You don't know how many times I've struggled over this ground. But this is the bottom line: the end result was the same, no matter who's to fault." She paused for a moment. "Isn't it?"

"The result may be the same, but perhaps the solution would be different."

"Oh yes, of course. I've heard that one, too. If God did the deserting, or if there is really no God at all, then that's that. But if I left God, then I can choose to return. Right?"

"You're not looking for answers now, are you, Irene?"

"No. I don't even know why I'm sharing all this. I guess this is just your lucky day."

"It might be," he murmured softly.

She tried to ignore the gentle, almost hopeful timbre of his voice. And the odd, pleased, feeling it gave her. "Have you always been a Christian, Joel?"

"When I was five years old, I stumbled up to the altar at church. My parents set me on the right path, both literally and figuratively. They've got a remarkable relationship with God. But I have to admit, mine never seemed as smooth as theirs. I had a lot of struggles."

"But you stuck with it?"

"I don't know what else I would have done."

"Is that a good enough reason? I used to think that, too. Where else would I go, Lord? But there came a point when I couldn't accept that any longer."

"I guess I never got to that point."

"Maybe you had a stronger base than I did."

"I doubt it. Do you remember when you asked me about my faith being a crutch? I wasn't completely honest with you—at the time, I didn't feel I could trust a stranger with the whole story."

"And now. . . ?"

"You don't seem like a stranger at all, anymore. Maybe the intensity of our present situation has forced us to bypass the usual formalities."

"I think that's an understatement."

"Well, nevertheless, I won't bore you with my whole Christian testimony—at least not in one fell swoop. But I sense you want to know a little bit. You probably know the story in the Bible about the man born blind."

"Yes. The disciples thought he was blind because of his parents' sin, but Jesus said it was so that God could be glorified."

"And after the man was healed, the Pharisees got into an uproar because Jesus had healed him on the Sabbath. They gave the guy the third degree and tried to convince him that Jesus was a sinner. His answer was in effect, 'I don't know if he is a sinner or not; all I know is that once I was blind, but now I can see.' "

"But you're still blind, Joel."

"I realized a long time ago that blind man wasn't talking about his *eyes*. Believe me, I've tried many times to get healed." He closed his eyes, remembered pain etched on his face. "I've accused God; I've even hated Him for my handicap. But it always boils down to that blind man's simple statement. Once I glimpsed God, I could never shut Him out again. I don't know why God does some of the things He does; I certainly don't have a perfect knowledge of His character. I only know what I can *see*."

"And when you can't see anything?"

"You ask some tough questions, Irene. I don't know the answers. I guess I've come to the place where I don't have to know all the answers."

"Blind faith?"

" 'Now we see through a glass, darkly; but then face to face . . .' " He quoted as if those words were never far from his lips or heart. "It's not blind faith when you *know* how it's going to come out."

Irene thought about the kinds of struggles a blind man might have suffered. She thought of the death, at such a young age, of Joel's wife, the woman he loved. She thought of this recent upheaval in his life, his confusion, even his sense of self-recrimination. How she envied his assurance. How she wished she could go back ten years to when she had that same kind of assurance.

They walked in silence for a few minutes. Irene had noticed for some time the barking sounds of sea lions, but now it was louder than ever, a pervasive riot of sound that was oddly pleasant and cheerful. A few years back, some sea lions had taken up residence on the pier; before long, their friends joined them, until now they had completely taken over Pier 39.

In an obvious attempt to change the subject, Irene said, "Do you want to go watch the sea lions?"

"Lead the way!" He smiled somewhat ironically. "But do you mind if I just listen?"

"You do that very well, Joel." She spoke earnestly, not glibly.

They came to a place where there was a bench from which they could view not only the animals but also the moonlit bay. They sat there for a few minutes, laughing over the antics of the lions while Irene described them in humorous detail, both seeming glad for the pleasant interlude. Then they started talking again and left that place so they could hear each other over the din of barking. When the fog rolled in and the damp air grew too chilly, they stopped for decaf mocha in a little coffeehouse. Irene couldn't remember feeling warmer or safer. It had surprised her when she realized it was almost midnight. They were both reluctant to end the evening, but Joel had an early appointment in the morning.

Yes, she'd had a wonderful time. Better than any date she could remember. Probably because this *wasn't* a date. What it was she couldn't say, but did it need a label? If her mother were here, she'd insist on categorizing it some way.

"Don't kid yourself, Irene," Millie would say. "When a handsome man like that and a good-looking gal like yourself get together, there's bound to be something more than friendship brewing. Two and two always make four—there's no way around it."

But this was different, on an entirely different level. It had to be. This was the wrong time, the wrong place for romance.

Joel was just a very nice man—warm, interesting, and charming. He—

A sudden knot formed in Irene's stomach. Charming?

Could it be. . . ?

She physically shook her head. No. Of course not.

But Joel might well be Greg's brother. Were they more alike than she wanted to believe? There *were* similarities. Joel had won Irene's sympathy and even her admiration from the beginning. As had Greg. And Joel was a Christian. As Greg had been.

"Irene, you're nuts," she said aloud.

Then to distract her mind from the unwelcome train of thought, she moved to the window, pulled back the corner of the drape, and saw it was overcast outside. She had to remember to make sure the boys took their jackets to school.

After making sure Adam and Mark were awake and eating breakfast, Irene showered and dressed quickly. She could drop them at school on her way into the city. Before leaving, she called her office to let them know she'd be late. Then, grabbing a travel mug of coffee and a leftover piece of toast for her breakfast, she herded everyone into her car.

She arrived at the police station at exactly eight-thirty.

"Glad you could make it, Miz Lorenzo." Reiley seemed more congenial than he had the previous day. He still had that rumpled look and a five o'clock shadow which, if it was intended to appear stylish, had just the opposite effect. He looked more like a derelict—or an overworked, underpaid civil servant.

"Yes . . . Mr. Reiley." She was still a bit sluggish. One cup of coffee was hardly enough to face the morning, much less the police.

"You want some coffee?" In Irene's book, Reiley's personal stock went way up with that question.

"Yes, thank you."

"Cream and sugar?"

"Just black."

He went across the busy room, where several other detectives and uniformed officers were already hard at work, and poured her a cup from a big coffeepot. She accepted the steaming brew with a grateful smile. It tasted awful, but it was strong enough to disperse any remaining shackles of sleep.

After a couple gulps she asked, "So, Mr. Reiley, what did you need to talk to me about?"

"Mitchell's autopsy report came back. It's not good. It appears he was dead before the crash took place."

"What does that mean?"

"The crash didn't kill him, Miz Lorenzo," Reiley replied with great patience, as if speaking to a child.

"That's obvious. Do you know what did kill him?"

"A blow to the head. And it's possible some of his contusions and bruises were inflicted before the crash. The coroner is performing further tests to confirm that."

"But they couldn't have been self-inflicted."

"Impossible."

"That could only mean . . ." The idea was too awful to complete.

"I'll be blunt, Miz Lorenzo—I think we're looking at a homicide."

"That can't be."

"Why's that?"

Irene shook her head. What did she know? Greg could have had any number of enemies. While they were married he'd associated with many shady characters and was involved in schemes and deals that Irene made a point of not looking at too closely. Since their divorce he had done nothing to indicate that he had changed.

"I don't know, Mr. Reiley. It's just hard to fathom that happening to someone you know."

"Are you aware of any enemies your ex-husband might have had?"

"No, but . . ."

"Yes, Miz Lorenzo?"

"I suppose it's possible. Greg could have been mixed up in anything."

"Like what?"

"I couldn't tell you specifics. I hadn't seen him in a long time."

"What about while you were married? Did he do drugs?"

"I never knew for certain. He could have, but I don't think he was ever heavily into it. Not while we were married." She concentrated on her coffee for a moment, trying to let everything sink in. Greg murdered? It seemed inconceivable, yet not impossible. Poor Greg . . . it was all *too* possible.

"How long have you known Joel Costain?"

Reiley's question came so abruptly, Irene wondered if she had missed something. But she hadn't. Had it been the detective's intention to catch her off guard?

"A few days."

"Really? You seemed pretty chummy. . . ."

"Only a few days . . ." Her voice was dry, brittle. Her stomach knotted.

"What do you know about him?"

"Joel. . . ?"

"Yeah."

What did she know about Joel Costain? She had opened her heart up to him last night, and he had responded with tenderness. He had held her trust like a precious gem. He had been sensitive and earnest—and vulnerable. She had only known him a few days, but he was filling her consciousness as if he were becoming an important part of her life. And she felt suddenly defensive toward him in the face of Reiley's clear implication.

"What are you saying, Mr. Reiley?"

"Just a simple question, Miz Lorenzo. What do you—"

"I know just what you know." But that wasn't true. Joel had opened a part of his heart to her as she had to him.

"I don't know much." Reiley picked up a paper from his desk. "A partner in a big Montgomery Street law firm for the last seven years, been with the firm for ten. Tax lawyer. Deals with a lot of big names. He's probably worth a few bucks—major bucks. Graduated from Stanford, made Law Review. Did you know he practiced criminal law his first year out of law school, then took some additional classes and switched to tax law? He himself has no criminal record, not even a traffic violation—"

"I doubt he drives, Mr. Reiley," Irene interjected drolly.

"I suppose not. Anyway, his record's clean as a whistle. Almost too clean."

"What's that supposed to mean? I haven't got a police record, either."

"Three speeding tickets in the last two years."

"You have certainly done your homework, Detective."

Reiley shrugged then went on, ignoring her comment, "Can you tell me anything about Costain's relationship to your ex-husband?"

"Joel already told you everything."

"That you know of . . ."

"Well, yes, but—"

"You believe him?"

"I've no reason not to." But why wouldn't that ache in her stomach go away?

"He admitted that Mitchell threatened him."

"Sometimes Greg could get kind of belligerent toward men. He was smooth and suave around women."

"Interesting." Reiley shuffled through more papers.

"Can I get some more coffee?" Irene asked.

"Sure." Reiley started to rise when his phone rang. "Just a minute," he said to Irene, reaching for the phone.

"I can get it." She had to stand, move around. She felt as if she were being pummeled.

Reiley was hanging up the phone as she returned to her seat. "That was the coroner, Miz Lorenzo. They've found traces of blood on Mitchell that don't belong to him. We are definitely playing a whole new ball game now. I want you to think of everything you know about this situation between Costain and Mitchell."

"What makes you think Greg's death is related?"

"I don't believe in coincidences."

"Is Joel a suspect?"

"Everyone's a suspect. Even you, Miz Lorenzo."

Sixteen

When Irene finally left Reiley an hour later, she was a wreck. She didn't know why she went directly to Joel's office, except that she recalled how last night she had felt so safe with him. However, she tried to ignore that by thinking of more practical reasons for seeing him—such as the fact that Joel would want to know about the autopsy report. Reiley said he'd be in touch with Joel, but Irene knew the news would be better coming from her.

Riding up the elevator of the impressive TransAmerica Building on the corner of Market and Montgomery, Irene thought of what Reiley had said about Joel. She had assumed he was no ambulance chaser, but it hadn't really dawned on her until now just how well off Joel actually was. As she stepped out of the elevator into the plush reception area of the law office, Irene felt her stomach knot up again. She didn't know why.

"May I help you?" asked a receptionist.

"I would like to see Mr. Costain."

Irene was directed to another suite of offices where another secretary, an older, dour-looking woman, not Linda whom Irene had met earlier, greeted her.

"Mr. Costain is with a client. Do you have an appointment, Miss Lorenzo?"

"No, I . . . hoped to meet him for lunch."

The secretary glanced at her watch. She didn't have to tell Irene it was not even ten o'clock. A slightly raised eyebrow said enough.

"I'll let him know you're here," the secretary said coolly, then picked up her phone, pushed a button, and spoke. "Mr. Costain, there is a Miss Lorenzo here to see you. Shall I have her wait?" She paused to listen. Then, "Yes, of course." Glancing back at Irene, there was new respect in the secretary's eyes. "Mr. Costain will be out in a minute."

Within seconds the inner office door opened and Joel appeared, preceded by an older man who looked vaguely familiar.

"Dewy, thanks for being flexible," Joel said to his companion, shaking the man's hand.

"No problem. We've got the big issues worked out. I don't think anything's going to come back to haunt me at election time."

Irene realized that the man was Dewy Anderson, U.S. Senator. He said a friendly good-bye to the secretary, then nodded toward Irene, giving her an uncomfortably long appraisal before grinning.

"Joel, I didn't mean to interrupt your work," Irene said when they were in his office. "That was a United States senator."

"Yeah," he said casually.

"You didn't cut short his appointment because of me?"

"I've saved him almost a hundred thousand dollars in taxes this year—he won't hold a canceled appointment against me. Have a seat."

She sank onto the soft leather sofa, and Joel sat in an adjacent chair. Even in her frazzled state, she took note of the richly appointed office.

"So, to what do I owe this unexpected surprise?" he said lightly.

"I'm afraid it's nothing good. I've just come from the police station. That detective, Reiley, called me this morning. Greg's autopsy report came in. They're pretty certain he . . . was murdered."

"Oh, Irene . . ."

"That's not all. He said we are suspects."

"I wouldn't worry about that, Irene. It's just routine."

"Routine!" she blurted, having heard that word too many times lately. "Well, it's not routine to me! Murder, Joel! And Reiley asked a lot of questions about you. He seemed to know your life history."

Joel sighed and shook his head. But before more could be said, Joel's phone rang. He rose and answered it.

"Send him right in, Martha," he said into the receiver. Then turning toward Irene, he began, "It's my investigator—"

The door opened and a man entered. He was in his early thirties, muscular, with blond hair and a florid, boyish face.

Joel greeted him and shook his hand. "Irene, this is my firm's investigator, Jim Kincaid." Then to Jim, "Jim, this is Irene Lorenzo, Greg Mitchell's ex-wife."

Kincaid thrust out his hand, offering Irene a strong grip from a big, meaty hand.

Joel said, "Jim, it's timely that you've come now. We've just heard from the police that Greg Mitchell's death is being considered a homicide."

"You don't say."

"And I'm the prime suspect."

Kincaid chuckled. "What planet did you say that cop is from?"

"It's not impossible, you know."

"Last I saw, your aim isn't so great, Joel."

"Oh, I'm sure Detective Reiley has the answer to that."

"Which is?"

"I could have hired someone."

"And the motive?"

"Yesterday, he implied blackmail."

"He *is* from another planet or another century—"

"This is nothing to joke about!" Irene erupted.

"Irene," Joel breathed contritely, "I am so sorry."

"Oh, never mind. You didn't do anything—it's me. My nerves are frayed. I've had an awful morning."

"May I get you something?" asked Joel solicitously. "Do you need to leave? Do you need to be alone?"

"I don't know what I need."

"Can I take you somewhere?"

She almost smiled at the sincerity of his offer. Imagine a blind man taking her away, leading her to some safe place.

"Hey, before you take off," said Kincaid, "you wanted to see me, Joel, remember?"

"Yeah, that's right. Let's sit down." Before Joel resumed his seat, he took a large envelope from his desk. "This"—he tapped the envelope—"came in the mail yesterday. I wasn't in the office much so I didn't get it until this morning."

He gave it to Jim, who took a sheaf of papers from the already opened envelope. The investigator glanced briefly through the papers then whistled. "Another little bombshell for the day, eh?"

Irene closed her eyes. Maybe if *she* couldn't see, she could close out the world, too, and all its battering. It didn't work.

"What is it?" She had to ask.

"The contents of that envelope confirm that Charles Sullivan, convicted robber and murderer, is indeed my father." Joel's words were forced, difficult.

"Which, of course would make—" Jim began.

"Greg Mitchell my brother . . ." Joel finished. The final word *brother* was ragged, as if it took all Joel's courage to say it.

"This stuff looks pretty official," said Kincaid. "But who sent it? Mitchell? Or Sullivan?"

"Sullivan would be my guess. But my adoption was under the Closed Adoption Law—there's no way just anyone could have gotten ahold of these records without, at the very least, a release from either myself or my parents. More than likely, though, a court order would be needed. It definitely could not have been done without us knowing."

"Maybe they're forgeries."

"Someone's going to an awful lot of trouble on such a crazy hoax, then."

"Joel, do you think it's time you spoke to your parents?" asked Jim.

"A task I've been avoiding."

"I could try to manage—"

"No. I'll do it. They've been home from Hawaii a couple days. But back to these documents, Jim. Linda's gone today and the temp isn't as experienced. She read them to me but couldn't tell if they are authentic. What do you think?"

"They're poor copies, and I'm no expert, but they sure look like they are."

Kincaid gave the envelope back to Joel, who, in turn, handed it to Irene. She tried to focus on the papers, but all the legalese made it hard—especially since her mind was whirling from all the other events of the day.

Then Kincaid held out a manila folder he'd been carrying. "Here are the fruits of my labors. I've photocopied newspaper clippings, old police reports, anything I could find pertaining to Sullivan's case. It's all in the folder. I also went up to San Quentin."

"I'd like to hear about that visit, Jim," said Joel, "but maybe later."

"Sure." Jim stood and started to leave, then paused at the door.

"Listen, Joel, I don't know what's going on. It may be Mitchell's murder has nothing at all to do with either you or what's in that envelope. But it seems too much of a coincidence not to at least consider the possibility of a relationship."

Irene remembered Detective Reiley had said almost the same words.

"And?" said Joel.

"I don't know. My gut just tells me we might be opening up a Pandora's box here. I just think we all better be careful."

"I'll remember that, Jim. Thanks."

Several moments of silence followed Kincaid's departure. Irene's mind was in complete disarray. Panic gripped her. It was all so foreign to her—police, murder, deception. Suddenly the tensions of the day spilled out. Tears dripped from her eyes; she took a ragged breath.

"What's happening, Joel?" A sob caught in her throat and she could say no more.

Joel moved next to her and put an arm around her trembling shoulders. He said nothing, and Irene let herself rest against him, absorbing the strength and calm emanating from him.

"Are you going to be okay?" he said softly. She looked up at him. Was he real? Could a man truly be this tender, this sensitive? He brushed his fingers across her damp cheek. "I wish I could make the fear and pain go away as easily," he murmured.

When his lips found hers, she melted into him, oblivious to all else. His sudden passion was unexpected, as was her own hungry response. But more than that—far, far more—was the response within Irene that went deeper than physical longing. There in his arms she felt she could hide, absorbing his protection. He was a haven from the buffeting storm, a shelter, a strong tree on which to lean. Nothing could touch her here, not even—

Suddenly Joel pulled away.

"Oh, Irene—I'm sorry. I didn't mean—"

Irene jumped up, frantically gathering her walls and wits back around her. "Don't give it a thought." She paced to the window. "No one could blame either of us for getting trapped by the tension and emotion of the moment."

"Yeah . . . emotions."

Irene stole a glance at him. He seemed confused, too. Maybe he wasn't such a hiding place after all. Maybe he also needed sheltering and comfort. But why seek such things from her? Couldn't he see she barely had a grip on her own life, much less another's? Certainly even he wasn't so blind that her blaring weaknesses weren't clearly evident. What *did* he see? But Irene doubted she'd ever have the courage to ask him.

"I could use some fresh air," she said.

"Okay." Was that dejection in his tone?

"I wouldn't mind company."

His ready grin warmed her . . . and scared her—it was so much like Greg's.

Seventeen

*A*cross the street from the TransAmerica Building, he bought a copy of the Chronicle from a newsstand and feigned interest in reading it. But his mind couldn't have been further from the printed words before him. Charlie Sullivan's mind, maybe even his whole being, was focused solely on the entrance to the tall skyscraper. Though he'd only been standing by the newsstand for ten minutes, he had been moving around to various other locations within sight of the building for the last two hours.

Earlier he had called Joel's office.

"I'd like to confirm my twelve o'clock appointment," he had said.

"Your name?" asked the secretary.

"Garnet."

"I don't have anyone by that name down, and I'm fairly certain Mr. Costain won't be in the office at noon."

"Costain. . . ? This isn't the office of J. Compton?"

"No, it isn't."

"Compton and Rothchild Accountants?"

"Sorry, no."

"I apologize for bothering you."

Charlie hoped that if he was patient, he'd see Joel leave the building for lunch. If he missed him, he could camp out on Montgomery until Joel left at the end of the day. It was only ten A.M., but Charlie had nothing better to do with his time.

He took a scrap of paper from his pocket and studied it again for the hundredth time. It was a newspaper photo—actually, it was a copy made from the microfiche at the library. It was a dozen years old, a wedding photo of Joel and his new wife. The copy wasn't very good, but he remembered enough details from the original so he was confident he'd be able to identify Joel. As he folded up the paper and replaced it in his pocket, Charlie couldn't help thinking of all the significant moments in Joel's life he had missed. Graduations, a wedding, winning his first case, becoming partner in the firm, maybe the birth of children.

Would all he ever have of his son's life be nothing more than a crummy, distorted copy of an old photo?

His eyes shifted toward the office building. He felt like a fool, lurking in the shadows, trying to catch a glimpse of his own son. He reminded himself of the possible risks of approaching Joel directly. But they seemed remote just now, considering he'd had no repeat of the incident on the Embarcadero. Why couldn't he go right up to Joel, introduce himself, maybe even give him a hug, and tell him he was sorry for all that had happened? Why not get everything out in the open? Forget the nameless, faceless, perhaps even imaginary ghosts he feared.

But Charlie realized it was more than those fears keeping him from approaching Joel. He was scared—but it was a different kind of fear. What if Joel rejected him? He was a jailbird, a convicted killer, a man who had spent the last thirty-seven years in hell, with others of his kind—lowlives, reprobates, derelicts, scum. He was deluded to even entertain the idea that he could be accepted by a man like Joel Costain.

A few minutes later Charlie spotted the seeing-eye dog. It took a couple heartbeats before he could lift his gaze to take in the man holding the dog's harness. A knot rose in his throat, and tears actually welled up in his tired, old eyes.

How straight and tall the blind man was, walking with a confident step. Yes, perhaps led by the dog, but also very much in control. Even the woman by his side seemed to be following his lead, though he was walking about half a step behind her as he held her elbow. Joel's features were more seasoned than in the photo, accounting for the intervening years, but they hadn't hardened with age and experience. In them was still the open warmth of a young groom, the look of a man at ease with himself and a world of darkness.

A sudden impulse to emerge from the shadows and face this man coursed through Charlie. But he had only wanted to look. He wasn't ready for anything else.

"Son . . ." he breathed, but no one heard him.

And he remained where he was, an awful ache burning inside, worse than the pain of his cancer.

∽᷂᷂᷂᷂᷂᷂᷂᷂᷃ↄ

Joel and Irene walked down Montgomery to Market Street. They had no specific destination in mind. Irene thought a short walk around the block might help clear her head, but it had been a mistake not to go alone. All her senses were acutely aware of Joel. Her lips still felt the tender passion of his kiss. Her mind still reeled at his similarities to Greg, suddenly so obvious. Was it more apparent now only because Joel's relationship to Greg had been confirmed? She'd seen it before, of course. Why did it disturb her now more than ever? Why did it frighten her so?

"Irene, I think we need to talk about what happened in my office," Joel was saying.

"Nothing happened."

"Are you sure about that?"

"Don't make a big thing out of a silly kiss. We're both simply wrung out—it meant nothing. Let's move on."

He was silent—a silence she felt with an intensity that made her reel a bit. Irene knew she was not being fair. She was being too hard on him, but she had to protect herself against getting involved in something she knew she'd later regret. Everything was wrong about Joel Costain. He had too many strikes against him. Irene was a more mature, clear-headed woman than she had been twelve years ago when she mistakenly thought she could fix a man's weaknesses. And she had certainly grown beyond succumbing to physical attraction or, for that matter, even to love.

"Irene," Joel said at length, "do you think I'm incapable of being attracted to a woman because I'm blind?" Then he added before she had a chance to respond, "I guess that's a rhetorical question. I don't expect you to answer."

"Even I know what the answer would be, Joel. I don't understand it fully because I operate on a different level when I think of attraction between the sexes—"

"Believe it or not, Irene, I don't operate on a different level from the sighted. I just have different criteria for what stimulates me."

"So, I stimulate you, Joel—and that's supposed to make everything better?"

"I didn't mean—"

"What do you think we're on, some romantic romp?" she railed, suddenly venting all her frustrations. "There's been a murder, Joel! My children's father has been murdered. And all you can think of is whether you are physically stimulated or not? How can you—?"

"Never mind!" Joel snapped. "Just forget it, okay? I'm going back to the office." Then to his dog he said, "Ebony, back to the office." He turned and started back.

"Joel. . . !"

But he didn't respond and she let him go. To do anything else would have sent the wrong message. It might have indicated that she cared. And that would have been the biggest mistake of all. She couldn't care for Greg's brother. She just couldn't!

Irene spent the rest of the afternoon checking out several funeral homes and making arrangements for the disposal of Greg's remains. Detective Reiley still wasn't ready to release the body, but she arranged for the police to send the body directly to the funeral home, where it would be cremated. She wanted to get this over with. Move on, as she had told Joel. Get back to her normal life.

When she got home, Reiley called and wanted to see her again. But when she got to the police station, she found out after a long wait that Reiley had been called away on a case and would probably be gone the rest of the evening.

Several times, Irene was tempted to drive back to Joel's office. She should at least apologize for her harsh words. But she kept telling herself that would be a mistake. Yet, regardless of how often she told herself she would do them both a favor by never seeing him again, she could not shake a strong urge to see him just one more time.

Instead, she threw herself into helping with Adam and Mark's homework and working on a puzzle with them. After she put them to bed, she tried to get involved in some artwork. She picked up her sketchbook and spent a half hour drawing her cat. When she tired of that, she flipped the page and started a face. It wasn't long before it grew into a likeness of Joel. She shook her head.

"You're pathetic, Irene," she chided herself. And she didn't finish the sketch. Why should it be any different than the other work she never completed?

It was easier, however, to ignore a drawing than reality. She realized it just wasn't in her to be so heartless. Whatever else had happened between her and Joel, she knew she owed something, at least, to their budding friendship. And she knew it would hurt him if she left things as they were. Almost the same thing had happened between Joel and Greg, and Joel was suffering because there was no way he could repair the damage his rejection might have caused. It was important that between her and Joel there be proper closure.

She called Connie, who readily agreed to watch the boys for Irene.

Eighteen

*J*oel returned to his office after the walk with Irene.

"Hold my calls," he told the secretary as he opened his door.

"Okay, Mr. Costain. But a Detective Reiley has called several times—"

"Especially hold his calls."

Joel ducked into his office.

He hated himself for being such a jerk, for letting his emotions supersede good sense. Irene had been right that his timing was all wrong. She had been right to be indignant at how insensitive his actions were. She had been justified in misinterpreting him.

But she had been very, very wrong in believing that kiss had meant nothing. Joel knew himself too well to believe that. He had gone out with other women since Ellen. During those first dates, his heart hadn't been in it at all. Friends had played cupid for him, trying to help him get over his grief, but for two or three years it had been very easy for him to find things wrong with the women, small things or big, it didn't matter so long as it provided an excuse for him to end the fledgling relationships. Then, when the hurt of his grief began to disperse, he began to think he would like to marry again, to have a companion, perhaps even some children. Trying to make a relationship happen had been no easier. He still could find no one who could fill the empty void left by his wife, no one who could stir him emotionally and spiritually.

His friends chided him for being too picky. His parents worried that he would go on forever clinging to the past. He didn't think his desires were too exorbitant. All he wanted was a soul mate, a woman who could fulfill his needs as much as he could fulfill hers. But he supposed because of his handicap he wanted less emphasis on *his* needs. Although a strong woman appealed to him, he didn't want someone with a need to mother him and care for him. There had been several of those along the way, and they scared him off like a skittish jackrabbit. Maybe he *was* arrogant, but he saw no reason for anyone to mother him or protect him. He'd settle for nothing less than a completely normal relationship, just as he'd had with Ellen. If that was being picky, then so be it.

So, where did Irene fit in to this?

With so much going on right now, maybe he was crazy to even think about her. But Joel hadn't asked for their worlds to cross—or collide. He was no more looking for a woman right now than he had been looking for a brother.

Irene just happened.

There was no explaining it, except he now was going to have to find some way to explain it to her. To make her understand that she was touching him in a way he had not felt since Ellen—on all the levels he could possibly hope for, even spiritual. That was odd, too, given her ambivalence about God. Irene claimed she was spiritually dead, yet when they talked about faith, Joel sensed something very much alive in Irene. No matter what she said, he knew she hadn't stopped reaching out for God or longing for the joy and peace of that first love she had once felt.

Would Irene listen to him? Why should she? Hadn't she made it clear she felt nothing toward him? Yet, when they had kissed, she had responded to him. And though Joel was no schoolboy to place huge stock in such responses, he simply could not ignore all that had accompanied it the last few days. True, this *was* a bad time. And his relationship to Greg probably made him less than appealing to Irene. He supposed the best thing to do was to let it go—rather, leave it in God's hands. In fact, that was the one thing he hadn't done yet. Pray.

Then his phone rang. Joel rolled his eyes and murmured, "You know my prayer, anyway, don't you, Lord?"

He lifted the receiver.

"I'm sorry, Mr. Costain," said the secretary. "But your one o'clock appointment is here."

"That's okay, Martha. Give me a minute, then send him in."

The day got completely away from Joel after that. Life wasn't about to stand still for him to resolve all the conflicts of his own life. Although part of him fully realized he was using his busy schedule as a shield against those conflicts. He did try to call Irene. But there was no answer. Why didn't she have an answering machine like everyone else?

Another problem also nagged at him throughout the afternoon. His parents. Since talking with Jim, Joel knew he could no longer put off facing them. Perhaps they had some answers. He just wasn't sure he wanted to know anymore. His mother had called him once that afternoon, but he had been with a client and managed to avoid the call.

One caller he hadn't been able to dodge was Reiley. The detective had tried calling several more times, then he had arrived in person, forcing Joel to cancel an appointment in order to talk to the man. Then Reiley grilled Joel for a half hour, making it clear that, though he didn't have enough evidence to support an arrest, he considered Joel his best suspect.

"Mitchell was beaten to death," Reiley told him, "then put in his car and sent over a cliff."

"And you think I did that?"

"I didn't say that, but it is conceivable that someone with a bank-roll like yours could have hired killers. I've seen everything, Costain—killers of all sizes, shapes, ages, and physical conditions. Don't think being blind is gonna protect you, if you did it."

"*If*—but even you, Detective Reiley, have to admit that's a big assumption. And I must say, I don't have to put up with the direction of your questions without the formality of charges against me."

"I'm not accusing you of anything."

"Good. However, I do want to cooperate in any way I can because I have nothing—*nothing*—to hide. For instance, you ought to know that recently—this morning, in fact—it was all but confirmed that Greg Mitchell was my brother." Joel slid a folder across his desk. "Here are supporting documents, in addition to a few other items that might be of interest to your investigation. Those are copies for you to keep."

"That is cooperative of you, Costain," said Reiley with a slight edge of irony to his tone. Nevertheless, he scooped up the folder.

"One person, who is mentioned in that folder, could probably help your case considerably. Charles Sullivan."

"Yeah, we know about him. And, guess what? He's disappeared."

"I know."

"I sure hope I don't find his body at the bottom of some cliff."

"I have an investigator working on locating him," said Joel, ignoring Reiley's implied accusation.

"I guess he'd be your father."

"Right."

"Ex-con, convicted killer—some family tree you got, Costain."

"We can't all have your impeccable credentials, Reiley."

"Okay, Costain, that's all I've got for now." Reiley pushed his chair back sharply and stood. "You're not planning any long trips, are you? I'd like you to stick close to town."

"I'm not going anywhere."

"And you will keep us informed of anything your investigator uncovers."

"Gladly."

The encounter had been disturbing, not only in being suspected for something of which he was completely innocent but also in the memories of the past it conjured—his ill-fated career in criminal law. One of the few times in his life he had yielded to his handicap, admitting that maybe, just maybe, there was one realm where the blind could not venture.

When Joel's last appointment left at six that evening, he was ready to go home, turn on his stereo, and lose himself in the world of music. Then one of his associates came in and reminded him about the gathering to celebrate Arthur Eberhard's birthday. Had it been for anyone else, Joel would have politely declined, but one simply could not slight the firm's senior partner in that way without a major excuse. Joel at least had to make an appearance. But what if Irene tried to reach him while he was at the restaurant where the party was to be held? What if he missed her?

When he finally returned home at nine o'clock, all he could think of was getting to the answering machine and checking his messages.

Nineteen

Joel's key did not fit into his lock as smoothly as usual. Ebony was suddenly restless, whimpering.

"What's wrong, girl? Did someone feed you pâté at the party?"

Joel wiggled the key, but nothing happened. His ride had already driven off, so he'd be stuck if he didn't get the key to work. He turned the doorknob, then tried turning both the knob and the key, and finally it gave way. Immediately upon stepping inside, he heard sounds. He took a few more steps.

Then Ebony barked and held back.

Joel knew better than to override his dog's good sense and would have exited right then, but before he could turn, a voice stopped him.

"Let's get outa here!" said a male voice.

"Hey!" Joel yelled.

"He's seen us."

Something struck Joel. Staggering back, another obstacle made him lose his balance. As he hit the floor, he flailed wildly, hoping to strike his attacker. Instead, he was struck again, this time full in the face. The blow disoriented him, though he was certain he heard Ebony snarling.

One of the attackers screamed. "Get this blasted dog off me!"

Then there was a sharp sound, followed by a terrible "Yelp" from Ebony.

"Ebony!" Joel yelled, but there was no answering bark, only a few more pitiful whimpers. Joel tried to crawl toward the dog, reaching out his hands, hoping that at any moment he would feel Ebony's warm, soft fur.

"I'm bleeding!" said one of the men. "That dog bit me!"

And, without thinking, Joel struggled to his feet and leaped in the direction of the sound of that voice. He was shocked when he made contact with one of his attackers. But he knew he had to act quickly because whatever advantage he had through surprise wouldn't last long. He sent his fist flying and clipped something soft and fleshy.

However, he experienced only a moment's gratification from that success before being grabbed from behind and yanked away from his prey.

"Lenny, he broke my nose!" said one of the interlopers, and from the direction of the man's voice, Joel could tell he was lying on the floor directly in front of Joel. Joel experienced a grim satisfaction that he'd hurt the man. But he had no chance of getting at him again because firm hands now gripped Joel's arms, wrenching them firmly behind him.

"Shut up, you idiot!" said the man holding Joel.

"He isn't gonna identify us, stupid, he's blind. Put him out so we can get away."

"You don't want to do that," said Joel desperately. "Burglary is one thing, but assault—"

"That's right, I forgot you're a lawyer," said the man holding Joel. "I don't need no free legal advice. But maybe you can tell us *something*."

"You want me to loosen his tongue?" asked the other man who was now standing in front of Joel.

"Yeah, but not too much—remember he's a lawyer, and we might never get him to stop talking once he starts." The man laughed at his humor. Then he added, "And, don't make the same mistake you made last time."

"So, Costain, you gonna be cooperative?" A voice growled in Joel's face.

Before Joel could answer, a fist smashed him in the ribs. He gagged and doubled over. The other man's big hands still held him firmly, yanking him upright.

"Where is it?"

"My wallet . . ." Joel gasped. "In my back pocket—"

Another blow clipped him across the chin.

"I ain't talking about chicken feed. Now where'd the old man tell you to put it?"

"I . . . don't know what you mean."

"So, you're gonna be stubborn."

"I don't know—"

Joel struggled mightily against his captor, but the stronger man held firm. Then the blows started coming without letup, raining on him from out of the darkness like cruel reminders of his weakness.

"Okay, I said don't get carried away," said Joel's captor, his voice barely penetrating the fog descending over Joel's brain.

Then they dropped him in a heap on the floor and the fog became impenetrable.

⟨ᏇᏇᏇ⟩

Joel had no idea how long he lay there unconscious. It might have been minutes, or it could have been morning already. How could he know if light penetrated the windows of his home? Joel tried to move, but he retracted against the pain, in his chest mostly, but also in his head and limbs. He had to get up, he couldn't just lie there. He had to do something.

Groping about, he found something solid—an overturned arm-chair. He gripped it and forced himself first to his knees, then painfully to his feet. Taking a step, his foot crunched something like broken glass. Another step.

All right, he silently told himself, this is my house—I can find my way. Then an awful thought occured to him. Maybe he wasn't in his house at all, maybe the theives had dragged him away—but that was irrational, they'd have no reason to do that. He had to start thinking straight. Logically. He must be in his house, in the living room, judging by the armchair. Hoping the chair hadn't been moved too far from its usual location, he turned a bit to his left. There should be an end table—but his foot struck a smaller obstacle, lower to the floor, and he was thrown off-balance. He started to go down, reached out—grasped only air. When he fell, he didn't hit the floor, but rather struck thin hard objects that stabbed into his bruised, sore chest. Catching his breath, he tried to calmly identify this new obstacle. He moved his hands up and down the thin projectiles, finding at the bottom a somewhat flat surface. The end table. He pushed away from it, rubbing the new bruises the table legs had made in his already aching chest.

And now he began to worry as he realized the upturned end table indicated his attackers had no doubt ransacked his house. There was no telling where he was in relation to anything else. Hope of finding his way to a telephone diminished. But he had faced larger obstacles in his life and was not daunted—at least not yet.

"Ebony," he called, suddenly remembering he wasn't alone.

Or was he?

There was no answer to his call. No friendly bark, no sound of harness jingling as his dog jogged to his rescue. Joel reached out as if to welcome his friend's exuberant approach. But Ebony never came.

Momentary panic caught at Joel. He was lost in his own home, helpless.

"Oh, God! Help me!"

He took a breath and swallowed back the fear. Then, with renewed determination, tried again to make the journey across the unchartered jungle his living room had become. He remained on his hands and knees so as not to fall again, but the floor was littered with broken glass. His hands were cut to ribbons when a few minutes later he paused by a doorway. He had hoped to find his kitchen and the cordless phone he had left there that morning. But there was carpet on the other side of this doorway, not linoleum as was in the kitchen. He had been heading in the opposite direction of the kitchen. This was a guest room he hardly ever used. At least now he had a direction to follow.

Using the wall as a reference point, he hugged as close to it as the many scattered obstacles—torn books, picture frames, lamps—would allow. He had only gone two feet, however, when he encountered an obstacle that made him stop in horror.

"Ebony!"

The dog didn't move.

"Oh no!" he groaned and bent over the sleek, furry form and wept.

Twenty

*I*rene had never felt more foolish as she drove up to Joel's house. She should have called instead of barging in on him unannounced. Yet, it had seemed easier this way. Nonetheless, she had taken her time on the drive from San Bruno, driving the speed limit on the freeway—she couldn't remember when she had done that when it wasn't rush hour. Then she meandered through the streets of San Francisco with uncharacteristic patience. She wasn't even certain she would go through with it until she turned on to Greenwich Street.

What is the big deal, anyway? Showing up at his house at ten o'clock at night is only making that much more of it. . . .

"Go home, you idiot," she told herself, "before you set something into motion you will only regret."

When there was no parking on his street, Irene decided she had the perfect out. But, for some reason she couldn't fathom, she drove around the block, returning again to his street. Only after driving around the block twice was she seriously convinced to keep on going, abandoning her impulsive mission. Then a parking spot opened up on his street, a few doors down. Parking the Toyota, she tried to shake the feeling that something was conspiring against her—or was it conspiring *for them*? She took a breath and stepped out of her car.

Joel's door was slightly ajar, as if he had tried to kick it shut as he hurried in, not latching it completely. At least he must be home. . . . She knocked.

No answer.

Maybe he was asleep. It *was* ten-fifteen. But the lights were out, and Joel usually kept his lights on when he was awake, for Ebony's benefit. Irene recalled him once mentioning that he was a nocturnal creature, needing only a few hours of sleep a night. Why she didn't quit then, she didn't know. She was probably going to wake him up and feel terribly embarrassed. Yet an unsettled feeling nagged at her. Gathering her courage and determination, she knocked again.

The door creaked open. Now she really felt awkward.

"Joel?" she said tentatively, softly.

Certainly he would have checked his lock before going to bed. Maybe something *was* wrong. Even if Joel hadn't heard the squeaky door hinges, Ebony surely would have and responded protectively. She stepped inside and was about to call Joel's name again when she heard a voice, muffled and raspy.

"Oh, God, what now. . . ? What. . . ?"

"Joel?"

"Irene!" The sound of hope in his voice was enough to dispel her awkwardness.

She strode forward with more confidence and urgency, then, unexpectedly, tripped and would have fallen had she not grasped at a nearby shadow that proved to be a coatrack. Steadying herself, she cast about for a light switch. Finding it, she flipped it on and gasped at what met her gaze. The entire room was torn apart. Every piece of furniture was overturned, and upholstered pieces had been slashed, the stuffing pulled out. Books had not only been tossed from their shelves, but they had been torn from their bindings as well, including what must have been costly Braille editions. Pictures had been torn from the walls and from their frames. Broken shards of glass, dishware, and lamps were strewn all over the white carpet. The fine, tasteful room was destroyed. And beyond that, Irene could see similar destruction in the kitchen.

Far worse than that was Joel's fallen form.

"Oh, Joel!" She rushed to him and dropped down next to him, only vaguely aware of the sharp pain from the broken glass as it cut through her jeans into her knees.

"Irene . . ." he spoke in a shattered, shaky tone, "Ebony's dead. . . ." Tears spilled down his bruised and cut face making tracks through the blood.

She wrapped her arms around him, gently patting his head and cooing soothingly as she would to one of her children. "It's okay . . . it's okay. . . ." Even as she spoke she realized how empty her words were . . . but what else could she say? What other comfort could she give?

She looked down at the dog and instinctively touched her silky black fur, Irene's gaze resting momentarily on a bloody splotch on the dog's abdomen. Irene felt overwhelmed at the thought of Joel's loss. Far deeper than losing an important tool, Joel and his dog had a powerful bond between them. Irene had seen them interact, the companionship between them, how they both seemed to know instinctively the other's needs. She had even envied their relationship. But Ebony's loss was also devastating on a practical level. The dog meant independence to Joel, and without her Joel would be handicapped indeed. It might take weeks or months for him to break in another guide dog.

Joel lifted his head away from Irene. He took a breath and swiped a hand across his face. "I'm sorry," he rasped. "I'll be okay." But his voice lacked its usual confidence.

"What happened, Joel? Should I call the police?"

"Yes—but don't go just yet." There was a desperate quality to his tone as he clutched at her arm. "You don't know how good it was to hear your voice a minute ago, Irene—and I mean *your* voice. Anyone's would have been welcome, but it wouldn't have—"

"I'm just glad I was here." She cut him off, afraid to hear more.

Joel reached out and touched Ebony. "Irene, I feel so lost, so empty—she was just a dog, but—" His voice caught on a sob he could not repress. "Do you know I never cried for Greg? I never shed a single tear. . . . What's wrong with me, Irene? I've cried for my dog but not for my brother."

"He was a stranger."

"He was somebody . . . my brother. Irene, he's dead! My brother is dead. I can never get him back, never have even as much of a relationship with him as I had with my dog." He reached up with a trembling hand and fingered the moisture on his face as if ashamed. Then he buried his face in his hands, silent sobs wrenching at him, all the emotion his stoicism had prevented before now pouring out. "God, forgive me . . . for letting him go. . . ."

"Don't do this to yourself, Joel," Irene murmured, still holding him. Then, desperate to do something to distract him, she added, "Why don't we get out of here? We can call the police from a pay phone."

"I don't want to leave Ebony!" His tone scared her a little, as if he had lost rationality.

"No . . . we won't," she soothed. "We can put her in the backseat of my car." It wouldn't be easy lifting the seventy-pound animal, but Irene was trying to understand how cold it would seem to leave her, even dead, in that pathetic room.

However, it was obvious she couldn't do it alone, and Joel was in no condition to lend a hand. When he finally managed to stand, with Irene's help, he could only do so by remaining somewhat doubled over. He winced painfully with every breath.

"I think I should take you to a hospital," she said.

"I'm okay." His words came through gritted teeth.

"Yeah . . . right," she responded skeptically. She took a tissue from her purse and dabbed at a bleeding cut over his right eyebrow, catching the drips before they hit his eye. He laid his hand over hers and brushed his lips over it. She didn't pull away, though the simple intimacy of that gesture reached something inside her that hadn't been touched in a long time, igniting a rush of confusion within her. She said a little more brusquely than she intended, "Okay, I want you to sit while I figure a way to move Ebony." She turned a chair upright and guided him into it.

"I'm not going to be able to help," he said reluctantly, apologetically.

"I'll figure out a way."

"I wasn't thinking straight, Irene. It'll be too much work. Forget it—"

But she was already trying to scoot her arms under the animal. If she could get the right leverage—

She stopped suddenly. Did she feel movement?

"Ebony!" she cried.

The animal's tail lifted a mere fraction of an inch from the ground then flopped down again.

"Joel! She's alive!"

"Thank God!" Joel breathed, and in a moment was again kneeling on the floor beside his dog. It was as if Ebony's sudden "resurrection" had brought something back to life in Joel, curbing his plummeting despair. Almost as though in answer to Joel's prayer of forgiveness. Joel rubbed his hands up and down the furry flank and felt the animal's movement for himself. But as his hand brushed Ebony's wound, she whimpered. "I'm sorry, girl. . . ." Was he apologizing for *all* his mistakes?

"Irene," Joel said, with vigor and determination, "call my vet. There should be a phone in the kitchen." He called out the number when she had recovered the cordless phone from the rubble.

The vet assured Irene he would open his office and be there to receive the wounded dog. Joel seemed to rally his frayed emotions around the urgent need of his dog, thinking more rationally, with more hope. He told Irene to see if the next-door neighbor was home. She hurried away and enlisted the aid of the woman there. Together they were able to lift the dog onto the backseat of Irene's car. The woman also said she would call the police and wait for them and explain what had happened. With Joel beside her in the Toyota, Irene pulled away from the curb with a screech and dashed across town to the veterinarian's.

Twenty-one

Joel looked pale as he limped back and forth across the floor of the veterinarian's waiting room. Irene had tried to get him to go to an emergency room for himself, but he insisted on staying until he knew if Ebony would make it. Finally, the doctor made an appearance.

"I think she'll pull through. The bullet nicked some organs, and there's been a significant loss of blood, but Ebony is a tough, strong animal. I'm giving her a transfusion now. In a few hours, I'll be able to perform surgery."

The relief was evident even on Joel's drawn, pale visage. "Thanks, doc."

"Now, Joel," the doctor continued, "it looks to me like you could use some first aid."

"Are you offering, doc?"

"You're not furry enough for me. Get yourself to an emergency room." When Joel shrugged non-committally, the vet turned to Irene. "See that he gets to a doctor tonight, young lady."

"Don't worry, that's our next stop," said Irene.

"Doc, I'm going to call you in an hour or so to check in," said Joel.

"I would have been surprised if you didn't."

Joel left reluctantly, and Irene knew he wouldn't have gone even then, except that he must be starting to feel rotten himself. His breathing was becoming more and more labored, and he grimaced painfully every time he took a deep breath. As they drove away from the vet's, Irene pushed hard on the Toyota's gas pedal.

It was after eleven, a clear night with a moonlit, star-studded sky overhead. The traffic was heavy at that late hour, even for the city. But then Irene realized it was a Friday night. How easily she had lost track of time in the last few days.

"I shouldn't have left my house before the police arrived," Joel said as they sped to Mission Emergency.

"Oh, let them sue us if they have a problem with it," Irene quipped.

"You sure are getting bold toward our law enforcement officials. Just a few days ago you were quaking just to be inside their station."

"I guess it doesn't take more than a few encounters to get cynical."

He smiled, then winced as the movement caused a cut on his lip to split open again. Irene quickly handed him a tissue.

Dabbing the wound, he murmured, "I could get used to you being there for me, Irene."

"I don't think you'd like it at all, Joel. You're too stubborn and independent."

"We both are. Maybe that's why I feel safe with you. You understand me too much to want to smother me."

"I suppose so."

"But that's not the real problem, is it? Neither of us is afraid of losing our independence. It's something else. . . ."

"I think we have more pressing matters to discuss."

"You're right, but I don't plan to let go of this. We're going to confront it later."

"We'll see. . . ." She pretended to concentrate on making a turn, then a car pulled out in front of her and she really did have to focus on driving. So nothing more was said until they reached the hospital.

Inside, the place was a hive of activity. More than twenty people stood, sat, slumped, or paced in the waiting room. A receptionist told them they might have to wait an hour—longer if a more urgent case came in. Irene called her sister and explained the situation.

Connie assured her, "Do what you need to do, Reenie. I'll stay with the kids all night if I have to. In fact, since tomorrow is Saturday, why don't I spend the night here? If you're not back by morning, I'll take them home with me."

Relieved and thankful, Irene returned to where Joel leaned against a wall. There were no vacant chairs in the overcrowded room.

"Maybe if I came back in the morning—" Joel began.

"No way!" said Irene firmly. "But I am sorry you have to stand. Would you like to sit in the car? I'll come for you when they call—"

"No way!" he echoed, followed by a taut grin. "We've come this far together. . . ."

"Yes . . ."

Silence intruded for a moment, then Joel asked, "You never did say why you came to my house tonight, Irene."

"That's something we ought to discuss later, too. I have a better question—what happened at your place?"

Joel shook his head, obviously not happy about the subject change, yet resigned to the necessity of discussing Irene's question. "I'm not entirely sure, but I have a sick feeling it was somehow related to everything else that's been happening."

"How?"

He recounted what he remembered about the attack and the conversation of his assailants before he passed out. "It wasn't a run-of-the-mill robbery. They were looking for something specific—they asked me about *it*, very pointedly, and they weren't talking about what I was carrying in my wallet. Besides, I'm sure they destroyed some pretty valuable items—the artwork on the walls alone would have more than compensated their efforts, but they destroyed it."

"Maybe they weren't art connoisseurs."

"How about their comment about 'the old man'?"

"What exactly did they say?"

Joel rubbed his chin in thought. " 'Where did the old man tell you to put it?' or something like that."

"But what old man?"

"I can think of only one old man in this whole affair—Charlie Sullivan."

"So, they thought Sullivan gave you something. What? And who would give them that idea?"

"They probably found out he's my father. It would logically follow then that he might entrust something to me. What I'd really like to know is who those thugs are working for."

"What makes you think they weren't on their own?"

"The way they ransacked my house, the beating they gave me . . . it just seems too professional—and guys who are in that business usually do it for others."

"Is that important?"

"If that's the case, we're not up against two-bit hoods or con artists. Whoever is involved in this has the means to do some serious damage. It's very likely they're the ones who also killed Greg. In fact, I remember one of them saying something about 'not getting carried away like last time.' "

"Joel, do you think they also killed Charlie Sullivan?"

"I . . . don't know."

"You could be in danger."

He rubbed his bruised chin. "Another logical assumption." A nurse called a name, and an elderly woman with a dish towel wrapped around her bloody hand ambled forward. Joel shifted restlessly from one foot to another. "I wish I knew what was in Jim Kincaid's folder," he said distractedly.

"You haven't read it yet?" Irene knew she would have been so curious she would have read it immediately.

"I was going to have you read it to me when we returned to the office, but . . ."

Irene hadn't forgotten about what had happened between her and Joel earlier in the day, but it seemed so long ago. She realized that if she hadn't run off, the day might have turned out differently. Maybe Joel wouldn't have been attacked. They might have gone out to dinner together and not reached his place until after the criminals had gone. Ebony wouldn't have gotten shot—

"Irene," Joel said softly, "don't blame yourself."

Surprised, she lifted her eyes to study him. How could he have known what was in her mind? Did he truly have some kind of sixth sense that miraculously compensated for the one sense he lacked? Or did it spring from a more personal source? Was there an emotional connection between them? But they were practically strangers. How many times had she reminded herself of that over the last few days? It was becoming harder and harder to believe. As she gazed at him now, she felt familiar with every feature of his strong, handsome visage. As though she had been observing and discovering him for years.

Was it his similarity to Greg? But she'd never felt quite this way with Greg, not for many years. It was Greg who had been a stranger. Joel was . . .

Who are you, Joel Costain? Am I willing to take the risk to find out?

"I'm not blaming myself," Irene said, trying to shake the spell capturing her. "But I did walk out without a word. You didn't deserve for me to blow up at you like I did."

"Why did you come back?"

"To rescue you, of course," she answered lightly. But it was the wrong reply at that particular moment. He recoiled.

"I don't need you to rescue me. I don't need to be protected. I—" He stopped abruptly and turned slightly away from her. His voice was dry and hollow when he added, "What a joke. And with Ebony gone, that statement is quite a riot." No amusement was evident in his tone.

"You're not feeling sorry for yourself, Joel?"

"It can happen even to arrogant lawyers."

"There's nothing wrong with an occasional lapse."

"I've spent my life trying not to be helpless, running from women who wanted to *help* me." He spoke the word *help* as if it was a foul obscenity. "Never mind. I don't want to whine—that would be worse, by far, than helplessness. But, Irene, I sensed from the beginning that you were different, that you saw me not as a *blind* man— but as a *man*."

"I think you're being overly sensitive because of all that just happened." Impulsively she took his hand; they couldn't make eye contact, and she needed some connection with him. "Joel, those thugs yanked your secure rug out from under you. It's no wonder your confidence is a bit shaky. In a way, my relationship with Greg has made me feel the same way about relationships with other men. . . ." Her voice trailed off. "You have to give yourself a break, and maybe, just maybe, you are going to have to accept some help—There! I've uttered the horrible word. Everyone has to submit to their weaknesses now and then. I don't have much going for me—no money, no spiritual foundation, and my emotional balance has been pretty shaky lately, too. But I've got eyes—and I gladly offer them to you. That's all, just eyes.

"I've already got two children, Joel—I don't need to mother anyone else."

He lifted her hand to his lips, and an interchange occurred between them, like two lovers gazing into each other's eyes, opening their hearts and an avenue of trust. She sensed he was looking as deeply into her as she was into him. And the level of intimacy in that exchange made her both want to run away from it and wrap herself up in it. Then Joel moved almost imperceptibly away from her, leaning back against the wall, still holding her hand.

Before another word could be said, the nurse called Joel's name.

Twenty-two

*T*hey left the hospital at two in the morning. Joel had received stitches for a cut over one eyebrow and had a cracked rib taped. He had called the veterinarian's office several times and, when he called again before leaving the emergency room, received word that Ebony was in surgery. Joel insisted on going there and waiting until it was over.

The veterinarian came out an hour later to inform them that the surgery had gone well.

"Now, go home and get some rest," the doctor admonished Joel. "You look like you need it more than the dog."

Joel, completely exhausted, had little difficulty obeying the order. He and Irene climbed back into the Toyota. As Irene started up the engine, she suddenly realized Joel had no home to go to.

"I know of a place where we are sure to receive a welcome—even at this hour," Joel said.

"Lead the way—" Irene stopped awkwardly.

Joel laughed, then directed confidently, "Head north to the Golden Gate. We're going to Sausalito—to my parents' house."

"They won't mind us barging in on them in the middle of the night?"

An affectionate smile played across his lips. "Not Mom and Dad."

Irene remembered Joel mentioning how close they were and how his parents had always supported him. But she couldn't help being a little nervous. She also assumed from his description that they were affluent—far removed from her blue-collar world. Not that such class differences had interfered with her and Joel. So, if they were anything like him there was nothing to worry about—they would probably capture her heart just as Joel was starting to do. Then again, maybe that *was* cause for worry.

Well, she convinced herself, I'm only going to drop Joel off and go home. No sense getting sucked any deeper into this family.

The Toyota's headlights cut through the thickening fog as it crossed the Golden Gate Bridge, all but deserted at that hour. Only a handful of cars traversed it in either direction. The knots of pedestrians usually strolling across the bridge and enjoying the view were also absent. But it wouldn't have been a great night to walk over the bridge with its fog-wreathed spires, looking out upon a bay blanketed in eerie, cloudlike wisps. Within a couple hours the clear night had been transformed into something ethereal, moody, like a scene from a Gothic novel. Melancholy crept over Irene, giving her a little shiver and turning her thoughts to sad things—Greg's troubled life ending so unfulfilled; the fact that Joel could never enjoy a sunset; the sweet kiss from a man she could never accept; and, perhaps saddest of all, her own life ending up like one of her unfinished paintings, begun with such promise but cast aside because she didn't have the courage to risk failure.

Irene directed a sidelong glance at Joel, sitting quietly, no doubt absorbed in his own thoughts. She wondered about a painting that included him, with all the things that made a fine work of art—texture, depth, focus, interest. Yet the blank canvas was safe, no chance for error with that. She could be content with her sons and the life they had together. Couldn't she? But that wouldn't last forever; Adam and Mark would grow up and lead lives of their own. She told herself there was nothing wrong with being alone. She'd already learned there were a lot worse things than being single. She let out a frustrated sigh.

"You okay?" asked Joel.

"Yes, sure," she lied.

"Where are we?"

"Just crossed the bridge. We're almost at the tunnel."

"The exit will come up in a minute, the second one after the tunnel."

Irene was familiar with Sausalito, though only as a quaint little town where she brought out-of-town visitors to impress them. This town had always been filled with romantic allure, catering to the Bay Area rich with its spendy shops and elite air. Irene had come here a couple times since she had started painting, to draw the colorful marina filled with elegant yachts and the lovely hills peopled by the masters of such vessels.

She took the Monte del Mar exit, and, as Irene might have guessed, Joel's directions led them into those very hills. The narrow and winding two-lane road would be difficult enough to manage on a clear day, but, in the fog, it was harrowing at best. Even Irene was forced to take a cautious approach, especially when they turned down a road that quickly disintegrated into one lane. It was hard to tell now, but Irene imagined that the homes tucked into the hills all had spectacular views. At last they came to a two-story house sitting on a bluff, facing the bay. Joel described it so accurately, Irene could hardly believe he had never before seen it.

"When it's clear, you can see Angel Island," Joel said.

"I'll bet it's fantastic."

Irene pulled down a steep driveway and parked before a house that gleamed white even in the foggy darkness. It was very streamlined in design, as if the architect realized that in competing with the glorious view of the bay, any house but the simplest would be dull by comparison. Irene stepped out of the car and immediately noticed the scent of roses. Instinctively, she took in a deep breath of the sweet smell.

"It's great, isn't it?" Joel said. "The rose garden is one of my favorite places. I'll show you in the morning."

He seemed to be expecting her to stay, so she said nothing just then to dispel that expectation. A subtle change seemed to be infusing Joel. The taut lines around his mouth were relaxing, and that easy confidence was returning. Only then did Irene fully realize how these last days had weighed upon him. In a few quick, eager strides he reached the door.

Irene could not match his enthusiasm. No matter how nice he claimed his parents were, it didn't settle well with her to wake them from a sound sleep, greeting them with Joel's injuries and the incredible tale of recent events. Joel rang the bell, apparently unaware of her reluctance.

Three long minutes passed before the sounds of padding feet could be heard inside.

"Who is it?" came a man's voice, still thick with sleep. "Joel?" He must have made use of the peephole in the door.

"Yes, Dad, it's me."

"Let me turn off the alarm."

In a moment the door swung open, and the two men embraced each other without another word. Irene observed the intensity of Joel's embrace, even in spite of his injured ribs, lingering longer than a greeting after a couple weeks' separation could account for. Joel's father must have noticed it, too.

"What's wrong?" he said. Then he noticed Irene. "Hello," he added with more warmth than she had dared expect.

"Dad, this is Irene Lorenzo—"

"Good Heavens! Joel, what happened to you?" Mr. Costain exclaimed as he got a view of his son in the light of the entryway.

"Long story—"

"Come in . . . come in," Mr. Costain said, adding as he closed the door behind them, "Let me tell your mother you're here." The elder Costain jogged up the steps that led from the entryway. Halfway up, he called, "Adrianne! It's Joel."

Joel's mother appeared around a corner, knotting the belt of a lavender, quilted satin dressing gown. Irene had a good look at the couple as they descended the stairs. Walt Costain was a tall, thick-chested man with plentiful iron gray hair and a matching moustache. His suntanned face made him appear as if he spent much time outdoors, perhaps on one of those yachts in the Sausalito marina. Joel's mother also had a tanned, attractive face. She was taller than Irene by several inches, trim, and even after being woken in the middle of the night, every strand of her short, graying pale hair was in place. They looked exactly as you might expect an affluent city couple to be.

And they intimidated Irene.

Then Joel's mother spoke, the warmth of her voice diffusing even Irene's fears. Adrianne rushed ahead of her husband down the stairs.

"Joel! What on earth happened to you?" Without waiting for an answer, she embraced him.

"Not so tight, Mom," Joel said with a wince and a slanted smile.

"Oh, dear!" She stood back, but grasped Joel's hands and didn't let go. Then she turned kind eyes toward Irene. "I'm Adrianne," she said, offering one of her hands to Irene while she still held on to Joel with the other.

"I'm Irene Lorenzo." Irene took the hand, shook it briefly, and let go.

"I'll put on a pot of coffee," Adrianne said.

"Mom, we feel bad enough waking you at this hour. We can talk in the morning."

"You don't think I can go back to sleep, do you? But if you're tired—"

"It's not that—"

"Joel, no use trying to argue. Your mother is determined to talk. We can all sleep until noon tomorrow if we want," said Walt.

In the darkness, Irene only caught shadowed glimpses of some of the rooms as they crossed the entryway and walked down a hall to the kitchen. But she was left again with the distinct impression of taste and affluence and an ambiance not unlike Joel's house. Irene was almost certain his mother must have decorated both places herself or at least been integral in the choices of decor.

The kitchen, however, had a warmer, cozier feel. Besides the oak cabinets and large counter-island, there was a big, round oak table and matching captain's chairs in one corner and a well-worn plaid sofa and chair facing a television in another corner of the room. On a coffee table in front of the sofa there was a recent issue of *TV Guide*, a couple newspapers, and several magazines, including *Sunset* and *Cruising World*. This room was lived in, and unlike the living room and formal dining room which looked more like photos from *House Beautiful*, Irene could easily picture children running through the kitchen or Joel seated at the table with a peanut butter and jelly sandwich in hand or Walt reading the paper with feet propped up on the coffee table.

While Adrianne busied herself fixing coffee, Joel flopped down on the sofa as he must have done countless times before. Irene sat next to him while Walt took the big matching chair.

"So, Irene, how do you know Joel?" asked Walt, who seemed more interested in filling the silence than in gleaning information.

Irene glanced at Joel, then said, "Perhaps Joel should tell you. . . ."

"Let's wait until the coffee's done," said Joel.

Another silence ensued, and after a minute, Irene tried to fill it. "I live in San Bruno now, but I grew up in the city—in fact, I was born at St. Francis Hospital."

"Well, it's not often these days you meet a born-and-bred San Franciscan."

After a couple more minutes of chitchat, Adrianne joined them with a tray of steaming mugs of coffee, cream, sugar, and even a plate of cookies. Irene could tell she was a woman who took entertaining—even at three in the morning—seriously. She sat on the other side of Joel on the sofa.

Joel and Walt both doctored their coffee with cream and sugar while Irene and Joel's mother took theirs black. Everyone seemed quite interested in their cups—or, as was more likely, reluctant to plunge into what promised to be an involved discussion.

Joel finally took the initiative. "My house was broken into." Even now he was taking the round-about approach. "I stumbled in on them in the act."

"And they beat you up?" asked Walt.

"Yes. And shot Ebony—"

"Oh, Joel!" Adrianne's hand went to her mouth in horror. "She's not—"

"We got her to the vet in time. It looks like she'll be okay. I was suddenly homeless—the house-breakers also tore my place apart—so, we came here."

"Did they get away?" asked Walt.

"Yes . . ."

"But that's not all there is to it," prompted Adrianne.

Joel shook his head. "Where do you want me to start?"

"How about the beginning?" said Walt.

"Like maybe thirty-seven years ago in a San Francisco adoption agency?"

Adrianne and Walt exchanged a poignant but resigned look.

"The break-in and your adoption are related," said Walt, his words more a statement than a question.

"I think so."

"Walt," said Adrianne, "we shouldn't have ignored that phone call—"

"So, they did contact you?" Accusation infused Joel's words.

"Before we left for Hawaii," said Adrianne. "The agency told us there had been inquiries and wanted to know if we were interested in signing a release-of-information form."

"And you told them no, then left for a vacation," said Joel sharply.

"I don't like your tone," said Walt, a bit indignant.

Joel laced his fingers through his hair. "I'm sorry." His voice was still tense.

"We told them," Walt continued, "that we'd like to think about it. We went away so we'd have time to really consider all the possibilities before we saw you. How did you find out, son? What's going on?''

"I had a visit from a man named Greg Mitchell who claimed to be my brother. He informed me about my birth parents—a mother who died giving birth to me, a father who's been in prison for thirty-seven years. I have since verified most of his story, and, to some extent, his claims about being related to me. But not before Greg Mitchell was murdered.''

A little gasp escaped Adrianne's lips.

"There's more,'' said Joel. "Irene, here, is Greg's ex-wife. I met her several days ago when I was trying to find Greg, who had disappeared—of course, that was before we learned he had been killed.''

"Your brother . . .'' Adrianne murmured, shaking her head.

"Did you know about him, Mom? Did you realize I had a brother all along, someone I could have met—''

"Joel, please don't,'' begged Adrianne, nearly in tears.

"You can't lay recriminations on us, Joel,'' said Walt. "We did what we felt was best—for you. Think of the position we were in. Long ago, adoptions were highly secretive affairs. Typically no information whatsoever was exchanged between birth parents and adoptive parents. We happened to know more than many because of your peculiar situation.'' He sighed before continuing. "Let me tell you exactly how it was. Your mother and I had tried to have children for years and, finally giving up on that, turned to adoption—we've told you all this—but what we may not have told you was how difficult it was to get a child. I was a fledgling architect, a small fry in a big firm, with a small income. That, along with the fact that we didn't own a home, made it difficult to qualify. Anyway, we finally did qualify, at least to the point where we could get on a waiting list. Then you came up for adoption. You would have met the most particular qualifications—blond, blue eyes, white—the perfect child to fit in to many of the typical families seeking children. Except for one thing—''

"I was flawed merchandise.''

"We never considered you flawed,'' said Adrianne. "We had a home and love to give; you needed a home and love. It was that simple. There was no way under heaven that we could have turned you away.''

"We still had to go through another battery of tests,'' added Walt, "to prove we'd be fit parents for a handicapped child."

"It must have been grueling and frustrating," said Irene.

"Joel was two months old before we took him home," answered Adrianne. "I truly felt as if I'd experienced labor and delivery."

"During that time," said Walt, "the trial of Charles Sullivan was fairly big news in town—" he added to Irene. "We lived in the city at the time. Didn't move here until Joel was two and my career began to really take off. Anyway, the trial was in the newspapers. It didn't take a genius to put the pieces together—a woman gives premature birth to a child who is blinded in the process, after her husband is arrested for robbery and murder. We asked the agency about it, but they couldn't tell us. However, they pointedly didn't deny it either. Our social worker felt we had a right to know we were adopting the child of a murderer. It wouldn't have mattered, though. We considered you our son the moment we first laid eyes on you, before we ever heard about Charles Sullivan."

Joel chewed his lip for a long, silent moment. The muscles in his jaw twitched as he apparently absorbed his father's explanation. "How come you never told me about him?"

"You never asked," said Walt, with a slight edge, then he added more gently, "Believe me when I tell you we wrestled with that question—right up until a month ago when we received that phone call. From the beginning we decided it would have done you no good to know. In fact, we sincerely believed it might have done you harm. You already had a lot stacked against you. How much worse would it have been for you to grow up knowing about your birth father? Knowing you were the child of a killer? We decided not to take that risk."

"But what about now?" asked Joel. "Was there never a point in my adult life when you thought I might be able to handle it?" Lurching to his feet, he strode across the familiar room, finally halting at the island counter, where he rested his hands on it, his back toward the others. The muscles in his shoulders bunched tensely.

"Can you forgive us, son?" asked Adrianne plaintively.

"There's nothing to forgive." He shook his head. "You would have told me anytime, but I never asked. I never asked. . . ."

"Now, don't start blaming yourself," said Adrianne.

"I'm tired," Joel said abruptly. "I've kept everyone up long enough. Mom, would you show Irene to a guest room?" He swung around and made his way to the kitchen door where he paused and briefly turned toward the others. "Good night," he said, making an effort to somehow soften his previous abruptness. Then he continued on his way. He needed no help, except for his cane, to find the bedroom he had occupied half his life.

Irene was too tired to argue when Adrianne led the way to a second-floor guest room.

Twenty-three

Joel awoke at about seven in the morning. He followed the fragrance of freshly brewed coffee down to the kitchen. His mother was there humming—off-key—the Gaither tune "Something Beautiful," his mother's favorite.

"Beautiful!" he said as he ambled into the room, cane loosely held in his hand, though he hardly needed it in these familiar surroundings.

"Even if I can't carry a tune?"

"When did that ever matter?"

"Here." Adrianne had poured him a cup of coffee and held it out to him.

He took it and went to the oak table and sat down.

"The bowl of sugar and a pitcher of milk are at twelve o'clock," Adrianne casually instructed Joel, then just as casually added, "Your friend, Irene, seems like a nice person."

Joel grinned. "I love your subtlety, Mom!"

"So. . . ?" she prompted.

"I met her less than a week ago. She's my brother's ex-wife. I can't begin to list the complications—"

"But you're in love with her nonetheless."

Joel deliberately stirred his coffee, then brought his cup to his lips and slowly sipped the rich brew. "Is it that obvious?"

"To me, it is. I guess I know you too well, Joel."

"Then, can you tell me what I'm going to do about it?"

"Be gentle, understanding, and give her time."

"That won't be easy to do. I've been waiting a long time for her—and now that she's here, I'm ready. Unfortunately, she wants to run in the other direction. She's scared. Her ex-husband was a real scoundrel and brought a lot of havoc into her life. That alone would make it hard enough for her to want to get involved with someone, anyone! But the man's brother? I wonder if I have a chance.''

"It won't help to push.''

"I know. If God wants this to happen, it'll happen,'' Joel said, his tone slightly colored with sarcasm.

Adrianne finished wiping off the counter, then poured herself a cup of coffee and brought it to the table. Sitting, she laid her hand on Joel's. "It could be worse, you know. It could be your handicap that scares her.''

Joel chuckled. "I love you, Mom. You always know the right thing to say.'' He paused and drank his coffee. He had to broach another subject that wouldn't be as easy. "Mom, I have to apologize for my behavior last night.''

"There's no need, Joel.''

"It was wrong to even hint that you or Dad might be in any way responsible for my ignorance. I let it happen, not you.''

"And for good reason.'' Joel heard her chair creak as she shifted her position before taking another drink of coffee. Then she continued. "I'm no psychology expert, but I think it's pretty common for children, even in the most functional families, to fear abandonment. That's why babies scream so when their mothers leave them at a sitter's. You went through that, too, but it lasted longer than your infancy. You were five or six before I could leave without you raising a ruckus of some sort. You were five when we told you we had adopted you.''

"I remember that,'' said Joel. "You said you looked at lots of babies, and out of them all you had chosen me. Boy, was I proud! A couple of months later, when I accepted the Lord, I could really understand the concept of being an adopted child of God.''

"Yes, you seemed to have accepted it very well. But there were deeper insecurities hidden below the surface. Imagine the normal childhood fear of abandonment compounded by being adopted—in your little mind you had already been abandoned once. To make matters worse, abandonment is a common fear of blind people—children and adults. You had a triple threat working against you. You had a very good reason for not asking about your roots. What if your asking upset us and we withdrew from you?''

"I should have known that would never happen.''

"Perhaps on a rational level. But the heart and emotions aren't always rational. Had I realized all this at the time, I might have decided differently about how to deal with the question of your birth family. You know when I was first enlightened? While we were in Hawaii last week. We actually met a retired child psychologist and we talked a bit about these things. It was the first time I ever connected the idea of abandonment with your reticence about your birth family. Still, I'm not entirely sure we would have decided any differently. The fact that your father was a convicted killer still hung over us. The fact that he could have gotten paroled at any time was a nagging fear I had. I was always relieved you didn't inquire."

"I understand."

"Do you, Joel? Do you see that no one can be blamed?"

"I suppose so." But he was still not entirely convinced.

That morning Irene woke at nine. She dressed, then went to the kitchen where Walt and Adrianne were eating cereal and toast. She assumed Joel was still sleeping. After Adrianne showed her where to find things, Irene fixed herself some toast and a cup of coffee and joined them. Their conversation was pleasantly trivial—Irene telling about her children, and in turn, Adrianne and Walt telling about Joel's childhood. Irene learned more of Joel's hardships and disappointments—things he spoke little of, perhaps because he didn't want her to feel sorry for him. But as Irene listened to his parents, it only deepened her respect for him. He usually gave the impression of simply striding through life, causing Irene to forget that achievements such as his were made not without crashing into more than a few brick walls.

"When he was in college he had to have readers," Walt told her. "It was especially harrowing in law school. They would tape record chapters from his law books—of course, he had to tear apart his books and pass chapters around to maybe a dozen readers so he could get everything done. Half the time, the readers would forget to say what chapter they had so when he got them back, he had to piece everything back together like a puzzle. And then there were the background noises that would distort the tapes—crying babies, appliances, radios, and TVs. For everything a sighted student had to do, Joel had to do double. Exams were another nightmare. Usually his readers knew nothing about the law, so they could easily read things wrong. Just changing the tense or mixing up first party and second party could make a huge impact on a test.''

"But he passed the Bar on his first try,'' said Adrianne proudly.

"And that was in spite of the fact that his reader got laryngitis halfway through it and had to repeat half of what she read. I won't listen to anyone who says Joel made it because he had help. Of course he had help, and Joel is deeply grateful to those who read so faithfully for him. Yet that in no way diminishes his success. We who can see forget that daily we receive the help of a world geared toward the sighted. What would we do if society were organized to benefit the blind? We'd be lost, fumbling around in darkness. In the country of the blind, the one-eyed man isn't always king.''

Irene wanted to ask about Walt's provocative final statement, but she suddenly remembered something Detective Reiley had told her. "Why did Joel decide to practice tax law instead of criminal law?''

Joel's parents glanced at each other, appearing to silently debate how they should answer such a question. Irene instinctively realized she had stumbled onto a sensitive subject.

"Maybe it's none of my business,'' she said quickly.

"Have you asked Joel?''

"No. I just heard it from someone and forgot about it until now. As I said, it's none—''

"Ask Joel,'' said Adrianne. "I think it would be good for him to tell you.''

Irene didn't know what to make of that statement but decided to let it drop. There was no need for her to even ask Joel. It might only cause things to become too personal, and that was something she wanted to avoid. Yet she had listened avidly to his parents, to their insights about their very special son. She felt almost helpless to maintain her resolve. With each passing moment Joel Costain was taking a firmer and firmer hold on her . . . and on her heart.

"He's out in the rose garden,'' Adrianne said.

"Well, I need to make a phone call before I do anything else,'' Irene hedged. "Do you mind if I use your phone? I want to check on my kids.''

"I'll show you the way,'' said Walt, rising.

But when Irene finished with her call, she found herself wandering out to the garden. The morning was clear, all traces of the early-morning fog gone. The garden was terraced into the hillside sloping down from the back of the house. A brick-lined path wound through the garden, which, if laid flat, would have been nearly the size of a tennis court. The garden faced the sea, and the view was even more spectacular than Irene could have imagined.

Joel was sitting on a stone bench, situated about halfway down the slope, his white cane next to him. His head was slightly inclined and his eyes were unfocused, very much turned inward as if deeply absorbed in his thoughts. Irene thought he looked more like a blind man at that moment than he ever had before, and the realization shocked her. It unnerved her to feel sorry for him. How he would resent her for thinking that! She reminded herself of her discussion, only minutes ago, with his parents and the sense of admiration it had instilled in her.

As Irene approached, she recalled Joel mentioning how he loved this garden, and she could easily see why. Even of the late-blooming roses, there were many colors and varieties. But then Joel's impressions of the garden must be far different from hers. She briefly closed her eyes in a frivolous attempt to experience it as he must. Even with closed eyes, rose-shaped, vibrant images reflected in her mind's eye, something that would be impossible for Joel who, being blind all his life, had not the slightest idea of what a rose actually looked like, nor even what yellow or red or orange were.

"Mind some company?" she asked.

In reply he scooted over on the small bench, but even at that, she had to sit very close to him—disconcertingly close. She tried to concentrate on the view. Angel Island sparkled like some remote hideaway. Her father had once owned a small sailboat and the whole family used to sail out there for picnics.

Then Joel spoke, and oddly, his thoughts were also on his childhood. "One of my first memories of pain came from here," he said quietly, as if giving voice to an on-going train of thought. "I wandered away from the house by myself—I must have been three or four years old. I wanted to find out where that delicious smell came from. My mother found me tangled in a bush, screaming."

"You said you loved the rose garden. . . ."

"I do. Maybe I'm a glutton for punishment. If I avoided everything that caused me pain . . . I might just as well be locked up in an institution." He held out his hand, and in it was a partly open Cup of Gold bud. A fresh drop of blood clung to a scratch on his hand, and though there were other scratches there from last night's attack, Irene knew this one was recent. "I get pricked nearly every time I reach for a rose, but I always reach for them. Feeling and fragrance—and thorns, too—that's all a rose is to me. It's impossible for me to admire them from afar. There must be a moral in there somewhere."

They were quiet for a while. A bee buzzed nearby, then flew away. Irene enjoyed the sense of peace surrounding them. She wanted to bask in it, let it do its work in her, though she knew it couldn't possibly last. When Joel spoke again, it was in a soothing tone that indicated he, too, was benefiting from the ambiance of the moment.

"I've been thinking of Charlie Sullivan. I hope he's alive, Irene. I want to find him, get to know him."

"Despite what he's done?"

"When I was a kid—you have to forgive all these childhood stories. I guess being home brings them out."

"I don't mind." She longed to know everything about him, though she couldn't tell him so.

"Well, when I was a kid, my dad thought I could learn how to play baseball—he's crazy about baseball. But the thought of something I couldn't see flying in my face terrified me."

"I can't imagine how you'd ever catch a ball."

"Well, even my dad decided to concede to my handicap in that area. He gave up after a while, but I thought it really disappointed him. And, like any kid, I wanted to please him. So, I got some of my friends to try and teach me how to catch. I thought it would be fun to surprise my dad with my new skill. It took every bit of grit I had not to duck or cover my head when my friend hurled that first pitch at me. It smashed me right in the face and broke my nose. However, my worst fear having been realized, there was nothing else to fear. I had many more bloody noses, fat lips, even concussions. But it taught me that life is better lived than avoided. A lesson I somehow failed to apply in one important area. All along I avoided my origins. I never asked, Irene. Never. And now it may be too late. I've lost Greg. Maybe Charlie Sullivan is dead, too. But I can't avoid it any longer—I can't avoid him."

"Maybe it won't hurt as much now that you know what to expect."

"Oh, it'll hurt . . . but I think it's about time I began to apply a childhood lesson."

"Joel, what I said yesterday about being your eyes—"

"No, Irene, I'm not going to hold you to that. You need to be home. You have a job, don't you? Responsibilities."

"I want to help you find the answers. I can drive you around, whatever. It must get expensive using taxis all the time."

"Thank God I can afford that kind of independence."

"Maybe you don't need me, but—"

"I need you, Irene, I admit it." His intensity was unsettling.

"You don't have to admit to anything, Joel," she said lightly. "Plead the Fifth."

"I said we'd have to talk about this eventually."

Irene stood abruptly and wandered to a nearby bush, pretending to admire its blooms. Why did he have to be so persistent about this? But, then, that was Joel's nature. If it bothered her so, why didn't she just take the initiative and leave? How could she be so strongly drawn and repelled at the same time?

She jumped when she felt him come up behind her. She hadn't even heard him approach.

"Irene, you're going to have to do better than that if you want to hide from me."

"Who said I was hiding?"

He gently placed his hands on her shoulders and nudged her around to face him. It made her breathless to be so close. He could have bent down so easily and kissed her again, but he didn't. And she was relieved because she desperately wanted him to. She could have drawn away at any time, but she didn't.

"Am I expecting too much of you, Irene?"

She nodded.

He was close enough to sense the movement of her head because he answered, "I'll back off a little. But I do have to tell you one thing—I don't put on relationships like I do clean socks in the morning. I couldn't have a 'romantic romp' even if I wanted one. That's not what this is about."

"Okay . . ." She felt weak and uncertain.

He eased his hands from her shoulders. And, oddly, she felt more of a weight after they were gone. Then he gave her the rose he had been holding.

"Yellow," he said. "For friendship."

"How did you know the color. . . ?" It wasn't what she wanted to say, but it was all she *could* say.

"I just know." There was so much more meaning in his simple statement it made Irene's head swim.

No more was said because Joel's father called from the garden gate. "Joel, there's a police detective on the phone for you."

Twenty-four

*I*rene and Joel drove back to San Francisco reluctantly. The atmosphere at the Costain home was for both a soothing balm. To have that disrupted by a visit to the police made it even harder to leave.

"You're a hard man to nail down, Costain," Reiley said when they met at his desk, and, as always, his words seemed to be loaded with ulterior meaning. "Heard you had a bit of a row at your place last night."

"You could say that. Have you come up with any leads yet?"

"Well, that's burglary's department. When we're done talking, I'll send you down there."

"Why aren't you involved?"

"Like I said—"

"It never occurred to you there might be a connection?" Joel shot back, not hiding his frustration.

"Is that what you think?"

To Irene the answer seemed pretty obvious, even without Joel's side of the story. It was just too coincidental not to be related. Joel, of course, felt the same, but he patiently recounted to Reiley the conversation between his attackers.

"Maybe you heard wrong."

To which Joel retorted, "Better still, maybe I staged the whole event to deflect any suspicion about Greg's murder away from me!"

Reiley scratched the bald spot on his head as if he was really considering Joel's suggestion. "In that case, the break-in *would* be of interest to me."

"Are you going to do anything about this or not, Reiley?"

"Well, now that I've heard your side . . ."

Joel gave a frustrated shake of his head, then said, "Have you learned anything more about Charlie Sullivan?"

"Nothing. For an old codger, he's a slippery devil. I've posted notices at hospitals, the medical center, and with cancer doctors in the city. Maybe that'll get us somewhere."

"Could you trace any fingerprints on Greg's car?"

"The car burned."

"But Greg wasn't—" Irene began.

"He was thrown from the car," Reiley cut in. "That might have saved him if he had been alive to start with." He was momentarily distracted as he searched through the rubble on his desk for a pencil. "Tell me again what those hoods who ransacked your house said?"

After Joel did so, Reiley went on, "Okay, burglary might have some fingerprints. And, who knows? Maybe we'll get lucky and find something left on the burned-out car."

"I believe," said Joel, "that the men at my house were wearing gloves—at least the man who hit me was."

"Well, so much for that." Reiley scratched something off his paper. "They were probably professionals—knew what they were about." Reiley stood. "I guess that's all for now."

"Mr. Reiley," said Irene, "what about Greg's body? When can it be released?"

"Now that all the final reports are in, we can do that at any time."

"This afternoon?"

"I'll push through the paper work."

"I want him sent to this funeral home." She handed him a business card.

"No problem." To Joel, Reiley said, "I suppose we're gonna want to go through your house again because of this new light you've shed on the case. So, I'm gonna keep the police barrier up for a day or two more."

After Irene and Joel left the police and headed to her car, she asked, "What are you going to do if you can't get into your house? Do you need anything?" He'd had a change of casual clothes at his parents, which he was now wearing, but he had little else.

"Even if Reiley would let me, I'm not sure I want to go back to my house as it is now. Anyway, they might well have ripped up my clothes, too." He paused as he considered his options.

Irene said, "Why don't I take you shopping?"

"Excellent idea!"

They picked up Adam and Mark, then drove to the mall.

"Have you ever gone shopping with a blind guy?" Joel asked.

"Nope," said Irene. Then, with a twinkle in her eyes, added, "But you know, of course, that purple and orange is all the rage this season for men's clothing?"

"Mom!" scolded Adam, "that's a terrible thing to say."

"I was just joking."

"You wouldn't be the first to get me with that," said Joel. "Not that I didn't deserve most of the abuse I got in my youth. I did everything but ask for it. Once my roommate switched all my socks so each pair was two different colors. Then there was the time I really got my comeuppance."

"What happened?" asked Mark.

"We had a little row in the cafeteria one day that evolved into a huge food fight—which I caused. But when all the perpetrators were rounded up, I pleaded 'poor blind kid' and got off without so much as a lecture. The others spent hours cleaning the cafeteria. But they got back at me. They put dye in my shampoo—the permanent stuff, too—and I walked around all day with green hair before some kind soul mentioned it to me. It was a long time before my hair was normal again."

"Bet you never did that to your friends again," said Adam.

Joel shrugged sheepishly. "I'll plead the Fifth on that."

After a moment of silence, Adam asked, "How do you know what color clothes you're wearing?" He was hesitant, but Irene could tell he was too curious to restrain himself.

"Everything I have is very organized—at least it was. It all has Braille markings on it with the color or if it's a plaid or stripe. But even now, my mom helps me shop and get organized."

Joel's answer was so easy and open that it broke down the boys' remaining reserves. They freely asked questions throughout the rest of the afternoon.

"How does Ebony know when to cross the street?" Mark asked. Crossing streets was still an adventure for the six-year-old.

"I tell her," said Joel.

"But what good is she, then?"

"I should say, the final judgment is mine. But she's been trained to watch and listen, too. The best way I can explain it is that we are a team. We've become very sensitive to each other. There have been times when I've given the 'forward' command and she held back because she saw a car turning a corner—one that I perhaps couldn't hear because it had slowed down."

"Have you ever been hit by a car?" Mark asked, eyes wide.

"Never."

"Maybe Mark should have Ebony," said Adam with a haughty tone. "He's scared of crossing the street."

"So am I, at times," Joel said. "But by exercising caution and good sense, I've learned to deal with my fear."

As they wandered from store to store, it surprised Irene that Joel had definite ideas about what he wanted. He knew what looked good on him and what was in style. But she was also struck by the amount of trust he had to exercise.

He said glibly, "I only shop with those who love me." Obviously wishing to retract the thoughtless slip, he rushed on, "I didn't . . ."

She rescued him. "Just wait till you put on those red polyester pants you just bought."

Relieved, he joked back, "I don't know about red, but I felt everything very carefully, and I'm certain I haven't bought any *polyester.*" He gave a theatrical shudder as he said the final word.

"Don't worry, Mr. Costain," said Adam. "I wouldn't let Mom do that to anyone."

"We men have to stick together," laughed Joel.

Irene marveled at the easy interaction between Joel and her boys, especially Adam, who was the more introverted and sensitive of the two. Perhaps it was just that he needed, as much as anyone, a release from the heaviness of the last few days. Perhaps it was Joel's disarming manner. She knew Adam and Mark were hungry for an adult male in their lives. Of course, there was Norm and their grandfather. But Norm worked long, hard hours at his construction company, and the boys saw him too seldom. And their grandfather just didn't have the energy they needed.

Irene wondered if, and when, it would be appropriate to tell her sons about their relationship to Joel. Why not? But she knew the answer to that immediately. *She* wasn't ready for it. It would draw Joel into their lives. And the way blood stains cannot be removed, a blood relationship couldn't easily be severed.

Twenty-five

"You idiots!" The man's hand shook as he tightened his grip on the telephone receiver. "Why didn't I just hire Abbot and Costello for the job? You clowns are the most inept—"

"Hey, it wasn't all our fault."

"I told you to maintain a low profile. You kill one man, assault another—and it isn't your fault. What were you thinking?"

"I thought you wanted results. Things were starting to stall. Anyway, Mitchell's death was an accident."

"The police don't think so."

"So, when we gonna get paid?"

"You have real nerve."

"You can't renege on us!"

"Sue me."

"Why you—"

The man moved the receiver away from his ear as the irate party at the other end of the line vented his anger loudly and explicitly. When the tirade tapered off, the man holding the phone said with icy cool, "We're finished, do you understand? All ties severed. And don't get any ideas, because nothing can be traced back to me."

He hung up the receiver quietly, then turned in his swivel chair to face a large glass-topped, very organized desk.

"That's that," he said to the only other person in the room.

"Do you think it was wise cutting them off like that? They're tough characters."

"There's really no other way to deal with such types. They only respect toughness."

"I still think they could be useful—"

"What's done is done," said the man with finality. "Now, we must decide where to go from here."

"We have to get to Costain. With Mitchell dead, he's the only connection. That is one thing those two thugs did for us—lead us to Costain. I can't quite figure out what Sullivan's game is—why all the coyness—but I believe we can forget Sullivan, for now, and concentrate on his remaining son. There's no way Costain can slip away from us. Sullivan has got to contact Costain sooner or later—sooner, if his illness is as progressed as we think. If we watch Costain, who won't be able to hide as easily as Sullivan, we will be rewarded."

"You are a daughter to be proud of," said the man, the pride in his eyes only partially masked by his hard edge. He tried to forget that it had been her idea to hire the two worthless thugs. "How do you propose we watch him?" He couldn't help adding, "Certainly not by hiring more—"

"All right! I admit that was a mistake."

"Haven't I always told you, Lena, 'If you want something done right, you have to do it yourself'?"

"And Daddy is always right, isn't he?"

The woman chuckled lightly, giving her head a demure shake, causing her blond tresses to ripple like satin. She uncrossed her long, shapely legs and stood, walking around the barrier of the desk until she was standing inches from the man. She bent over and kissed his deeply lined forehead.

"For all your faults, Daddy, you have many more redeeming qualities," she said affectionately.

"I hope you're speaking of my best qualities—greed, ruthlessness, pride, and, the best of all, the charm to blind others to those qualities."

The woman laughed. "Of which I am a true beneficiary."

"I've given my daughter only the best."

"I do have one concern, Daddy. What if Charlie Sullivan has more on his mind than simple blackmail?"

"He's a worthless, sick old coot. I'm sure I have nothing to fear from him. If he did try anything, do you think he'd get far?"

"Daddy, I saw the copied page from that notebook—Sullivan could hurt you, and I don't mean physically."

"He can be bought. And I suppose I do owe him something, he paid—"

"Don't even say it, Daddy! You were just better than him. You owe him nothing."

"A payoff may be our only recourse this close to the election."

"Whatever you do, don't underestimate Sullivan. And please," she added with real concern, "stay close to your bodyguard."

"I will. And you will keep close to Costain, right?"

"Of course. I don't expect it to be difficult. The man is blind. How much trouble can he cause?"

She walked back to her chair, picked up her Gucci handbag, then strode to the door. "I'll make an appointment with the man today. Actually, this should be rather amusing."

Her full lips, colored deeply red, bent into a cunning smile before she opened the door and exited.

Twenty-six

Three mornings a week—Monday, Wednesday, and Friday—Joel had a standing date to meet an old college friend at the gym. He'd missed the previous week, and his body was starting to feel the lack of exercise. If it wasn't for that he might have again put off his appointment. His excuse had been all the other events happening in his life, yet he knew he was avoiding Kevin for an entirely different reason. A sensitive subject had come up during their last meeting, which Joel had been reluctant to confront. His insights the other day at his parents' were just as applicable to this particular situation as to the affair with his birth.

"It's been a long time *old* man," Kevin sneered jokingly. "I think you're already starting to get flabby."

"I feel flabby."

"So, what's been keeping you away? Big case?"

As they worked out on the weight machines, Joel related the high points of the recent events.

"That's heavy, man." Of Joel's former classmates, Kevin was one of the few counter-culture holdouts. Maybe that was because he had gone into teaching law instead of practicing it. He wore his hair in a long ponytail, with an earring in his ear, and a long, drooping moustache. Usually he wore corduroy trousers, tweed sport coats with patches at the elbows, colorful plaid button-down shirts with neckties, and loafers on his feet. He conceded only as much as his job absolutely required to the establishment. He no longer smoked marijuana because a few years ago he'd turned his life over to God, but he still drove an old Volkswagen van.

"What're you gonna do about it?" asked Kevin, puffing between each word as he did leg curls.

"I'm trying to find Charlie Sullivan. I think that's all I can do."

"What about your brother's ex?"

"What about her?"

"I ain't blind, buddy. I saw your love-struck expression when you mentioned her. I haven't seen you look like that since—well, you know."

"I know. . . ." Joel pretended to concentrate on flexing his arms under the strain of the weight machine.

"It's been a long time coming," said Kevin.

"Well, don't start making wedding plans. She's not just reluctant to get involved with me, she's scared stiff."

"She'll get used to your blindness."

"That has little, if anything, to do with it. I'm afraid that every time she looks at me she sees her ex-husband."

"You two look that much alike?"

"I'm not sure. No one can say. I wish that the moment Greg and I met I could have had my sight. Just for one brief instant."

"See if you can get a photograph of him. I'll tell you."

"That's a good idea, because I don't think Irene wants to discuss it."

They moved to side-by-side treadmills, but their conversation gave way to the exertion of their effort. Joel set his treadmill to the same tension he'd used before his absence, and he felt every moment of it. But it felt good, too, as sweat poured off him, drenching his T-shirt, and his every muscle tingled. When he and Kevin finished in a half hour, Joel thought he was off the hook regarding that other matter they had discussed over a week ago.

But after they showered, while they were dressing, Kevin brought up the subject.

"Joel, have you given any more thought about that professorship?"

"Not hardly."

"I know you've had a few other things on your mind, but if you're at all interested, you will need to act soon."

"It's a big decision, Kev."

"I thought you were unhappy where you were."

"I don't think 'unhappy' is quite the right term. Bored or unfulfilled might come closer to reality."

"As far as I'm concerned, it all adds up to unhappiness."

"Maybe I'm waiting to see what God wants me to do."

Kevin laughed. "Come on, bro! You're hedging, not being spiritual."

Joel stuffed his workout shoes and clothes into his dufflebag. "Okay! Guilty as charged. I know I don't want to keep doing what I'm doing. But this is a bad time for changes, especially with all that's happening right now—oh, I know, that's just another excuse. I guess I'm not sure if I *can* change. Or whether teaching is the change I should make. I've never had a desire to teach."

"I bet you keep thinking of the adage: 'Them that can, do; them that can't . . . teach.' You're afraid that by teaching you're admitting failure. But you haven't failed at anything. You made partner by age thirty at one of this state's most prestigious law firms—that's success whether you're blind or sighted."

"You were always a teacher at heart, Kev. In law school, you tutored everyone whether they wanted it or not."

"I think you'd be a fantastic teacher, too. And I spoke to the dean of the law school—"

"You spoke to him?"

"I didn't think I shouldn't. And he'd be thrilled to have you fill the opening. I think all you have to do is say the word. But they need someone for the spring semester, and they are going to begin the selection process soon."

"I'll think about it."

"What else is there for you, Joel? Unless you tackle criminal law again. That's still eating you, isn't it? You can't bear having a single challenge out there you haven't conquered."

"I guess it's what you can't have that you want most."

Joel thought about that as he returned to his office. Hadn't he matured beyond that shallow perception of life he'd once nurtured? Or was challenge still the consuming force of his life? Having a job that challenged and stretched was one thing, but seeking such a job *simply* for the challenge was another. On one level that had been part of why he had gone into criminal law in the beginning. His professors had told him it would be next to impossible for a blind man to be a successful criminal attorney. One of the key facets of criminal practice was the ability to read people's expressions. A voice might say one thing, but accompanied by a slight narrowing of the eyes it could have an entirely different meaning. Then there was the jury. They never talked, but their facial expressions and body movements could make or break a lawyer's case.

It was Joel's nature, especially when he was younger, that when anyone said the word *impossible* to him, he took it as a challenge. In school and during his short criminal practice, he learned ways to compensate for the times when sight was necessary in a courtroom. But it hadn't been enough. However, before he realized that, he had been cocky enough to open his own practice immediately after passing the Bar. He'd won a couple of cases—petty theft, DUI, some juvenile cases. These successes made him think nothing of taking on a rape and assault case, his biggest challenge yet. That's when it had all begun to unravel.

Even after all that happened, it had been, and still was, hard to admit defeat.

Maybe that's why Joel had never been completely content with his present position. He had *settled* for tax law. Oh, there were times when it proved quite fascinating and challenging. But when he asked himself about what good he was doing in the world, his answer wasn't satisfying. He was helping people—rich people—get richer. Precious few poor people could afford the services of Eberhard, Wilson, Petri, and Costain. Even the pro bono cases he handled were too few to make enough of a dent into his longing for more meaning.

And aside from all else, that too had been among his motives for desiring criminal law. Joel had considered working as a public defender—overworked and underpaid, yes—but in a position to offer the best legal assistance to those who could not afford it. He'd had a few ideals in his youth; he hadn't been entirely driven by his own needs. And in those times when he most felt his inadequacy to fulfill those ideals, he most cursed his handicap.

His morose thoughts put him in a proper mood for what he had to do that afternoon—Greg's funeral. But as Greg entered his mind, Joel was reminded that he had been blessed in more ways than he certainly deserved. How many blind men—or for that matter, how many sighted men—had the number of choices he was now faced with? Should he remain at a prestigious law firm, or should he teach at a top-notch law school? He had so much, not only materially but in quality of life. And he had a God to lead him upon the right path, so he need not stumble on rough places. But, if he should stumble, he had a Lord who would help him stand and continue leading the way.

If only Greg could have had such opportunities, too.

Twenty-seven

*I*rene kept thinking about the song lyrics "Rainy Days and Mondays." She did indeed feel like crying. She peered through the rain-splattered windshield and wondered why Greg could not have gotten a break, at least in the weather, for his funeral.

Yet Irene was not prepared to postpone the day for better weather. This chapter in her life had to be closed once and for all. Of course, she knew better than to think it would completely wipe Greg from her thoughts. If for no other reason than for her sons' sakes, she would have to continue confronting the specter of Greg Mitchell. She was Irene Lorenzo, but her children still bore the name "Mitchell."

No, a funeral would not completely bury Greg.

But Irene hoped it would be, if nothing else, a step toward taking a more phlegmatic view of the man. All that she had been going through since learning of his death might be more a function of his manner of death and its suddenness, and less of how she felt about Greg himself. She hoped so, at least. She thought about when Joel had asked her if she still loved Greg. She had truly believed she had stopped loving him years ago, long before their divorce. But if that were the case, how could she explain her grief and pain now?

She had to get beyond all that. Maybe then . . .

Joel flashed through her mind. And a knot lodged in her throat. How could she even consider a relationship with Greg's brother? It was insane. Yet, why did Joel tug at her heart so? Did she feel sorry for him? Hardly. That was one emotion she was certain she didn't have regarding Joel.

"Reenie, are you okay?"

Irene had almost forgotten her sister seated beside her in the car. Adam and Mark were in the back, too. She had to pull herself together. For them.

"Yes," Irene said.

"Well, you're going fifty in a thirty-five mile zone. . . ."

"Oh, my goodness!" Irene hit the brakes. She wondered how Connie would respond to her thoughts just then. What wisdom would her sister dispense? She hadn't met Joel yet. What would she think? Like everyone else, Connie had been taken in by Greg. She was no astute judge of character. Connie would like Joel; there was no reason not to. Irene talked to Connie about everything—why hadn't she mentioned this subject yet? She had only told Connie about Joel's relationship to Greg, and then only because Connie had already heard about him through their mom.

She wanted to tell Connie more, but she was afraid that by verbalizing her feelings, it would make them more real, harder to deny. And she had to keep a back door available.

A simple service was planned for Greg in the chapel of the funeral home. Since his ashes would be interned in a small vault, there would be no graveside service. They gathered in the smallest room of the chapel, needing no more space than that. Along with Irene and Connie and Adam and Mark, Irene's parents were there, and Norm had driven over separately from work. Joel was there, too, as were his parents. Irene had assured them she didn't expect them to come, but they wanted to attend, for Joel's sake.

Ten people. And a minister who was a stranger to all of them, including Greg. That alone was sad enough to stir emotions. But Irene didn't cry, not even when the minister intoned such hackneyed phrases as, "From dust to dust," and "I am the Resurrection and the life." The word "generic" kept flitting through Irene's mind. She started to feel guilty, then she reminded herself that there could well have been no funeral at all. She could have turned her back on Greg, as his second wife had. At least Irene had done *something*.

After the service they all gathered at Irene's parents' house. Theresa, who had not felt up to going out into the wet weather, had laid out a snack of sandwiches and other finger foods. Irene was a little nervous about Walt and Adrianne—and even Joel, to some extent—entering her family's very blue-collar world. But Walt and Ray immediately discovered their mutual love of baseball and boats, and any differences between them were never noticed. Norm and Joel started talking and before long were deeply involved in a spiritual conversation Connie eventually joined and from which Irene stayed far away.

The older women took a little more time to warm up. Millie had been put off a bit when the elder Costains drove up in their Mercedes. One thing Millie couldn't abide were snobs, and she had prejudged the Costains as such.

Then Mark broke a glass in the kitchen, and when Millie came to see what the disturbance was about, she was shocked to find Adrianne kneeling on the floor picking up the scattered shards.

"You don't have to do that," said Millie.

"Not a problem," said Adrianne. "Raising a blind child, I've become quite adept at picking up broken glass. Where's your broom?" And Adrianne swept the floor, forever softening Millie's prejudgments.

Irene, who had come in to see if she could help, watched in amazement. But it also disturbed her that it pleased her so much, as if it mattered whether her parents and Joel's parents got along. In fact, of the entire mismatched group, she was the only one at loose ends, not feeling as if she belonged anywhere. And she was relieved when, after an hour, the Costains departed, taking Joel, who had to return to work, with them. Only then did she relax enough to flop on the living room sofa, put her stocking feet up on the coffee table, and enjoy a cup of coffee. It didn't even bother her that her mother and grandmother were in the kitchen cleaning up. She'd give them a hand in a few minutes.

Connie sat down beside her. "Looks like you're unwinding a little."

"I'm glad it's over."

"You never told me what a nice guy Joel is."

"Huh?" The statement caught Irene off guard. "It . . . never occurred to me."

"To tell me? Or that he's a nice guy?"

"I don't know."

"Reenie, are you blushing?"

"No way!"

"You are." Connie paused, and when she spoke again, her voice was lower, despite the fact that they were alone in the room. "Irene, do you have a thing for this guy?"

Irene chuckled dryly. "Connie, you do have an imagination."

Connie just rubbed her chin slyly. "What's that saying about protesting too much? That's got to be the only reason why you've said next to nothing about him. You would have told me everything if you weren't afraid—"

"I don't want to talk about it."

"Wow! It's that bad?"

Irene rolled her eyes and turned slightly away from her sister. Then she said in a small, hollow voice, "He's Greg's brother, for heaven's sake."

"That must make it hard for you," Connie replied quietly.

Irene nodded, torn between wanting to pour out her thoughts to her sister and remaining silent.

"Are you in love with him?"

"I've only known him a week!"

"That doesn't always matter."

"Of course. I fell in love with Greg right away, too. Do you remember, Connie? I was so starry-eyed. He charmed the socks off me. My heart went pitter-patter every time I saw him, and I thought only of him, day and night. You remember, don't you, how it was. . . ?"

"And is that how it is now?"

"I . . . I don't know."

"Irene, you're older now, far more mature. You could not make the same mistake again. Just the fact that you are wrestling with these things is confirmation of that. You are approaching this far more rationally."

"I don't feel very rational. Why does this have to happen now?"

"Maybe because now is the only time it could have happened. How else would you have met Joel?"

"And that's another thing. Our lives and our backgrounds are far removed from each other, practically two different worlds."

"Just because his dad is a rich architect who drives a brand-new Mercedes, and your dad mows lawns for a living and drives an old Ford pickup? You're just as bad as Mom if you allow such things to interfere with your judgment. You're a reverse snob. There's only one element that matters, and that's how you both are *inside*."

Irene smiled at her sister's endearing simplicity. But she was right. Irene had hardly noticed the class differences between herself and Joel, at least not until she had met his parents. That level had been inconsequential in the wake of the way their hearts and minds and spirits had touched.

"You know what I think?" Connie said. "All this 'two different worlds' stuff is just a convenient excuse for you to avoid him. Just like you've done with every man you've met."

"I'm a pathetic mess, aren't I? So, do you think my fears about him being like Greg are just an excuse, too?"

"That's more valid. Even I tried to see if he was anything like Greg. But aside from the fact that he looks a little like him, they are two totally different people."

"I'm supposed to trust *your* judgment? You practically fell in love with Greg, too, remember?"

"Well, here's the acid test. Mom cornered me in the kitchen a little while ago, and you know what she said? 'Connie, I talked with Joel for a few minutes and he's such a nice man. I can hardly believe he's Greg's brother.' "

"Really?" This was a surprising turn. Still, Irene tried to resume her previous skepticism. "Nevertheless, I'm not in love with Joel Costain, so this whole conversation is moot."

Connie stretched languidly as if she was bored anyway with the conversation. But a moment later she asked in an offhanded, casual tone, "So, how does Joel feel about you?"

Irene reddened immediately.

"I see . . ." said Connie, then she stood. "Well, I better go help Mom and Grandma."

Irene let her head fall back against the sofa. Was life really as simple as Connie made it out to be? Maybe Irene did make it more complicated than it should be by mulling over it, agonizing about it. But she couldn't be as simplistic as Connie, nor could she be as sure about her heart as Joel was about his. She had to work through things, ponder all the various facets. And, even then, she wasn't always sure of herself. That had been one frustrating aspect of her Christianity. She could pray and pray about God's will and still not be certain. She had often quoted the verse that said the steps of a righteous man are ordered by God. She figured as long as she was trusting God He would direct her when she was uncertain. It worked—until she'd hear some Christians talk about how "God told me. . . ." Or, "I prayed about it and I know God wants me to do this. . . ." How did they get off being so certain of God? Part of her was always quite skeptical about their confidence.

But where did all that leave her now?

In pretty sorry shape. She no longer had even the certainty of knowing her steps were being ordered by God. She had nothing, no foundation. Only herself to rely on for guidance.

"Well, almighty Irene," she murmured acerbically, "what will you do now?"

A gnawing emptiness accompanied her into the kitchen.

Twenty-eight

Two days later Joel arrived at his office to find a memo from Arthur Eberhard asking to see him as soon as possible. Joel had no overt reason to worry about the concise note, except he had been extremely remiss in not informing Eberhard about the recent events in his life. The senior partner of the firm did not demand to be involved in his colleagues' personal lives; however, Joel's relationship with Eberhard was on such a level that, at the very least, his silence might hurt Arthur's feelings.

Upon entering Eberhard's office, Joel was greeted warmly. The senior partner shook his hand and directed him to one of the antique velvet chairs in the office's spacious sitting area. At least Eberhard chose not to conduct the meeting behind his huge oak desk reputed to have belonged to Harry Truman. Eberhard was in his eighties, but quite fit for an octogenarian. He was almost a foot shorter than Joel, with soft, pink skin, and hands calloused only where he gripped his golf clubs. He was soft-spoken and somewhat effeminate in his manner. He might have come off as quite inconsequential, except for his iron gray eyes, hard and calculating. Of course, this description had only been passed on to Joel from others. The soft manner and the hard eyes were somewhat lost on Joel; however, he had long ago gauged the man as a force to be reckoned with. The first time he met Eberhard he had heard the steel in the man's soft voice, felt it in the firm grip of his handshake.

"It's been a while since we've had a little chat, hasn't it, Joel?" said Eberhard, rather warmly.

"Yes," said Joel, "and it's my fault. I've had a lot going on."

"So I've heard."

"What have you heard, Arthur?"

"About the appearance of your brother and his murder . . ."

"It's all pretty sordid, I suppose. Difficult to believe, really."

"Had you hoped to keep it quiet?"

"No, not at all. I've simply been so caught up in events—I should have said something to you, Arthur, at least about the police. I'm sorry."

"What's done is done."

"I'm afraid it's not done yet. They haven't found his killer. And you must know I am a suspect; however, I doubt seriously so."

"Perhaps you are unaware of just how serious this is or can become. I've had a call from the managing editor of the *Chronicle*. They were going to print an article about the break-in at your house and the possible connection to the murder of Greg Mitchell, your brother."

"No one contacted me for an interview."

"Well, it's a moot point now. In deference to my long-standing friendship with the editor, he wanted to run the article by me first. I asked him to drop the story."

"I don't see why."

"The firm doesn't need to be mixed up in an affair like this."

"But I am involved, and thus, by default, so is the firm."

"It does not have to become a public spectacle. You've always been one to downplay the importance of your position in the legal community, and that of your firm. But despite our substantial place in the community, the press would love to have a field day with us. They could very easily turn this into a scandal—"

"Oh, Arthur! I just can't believe that."

Eberhard shifted in his chair and crossed his legs. Joel sensed by the man's movement and a slight edge to his voice that he was uneasy about this conversation. "Do you recall what happened when George Petri and his wife divorced two years ago? It made big news."

"The custody battle over the children was as ugly as they come."

"I agree. But, Joel, your situation involves *murder*—far juicier fodder for the press than a divorce."

"I'm still not convinced, Arthur, but suppose what you indicate does happen, what can I do about it? I can't change what has happened, nor my involvement. I've kept this a low profile for my own reasons. Yet, I can't change the fact that my brother has been killed."

"I just want you to be aware of all the possible ramifications."

"I am."

"And I want to impress upon you the importance of making no statements to the press."

"I don't intend to."

"Good, I'm glad we understand each other." Eberhard poured himself a glass of water from a decanter on the table in front of him. "Can I get you some refreshment, Joel?"

"Thanks, I'm fine, Arthur." Joel paused, waiting as Eberhard drank his water. Another moment of silence passed before Joel asked, "Was there anything else?"

"Yes . . ." The senior partner's tone indicated great reluctance to continue. But, with a sigh, he did so. "Did you know I have another friend in high places?"

"I know you have many."

"This particular man happens to be the dean of Carlisle Law School. We play golf together every Friday."

Joel just nodded. He knew what was coming, but he decided to let Eberhard continue so Joel might better judge the man's reaction.

"Joel . . . Joel . . ." Eberhard shook his head. "Do you know how distressing it is to learn from an outsider the dissatisfaction of one I thought was close to me?"

Joel sank down an inch in his chair like an errant schoolboy. "What exactly did Lowenfeld say?"

"That you had inquired about a professorship opening up at the school."

"Well, Arthur, I didn't inquire. I was approached by a friend of mine who teaches there. I never spoke to Lowenfeld, nor did I say I was interested. I'm afraid my friend was more enthusiastic than me."

"So, you aren't considering the position?"

"I thought about it."

"But, why? Certainly you must realize what a demotion that would be."

"That aspect doesn't matter to me, Arthur. It would not be a demotion if that's where I belong. I'll be frank with you. I've been dissatisfied with where I am for some time. It's not the firm, mind you. It's just—" How could he say what he was feeling without stepping on Arthur's soft toes? "Do you recall, Arthur, that when I finished law school, my first choice was to practice criminal law?"

"Of course I remember, and we know how disastrously that

turned out. I should have thought that sad incident would have showed you once and for all your limitations."

Joel rankled at the word *limitations*.

"I'm sorry," Eberhard continued, "for *my* frankness. But you were pretty shattered after what happened. You thought you should give up law altogether. But I saw you were an intelligent, talented young man, and that there was a place in this profession for a blind person. I took you in, Joel, when many wouldn't have—"

"Is that what it was all about, Arthur? Helping out the blind man? I never asked for sympathy or special treatment."

"And you never received any beyond my twisting a few clients' arms at first to give you a try. You quickly proved yourself—*by yourself*. Do you think I'd take in a thirty-year-old partner every day? You earned it. And that is why I cannot understand why you want to throw it all away now."

"It's never been easy for me to accept my limitations, as you put it." There was much more to it, Joel knew, but Arthur would not be able to hear all of it without taking offense—how Joel was tired of helping the rich get richer and the poor—well, hardly helping them at all. That's what Eberhard's firm was all about. That's what put the Armani suits on their backs, the BMWs in the garages, the expensive antiques in the offices, and what paid for the condos the firm owned in the Caymans. Arthur Eberhard had been living this life too long to hear about the shallowness of it all. So instead of saying more, Joel felt his Braille wristwatch and said, "I have an appointment in a few minutes."

"Yes, of course." Arthur stood and walked Joel to the door. "I hope we can keep an open dialogue about these things, Joel. You are like a son to me."

"I will, Arthur." They shook hands. "And I hope you can forgive my silence in the past."

"Forgiven and forgotten."

⁓

Joel had just arrived back in his office when his secretary called to tell him his client had arrived. Giving himself five minutes, he spent the time reviewing the information, some Braille notes, and a tape Linda had prepared. It was a new client, the owner of a large and prosperous restaurant chain called Alexander's, dedicated to fine, upscale dining.

He rose from his chair as the woman came into his office. She extended to him a slim, well-manicured hand, with rings on three of the fingers. Expensive perfume lingered about her. Joel judged she was tall, five nine or ten, and trim, if her graceful movement was any indication.

"Miss Westfall," Joel said as he took her hand.

"Please, do call me Lena. And if I may call you Joel. . . . That's the kind of business relationships I like to have."

"Sounds very good. Please have a seat."

She slipped into one of the leather chairs facing his desk, and he heard her straighten her dress as she crossed what he guessed were long legs. By the sound of her voice, which was rather throaty and rich, he guessed her age to be in the early or mid-thirties.

"I'm so happy, Joel, that you were able to see me with only two days' notice." She gave her head a little shake and patted her hair.

"I could hardly turn away a client such as you. I've dined at Alexander's and loved it."

"One of the perks of our patronage with you is that you will be welcome to dine with us any time—as our guest, of course."

"That's generous of you. Tell me, Lena, why you've decided to come to our firm? Aren't you presently represented by Abernathy and Carter?"

"We are planning to expand. Restaurants in Phoenix and Seattle are nearly complete. And there are three more in the works. That would bring our total to twelve. We are also considering expanding as far as the East Coast."

"Don't you feel Abernathy and Carter could handle an operation that large?" It was a leading question. Personally, Joel believed that firm should be more than adequate. He sensed there was more to it.

"We haven't been entirely happy with them for some time," Lena replied without hesitation. "Fred Abernathy was an old family friend, and my father has stayed with the firm out of loyalty. I've been trying to sway him away from them for years."

"And you've finally succeeded?"

"My father is scaling back his involvement in the business. I became president of the company recently, and major shareholder."

"Is this change, then, contrary to your father's wishes?"

"Why, Joel, it almost sounds like you don't want Alexander's business!" She laughed lightly, giving her hair another shake. Joel decided that the way she liked to flip her hair and fondle it, she must have a head of lovely locks. Perhaps blond or red. He'd have to ask Linda later to see if he guessed right.

"I can assure you that is not the case at all," he said.

"Good! And you can rest assured you won't be immersing yourself in some family squabble. Father has given his blessing to this change. He's even admitted that he was never entirely happy with our former attorney." She paused, then opened her handbag—or was it a briefcase?—and laid something on Joel's desk, sliding it toward him. "All of Alexander's accounting and tax records are on this computer disk. I'm sure you'll want to review it—that . . . uh . . . won't be a problem for you, will it, Joel?"

"Not in the least."

"You'll have to forgive me. I've never worked with a blind attorney before, and I'm not sure what to expect. However, you did come highly recommended."

"You can expect no less from me, Lena, than you would from any attorney." Although it was an effort, considering his recent conversation with Eberhard, Joel managed to keep an annoyed edge from his voice.

"You know, Joel, I am simply famished. I realize it's a while before lunch, but I would much prefer to continue our business in a more relaxed atmosphere. I've never liked offices. Would you care to join me for a bite?"

He didn't want to. Miss Lena Westfall, though he guessed her to be an attractive woman, was a bit too high society for him to enjoy being around for long. However, he understood well the importance of taking care of clients. And Alexander's, with a dozen restaurants in major cities, would no doubt bring in sizable revenue to the firm. Besides, he was on uneven enough footing at the moment to risk incurring another strike against him at the firm. Unless, of course, he wanted to get forced out. The idea was both appealing and unnerving.

"Let me check my schedule, Lena," Joel said. Then he called Linda who assured him that, as he already knew, he had no more appointments until after lunch. "Apparently I'm free," he said to Lena.

"Where do you recommend we go?"

"That's a loaded question from someone in your position, Lena. Why not Alexander's?"

"Another time, Joel. I'm sure you'd prefer neutral territory for now."

He shrugged. "It wouldn't be a problem."

"You're not nervous about choosing a restaurant, are you?" She tittered lightly. "I do like checking out the competition occasionally."

Joel had the feeling he was being tested. "Well, let me see if I can come up with something that would come near your standards."

He rose from his desk, picked up his folded cane from off the desk, then walked around. Lena immediately linked arms with him, and he sensed it was not as much a gesture of assistance as it was her way of being friendly, even chummy.

Her words punctuated the gesture. "I feel this is going to be the start of a fabulous relationship, don't you, Joel?"

But Joel only nodded and smiled; he was busy thinking of where might be the best—or perhaps the second best—restaurant in San Francisco.

Twenty-nine

*I*t turned into a long day. Joel had been reluctant to call Irene at the end of it to ask if he could spend the evening with her. He was unsure of where the line between pushing and pursuing was drawn. The chapter in their lives that had brought them together seemed to be closing, especially now that Greg was buried.

But Joel wasn't ready to let that happen, and he innately sensed that as much as she said she wasn't ready for a serious relationship, she also was reluctant to cut Joel off completely. And when he finally did call her, he thought he heard a hint of pleasure in her voice. He prayed it wasn't his imagination.

Joel tended to a few errands, and by the time he arrived at Irene's apartment that evening, he had Ebony at his side. The taxi driver brought up the rear, carrying two large pizzas and a grocery bag.

Irene opened the door. He knew she was grinning and he imagined her eyes were sparkling.

"And Ebony, too!" she exclaimed after greeting Joel. She bent down and scratched the dog's ears.

"The doctor released her on the proviso that she didn't work for at least two weeks," Joel explained when Irene asked about the missing harness. "She's still stiff and weak, and the vet wants her to take one walk a day at first, increasing gradually, to ease her back to normal. So this is her first big outing."

"I'm so glad she's better." Irene then unburdened the taxi driver while Joel paid the man.

As Irene carried the pizza to the kitchen, Adam and Mark came out from their room, the fragrance of pizza enticing them. From the grocery bag Irene took a six-pack of A&W root beer and a carton of vanilla ice cream.

"I have a terrible weakness for root beer floats and pizza," said Joel. "Hope no one minds."

Of course, no one minded.

They finished off one pizza—the boys were thrilled there would be leftovers for later, as Joel had planned. They watched *Jeopardy!* on television while they had their floats, and Joel learned that he and Irene shared the same interest in trivia games. Joel promised to teach everyone some Braille card games next time he came to visit. There was no protest or sense of hesitation from Irene about the mention of another visit.

"Joel, are you still staying at your parents'?" Irene asked.

"Yes, but I hope only for a few more days. I love them, but . . ."

"Parents are always parents, aren't they?"

He nodded. "My insurance will make good on most of the damage, but I'm not going to wait for their check. The police are through so I've got a janitorial service cleaning up, and when they're done, I'll re-furnish the place."

"It was so lovely. Are you going to change it?"

"Probably. Mom is already chomping at the bit to get at it. She loves that sort of thing."

"She must have decorated it before."

"Yeah. Say, Irene, how would you like to give her a hand?"

"Me? Oh, I don't think I'd—"

"Mom's an artist," put in Mark, who was half listening to the grown-up conversation and half-absorbed in playing with some action figures. "She knows all about making cool stuff."

"It's not the same, Mark," said Irene.

"I didn't know you were an artist," said Joel.

He heard her shrug before saying, "I'm hardly a real artist. I've never even finished a project."

"You should see some of her pictures—" Mark began, then stopped, flustered, and added apologetically, "I'm sorry, Mr. Costain. I didn't mean—"

"That's okay, Mark. Maybe you can *tell* me about them."

"Really," protested Irene, "they're no big deal."

But Mark was already grabbing Joel's hand as Joel stood. "Come on, they're in the bedroom."

"You don't mind, do you, Irene?" Joel asked.

"Well . . ." And she followed them down the hall to her bedroom-studio.

"Show him the one of us," said Adam, joining them a moment later.

Joel heard some scraping and moving. He guessed it was rather frivolous to make Irene go to this trouble to show him her work, yet he wanted to know everything about her, her heart and her soul, and he sensed, by her sensitive nature, that art was an important expression of who she was.

"I painted this at Stinson Beach not long ago," Irene said. "I love doing seascapes. The beach is in the background, waves breaking on the sand. The sun is trying to break through the clouds—but I haven't captured that very well. Adam and Mark are in the foreground building sand castles."

"You can only see my back," said Mark. "But you know it's me because I have on the Giants T-shirt Grandpa bought me."

Adam asked, "Have you ever seen the ocean, Mr. Costain?"

"No," said Joel. "I've been blind since I was born. I've never seen anything."

Both boys let out low sounds of awe at this mind-boggling concept.

"But I love the ocean," Joel added. "In fact it's one of my favorite places, too. Next time you go, close your eyes for a few minutes and you'll discover much more to the ocean than merely what you can see. The sound of the waves crashing, the wind blowing, the birds. And the smells—fish and salt and even suntan lotions."

"I like to feel the wet sand squish between my toes," said Mark.

"Me, too," said Joel. "If you think about it, what you see is only a small fraction of what the ocean holds."

Irene showed a few more of her unfinished paintings, then Adam and Mark grew bored and wandered away.

"Well, I guess that's all," said Irene.

"You've nothing else?"

"I don't see the point, Joel. It pleased the boys, but you don't have to do this for my benefit."

"I'm not. I'm truly interested. What else have you got?"

"Well, I've drawn a picture of you," she said with some reticence. He heard the pages, probably of a sketchbook, flip open.

"I wonder how you see me," he mused aloud.

"I'm not a good enough artist to properly express it."

"How much does it resemble Greg?"

She was silent for a long moment before replying, "You've been wanting to ask that for a long time, haven't you?"

"Yes . . ."

"There's a resemblance . . . I suppose. . . ." Her tone was forced, hesitant. It was easy to perceive she didn't want to broach this subject.

So he took a different tact. "Is this picture unfinished, too?"

"Of course."

"Why don't you ever finish anything, Irene?"

"Just lazy, I guess. Undisciplined."

"You're not afraid of the risk involved? That you'd no longer have an excuse?"

"Maybe so. I don't think I could handle rejection."

"Or acceptance?"

She sighed, then began moving, putting things away. There seemed to be a nervousness in her sudden activity. He knew he had been too harsh. How hard it was *not* to push when he saw so clearly the possibilities that existed between them, when he felt so deeply the tug she had on him. And even harder to ignore was the strong urge he had to touch her—not in a sexual way—rather it was the need of a blind man to connect in the only way he knows. Surrounded by his world of darkness, Irene sometimes seemed so very distant, especially now that she was purposefully pulling away from him. He heard her sounds of movement, smelled the fresh fragrance about her, but she was as far away as the birds in "The Country of the Blind." He thought of the H.G. Wells story he had discovered while in college, about the isolated land where the citizens had been blind for so many generations they no longer even had words in their vocabulary for the forgotten sense of sight. And in that country they heard the singing of the birds overhead and the fluttering of their wings and thought these must be angels, which they could not touch.

"Irene, I'm sorry," he said quietly.

She was silent for a moment, even ceasing her busy movements. Then she murmured, "You're probably right."

"It doesn't matter." But it was like talking to someone across a chasm. He hated it, and he couldn't help his next words. "I want to touch you."

Would she understand?

He added softly, "I don't want you to be an angel in the country of the blind, who is nothing more than distant sounds."

"Your father mentioned something about the country of the blind," she said, obviously hedging. "What is that?"

Joel answered, though he knew the question was just her way of avoiding what was truly happening. Maybe it should be avoided. "It's an H.G. Wells story." He told her about the land isolated in the Andes and about the birds thought to be angels. "The story tells of a sighted man who gets lost in the mountains and stumbles upon the land."

"Did they make him king? Your father said something about a one-eyed king."

" 'In the country of the blind, the one-eyed man is king,' " Joel quoted. "That's what the fellow thought would happen. But in reality, the people considered him to be something of an idiot, clumsy and talking gibberish about something called *sight* and *seeing*. They treated him as an inferior, capable of only the most mundane tasks. They did their work when it was cool, which happened to be at night, and they slept during the warm part of the day when the sun was out. So the sighted man was forever bumbling about in the darkness. Thus, they were not impressed at all by the fact that he could see, because they had no concept at all of what that meant."

"What happened to the man?"

"He fell in love with a girl of that world, and she with him. But the elders could not consent to a marriage between one of them and such an inferior. Then they figured out a way he could be made equal to them—"

"Oh no!" said Irene as she deduced the solution.

"All he had to do," Joel said, ignoring her reaction, "was allow them to remove his eyes, which they considered quite useless, anyway."

"And did he?"

"He was ready to do it . . . for love. But on the day that the surgery was to take place, the man went on a walk to have his last look at the beauties of the world. And he just kept on walking. The wonders his eyes beheld were simply too precious to sacrifice . . . even for love." A knot rose in Joel's throat as he finished. The idea of sacrifice lay heavily upon him. "She was asking too much of him," Joel said at length.

"How could she realize that, if she had no idea what sight meant to him?"

"It was one of the reasons she fell in love with the man. She alone, of all the people, had been captivated by his strange tales of sight."

"You didn't mention that. She was in a terrible position, then. The very thing she loved about him was also keeping them apart."

"Ah, fiction!" Joel said lightly. "Thank God real life isn't like that."

"Yes . . ."

But they both knew differently. And Joel thought of what Irene had once said about timing. The wrong time . . . the wrong place. But what of God's timing? Joel could not give up, at least not until he could just once reach out and touch the elusive angel.

Despite the inner conflicts the evening generated, there was one very positive occurrence. Only one brief mention of Greg had been made the entire evening, and neither was Charlie Sullivan mentioned or anything regarding Joel's mystery. He took it as a good sign that he and Irene had something more to build upon than the events of the past few days. Joel relished the prospect of embarking on a more normal path with Irene. He thought of casual walks with her, home-cooked dinners, sitting together in front of the TV, taking the kids to a movie . . . and it all sounded marvelous. He didn't let himself think of the fact that because of his handicap they might never have a totally normal life. He would never ask her to make that sacrifice.

But Joel prayed constantly that God would work in Irene's heart so she would eagerly desire to do so—and wouldn't consider it a sacrifice at all.

Thirty

In a bar on Geary Street, two men nursed their drinks, one a beer, the other a Bloody Mary. They sat alone at a corner table, conversing quietly, not bothered by the happy-hour din in the crowded place. A recording of a Tony Bennett song blended into the general chaos. No one paid the men or their conversation any attention.

"I say we ought to cut our losses and split this place."

"We're in too deep, Lenny. We've got nothing to lose." The man absently rubbed a small bandage across the bridge of his nose.

Lenny gulped his beer, then wiped foam from his moustache with the back of his hand. "No one's on to us, yet. We got time to get to Mexico."

"I tell you, it's too late for that. We shoulda split long ago, if we wanted to make a clean getaway. There's one thing that kept us here—money. And that's still a problem. We ain't gonna get a cent out of our former boss. And we don't got enough between us even for fake passports, much less to cover traveling expenses."

"We don't dare shake down Fabroni." Lenny glared into his beer. "That rat stiffed us, and we can't do anything about it. But that's not what you're thinking, is it, Bobby?"

"We got murder one hanging over our heads; no way to implicate Fabroni. So, let's just forget him for a while—a little while at least, but I still want to pay him back for what he did to us." Bobby shifted his big, two hundred and fifty pound, muscular frame in his chair. "In fact, Charlie Sullivan is still the answer to our problems."

"Whatever you're thinking, Bob, is too big a risk—"

"So, you'd rather go to Mexico and live like a peon? Well, that isn't the life for me. I'd rather risk getting gassed or spending the rest of my life in jail."

"You're crazy."

"Crazy, but smart." Bobby finished his Bloody Mary, then signaled a waitress to bring more. "While you been shaking in your boots, Lenny, I've been doing my homework. I found out some stuff about that Sullivan we been tailing. I found out he's done thirty-seven years of a life sentence for burglary and murder."

"Who'd he kill?"

"A cop who got in his way while he was burglarizing some trucking company."

"What'd he steal?"

"The newspaper said the trucking company reported they were missing nothing."

"So, he came up empty-handed."

"Then, why is a big shot like Fabroni putting so much energy into tailing Sullivan?"

Lenny shrugged. The waitress came with fresh drinks. When she left, he said, "Maybe an old debt. Maybe that fink, Fabroni, just mentioned the money to lure us in. It could be he only wanted to even an old score—"

"Man, use your head for a change, Lenny! If that were the case, why tail him instead of just knocking him off? No, that isn't it at all. Sullivan was a two-time loser who never had nothing, much less the kind of cash that would interest Fabroni. That's why I'm thinking Sullivan has something else that very much interests the man. And here's something else, if anyone has an old score to even it'd be Sullivan, who did hard time—Fabroni has lived high off the hog all these years."

"You think Sullivan did time for Fabroni? That's pretty heavy."

"The possibilities are endless."

"What, besides money, would be worth anything, after all these years?" asked Lenny, still skeptical.

"I don't know. I don't have all the answers. But I think it would be worth our while to find out."

"You've flipped out now, Bobby! You want to stick your head in a noose on the off chance you'll score?"

"We're not that hot, Lenny. The cops are never going to trace us to Mitchell's death. And how's a blind guy gonna ID us over the break-in? We don't have to start running scared. We have time to see where this thing leads. And my gut tells me it's gonna be big. If nothing else, we can figure out a way to blackmail Fabroni."

"He is too careful for that."

"We'll see . . . there's no such thing as a perfect crime."

"I just hope that isn't what the cops think about us."

"I tell you, we are in the clear."

Lenny shrugged, not fully convinced. "I always start to worry when you talk like that, Bobby. It's a jinx."

"Would you shut up, Lenny, and hear me out? We know Fabroni is looking for something that Sullivan has. What if we beat Fabroni to it? We're already one up on him, and even if he hires someone else to finish our job, it'll take time for the guy to get oriented."

"We've lost track of Sullivan since Fabroni fired us."

"We can pick up his trail easy. Plus, we can tail Costain, too. Sooner or later he and Sullivan have to make contact. Then we can nail them—after they've led us to . . . whatever it is Fabroni wants."

"Sounds too simple."

"That's what I like about it."

Lenny rubbed his chin. "It would be nice to blow this country with some money in our pockets." He was, if nothing else, a practical man.

"And live in the style we deserve."

Bobby and Lenny finished their drinks, each imagining long stretches of sandy beaches, servants waiting on them hand and foot, beautiful women draped over each arm, endless days of piña coladas, sunshine, swimming in the surf, and absolutely nothing to do but dip into their very full pockets to pay for it all.

⟋◍⟍

Charlie stretched out on the bed of yet another cheap motel. He didn't know how much longer he could keep this up. Aside from his physical limitations, there was the problem of cash flow. He was running low. Greg had given him a couple hundred bucks in the beginning, but motels and booze weren't cheap.

He had been so close to approaching Joel. Now, he didn't know what to do. In one sense the break-in and assault on Joel was a good thing because it erased all Charlie's doubts about whether someone was on to him. It also indicated that perhaps all Charlie's caution was a waste of time now. If the break-in was indeed related to Charlie, then it was an effort in futility for him to be coy any longer. Whoever had found and killed Greg had now found Joel. Perhaps it was time to come forward, if for no other reason than to warn Joel. A mere phone call would be enough. No commitment in that, no face-to-face meeting.

He'd do it tomorrow.

Charlie glanced at his watch. It was only seven in the evening. Joel would probably be home now. The only reason to put off the call was that Charlie was a coward. The very idea of speaking to his son made him knot up inside. Yet, when would it be a better time? Tomorrow? Who could tell what might happen then. Charlie could be dead. Joel could be—

Charlie heaved himself from his bed. He had to do this now. It was foolish to put it off any longer. He slipped into his shoes, sat in a chair, and with a painful grunt bent over and tied the laces. There might not be a tomorrow for him. He then picked up his wallet from the dresser along with a handful of coins. Unfortunately this cheap room didn't have a phone; he'd have to use the pay phone in the lobby. But every step he took weakened his resolve. By the time he reached the landing to the stairs, he was nearly ready to turn back.

Then something struck him. Thirty-seven years ago, Charlie had been as self-centered a man as there was. He had ignored his wife's pleas to give up his shady activities. In his estimation, back then at least, guys with regular jobs were chumps who worked their tails off only to live like paupers. He was going to live high, have a brand-new car, fancy threads, all the latest appliances for his wife. He tried to convince Betsy he was doing it for her, to give her a better life, but he had never really fooled her. They both knew it was all for him, so *he* could feel like a real man. She hadn't wanted any of it. Thirty-seven years in prison hadn't changed him. He still could think only of himself. And because of that, he was thinking of putting his son in danger.

But could a phone call prevent that? Joel would still be in danger, even if Charlie met him personally. What could Charlie do?

More excuses.

For once in his life, he knew he had to do something for someone else. He had thought that sharing blackmail money would be the answer. But it was only a small part—the easy part. To make it all really mean something, he had to give of himself, too. An entirely new realm for Charlie Sullivan, ex-con.

He descended the stairs, his steps determined, but hesitant.

Someone was using the pay phone. He paced nearby for a couple minutes. When the caller finished, Charlie dug into his pocket for a quarter and approached the phone. He dropped in his money and began to dial. He had the number memorized for fear of writing anything down on paper.

Then Charlie saw him. The big goon from the bar several nights ago, the one who drank a Bloody Mary. He was leaning on the front desk, flirting with the pretty clerk. Charlie saw the man only in profile, but he could not be mistaken. It was the same man.

Charlie turned around sharply, so his back was toward the man. He still held the phone, but a busy signal was beeping in his ear because he had waited too long before completing his number.

He cursed silently. Had he been seen? The lobby was small and the phone was in full view of the desk. If the goon hadn't spotted Charlie, he would—and soon. But Charlie was trapped. His only hope was keeping his back to the guy. He pretended to talk into the receiver, in low tones as one would normally do for privacy, nothing too suspicious. He even chuckled a couple times as if he didn't have a care in the world. After a minute, he stole a glance at the front desk. The goon and the gal were really involved in each other. He might just be able to take advantage of the moment.

Quietly, Charlie hung up the phone, then casually sauntered toward the door. But when he was only two steps away from escape, the door burst open and a man and a woman came in.

"Made it just in time!" said the new man.

"I told you we should have taken the umbrella."

From the desk, the goon said, "Don't tell me it's raining! It was sunny a couple hours ago."

"That's San Francisco," laughed the clerk. Her next words made Charlie freeze in horror. "Hey, mister, you're not going out like that, are you?" She was looking right at Charlie.

Charlie had no coat or hat and was wearing just a thin cotton shirt. He hadn't been planning on going out at all. "Just running out for a newspaper," Charlie mumbled.

"You'll get drenched," said the woman who had come in.

He scowled and headed for the door. No choice now. But as he grabbed the latch, he twisted slightly—maybe it was some sick compulsion, but he couldn't help it. He turned enough so he could glimpse the goon once. And the man was staring straight at him. Their eyes met. And, had they spoken, they could not have understood each other better.

Charlie then dashed into the rainy evening. Within moments his thin shirt was soaked through, clinging to his skin like a cold shroud. Good, he thought dismally, now instead of dying of cancer, I'm gonna die of pneumonia. But not yet. He still had something important to do, and he wasn't going to allow his sudden flight to be one more excuse, one more reason for his failure.

His only other thought as he jogged down the street was that his few belongings were back in his room. He could never go back for them. His pain medicine was there, too.

Thirty-one

*J*oel shook the rain off his umbrella and set it on the porch by a
planter. Ebony gave herself a good shake, too. It felt good to be
home again. His key fit perfectly into his new lock.

Joel had been there earlier that morning with his father, who
helped him familiarize himself once again with his home. The cleaning service had cleared out all the debris, so there were few obstacles
to worry about. Most of the old furnishings were so damaged they
had to be hauled away, and he and his mother had not yet had a
chance to select any replacements. He did, however, buy a new mat-
tress to replace his old one, shredded beyond repair. The rest of the
bed and other oak bedroom furnishings had been salvageable. The
service had neatly put away his undamaged clothing, which amounted
to about half his wardrobe, and he had instructed them on his coding
system. So there was enough order for him to at least sleep comfort-
ably in his own house. The only other purchases he had made was a
new stereo system, several CDs, and two comfortable chairs for his
living room.

Joel fed Ebony, then went upstairs to his bedroom to change out
of his suit and into something casual. He picked a pair of brown Dock-
ers from his closet, and a brown-tone sweater from a drawer, hoping
the cleaners had gotten his code right. Then he padded, in stocking
feet, back downstairs where he put a Miles Davis CD in the stereo.
He had been eating his meals out, so there was nothing more to do
but put his feet up on the chair's matching ottoman and relax. There
was so often office work to do at home that he had no qualms about
taking full advantage of rare times like this.

However, it occurred to him that he used to enjoy kicking back,
absorbing his music, far more. But he was now struck with the sudden

sense that something was missing. Maybe it was the empty house. Maybe it was because he had finally found someone with whom to share these quiet moments, and they could no longer be as enjoyable without her presence. Whenever he thought of Irene these days, he could only think of how much she belonged in his life. His mother had advised him to be patient; his good sense told him the same. But his heart . . . it spoke a different message, that of a man in love.

Yes, love.

Joel dare not speak that word to Irene. He feared even to think it because the emotion was so strong in him that if he gave it the least rein, it might well push him to go against every ounce of rational sense he possessed. But he did love her, of that he was certain.

The phone rang, startling him from his thoughts. He reached down beside his chair where he had put the cordless phone, picked it up, and answered after the second ring.

"Hello," he said, hoping he'd hear Irene's voice. It wasn't.

"This Joel Costain?"

"Yes."

"I'm just calling to warn you that you're in danger."

"Pardon me?"

"Listen to me—"

"Who are you?"

"That don't matter. What matters is that your brother's death, the break-in at your house—they are all related. You gotta watch yourself or you could wind up like Greg."

The voice at the other end of the phone was raspy, strained, as if breathless or in some discomfort. It also held an urgency that made it believable.

"Why?" said Joel. "Why would I be in danger? What's going on?"

"The less you know, the better."

"Do you really believe that?" said Joel. "I know absolutely nothing and I've been assaulted—and, by your own admission, I'm still in danger. Tell me what this is about and maybe I can help."

"How could you help?"

"You'd be surprised."

"I gotta go."

"Wait!" Joel shouted desperately into the phone. "At least tell me who you are."

"Can't."

"Are you Charlie Sullivan?"

"I have to go."

"Listen, if you are Sullivan, you have to meet with me. I want to see you! Do you understand? We could help each other."

"No."

"You owe it to me, Charlie. Do you hear—?" But the only response to Joel's plea was a hasty click of the phone on the other end.

With a heavy sigh, Joel let his head fall against the back of the chair. Had he just been talking to . . . *his father*? He tried to recall every intonation, every nuance of that voice, searching for a sense of familiarity or anything that would reveal the truth. But all he could hear was that forced rasp. Maybe he was reading too much into that, but it sounded like the speaker was sick, probably in pain. And there was something else that perhaps only Joel's keen ear for voices could have discerned. The caller's warning sprang from more than a sense of duty. There had been concern in that broken voice, perhaps even *caring*.

It had to have been Charlie Sullivan. No one else but a man talking to his son for the first time in thirty-seven years would have sounded that way.

Joel pressed in a number on the phone.

"Irene," he said when she answered. "Is it okay if I come over tonight?" He listened a moment, then said, "Great. I'll be there in a half hour or so."

⟨∞∞⟩

Charlie hardly felt the rain beating against his coatless back as he hung up the phone. His heart was racing, his hands shook. It had taken every ounce of courage to make that call; yet he knew, from Joel's viewpoint, he must have appeared the definitive coward.

Why couldn't he have offered his son just one word of affection? Why hadn't he said something even as simple as, "It's good to hear you"?

Joel had said it all when he said Charlie *owed* it to him. For abandoning him, for causing his blindness . . . the least Charlie could have given Joel was one kind word. But wasn't it better this way? Charlie wasn't fit for any kind of relationship with a man like Joel, so why torment either of them? He'd been a fool to entertain the delusion that such a thing could happen, that he could have a son again.

And now that he knew there was no hope of a reunion, he could get on with the next phase of his final mission on earth. Which was another reason for distancing himself from Joel. It was time to set in motion his long-sought revenge against the person who—even more than Charlie himself—was responsible for destroying his life and family.

*　*　*

Irene had a strong urge to embrace him when she opened the door. She took his wet coat and umbrella instead. He had left Ebony at home, but he was familiar enough with her apartment to negotiate well with his cane and with a nudge or two from her.

"Whew! Is it wet out there. Autumn is here for sure," Joel said.

"I'll hang your coat by the heater so it'll be dry when you leave."

"Thanks." He was carrying his briefcase, which he laid on the coffee table.

They sat on the sofa.

"Where's Adam and Mark?" asked Joel.

"In bed. It's after nine."

"Bad habit of mine—losing track of time." He offered a sheepish smile.

She returned the smile, then said, "So, what brings you out on a nasty night like this?"

"I needed to talk, work some things out. Irene, I think Charlie Sullivan called me tonight."

"Really! You actually spoke with him?"

"He didn't identify himself, but it couldn't have been anyone else. He called to warn me that I'm in danger. He said Greg's death and what happened at my house are related, and I could end up dead, too."

"Oh, Joel!" He'd said the words so carelessly, as if he didn't take them seriously at all or had no fear of such a thing.

"It's no real surprise, is it?" he said.

"I guess since nothing more has happened, I thought—I hoped—it was all over."

"It won't be over until I meet Charlie Sullivan. I know that now more than ever."

"Why would he stay away, even now when it seems you're in danger anyway? If he was protecting you, it hasn't helped much."

Joel reached for his briefcase and opened it. "Irene, I want to look through all these papers Jim gathered again. Would you help me?"

"Of course."

He smiled.

"I guess I'm a bit curious myself. What are you looking for?"

"I'm not sure. Something that will tell me what's going on; maybe a clue about who is responsible for this so-called danger; and, in my wildest expectations, how to find Charlie. Irene, you can't imagine how it was to actually talk to him, to hear his voice, to realize *this is my father*. Up until that moment, it was all kind of a dream, not real. Now he's a person with a voice—and that's a huge percentage of the person for me. I've got to find him."

Irene took some papers from the briefcase. "Let's get started, then."

The briefcase was packed full. Newspaper clippings, mostly, but Jim Kincaid had truly proved his worth when he had produced transcripts to Charlie's trial. Jim had unearthed the transcripts and had been lucky enough to find the court reporter who had taken the transcripts years ago still alive and able to transcribe her work. They had been delivered to Joel that morning. Irene spent the next two hours reading to Joel, and they began piecing together the events of so long ago.

Charlie had been a ne'er-do-well working for underworld types, running numbers, collecting debts, any dirty little job that came along. It was never clear why he switched from being a wiseguy to being a burglar, which, in criminal circles, would probably have been considered a real comedown. He said at the trial that he was just tired of working for someone else. He wanted to go straight but couldn't get a break. When asked why he broke in to the trucking company office, he said he'd heard there was a payroll in the safe.

Who did he hear that from?

Charlie wouldn't say.

Was he working alone?

Charlie refused to answer.

Was he protecting an accomplice?

No comment.

The prosecutor questioned Charlie very carefully about his activities between his getaway from the scene of the crime and the time of his arrest—spanning nearly twenty-four hours. Charlie said he visited his family during that time and was also trying to get fake papers so he could leave the country.

"That's interesting," said Irene. "I guess I assumed he was arrested at the scene."

"I wonder if he was planning to take his family with him?" mused Joel.

"I doubt it, if his wife was pregnant. How far along was she?"

"I think my mother mentioned that Betsy was only six and a half months along when I was born. You're right, he wouldn't have taken a risk like that, either for her sake or his. A fugitive with a pregnant woman along would have really stood out. So he spent at least part of that time saying good-bye to his wife and son. It must have been hard."

"Do you think so?"

"Maybe it's because I want to believe it. After talking to him today, I sensed he wasn't a hardened, heartless criminal. He has a soul. And what if he was protecting an accomplice? It shows he was a man of some honor, too. Or, is it just wishful thinking on my part?"

"Joel, I just thought of something we haven't considered. If there was a partner in the robbery, whatever happened to him? Charlie had to bear the whole thing alone."

"I guess we better not get too sympathetic. He did kill a man."

"He was *convicted* of killing a man," Irene corrected.

"Interesting point—counselor!"

Joel leaned forward, elbows on knees, chin resting in his hands, his mind obviously working. Irene decided he was very much in his element, piecing a puzzle, mentally digging for answers. This must have been at least part of why he had become a lawyer. She wondered again why he had quit practicing criminal law. Did tax law give him the same thrill she now saw etched on his face?

"Want more coffee?" Irene asked as she stood to refill her own cup.

"Sure," he said absently, hardly noticing her.

She brought back two cups, set Joel's in front of him but said nothing, not wanting to interrupt his thinking process. He picked up his cup with the same absent air. In another minute or two, he finally spoke.

"Irene, I think I've figured it out—some of it, at least. The police report, the trial transcripts, even the newspapers all agree that Charlie left the trucking company empty-handed. It's also logical to assume that Charlie had no money to speak of—or he wouldn't have risked the robbery in the first place. That's assuming he wasn't the type to commit the crime just for the thrill of it, but everything points to the fact that he robbed the trucking place because he needed money. So, here we are thirty-seven years later, Charlie is out of prison. He tries to locate his sons and succeeds. He approaches Greg but not me—I'm still not sure why. Now suspicious things start to happen, including murder. Charlie disappears—not that he had ever really *appeared*. Nevertheless, we can pretty much conclude that Charlie fears for both his and my life. Someone killed Greg and may well kill Charlie or me. Why? It must relate to that robbery. He's been in prison, so what else could it be? Now, are you ready for me to be truly brilliant?"

"I can't wait."

"If someone wants Charlie or me dead, they could have done that many times over—at least they could have easily killed me. I think they—whoever *they* are—want something out of Charlie. And what is a major motivation of murder? Greed. Money."

"But you just said Charlie had no money."

"Unless he didn't come away from that trucking company as empty-handed as everyone thought. What if Charlie stumbled upon some money that the company owner couldn't report because it was ill-gotten? What if Charlie came away with a bag of loot that he managed to hide before the police arrested him? And now that he's out of prison, he wants to get to his money, but there's someone else who also wants it—someone who is willing to kill for it."

"I don't know, Joel, if that's brilliant or crazy."

"Isn't brilliance just the other side of insanity?" He grinned wryly. "I can think of only one other explanation. Charlie has something else these people want. Something valuable enough to kill for. Those thugs who broke in to my house were looking for something specific. Remember they asked, 'Where'd the old man tell you to put it?' "

"Yes, you're right. But it's so incredible—after all this time—that it should still interest people."

"That's why my first guess is that this involves money; however, it would have to be a lot of money, even by today's standards, if it is still enticing interest. But the big question I'd like answered is *who*, besides Charlie, would still be interested? There's the owner of the trucking company—what was the name? It's in one of those articles."

Irene shuffled through the clippings, scanning several. "Here it is—Banducci Trucking. Do you think they're still around?"

"I'll make some phone calls tomorrow." Joel rubbed his hands together, the eagerness apparent in his face, despite the lateness of the hour. "Then there is this possible accomplice. If he existed and is still alive, he'd certainly have a stake in recovering the money."

"Not that he deserves it, if he's walked around free all these years while Charlie was stuck in prison."

"Perhaps his interest is merely in protecting himself."

"That makes a lot of sense."

"If only we could talk to Charlie," mused Joel. "He could tell us. Why can't he realize we'd all be better off working together? No doubt he thinks his helpless blind son just needs protecting." Joel slapped his knee with frustration. "What a stubborn old cuss! I've *got* to talk to him again, but the ball is totally in his court. I *am* helpless."

All words of encouragement that rose to Irene's lips seemed so trite. Instead of saying anything, she just reached out and laid a hand on Joel's. The grateful expression on his face told Irene that had been the right thing to do. She was learning how important touch was to him and that it could be a very platonic kind of thing. Yet the warm vibrance of his hand beneath hers filled her with an inner warmth that could hardly be described as dispassionate.

"I guess I'll just keep looking until I find him," Joel said, his old confidence back.

"And you will, Joel, I'm sure of it. You seem to thrive on unraveling mysteries."

He smiled wanly. "I suppose so."

"Then, that can't be why you quit practicing criminal law."

His brow creased. "Where'd you hear about that?"

"Detective Reiley mentioned something. Maybe I shouldn't have said anything?"

Shrugging, he answered, "It's not my favorite subject."

"Then, forget I ever brought it up."

Joel said nothing for a long time, but his expression was one of intense thought. Finally, he replied, though with some hesitation. "One of the few times in my life I had to give up in utter defeat."

Thirty-two

*D*o you want to talk about what happened?" Irene asked.

Needing no more prompting, Joel plunged into the account as if meeting the inevitable. "When I finished law school, I set up my own practice because most of the established firms had reservations against hiring a blind man to practice criminal law. My clients were mostly poor people who couldn't afford the big firms. I didn't care about making money. Helping those who deserved quality legal counsel but who didn't have the means to obtain it was just what I wanted to be doing. And I was successful, at first. I won eighty percent of my cases—acceptable statistics for any attorney, blind or sighted. Then I took on the defense of a man accused of assault and rape—my biggest case. And I won. He was acquitted. Two weeks after his release, he was arrested again. This time for raping and killing a woman."

"And you blamed yourself?"

"If I had been able to see, maybe I would have clearly *seen* that he was guilty. I would never have defended him had I known that."

"But isn't it true that even a guilty criminal is entitled to a defense?"

"That's not the point. I missed something, and because of that . . ." Joel shook his head, apparently still finding it difficult to face what had happened.

"It must have been hard," Irene replied soothingly.

"Thank you for not trying to console me with all the pat answers. At the time some blamed me for taking on a responsibility for which I was unfit. But, largely, I heard the run-of-the-mill comforts like the fact that the guy had fooled many sighted people before me; or that I won the case because of foul-ups by the police, not because I was blind, etc. But I was afraid to take that risk again. Afraid . . ."

"Oh, Joel . . ."

"I am a blind man, Irene." He said it as if he was realizing it for the first time. "It irks me to admit it. But I'm handicapped—or visually disabled, visually challenged, or whatever cute term you choose to give it. I'm defective, flawed—"

"Stop it, Joel!"

"Why? Maybe my disability should scare you far more than how much I look like Greg. Then again, it wouldn't matter to you unless you cared for me."

"You hate self-pity, Joel. Don't let yourself fall into that trap." She wanted to tell him she did care, but she couldn't say the words. Instead, she said, "It doesn't matter. I don't see a blind man."

"Maybe you should."

"If I cared. If I loved you . . ."

"If . . ." He reached for his coffee cup, put it to his lips. Irene had noticed it was empty but hadn't said anything in time. He let a slanted smile diffuse some of his tension. "Just a minor inconvenience . . ." he murmured wryly. She wondered if he was talking about the empty cup or his handicap.

She took the cup and refilled it.

After taking a sip, he said, "Well, I've always thought that fiasco with my criminal practice was probably God's will for me, at least I hoped that. But if that was where He wanted me, then I really turned my back on His will. However, I did prosper in the path I finally followed, even if I haven't always been content."

"I can't begin to count the times I've struggled with *God's will*," Irene said. "My way of coping was to just plow ahead hoping He wouldn't let me go too far astray. I'm not sure about a lot of things, Joel, but is the kind of God you believe in the kind who would play such games with you? Would He really treat someone who loved Him that way?"

"That's a funny statement coming from you, Irene. But a very wise one."

Now it was Irene's turn to squirm uncomfortably. "Old habits die hard," she said lamely. "But I was talking about your belief, not mine."

"You know what I think?" Joel began. "You haven't stopped believing in God or loving Him. You've just temporarily lost confidence—in Him or in yourself, I'm not certain which."

"It has the same effect, doesn't it? Kind of like you losing confidence in your ability to practice criminal law. It's too much of a struggle to rebuild it. Perhaps it's even impossible. Fear can be a very debilitating thing."

"But not impossible to overcome."

"Not impossible, I guess."

"We're fighters, Irene. It is possible."

"We?" Irene shook her head with uncertainty. "How can you know that about me? I failed at marriage, at my faith—I can't even finish a painting. That's not fighting, that's giving up."

"How do you know until the last vote is counted? As long as you're alive, you have a chance to fight."

"As long as I don't fight God." She smiled.

He lifted his hand and traced the upturned curve of her lips with his finger. He lingered a moment, his hand gently caressing her cheek. Irene didn't flinch away, though she told herself she should. Instead, she leaned ever so slightly into his touch. He lifted his other hand also until her face was cupped in his palms. She gazed up at him, scanning his sightless eyes, feeling again that his eyes were seeing into her heart.

"It would be self-defeating," Joel said quietly.

"I don't want that. I want to fight. I want what I once had."

"I know."

"You've always known, haven't you?"

He nodded, a slight twitch of mirth on his lips. "I couldn't have loved you otherwise."

"Please, Joel, don't say it."

"It's too late. . . ."

"If only . . ." Her words were barely audible, but Joel heard.

"We believe in the kind of God who will take care of those 'if onlys'," he said.

We believe . . . was it true, then? Had she not wandered so far away that it was impossible for her to come back? She recalled the Scripture, "With God nothing is impossible." She thought of Joel, who was constantly defying impossibilities, and she knew he would give the credit for his accomplishments to God. Yet even a man such as Joel stumbled and doubted at times. The stumbling wasn't the problem at all. Difficulties only arose when you fell and refused to get back up and keep going. Joel had done it once in his life, but Irene had done it with her *whole* life.

Was she a fighter?

She laid her hand on one of Joel's and nodded. "I think you may be right."

He gave a pleased sigh and smiled. "I'll be here for you, Irene. It may be like the blind leading the blind—"

"No, Joel. In spiritual things I am indeed in the 'Country of the Blind.' You see far better there than I."

She brought his hand to her lips and kissed it tenderly. She had no idea what would happen next or what kind of commitment she had made, either to Joel or to God. All her confusion would not dissipate overnight. Yet she felt infused by a strength that had not been there before. She had a desire, at least, not to give up.

Thirty-three

*T*he next day after work, Irene called Joel at his office to invite him to her place for dinner.

"I have to take a client out to dinner," he said, clearly disappointed.

"Well, maybe tomorrow, then."

"Irene, why don't you join us tonight?"

"I'd be out of place. . . ."

"Believe me, you would help brighten an evening that's sure to be boring. I'll treat you to a decadent dessert afterwards, just you and I."

"Root beer floats?"

"Your choice."

"Cheesecake?"

"Done."

Irene laughed and couldn't refuse. He told her when and where to meet them. And she found she was eagerly anticipating the time to arrive. She simply couldn't obliterate what was growing in her heart. Since last night, a change was slowly but very surely creeping over her. Joel was becoming less and less Greg's brother, more his own man— a decent, sensitive, gentle man. The better she knew him and the more she scrutinized him, trying to find his fatal flaws, she realized that, if he had flaws—and he most certainly did—they were not identical to Greg's. Joel might let her down, he might even hurt her, but it wouldn't be in the same way Greg had. Joel simply wasn't a carbon copy of Greg; he never had been and never would be.

But that didn't absolve all risk.

Her rational mind kept telling her all relationships held some element of risk. There was no way around it. For the last year she had been dismissing men—the few she had even allowed into her life—for all manner of flaws, major and minor. But never before had a man been more difficult to dismiss than Joel. Not so much because of his persistence, but rather because of a special, indefinable draw he had on her. The other men simply hadn't been worth the risk, the danger of taking that precarious step into a real relationship. Was Joel?

There was no question in Irene's mind that he was. The only remaining question was whether she was *willing* or not. Maybe she didn't have to answer it right away. She knew Joel was giving her time—and she would need lots of it. She had made one hasty marriage, and she wouldn't do it again.

To distract herself, Irene went into her bedroom to try to find something to wear for dinner. Opening her closet, she scanned her selections. They would be dining at Alexander's, a five-star establishment, so she definitely wanted something classy. She took out a red silky dress that was hanging toward the back. It had simple lines, flared skirt, long sleeves. It was very "dressy." Maybe it would be appropriate for where they would eat tonight, but . . . was it was *too* much? It was a hand-me-down from Connie, who didn't want it because it was too short. It fit Irene's more petite frame perfectly, but she had never worn it—now she saw why. She hardly ever dressed up. Cotton pants or Levi's were her usual garb. Even for work, pants with a shirt and blazer were quite acceptable. It occurred to her that Joel probably attended many functions that required evening attire. Was that another strike against him or a plus? She couldn't decide.

She tossed the dress on the bed. Returning to the closet, she dug around some more. Within a few minutes, several discarded outfits lay on the bed.

Chomping on an apple, Mark ambled into the room. "What's for dinner, Mom?"

"Hot dogs and macaroni and cheese. Lisa will fix it when she comes to stay with you this evening."

"What're you doing?" he asked, eyeing the pile on the bed.

"Trying to decide what to wear tonight." She held up a blue skirt and matching mohair sweater. "What do you think?"

Not a fashion maven, Mark just shrugged. "Mom, if Joel is blind, what's the big deal about what you wear?"

His logic surprised her, then amused her. She chuckled. "Well, Mark, I know it doesn't make sense, but there's a lot of factors to consider in this process. You don't really want to hear them, do you?"

He shook his head and took another bite of his apple.

Irene finally decided on a black rayon flared skirt with a Victorian rose print. With it she wore a black cashmere sweater with pearl buttons down the front. Classy, but casual enough for her to feel comfortable in.

Alexander's was located on Nob Hill, surrounded by San Francisco's best hotels, including the Fairmont and the Mark Hopkins. Irene had often taken out-of-town guests to the Fairmont for a ride in their glass elevator to view the city from the top. Once, early in their marriage, Greg had taken her to the Top of the Mark for a drink to celebrate something, she couldn't remember what now. She couldn't afford to patronize these fancy establishments except as a tourist passing through.

She entered Alexander's and a hostess in a stylish black crepe dress approached her. Suddenly Irene felt rather commonplace, not classy at all. She told the hostess she was joining Joel Costain, and was immediately taken to a booth in a secluded corner of the dining room. On the way she caught sight of Joel and an attractive blond woman seated opposite him and realized anew how easily Joel fit in to this world. Giving her sweater a nervous tug, Irene squared her shoulders and took a breath before trying to plunge into that world.

Introductions were made, and Lena Westfall offered Irene a cold, limp hand before she gestured for Irene to sit in the plush, red velvet booth.

"I am confused about your relationship to Joel," said Lena. "His fiancée, is it?" Her tone was unmistakably condescending.

"No, just friends," Irene replied, crimson infusing her cheeks. She hated for this cool, well-bred woman to see her so flustered. At least Joel couldn't see it.

"The best of friends," added Joel, giving her a smile meant to be encouraging, but its warmth and intimacy only made Irene redden more.

A waiter came and took their orders. He was extremely attentive to them, especially when Lena made several special requests that weren't on the menu.

"Irene, did I mention that Lena owns Alexander's?" Joel asked.

"Really?" said Irene, then, because she felt a further comment was called for, added, "I'm sure it's a wonderful restaurant."

"You've never dined here?" asked Lena.

"I'm afraid I haven't." Irene didn't mention that one dinner here would have destroyed her weekly food budget.

The meal was so awkward and uncomfortable that it was a relief when Joel and Lena began to talk business. The discussion of taxes and the IRS was refreshing compared to the condescending words and looks Lena seemed to be casting Irene's way. When the main course was finished and the waiter asked if they wished for dessert, Joel quickly declined.

"I really couldn't eat another thing." Had he remembered their plans for after dinner?

No matter, Irene also politely turned down another course. In fact, she didn't care if there would be no dessert at all that evening, she just wanted to leave as quickly as possible. Lena insisted they at least end the meal with a cappuccino. And she was the kind of person who was difficult to refuse. When they were finally finished and it was time to depart, Irene made an effort not to dash away. She forced her pace to match Lena's relaxed stroll as they exited the restaurant. Irene did manage to assert herself when the valet arrived with Lena's silver-gray BMW. Irene offered to give Joel a ride home. He accepted, and it appeared as if he, too, was anxious to escape his client.

"I don't want it to appear that I am deserting you, Joel," Lena said. "I did bring you."

"I'm going right by his place," Irene lied. "It would be a shame to make you go out of your way."

"You live on Greenwich, don't you?" said Lena. "It's not out of the way, at all."

"Well, well," Joel chuckled, "usually I have trouble getting rides, now I have two beautiful women vying for the honor! But, Lena, I didn't want to put you out, so I already arranged for Irene to drive me home. Thank you again for an excellent dinner."

Lena smiled a bit stiffly. "Let me at least take care of the valet for you, Irene."

"I didn't use the valet. I parked on the street, not far away."

"Really?" Lena arched an eyebrow, as if she had never heard of such a thing.

"I like to walk," said Irene lamely. No need to explain how she was embarrassed to have the valet park her beat-up old car.

At last Lena slipped behind the wheel of her shiny car and drove away. Irene gave Joel a wan smile.

"That was kind of weird, wasn't it?" she said.

"The entire evening was weird. I couldn't wait for it to end."

"Then, I wasn't the only one."

"Hardly!" Joel lightly placed his hand on Irene's elbow. "Where's your car? I hope it's a mile away—I really do feel like walking."

"We have to walk off that dinner and make room for cheesecake."

He laughed. "Let's go."

They walked past her car, down California Street. The recent rain had brought with it a more definite fall season. The air was brisk and chilly enough that Irene was glad she had her gray wool coat. A cable car rattled past, and some tourists hanging off the handrails waved. Irene waved back. She suddenly felt very good, the pall of the earlier part of the evening now completely diffused. She could almost believe she had at last made it through a dark time. She had tried to pray last night after her talk with Joel, after her realization that she desired her old faith. And much to her astonishment, she had actually felt as if her prayer had at last broken through some barrier. Her words no longer echoed as if rebounding futilely against steel walls.

No wonder she was in a good mood. Years ago she had lost her dearest friend. And now she was reconciling with Him, with her Lord. The lightness of spirit she felt now made her realize just how heavily that loss had weighed her down. She still felt tentative and unsure at times, but with the wall around her crumbling by degrees, hope was gaining a sure foothold in her.

"Let's walk through Chinatown," Joel said.

"That's right where I was heading."

"Great minds, eh?" His hand dropped from her elbow and inched around her waist.

"You sure you won't trip walking that way?"

"I'll never stumble with you at my side, Irene."

"I'm not even going to respond to that!"

They turned up Grant Street, into the thriving Chinese community of San Francisco. The sudden bustle of activity here was jarring after the comparatively quiet street they had been on. Even at nine at night the street was crowded with pedestrians, mostly tourists. All the shops were open, with tables and bins also on the sidewalk. Jade and ivory Buddhas, ornately carved teak, painted fans, silk clothing, all bright and enticing, filled the senses. Joel commented on the cloying fragrance of incense coming from the shops and the babble in at least two languages.

Joel and Irene acted like tourists. Joel bought Irene a beautiful fan trimmed in lace with white lotus flowers painted against a black background. From a bakery Irene bought sesame cookies for her boys, and Joel bought some very un-Chinese chocolate fudge.

"This can take the place of cheesecake," Irene said as she tasted a small piece.

"No way. I promised you cheesecake, and cheesecake you will get!"

But there was no cheesecake in that neighborhood, so after traversing half the length of Chinatown, they returned to the car. No bakeries were open and they had to settle for frozen cheesecake from an all-night market. They brought it back to Joel's house.

Ebony greeted them at the door, her tail wagging happily. She was looking better, but still walked stiffly. The answering machine was beeping, signaling with sound for Joel's benefit, rather than the usual light. He went into the kitchen and switched on the machine.

Jim Kincaid's familiar voice greeted them. "Joel, this is Jim. Where are you? I'm going to call you every half hour until I reach you. Stay put until we talk. Got big news."

Thirty-four

There were two more messages on the machine, the final one at nine-thirty. It was now nine thirty-five and a long wait until ten, when Jim would call again. Joel and Irene had their dessert, but hardly enjoyed it. They were both suddenly tense. What big news? Why hadn't Jim mentioned if it was good or bad news? Irene wondered if her previous good mood was premature. Was a dark cloud about to shadow her life again?

They attempted to speculate about what Jim wanted, but when their attempts fell lamely away, they gave up and hardly talked at all. Silently, then, they drank their coffee and waited.

Joel's clock had just finished announcing in its mechanized voice, "It is ten o'clock P.M.," when the phone finally rang. Joel's hand was only inches from the cordless receiver, and he grabbed it as if it might escape before he got to it.

"Jim?"

"Man, I'm glad you're back! I was afraid he'd get away before I talked to you—"

"He? Who—?"

"Sullivan. I've found him."

"He's found Charlie," Joel said excitedly to Irene. Then back into the receiver, "Where?"

"I tracked him to a cheap hotel on Haight. He left there about two hours ago, and I've been following him while trying to get ahold of you. I didn't want to spook him until I found out what you want to—"

"I'll be right there! Give me an address."

"He's not in the hotel right now but in a bar on Stanyon." He gave Joel the number. "I'm directly across the street, trying to look casual at ten P.M. Not easy in this neighborhood, and me looking so much like a cop. I'd swear there was a drug deal going on a few minutes ago. You have my number, don't you? If I'm not here when you arrive, it'll mean I'm tailing him again. Call me, I've got my phone right with me."

"Okay, we'll be there in ten minutes."

Irene asked no questions until they were in her car, speeding across town. Joel made no comments about her driving this time, except to urge her to go faster. Charlie Sullivan had been so elusive until now that he had practically taken on the aspect of an imaginary friend. He could disappear into a puff of smoke at the slightest provocation. So keeping an eye on her rearview mirror, Irene pressed the Toyota's accelerator. Like a true San Franciscan, she slid through more than a few signals several moments after they had turned red. If she had not believed in God before, she certainly did now. Only He could have navigated her through the streets of San Francisco that night without mishap.

Stanyon Street bordered the eastern end of Golden Gate Park. A couple blocks farther east was Haight, of the famous Haight-Ashbury district where the flower children of the 60s had congregated. Back then it had been a disreputable area, in which once-stately old Victorian buildings had gone entirely to seed. Now, with even the whimsy of the flower children gone, the place had little left to recommend it.

Irene parked on Stanyon. Directly to her right was the park, dark now and forbidding. She wasn't surprised that even a physically capable man like Jim Kincaid was nervous standing about here, especially at this late hour. She had expected Joel to leap from the car the moment it stopped. But he hesitated, and Irene knew it wasn't because of the street people and derelicts who frequented this area.

"It just hit me, Irene," Joel murmured. "I'm going to finally meet him."

"Are you ready?"

"No . . . I'd like to run away. Would you stay with me?"

"Are you sure you don't want to be alone with him?"

"I'll play it by ear. For now I need some moral support."

"I'm with you, Joel."

They got out of the car. Irene walked around and Joel took her arm. He inhaled a deep breath before they started moving. Jim strode toward them.

"He's still in there," Jim said.

"I don't know if it'll be good or bad if he's drunk," Joel commented dryly.

"There's only one way to find out," said Irene.

"I knew someone would say that," said Joel. "Here we go, then."

All three crossed the street. The bar was an establishment called Fran's Place. Even if Irene were in the habit of frequenting bars, she knew she wouldn't go to a place like this. Of course, she doubted she'd be in this neighborhood in the first place. Jim waited outside, saying too many people might make Charlie nervous. Inside the bar, the small room was dimly lit and filled with cigarette smoke making Irene's eyes burn. There were about two dozen people, seated on stools at the bar and at the handful of tiny round tables. The room was noisy with the din of several conversations and loud, recorded music in the background.

Jim had given Irene a brief description of Sullivan—which could have described half the men in the bar. She was able to pick him out only by the outdated felt fedora he wore. He was seated on a stool, hunched over the bar, a shot of whiskey or something in front of him.

"I think I've spotted him," Irene whispered to Joel. "Now what?"

"Take me to him." The determination in Joel's tone was heartening.

They drew closer until Joel stood by Charlie's right shoulder, behind him. Joel said quietly, "Charlie Sullivan?"

The man noticeably tensed, but said nothing.

Joel went on, "I've been wanting to meet you for a long time, Charlie. I'm Joel."

Still Charlie did not respond or turn. He wrapped his hand around his drink as if for support, then brought it to his lips, taking a long swallow.

"Charlie, please talk to me," Joel entreated.

"You've done a foolish thing, finding me," Sullivan finally said in a low, forced tone. He continued to face forward.

"I don't think so. I believe we both wanted this moment to happen. Can you look at me, Charlie, and see what your son is like?"

"I've already seen you."

"I'd like to know that we met face to face."

"You ask too much. You want too much." Charlie drained off the rest of his drink and signaled the bartender to refill his glass.

"Charlie, let's sit together at a table and talk. Give me five minutes—that's all I'll ask."

Slowly, Charlie shook his head, and Irene thought that would be the end. But then, in a soft, forced tone, he said, "Five minutes."

Charlie turned and Irene saw him clearly for the first time. The face revealed was older than his years could account for and deeply lined beneath the two or three days' growth of salt-and-pepper beard. His crew-cut hair was gray and thinning, perhaps from the effects of some prior cancer treatment. His dull gray eyes were bloodshot, and their hard edge conflicted sharply with their mournful sadness. Irene saw that his shoulders and neck were perpetually bent, jutting ever so slightly forward to give him the appearance of a rather forlorn vulture. The sense of pity Irene felt for him was heightened by the ragged, black overcoat he wore and the scuffed shoes on his feet.

He swayed a moment as his feet touched the floor. Irene reached out a hand to steady him, but he shrugged it away, then shuffled to the only empty table in the room. He was seated, his drink in front of him, as Irene and Joel approached. Bringing his glass again to his lips, Irene saw his eyes lift, almost imperceptibly, to gaze covertly at his son.

Irene crowded two more chairs around the small table, and she and Joel wedged themselves in. All around, customers were laughing, talking, moving about, jostling them. She felt as if they were an island in a stormy sea. But the island itself was hardly calm or serene.

A waitress came to the table.

"What'll it be?" She dampened her pencil lead on her tongue and poised to write.

Joel shook his head, obviously annoyed at the intrusion.

Charlie said, "They don't like non-paying customers filling their chairs."

Joel took his wallet from the inside pocket of his leather jacket, opened it, and withdrew two twenties.

"No more interruptions, okay?" he said, handing the bills to the woman.

"Okay!" said the waitress, quickly palming the money.

"Hey, not so fast," said Charlie. "I want a double." He pointed at his now-empty glass. "Scotch." When the waitress scurried away, he glanced up sheepishly at Joel. "Guess you think your old man is, in addition to everything else, a drunk. But I'm not. I lost my medicine. Booze sort of takes its place."

"You don't have to explain," said Joel.

"I was real worried about the medicine making me into a drug addict. But hell—I'm sorry, I mean, heck—you gotta forgive me; when a guy spends as much time in prison as I have, you forget how to talk or act like decent people. Anyway, I'm gonna die, so I probably won't have time to become an addict or a drunk."

"You don't have to apologize for yourself."

"Yeah, I do. You gotta understand why I didn't want to see you."

"I understand. But you started this, Charlie. I'm just playing the hand you dealt. Before Greg came to me, I wasn't the least interested in my blood family. All my life, I seldom gave it more than a passing thought. It's all changed now that you opened the door. Once I knew I had a father out there, I had to meet you. I had to know what kind of person you are."

"Isn't that obvious? I'm an ex-con, a convicted killer."

"That's what you *did* or what you may have done. It's not who you are."

"What's the difference?"

"That's why I had to meet you. I had to find out if there was a difference."

The waitress came with Charlie's drink. He took a quick sip of the fresh drink.

Then he looked up at Joel, scanning his face as if hoping to find something there. Maybe hoping there was, after all, vision in Joel's eyes, or perhaps he simply wanted to see a reflection of himself in Joel.

"I'm sorry," Charlie said in a low, dismal voice.

"For what?"

"Come on, you know what. It's because I got arrested that your mother had you too soon and caused your blindness. You would have been normal, if—"

"You can't blame yourself—"

"Yeah, you're right. If it hadn't been for that weasel—" he stopped suddenly. "Anyway, I'm gonna set things right, make 'em pay—" He paused again.

"I don't understand," said Joel.

"Never mind. I think our five minutes are up."

"At least finish your drink."

"How'd you know—?"

"You'd be surprised what a man without vision can see. And you don't have to be sorry or feel sorry for me. I'm fine. Blindness is just a minor inconvenience."

"Minor, huh?"

Joel shrugged. "Sometimes more. But I've had a good life, Charlie. Good people raised me. I'm content. I'm happy." He paused, then added, "I just thought you'd want to know."

"I can see you're a good boy—a good man. You turned out well—" Charlie's voice seemed to catch. Irene saw emotion in his eyes, perhaps even rising moisture. "If I'd had anything to do with it, I'd be proud of you. It just doesn't seem possible that I could have a son like you." He glanced at Irene. "Is this your wife?"

"No. I was married but my wife died several years ago. I have no children."

"My name is Irene. I was married to Greg."

"You don't say?" Charlie pursed his lips and gave Irene a closer scrutiny. "How'd you get mixed up with a guy like that?"

Irene had no quick response and, searching in her mind for some answer, could only come up with, "I don't know. We had two children together," she added. "Boys. Your grandchildren."

"Greg mentioned them. Don't worry, I'll stay away from them."

"You don't have to—" Irene began.

Charlie cut in, "I didn't mean for Greg to get hurt. I still don't know what happened to him, but I've got an idea."

"Can you tell us anything about what's going on? Why are we in danger?" asked Joel.

"It's a long story, but soon you won't have to worry about that. I'm gonna take care of it."

"What are you going to do?"

"It's not your concern."

"You've got to give me some answers, Charlie. I'm in pretty deep, and my ignorance isn't doing any good. Did you realize the police suspect me of killing Greg? They haven't got much of a case, but I'd like to see all this cleared up. Do you want Greg's killer to get away with it? Tell me something—anything! I can help you. We can work together."

"I'm a loner."

Joel let out a frustrated sigh.

"I will tell you one thing," Charlie said. "I didn't kill that cop thirty-seven years ago. I was set up and betrayed. Your old man isn't no killer . . . I just thought you'd want to know. I'm rotten in every other way, but at least I ain't that."

"Who killed him?"

"It's time for me to go."

"Are you in danger?"

"I guess I'm glad you found me." Charlie started to stand, but Joel quickly laid a hand on his arm urging him back.

"Charlie, what was my mother like?"

Charlie was silent for a long time, rubbing his face as if trying to clear away cobwebs or painful memories. "You mind if I smoke?" he asked finally, digging a beat-up pack of Camels from his pocket. When Joel and Irene shook their heads, he proceeded to tap a cigarette from the pack and light it. After a couple of puffs, he spoke again. "She was a pretty girl," he said. "Only twenty-three when she died. So young. She was sweet, too, and I'm not just saying that—she really was. Innocent, you know. Naive." Charlie glanced at Irene. "Maybe like you were, honey, when you married Greg. She only wanted one of them little cottages with a picket fence and a brood of children. Instead, all I ever gave her was that dump on Haight Street."

"You lived near here?" Joel asked. "Where?"

"Yeah . . ." Charlie hesitated. "You don't want to know. It was a dump then, and it's just as bad now."

"Would it hurt for me to know? I found you, Charlie. I can easily find the house."

Charlie shrugged. "You're a persistent son-of-a-gun." His thin, dry lips almost bent into a real smile. "It's the second building from the corner of Haight and Waller. It's kind of a pea green color now, and it's empty, probably condemned. I can't remember the number."

"Thanks, Charlie."

"You were right when you said I owe you something. I wish I could give you more, but I don't have nothing to give." Charlie stood, this time with more finality in the action.

Joel took his wallet out again. "I don't have a lot of cash on me, but—"

"No, I don't want any money from you."

"A loan?"

Charlie shook his head; he had forgotten Joel couldn't see. But when Joel started to open his wallet, Charlie said firmly, "No!"

Joel reluctantly replaced his wallet. "I want to see you again," Joel said as he also stood.

"Promise me something," Charlie replied. "Don't follow me and don't let your man tail me. Just let me go."

"Okay, as long as you promise you'll call me again soon. I *don't* want this to be our last meeting."

"It's a deal."

Charlie started to walk away, but Joel reached for him and managed to lay a hand on the man's shoulder. Charlie stopped, turning. Joel held out his hand. Tentatively, Charlie took it. The handshake was formal, but it was filled with so many undercurrents of emotion and meaning that the two men might just as well have embraced. But Charlie let go before that could happen and started walking. Irene and Joel followed him outside.

Without a backward glance Charlie hurried away.

"I'll keep on him," Jim said.

"Let him go," said Joel. "I promised we wouldn't follow."

"You sure?"

Joel nodded, but he didn't look sure. He looked as if he wanted nothing more than to prevent Charlie—his father—from slipping away again.

Thirty-five

J oel would have made his next destination the house on Haight Street had it not been ten o'clock and a poor time to go prowling around that neighborhood. But Irene promised to meet him first thing in the morning to make the pilgrimage. She arranged for her work day to begin at ten, thankful her boss had always given her the latitude to have flexible hours.

At eight-thirty in the morning Haight-Ashbury was a bit more inviting than it had been the night before. The shops were opening and pedestrians were strolling along the streets. A homeless woman was pushing a shopping cart filled with what appeared to be junk but what were more than likely her only possessions. She didn't look at all out of place here. Neither did Irene's weathered Toyota, which she parked on Haight, across from their destination. Oddly, the only thing that did look incongruent to the surroundings was Joel in his expensive gray wool suit. He said he would have dressed more casually but he had an appointment in an hour and wouldn't have had time.

They had no trouble finding the building Charlie had described. Once it might have been a mansion belonging to a rich San Francisco socialite, probably built not long after the great earthquake in 1906. The original owner had long since fled this area along with the general exodus from city centers. The three-story mansion had been converted into an income-generating apartment house. There were four rusted mailboxes nailed up to the front wall next to the porch. The faded green paint had chipped in many places down to the bare wood. The windows were boarded up with what appeared to be fresh plywood.

"It looks vacant," Irene told Joel, and she described in detail what she saw. Then, momentarily leaving his side, she climbed the rickety front steps to read a notice tacked to the front door. Returning to Joel, she told him what she had read. "The place has been condemned by the board of health. That was last month."

"I suppose there's no way in."

"All boarded up."

They walked around to the side. There were about six feet separating it from the buildings on each side. The building on the right, at the corner of the block, appeared to be occupied, but the one on the other side was vacant and boarded up also.

Irene was about to suggest having a look at the back of the house when a young woman, exiting the house on the corner, caught her attention.

"Hi," Irene said with a friendly smile. "I was wondering if you could tell me anything about this house."

The woman was nineteen or twenty, dressed in worn jeans, faded flannel shirt, hiking boots, and a wide-brimmed felt hat over long, brown hair. "What do you want to know?" Her tone was wary, but no more so than was normal for a city person.

"Why has the house been condemned?" Joel asked.

"The earthquake last month."

Irene had forgotten about that, but it hadn't been anything major, only five points on the Richter scale. Too small to cause more than a blink of the eyes in a hardened San Franciscan. Yet even a small shaker like that, hitting just right, could cause havoc in already dilapidated structures.

"Didn't it affect the other buildings?" asked Irene.

"My building's been kept up pretty well. They did some retro fitting on it after the '89 quake. But I don't think anyone's touched that wreck"—she jerked her head toward Charlie's building—"in twenty years. That's what I've been told. I've only lived here two years myself. But, to tell the truth, most of the people in the neighborhood are glad to see it shut down."

"Why's that?"

"You some kind of real estate developer or something? You're not planning a renovation here—so no one can afford these apartments any more? They're not much, but I'm a student at S.F. State, and it's all I can afford."

"No, we're nothing of the kind," said Joel. "I'm just interested in this house for its . . . historical significance."

"Well, like I said, I haven't been here long, but since I've lived here, that house has been a crash pad for homeless and runaways; probably a drug house, too. I'm almost certain there was a 'shooting gallery' in the basement. The Board of Health found used syringes when they made their inspection last month."

"You see anyone else around here besides the county people?"

"Now that you mention it, there was an old man poking around here a couple days ago. I didn't talk to him because I was late for class."

"Did he go inside?"

She shrugged. "I really don't know."

"We don't want to keep you any longer," Joel said. "Thanks for talking to us."

As the girl continued on her way, Joel and Irene walked around the side of the house to the back. Since the front had showed no sign of recent entry, if Charlie had gotten inside, he must have done so from the back. In any case, it seemed the most likely place for Joel and Irene to make the attempt. There was a back door, and as Irene inspected the board nailed across it, she saw signs that it had been pried open, but whoever had done it had been careful to replace it to its original place. She worked her fingers under the edge and tried to pry it loose. It wiggled a little when she applied all her strength to it but didn't budge beyond that, and she only tore a fingernail for her effort.

"Maybe if we both gave it a tug . . ." she told Joel after telling him about what she saw. "I only hope we don't find the door locked behind it."

"I don't think it will be," said Joel. "Charlie was here. I can't believe he didn't get inside. Come on, let's give it a try."

Irene showed Joel where to place his hands, and together they gave the board several yanks until it finally gave way and the nails pulled out of the wood. Irene was then able to reach behind the board to grasp the doorknob. It turned easily. Pulling the board away from the doorjamb about a foot, they were able to squeeze through the opening. The board swung back into place, but they'd have no difficulty exiting by that way later.

Awful smells of age and disuse and filth greeted them as they straightened up in a small entry area where the back stairs were located. An old broom was propped up against the wall, a pile of rags lay in a corner, some cardboard boxes were stacked in another corner. Irene thought of the people who had recently been evicted. Homeless teens, drug addicts, the wretched, and the despised. But she was certain that Joel, at that moment, was thinking about other residents of this house, from a time in the more distant past. . . .

⟨≈⟩

"Now, Greggie, you be careful on those stairs," said the young woman. At twenty-three, she had a round, sweet face, flaxen hair, and eyes as blue as a sunlit sky.

"But, Mama, you go too slow," said the child whose hair was darker than his mother's, but who had very similar eyes, blue and twinkling with just a little mischief.

The woman sighed and smiled. Yes, she moved more slowly these days. A six-month pregnancy made any woman slow down a bit. She lay a hand on her swelling abdomen and her smile, filled with innocent delight, broadened as the child in her womb gave a little kick at that very moment. There was nothing better than being pregnant. She'd already told Charlie she wanted eight kids. He had only groaned playfully and said he needed to get a better-paying job. He wanted a lot of kids, too, she knew that.

"Come on, take my hand," she said, holding out her hand to the four-year-old who was already ahead of her by four steps.

"I'm a big boy, Mama!"

"I was only thinking you could help your mama up these steps. Your brother or sister is getting pretty heavy inside mama's tummy."

"It's gonna be a brother. Daddy says. And I want a brother, too."

"We'll see. . . ." She smiled again. Men always wanted boys. She didn't care either way, but she supposed a little playmate for Greggie would be nice. . . .

⟨≈⟩

Joel tried to imagine happy times in this sad, dismal old house. Maybe his need for this was greater because of his own happy childhood. He couldn't keep a sense of guilt from tugging at him. He wasn't to blame for all that had happened, but he'd had so much good in his life while Charlie and Greg and Betsy Sullivan not only had little, but had lost much. Was it possible there had been some happy moments here for them? Betsy had been a good woman and Charlie had loved her, obvious from the way he spoke of her.

Irene led Joel through the two small ground-floor apartments, describing them as they went. He could smell dust and mold, among other things, and his feet crunched on fallen plaster. They had to walk around a big crack in the floor of one of the rooms. They found the front stairs, but the banister was severely damaged and even completely missing in some places, so they returned to the back stairs, which were in a little better repair.

As they approached the second-floor landing, Joel tried to hear sounds of laughter echoing down through the years.

⌥

"Hey, baby, look what I got!" The young man waved a handful of bills in his wife's face.

"Charlie, wow! What'd you do, rob Fort Knox?"

Charlie laughed, his brown eyes twinkling. He was a handsome young man, twenty-five, strong, compactly built, with dark hair, combed like he'd seen James Dean wear his in the movies. But, unlike his hero, Charlie was dressed conservatively in a brown pinstripe, gabardine suit with wide lapels, narrow silk tie, wing-tipped shoes. It was his only suit, but he had bought the best because he was going places in this world. His recent cash windfall was proof of that. All he needed was to know the right people.

"I got a little part-time job."

"A pretty well-paying job?"

Charlie heard the skepticim in her voice. "Come on, Betsy, honey, we're gonna paint the town tonight."

"I don't know, Charlie. . . ." The amusement faded a bit from her bright, pretty eyes.

"What's wrong? It's been ages since we've had some fun."

"I know . . . but . . ." She looked down at her protruding belly.

"You're not embarrassed to go out, are you? Why, I think you are the most beautiful girl in the world—even more so now that you got our baby in you." Charlie paused, then thought of something else. "You're not worried about what to wear, are you? Because before we go anywhere, we're gonna buy you the finest dress in town."

"It's not that, Charlie. It's just that we need some things for the new baby. A layette, stuff like that."

"Oh, honey, don't worry about that. There's gonna be a lot more money like this coming in before the baby arrives. We'll be able to get him a lace bassinet like you saw at Macy's—and all the things you want."

"Really?"

"We are on a roll, babe. Our worries are over." He picked up his brown felt fedora and set it on his head at just the right angle. *"Get your coat. We're going shopping."*

"I gotta get Greggie," she said with renewed excitement.

"You bet! He's gonna get a present, too."

Joel and Irene reached the second-floor apartment. The door, with a tarnished brass number three, wasn't locked. Nothing, it seemed, was locked inside the building. They went in, and as with the other place, there was torn wallpaper, chipped paint, and severely cracked plaster on the walls. A few pieces of broken, torn furniture were scattered about. The windows were covered with old sheets, faded, torn curtains, broken-down venetian blinds, nothing that matched and often the coverings had gaping holes letting some daylight into the dingy rooms. As Irene described the place, Joel had a more and more difficult time trying to conjure up contented family scenes. Even thirty-seven years ago this wasn't the best place in town to live. He thought of his mother making futile attempts to turn it into a home—a vase of plastic flowers, a cheaply framed picture on the wall, a bright tablecloth on the Formica table. He thought of broken dreams and broken lives. . . .

"I gotta leave for a while, Betsy."

"Why? What's wrong?"

"I'm in a little trouble, that's all."

Betsy asked a dozen questions. *What happened? How can you leave me now? What will I do with two children?*

"I'm in trouble. But I won't be gone long. I'll be back for you soon—"

Desperately she threw her arms around him, tears dripping from her eyes. He wrapped his arms around her, too tightly, as if he feared what would happen if he let go. She felt his love, it was so strong. But she'd always known that. And she knew that if her dear Charlie was in trouble it couldn't be his fault. Charlie had a heart of gold. All he cared about was taking care of his family.

"Please, Charlie, don't go!"

He gently lifted her face from where it was buried in his shoulder, and he tilted her chin upward, kissing her tenderly. When she opened her eyes, she saw tears brimming in his eyes also. She knew then it was terrible trouble he was in—and if he went away, she might never see him again.

"Don't you want to say good-bye to Greggie first?" she said, pleading.

"I don't want to wake him."

But they went to his little closet of a room and peeked inside. The boy was sleeping peacefully, his sweet, round face looking so angelic. But that didn't weaken Charlie's resolve, his need.

"It's time," he said.

Betsy walked him to the door as if she'd really be strong enough to let him go. She ignored the shooting pain in her abdomen. She'd been feeling it for days now, and a friend said it was normal. But this time the pain made her wince involuntarily. Thankfully, Charlie hadn't seen, though she almost wished he had—maybe he'd stay, then. But somehow she was able to let him go, with one final kiss.

Then Betsy went into the house and wept until an hour later a knock came at the door. Opening it, she was greeted by two grim-looking policemen.

⌘

Irene took a couple steps into the room. Joel heard a loud crunch, and immediately Irene swayed then clutched at him.

"You okay?" he said.

"The floor fell in a bit," she replied, steadying herself. "I guess that's why this place is condemned."

"Let's go."

"You don't want to go up to the third floor?"

He shook his head. "It's too depressing here. I don't know why

I wanted to come in the first place. Was I trying to feel part of the past, part of a family that's supposed to be mine? If their spirits are haunting this place, I'm not sure I want to meet them."

"Maybe it won't be here, Joel, but I think you do want to meet them. You need to meet them, face them and their stories. But I think that meeting will be through Charlie. He's your link, not this broken-down old house."

"Will I ever see him again?" Joel felt as if the house was sapping all his hope and faith.

He never felt more relieved than when they exited the house and the crisp autumn air touched his senses.

Thirty-six

*T*he next day was Saturday, but that didn't prevent Joel from going to the office at seven in the morning so that he would have the proper resources available to untangle the mystery surrounding his birth father. Irene stopped in at eleven.

"My dad took Adam and Mark to a boat show, and I've got time to kill. Is it too early for lunch?"

"Maybe we can make a stop first," Joel said. "I've been on the phone all morning and finally got a lead on the owner of that trucking company Charlie robbed."

"That's great! What kind of lead?"

"The company itself went defunct years ago and the owner died. But I found someone who I think might be his daughter. I spoke with her on the phone, but she was kind of skittish. I suppose she has reason. I thought it best not to tell her everything, so I was a bit vague. She's going to think about it and call me back by noon. I hope it doesn't turn out to be a dead end."

"It's too bad Charlie wouldn't tell you more."

"There was absolutely no convincing him it would have been the best thing to do. Irene, I've been thinking about what he said—about setting things right, making someone pay, taking care of the danger. Had I realized it before, had there not been so many other things to absorb, I would have tackled him myself to prevent him from getting away. But . . . hindsight and all that. Anyway, I'm afraid he's plotting revenge for all that happened. He mentioned he had been betrayed, so a desire for revenge doesn't seem impossible. He's had over three decades to stew over this, for hate to build. He lost everything because of that robbery."

"Then, that would mean our speculation of him having an accomplice was true."

"I think there had to be more to it than an accomplice getting away while Charlie rots in jail. There isn't necessarily anything malicious in one thief escaping while the other gets caught. It would be an entirely different matter if his so-called accomplice had somehow lured him to the trucking company to set him up, to frame him for murder."

"And now it's payback time."

Joel nodded grimly. "I shouldn't have let him go. If he kills someone, or even hurts someone, he's going to get locked up until he dies—there won't be any mercy this time."

"If only we could prove he didn't kill that cop—and find the real killer."

"It's a thirty-seven-year-old crime—solving them makes for good Hollywood plots, but it would be next to impossible to solve one in real life. Witnesses die, memories fade. The building where the trucking company was located burned down ten years ago—more clues and evidence gone."

They fell silent. Dim, cobwebbed images of the distant past flitted through Irene's mind. They reminded her a little of the pale, gray face of Charlie Sullivan.

Suddenly the phone on Joel's desk rang. Joel grabbed it. The one-sided conversation was brief. At one point, Joel held a pencil out for Irene, then he repeated an address out loud, and taking his cue, Irene jotted it down on a note pad. It occurred to her what Joel had said about his handicap being a minor inconvenience. Writing without sight must be frustrating.

"That was her," Joel said as he jumped up. Grabbing his cane from his desk and quickly unfolding it, he strode from behind the desk. Then he paused as a little whimper came from near the window, and Irene noticed for the first time that Ebony was lying behind the desk. Joel turned back and bent, giving the dog a good rubbing. "Poor girl. I know you're bored, but take it easy while you can. I'll be back for you later and you can have a little outing."

Irene tore off the slip of paper with the address and they headed out the door. Their destination was Millbrae, a town about ten miles south of San Francisco, not far from where Irene lived. The place wasn't easy to find, and Irene's sense of direction was far from faultless. Wishing she had gotten directions from the lady, she stopped at two gas stations before she finally turned down the street whose name she had jotted down. The neighborhood was composed of tract homes that had been built in the fifties. Half the homes were rundown and unkempt; the other half made an attempt to show some pride of ownership. Since it was Saturday, a lot of children were roaming the streets, skating, riding bikes, playing ball in the middle of the street. Irene slowed for safety, and also so she could spot the nearly illegible numbers on the houses.

"There it is!" she said at last. It was three-four-one-one, though the three had slipped and was upside down.

The house was in better repair than its neighbors, though the paint was a bit chipped and the lawn needed mowing. A few flowers were blooming in a planter out front. Irene imparted a brief description to Joel as she parked.

The woman who greeted them at the door of the house was in her early thirties, attractive though she wore no makeup. Her hair was stringy and her clothes—jeans and a loose-fitting sweater—did not become her slightly overweight figure. Children were playing in the front room and the television was blaring.

"You are Heather Miller?" Joel asked.

She nodded and after only a moment's hesitation, Joel held out his hand. "I'm Joel Costain. This is Irene Lorenzo." He had to raise his voice considerably to compete with the television.

"Mama's got visitors," Heather said to the children, "so turn that TV off."

That drew a chorus of complaints.

"I said *off!*" the woman yelled. She gave a frazzled sigh and a woeful look at Irene. "Who invented Saturdays?"

"I know the feeling," said Irene warmly, trying to be personable and hopefully win the woman's confidence.

Plucking toys and other youthful contraband from the sofa, the woman invited her guests to sit. She flopped down on an aged leather recliner facing the sofa.

"I had my doubts about letting you come here," she said. "Do you have some ID?"

Joel handed her a business card and also showed her his photo identification. She studied them carefully, looking from the photo to Joel, especially at his eyes.

"You really blind?" she said.

"Yes."

"Don't see many blind people nowadays."

"Thank goodness."

"So, you're a lawyer interested in my father's old trucking company. Not a legal problem, you said, but personal. You got me curious. I had to let you come. What's it all about?" She seemed to be warming up, as if Joel and Irene were making a good impression.

"I'm interested in a robbery that took place at Banducci Trucking about thirty-seven years ago."

"That's a long time ago. I wasn't even born then."

"Do you know anything at all about your father's business?"

"He didn't talk much about it. He was very bitter about what happened—"

"The robbery?"

"I don't know much about that, but no, what got to my father happened after the robbery. He and his partner had a big falling out."

"His partner?"

"Well, he was more of a silent partner. My father owned the company first, and Fabroni came in later."

"Fabroni, you say?"

"Yes. Alessandro Fabroni—his nickname was Sandy."

"Not the same Fabroni who's running for mayor of San Francisco?"

"Yeah. Something, isn't it?"

"So, what caused the falling out?" Joel asked.

"My father was a good, honest man. It wasn't easy to run a clean business—you know, without mob involvement. But he wanted to keep straight. Fabroni just wanted to be a big shot, any way he could. As I heard it, he sold out to the mob but kept it from my father—until Dad finally found out. Daddy blew a gasket. He wanted Fabroni out, and it kind of surprised him when Fabroni bowed out so easily. Later, he realized why. Fabroni had bled the business of most of its profits so it was no loss for him to leave."

"Fabroni isn't still connected to the mob, is he?" asked Irene.

Heather shrugged. "Who knows? Isn't it 'once in, always in'? But it doesn't matter, you couldn't *prove* a connection if you tried. My dad never had solid proof. Isn't it just a foregone conclusion that most politicians are dirty?"

Joel deftly brought the conversation back to what was of most immediate interest to him. "So, did Fabroni get involved in your father's business before or after the robbery?"

"Gosh, I really don't know—wait a minute! I remember my father saying they broke up after ten years' partnership, and it was in sixty-four when they broke up." Heather squinted in thought as she tried to calculate the time.

"They got together before the robbery," said Joel.

"Is that significant?"

"I don't know. What happened after they broke up?"

"After Fabroni left, the business really took a nose dive."

"And you don't believe that was due merely to poor management?"

"Not hardly! My father was pretty naive in business, but he could have made it work if he'd been given a chance. Fabroni, and whoever he was connected to, made sure Dad's company failed by diverting contracts, even pirating trucks and merchandise. They basically squeezed the life out of Dad's business. The stress of it all eventually killed my father, but not before he lost everything. We were still paying off debts years after he died."

"But Fabroni obviously made out very well."

"Isn't that the way of it," Heather said with a cynical sigh.

"Your father never spoke of the robbery?"

"I was ten years old when my dad died, so if he did talk about it, it wasn't to his little daughter."

"I see. Did he ever mention anyone named Charlie Sullivan?"

"Sorry, no. I still don't see why a robbery that happened that long ago should interest you. Isn't there enough current crime for you lawyers?" Her last words were spoken lightly, good-naturedly.

Joel smiled. "Actually, Mrs. Miller, it was my father who was arrested and convicted for that robbery. He just got out of prison."

"Boy, that's tough. I wish I could help you more."

"You've been a big help. Maybe I'll find Fabroni and he'll be able to help me."

"Don't count on it. Fabroni was a rat when my father knew him; I doubt he's changed, though his election ads paint a glowing picture of the man."

Joel stood. "Thank you for your time, Mrs. Miller."

"Let me know how it all comes out."

As they were leaving, Irene thought about the day Joel had first come to see her. It seemed so long ago, but it had only been a couple weeks. That encounter was very similar to this. He'd asked his questions, she had apologized for not being of more help. They shook hands, and she walked him to the door thinking she'd never see him again.

Instead he had come to be an important part of her life. She couldn't imagine not knowing him, not being touched in her heart and spirit by his gentle smile, his tender soul. Was that first meeting a mere random act of fate? Had things been slightly different, might Heather Miller have been the one to capture Joel's heart . . . his love?

But Irene's revived spirit quickly told her more than fate was at work. God had been moving, prodding, guiding, just as He was now and would continue to do in both of their lives.

Thirty-seven

*I*rene had promised her parents that she would spend the afternoon with them. She invited Joel to join her, an act far less casual than she tried to make it sound. It was no small matter to bring a man to meet her parents, though technically Joel had already met them at Greg's funeral. Irene knew her parents, especially her mother, well enough to know they were already speculating about Joel. To bring him around again was tantamount—in Millie's eyes, at least—to a declaration of engagement.

By the time they returned to the office for Ebony and crossed town again, they arrived at Irene's parents' only minutes after Ray returned from the boat show with the children.

Adam and Mark pounced on Irene and Joel to chatter about their experiences.

"We got to go on some boats," said Mark. "But they weren't in the water."

"It was cool," said Adam. "Look what Grandpa bought me." He held up a white T-shirt with a sailboat printed on the front. Mark held up a similar shirt in red.

Ray said, "Joel, you ever do any boating—" he stopped, then fumbling awkwardly, added, "I'm sorry, I didn't think—"

Since there had already been a few instances of similar awkwardness which Joel had ignored, he said, "Please, you don't have to walk on eggshells around me. Say what you want; no need to apologize. You can use the words 'see' and 'look.' It doesn't bother me. I'd appreciate descriptions of what's going on, but that's all you have to worry about."

"We've never known a blind person," said Millie. "They still call it blindness, don't they?"

"You can call it anything, honestly. And, Mr. Lorenzo—"

"Wait a minute!" said Ray. "If we are really gonna relax, we insist you call us Ray and Millie."

"And you better call me Theresa," put in Irene's grandmother.

"I have no argument with that," said Joel enthusiastically. "Now, back to your question, Ray—I've done a lot of sailing. My father owns a boat."

"That's right, he mentioned it. A Hunter thirty-seven. Now, there's a boat!" Ray was clearly impressed. "And you like to sail, too?"

"For the most part as a passenger," Joel replied. "But I enjoy being out on the water. It can be so peaceful out there with just the wind in the sails to move you. No motor, of course!"

Ray laughed. "Your father must be a purist." Then he added, "I've been wanting my own boat since I was in the navy. I had a little twenty-four footer when the kids were younger, then both my truck and lawn mower broke down and I had to sell the boat 'cause I needed to buy the other things for my business."

"I remember that boat," said Irene. "We used to sail out to Angel Island and picnic."

"Grandpa, can you buy another boat?" asked Mark. "I want to sail on the water."

"Your grandma would have a conniption—she's not fond of the water."

"I went on the old boat a couple of times," Millie defended herself.

"I remember that, too," said Irene. "You had white knuckles the entire time."

Everyone chuckled and Millie just "harrumphed" dryly, but a little twinkle in her eyes indicated she wasn't as offended as her scowl might imply.

"I'm sure my father would love to take anyone sailing who'd like," said Joel.

"I'll stick to dry land," said Millie. "Thank you very much. But you men can talk all you want about boats—I've got to finish up dinner. Irene and Mom, would you give me a hand?"

Irene followed her mother and grandmother into the kitchen. The males were getting along fine and didn't need her, though she would have preferred remaining with them. She knew once her mother got her alone, there would be a barrage of questions and comments.

"I can't believe he's related to Greg," said Millie as she scrubbed carrots for a salad.

"He's a very nice young man," said Theresa as she set to work washing lettuce and breaking it up into a bowl.

"Yes, he is. . . ." Irene remarked noncommittally, pretending to concentrate on buttering a loaf of French bread.

"Irene, talk to us," demanded Millie.

"I don't have anything to say. . . ."

"Why do I always have to drag everything out of you? I'll bet Connie knows every detail."

"There are no details—"

"You're not getting involved with him?"

"I thought you liked him," parried Irene, more baiting than defensive.

"I do, but—"

"Well, we've just been working together, trying to figure out what happened when Joel was born and how Greg was killed."

"That's all?"

Irene shrugged. "Where's the garlic salt?"

"You know very well where it is." Millie picked up a knife and began slicing carrots into a bowl. "The kids seem to know him pretty well; you must be seeing a lot of him."

"This is a very intense time—"

"Irene Theresa Lorenzo!" Millie wagged the knife at Irene. "Are you ashamed of having a relationship with a man who's handicapped?"

"I never even thought of that."

"Then, you are having a relationship?"

"I didn't say that!" Irene sighed. "I don't know, okay? I just don't know how I feel. He's Greg's brother! It scares me."

Theresa said, "Reenie, those two are cut from entirely different bolts of cloth. Anyone can see Joel is a decent man. If you let him get away because you're scared he'll end up treating you like Greg did, you will lose more than . . . well, more than I don't know what."

"But, Grandma, how can I know for sure?"

"Honey, you'll never know for sure—no one ever does. You just gotta take your best shot. You sure don't have to rush into anything, but you do have to give it half a chance. That is, if it's what you want."

"Is it?" aksed Millie pointedly.

Irene tried not to feel as if she was being cross-examined, reminding herself that it was because her mother cared that she was asking the questions. Millie couldn't help it if her questions came out as though blasted from a cannon.

"I . . . I think so." Then Irene lifted her eyes until they peered directly into her mother's eyes. "I . . . care for him."

"Care?"

"Mom . . . I think I might love him." The words escaped before she could rein them back in. The feared word "love" tumbled off her lips in a rush, and she felt momentarily light-headed. It occurred to her how odd it was she should first speak that word, in reference to Joel, to her mother. Contrary to what her mother thought, Irene hadn't even admitted her feelings to Connie and certainly not to Joel.

Theresa dried her hands on her apron and gave her granddaughter a loving embrace. "It's about time, Reenie!" she said. "Time that you found real love and happiness."

Millie patted Irene's shoulder. "What does he think about this?"

"I haven't told him."

"How does he feel?"

"He's said he loves me." It sounded strange coming from her lips—and wonderful.

"I'll bet he doesn't have any doubts," said Millie.

Irene smiled. "None."

"Well, you better shake yours or you're liable to lose him."

"But, Mom, Grandma's right about not rushing into anything. I have to take it slowly. If he can't wait . . . I guess I need to know that, too. Greg rushed me, and I won't let that happen again."

"I don't think you've got a thing to worry about, Reenie," said Theresa. "He seems like a patient man."

⁂

There were a few more awkward moments when they gathered at the table for dinner. Millie had prepared steak, and she was a bit embarrassed when Joel had to ask Irene to help him cut his meat.

Joel easily diffused it with a joke. "Never let a blind man have a knife," he said. "That's how we lose fingers." And he held up his hand with the first knuckle of his ring finger bent in such a way that it appeared as if the tip of the finger was missing. Mark gasped. Then everyone roared with laughter.

Irene was nervous that her mother might blurt out their earlier discussion, but when it was apparent that Millie wasn't going to mention it, Irene relaxed. However, despite the fact that nothing was *said*, there were many meaningful looks exchanged by the elders and cast in Joel and Irene's direction.

When the meal was finished, Joel said, "That was a wonderful meal, but I was hoping for a taste of your Italian food. Irene has raved about it."

"You're welcome to come here any Sunday," said Millie, "and you can have your fill. I've even been known to cook spaghetti in the middle of the week for very special people." She gave Joel a grin that was meant to include him among that elite group.

"That means you, Joel," said Irene in an attempt to interpret the look Joel couldn't see.

"Irene said she ate dinner at Alexander's the other day," said Ray. "Well, I'll tell you, Millie and I have eaten there a couple of times on our anniversaries, and even *their* Italian food doesn't compare to Theresa's and Millie's."

"I didn't know Alexander's was Italian," said Joel.

"They got American food, but they have some Italian, too—at least the last time we were there they did."

"We had steak," said Irene.

"Good, no sense wasting good money on Italian—and I've never paid more for a dinner than I did there—when you can get the best for free right here at home!" Ray winked at his wife.

"Maybe I'll open a restaurant," said Millie.

When it was time to leave, Millie sidled up to Irene and said, "You know Irene, the evening is still young for you kids. Why don't you let the boys spend the night here, and you and Joel can have the evening free—"

"Mom!" said Irene in a low, warning tone.

"Well, I didn't mean—"

"Never mind, Mom," Irene said in an easier tone. "Thanks for the offer, but I think the boys and I will go to church in the morning."

"Church?" Millie raised an eyebrow. "That's a new one."

"I guess so."

Just then Ray arrived with Irene's coat and held it out to her. She gladly allowed herself to be distracted from her mother's scrutiny. She slipped into the coat and was heading outside before her mother could say more. But on the drive back to Joel's place the subject was revived.

"I couldn't help overhearing what you said to your mother," Joel commented.

"What's that?" For a moment the conversation in the kitchen flashed into her mind.

She was relieved when he answered, "About going to church tomorrow."

"Oh, that. It just dawned on me that tomorrow is Sunday. My only problem is I don't have a church to go to. Connie and Norm attend the church I used to attend, but I think I'd like to start someplace fresh."

"You could come with me. . . ."

"I don't know, Joel. Back when I was going to church, it always started tongues wagging when a single man and a single woman attended church together."

"We couldn't have that, now, could we?" But he said it with good-humored sarcasm.

"I could handle it, if you could handle it."

"Could you?"

"Maybe . . ."

He smiled, probably thinking a maybe from her was the prelude to a serious commitment.

Thirty-eight

*A*lessandro Fabroni was not difficult to locate. This close to the election, the man's presence was everywhere in the form of posters and television ads. Fabroni was turning into a prominent contender for the mayor's seat. Seeing the man in person, however, became a far greater challenge. Bandying the name of his firm, Joel got as far as Fabroni's campaign manager who promised to deliver Joel's request to speak with the candidate. But Fabroni wouldn't see Joel or even speak with him on the phone. Joel thought that odd. He remembered what Heather Miller had said about his possible underworld connections. Was the man in the Mafia or something? Joel wished he had known about him when he had spoken to Charlie. Perhaps he could have induced Charlie to tell him something more specific.

Thoughts of Fabroni nagged at Joel all that Monday morning as he tried to catch up on his neglected work. Irene also occupied his thoughts, and more than once his mind wandered during meetings with clients. It had been great attending church with her. It was as if the one gap in their relationship was filling. He tried to allow things to progress naturally. She had to find her own way back to God—he couldn't force it. In fact, because of her experience with Greg, Joel could do more harm than good by laying spiritual "trips" on Irene. Yet the excitement he felt inside about her journey back to faith was hard to contain. She was cautious, taking small steps, but he decided that was a good thing. "Flash-in-the-pan" faith wasn't always trustworthy and, if it was real, didn't always stand the test of time. He had no problem accepting her slow pace, her questions, her doubts and fears. Her heart was now truly set on God, and that's what mattered most.

"So, Joel," a voice intruded into his thoughts, "I think this tax shelter could prove to be a good investment. What do you think?"

Joel had entirely missed the client's previous statement, but he answered as if he hadn't missed a beat. "Let me study it a bit more, Phillip. I'll put together some figures. Why don't we meet again in a few days?"

After the client left, Joel felt his Braille watch. Almost noon. He pushed his chair away from the confinement of his desk, stood, stretched, then paced around his office. He was restless. Something kept eating at him, but he couldn't quite define it.

Fabroni?

That must be it. He was frustrated that he couldn't do anything about the man. He wondered fleetingly what would happen if he just appeared on Fabroni's doorstep uninvited. But he had seemed pretty adamant about not wanting to be bothered. Joel paused back at his desk, called his secretary, and asked her to get Jim Kincaid. But Kincaid was out. Joel punched in Kincaid's cellular phone number.

"Kincaid here."

"Jim, this is Joel. You busy?"

"Yeah . . . kind of . . ." There was hesitation in the investigator's tone. Joel wondered if he was starting to take advantage of Kincaid's aid. Jim did have other work with the firm, not to mention a private life.

"Okay, maybe when you have some free time, you can give me a call." Joel thought his voice was even, masking his sudden awkwardness.

"I can talk now. What do you need, Joel?" Jim's tone made a definite change, was more normal.

"I haven't had a chance to tell you about my new discovery." Joel didn't like having such a detailed and lengthy conversation on the phone, but it might be the only chance he'd get to talk to Jim. He told the investigator about his meeting with Heather Miller and her mention of Fabroni, and also about Joel's recent dead end with Fabroni. "I'd like some advice on where to go from here, Jim. Any ideas?"

"Fabroni always was a private person. In fact, I'm surprised he'd do something as public as run for office. I remember when I was on the force, there was an incident in which one of his bodyguards killed a trespasser. The bodyguard had a slick lawyer and got off. But I was impressed then that Fabroni didn't fool around where security was concerned."

"You ever hear anything about mob connections?"

"His wife's nephew is Donny Silvo, a big underworld figure on the East Coast. But Fabroni keeps a careful distance from him. If he's connected, he's done a bang-up job in concealing it. How else could he run for public office?"

"It wouldn't be the first time money and power bought an election."

"True. Anyway, you'd have a tough time getting past the gates of his estate, unless he invited you."

"I doubt an invitation is forthcoming."

"You think Fabroni is important?"

"I can't explain why, just a gut instinct, I suppose. But, yeah, I do. I wish I hadn't promised Charlie not to follow him."

"You do. . . ?"

"I'd like a chance to run Fabroni's name past him. Can you think of any way to get in to see Fabroni?"

"Not getting *in*, but maybe you can get to him when he's out. Look, I've got a friend I can ask to stake out his place, get an idea of his routine, that sort of thing. You might be able to confront him at a restaurant or the race track . . . wherever. I'd do it myself, but . . . ."

When Jim paused, again hesitant, Joel quickly said, "I don't expect that of you, Jim. You've already gone above and beyond. You ever get home these days?"

Jim chuckled dryly. "My wife doesn't think so."

"And she's probably right."

"I can sweet-talk Suzie." Several seconds of silence followed. Finally, Jim said, "Joel, did you really mean that about wishing you would have continued following Charlie?"

"Yes. But it's too late—"

"Not exactly . . . You remember how I hurried away from the bar that night you met Charlie?"

"You said you had to be somewhere."

"I lied. I kept on Charlie's tail—"

"All weekend?"

"I had a friend helping me. I'd put too much into finding Sullivan to give him up that easily. I'm sorry."

"I guess it's for the best. I just hope it doesn't undermine his confidence in me."

"I'm positive he's not aware of us. If he finds out, I'll tell him I did it without your approval. It's the truth. That is, if you want me to keep it up?"

"For the record, Jim, no, I don't want you to keep it up." Joel paused and smiled. "For the record, you understand."

"I got you, boss. Do you want to see Charlie?"

"I don't want to risk it right now. Let me see if I can talk to Fabroni first."

"And do you want me to put someone on Fabroni?"

"Sure, what'll it hurt? I'll have my cellular phone with me at all times. Have him report to me every hour, sooner if something significant happens. What's the guy's name?"

"Tony. He'll be there in less than an hour."

As Joel hung up the phone, he made a great effort not to rush off immediately after Charlie. But if he made the wrong move now, he could spook Charlie off, perhaps forever. It would be nice to talk to Charlie about Fabroni, but it just didn't seem worth the risk of losing him. Joel decided he'd made the right decision in waiting until he spoke to Fabroni. But the delay wouldn't be easy. If the Fabroni lead turned into a dead end, Joel would have to start thinking about giving up this cat-and-mouse game completely. He'd confront Charlie, take his chances. Have it out. Get this over with once and for all. Joel had to get his life back on track. But would even a final confrontation with Charlie make that happen? He still had the matter of Kevin's job offer to consider. Then there was Irene.

No matter what happened with Charlie Sullivan, it looked like Joel's life was bound to change, perhaps dramatically.

Thirty-nine

Jim was relieved his little deception was out in the open. Joel Costain was a good man and had given Jim more than a few breaks since they had become acquainted, so he hadn't enjoyed going against his friend's wishes. On the other hand, Jim had felt that Joel's decision regarding Charlie's request had been a purely emotional one. Not that he didn't understand. The man was Joel's father and it was hardly surprising that Joel wanted to win his confidence.

That's where Jim felt his involvement in this business was most essential. He was a fairly objective participant who stood to lose or gain nothing. An ex-marine who had served on the San Francisco Police Force for eight years, Jim Kincaid prided himself on his logic and objectivity. He had been a good marine and a good cop until, three years ago, a bullet received in the line of duty put him out of commission. A nerve had been severed, and he would never again have full use of his left hand. He'd been pretty depressed after the doctors had broken the news.

He and Joel had been in the same men's group at church, and shortly after his release from the hospital, Jim's wife had urged him to go to a men's retreat. He wasn't ready to face people and finally only went to appease his wife. In one sense, he'd been relieved when he discovered Joel would be his roommate. For someone who didn't want to *face* anyone, a blind man seemed the perfect roomie. However, he had never been close to Joel in the past and, in fact, shied away from him. Jim now realized Joel's handicap made him feel uncomfortable, confusing all his macho ideas of manhood. But that weekend, with no place to hide from Joel and his handicap, Jim was forced to confront his own self-image. By simply observing Joel, conversing with him on totally unrelated levels, Jim learned a valuable lesson in courage and self-acceptance.

The weekend gave Jim a whole new approach to life, allowing him to confront his future with optimism. And, of course, it had been Joel who had convinced the firm to hire Jim when a new investigator was needed. Physically, Jim was as fit as any marine or cop would be expected to be. His hand was still too stiff to make him eligible for the force, but it was normal enough for all practical purposes. He wasn't sure he'd want to go back to the SFPD even if he could. Suzie was thrilled that he was no longer on the dangerous front lines. He had no complaints.

Because of the bond between him and Joel, Jim truly wanted to do right by him. Why else had he committed himself to Joel's personal investigation, often at the expense of his work for the firm? And, lately, even at the expense of his marriage. When he had told his wife he was going to be tied up over the weekend with work, she was pretty upset. She'd thought the days of long hours and stress had ended with his job on the force, but he often put in just as many hours with the firm. As much as Suzie liked Joel, she wasn't thrilled with her husband taking on personal work in addition to his regular job.

But Jim had simply not been able to let Charlie disappear once more into thin air. So far, however, his attention to Charlie had reaped nothing significant. At least he knew where the man was, but his activities were fairly benign. He spent a lot of time in bars, three or four in a single day, obviously trying to make his trail hard to follow. He spent each night in a different hotel, too, mostly cheap places all over the city. For a dying man, he covered a lot of ground.

Charlie's activities had been aimless, purposeless, at least until this morning. After checking out of his hotel and carrying a paper sack that Jim guessed held all his possessions, Charlie stopped for breakfast in a "greasy spoon" diner. He hung out there for about an hour. Jim speculated that Charlie was waiting for stores to open because his first stop was a second-hand shop, and that's how he spent the morning—at pawn shops and thrift stores. He never seemed to buy anything.

When the bars opened, he broke up his "shopping" with a drink every so often. Charlie traveled mostly on foot, but he complicated Jim's efforts considerably when he hopped a bus. Jim almost lost him completely because he couldn't get a taxi in time to follow the bus. After getting a cab, though, he followed the bus route and managed to pick up on Charlie again.

Shortly after three o'clock, he visited a bar on Eddy in the Tenderloin, not in itself unusual. He was inside for about a half hour, then, upon leaving, he walked down an alley, glancing over his shoulder, appearing very nervous. Jim couldn't very well tail him there without being discovered, so he waited and watched from the street. Luckily there was a bus stop on the other side of the street where he could stand with his nose seemingly buried in a newspaper and keep an eye on the alley entrance. He hoped this wasn't Charlie's way of ditching Jim by escaping out the other end of the alley. But Charlie had given no indication until now that he suspected he was being followed. Nevertheless, Jim would give him a few minutes, just in case, and then investigate the alley if Charlie didn't return. He had learned enough about Charlie's movements so he was fairly confident that if he did lose him now, he could pick him up again later.

In five minutes, a hard-looking character ambled out of the bar. When he turned into the alley, the man tried so hard to appear casual it made it more obvious than ever that he was on a deliberate mission.

Had Charlie arranged in the bar to meet this man? That seemed pretty obvious. But why? That, too, seemed obvious. He was dealing something to Charlie. Two possibilities leaped to Jim's mind. The first—buying a weapon—he ruled out immediately. He could think of no reason Charlie would need or want a gun. But the second possibility seemed much more viable. Drugs. Charlie was ill, probably in pain. It had been weeks, to Jim's knowledge, since Charlie had been to a doctor. His prescription pain medication had to run out sometime. He was drinking a lot, if his visits to bars were any indication, but booze could only do so much. Charlie was probably tired of being drunk. He wanted relief from pain without inebriation. It wouldn't be too difficult to get what he needed on the street.

⌘

Charlie was nervous. Standing in this dirty alley, he felt vulnerable. The guy he had spoken to in the bar didn't look like a Boy Scout. More like the kind of man who'd feel more than comfortable slitting an old man's throat in a back alley. But Charlie had been everywhere trying to find what he needed, at a price he could afford.

He paced for a few minutes as he waited, but he was nearly too exhausted even for that. It had been an arduous day. But he hoped that in a few minutes all his efforts would be well rewarded. He'd have what he wanted; he'd be on his way to fulfilling his final act on earth. But it wouldn't happen today, of that he felt certain.

Tomorrow. He'd do it then.

Suddenly, Charlie heard a footstep. His heart leaped. The fellow from the bar turned into the alley. He had greasy hair, dark, ominous eyes, and an angry-looking scar down his right cheek. Charlie had dealt with many hard cases in prison, but it was different out here, alone, without the physical strength to either fight or run.

"You got it?" said Charlie in the tough tone that had aided his survival in jail.

"Yeah. What about the money?"

Charlie patted his chest. "Let's see what you got."

The dark man reached under his coat and pulled a twenty-two automatic pistol from the waist of his pants. Charlie reached for it but the man held back. "Money first."

"Don't I get to check it out?"

The man eyed Charlie carefully as if sizing up the danger he represented, then, seeming to come to the obvious conclusion that Charlie was harmless, he handed it over.

Charlie hefted the weapon. It was a Baretta .22 caliber semi-automatic. "Kind of small," he commented. It fit into the palm of his hand. He turned it over once. "And old, too, isn't it?"

"What'd you expect for the kind of money you have to pay? It's the perfect weapon for the inexperienced shooter. Very little recoil, accurate, and carries a big punch."

"What's the range?"

"You could maybe hit a target at fifty feet, but if you wanted to do some . . . you know, *serious* damage, you'll wanta get close."

Charlie had little or no experience with weapons. But he had no time for an education. He'd have to make do.

"How do you release the clip?" Charlie asked. The gun seller gave Charlie a few basic instructions, then Charlie asked if there was extra ammo.

"Just the one clip." The fellow handed it to Charlie.

Charlie took it and slipped it into his pocket; if he couldn't do what he had to do with eight rounds he'd be out of luck anyway. Finally, he took out his cash and handed over fifty dollars. The dealer quickly stuffed the money in his pocket and, without another word, hurriedly exited the alley. Charlie waited a few minutes before he did the same. He felt strange with that weapon in his pocket—powerful, potent, and oddly, frightened.

⟨ຓ⟩

Jim watched the stranger exit the alley. Five minutes later, Charlie also shuffled back onto the street. Jim hadn't noticed before, but the old man looked exhausted. The morning's activities had really taken their toll on him. That confirmed more than ever Jim's assumption that a drug transaction had just taken place. He felt sorry for the guy. He wondered if there was some way to obtain some legal medicine for Charlie. He'd mention it to Joel. He was tempted to run up to him now and give him some cash, but of course, that would probably only scare the man into permanent hiding. Jim just hoped this entire deal ended soon for the old man's sake.

If he was indeed getting drugs this way, it couldn't be cheap. How had Charlie come by the money? He was certainly not living like a man with much, if any, substantial resources. And even those cheap hotels cost something, not to mention what he must be forking out for food and, especially, booze. Jim doubted Charlie would be able to pay for hotels and liquor much longer—unless he had some bottomless pit of money, which seemed highly unlikely.

Still, what other explanation could there be for what had happened in that alley?

Jim tried to remember all Joel had told him about their meeting. Basically, Charlie had avoided any mention of the past. He had denied involvement in Greg's death, and for that matter, he had also denied killing the cop three decades ago. But that wasn't surprising. Every convict claims innocence. And Joel, of course, believed the man was innocent. Jim was fairly certain Charlie hadn't killed Greg; but as far as that cop went . . . well, it probably didn't really matter what *Jim* thought—that crime was too long past to worry over now. Besides, Charlie had already paid for it.

But maybe figuring that out wasn't as important as deciphering what other intentions Charlie had. . . . Why was he still hiding out? Why had he been so evasive with Joel, not telling him anything important? He'd left too many questions unanswered, and Jim's surveillance wasn't helping as he hoped it would. How much longer did

Charlie plan to keep up this hide-and-seek game? He was a dying man. Thus, it seemed highly unlikely he was just spinning his wheels. There had to be some purpose in his actions. But what?

Jim had no answers, and what was even more discouraging was the apparent fact that nothing was likely to happen in the immediate future. Charlie was exhausted. His breathing was more labored than it had been at the beginning of the day, and this was after pausing in that alley for several minutes. Also his complexion was grayish, and after taking a few steps, he had to lean against a wall for several minutes.

Jim followed Charlie a couple blocks to a bar where the old man remained for quite a while. Then he found another hotel and checked in. Jim waited outside for a while then called in the night shift.

Forty

Jim's man, Tony, watched the Fabroni estate for several boring hours. No action the entire time.

Then at six in the evening, the iron gates opened automatically, and a big Lincoln Continental drove through. The windows of the car were darkly tinted, so Tony couldn't tell if Fabroni was inside. He wished Jim would have had time to get the guy's license plate number. But Tony was going crazy just sitting there, so he decided to take the risk and follow the Continental. He started the engine of his tan Ford but waited until his subject had turned onto the street and was about a half a block away before he pulled away from the curb. He let another vehicle get between him and the Continental.

Keeping a safe distance, he followed the vehicle across town to California Street. Nob Hill. As the Continental pulled up to Alexander's Restaurant and a valet came to the car, Tony drove on by. Assured of his subject's destination, he parked down the street and walked back to the restaurant. He wasn't exactly dressed for this place, with his gray chinos and loafers. But he always tried to be prepared for everything on a surveillance, and so he wore a pinstriped button-down shirt and carried a necktie in the pocket of the sport coat lying on the backseat of his car. He was still pretty casual by Alexander's dinner-hour standards, but the necktie was his ticket inside.

When the *maître d'* asked him about his reservations, he said he was meeting someone in the bar whom he thought had already called ahead. The man checked the fictitious name Tony gave him, which, of course, he didn't find on his list. Tony acted perturbed at his "friend" and asked if he could wait anyway. On the way to the bar, Tony saw Fabroni, who looked just like his election posters. Average height, thirty pounds overweight, mid-sixties, completely bald with a rather homely face, save for his tiny, close-set eyes which made him look a lot like Nikita Khrushchev. Fabroni was being seated in a booth and, by the look of it, was receiving red-carpet treatment.

"Mr. Fabroni, so good to see you!"

"Mr. Fabroni, would you care for your wine, now? And will it be your usual selection?"

"Mr. Fabroni, the chef has a new delicacy he wishes you to try."

Tony slipped onto a seat at the bar that gave him a good view of Fabroni's table. He ordered a drink, then, nodding his head toward Fabroni, casually asked the bartender, "You treat all your customers like that?"

"Maybe so if they came in every night."

"You mean he eats here every night?"

"Yeah."

"Wish I had that kind of money."

Tony returned his attention to his drink and pretended to pay no further attention to the man in the plush booth. There wasn't much to pay attention to, anyway. Fabroni ate his meal alone, taking his time, seeming to savor every bite. By seven-thirty, Tony was wondering if the man planned on spending the night in that booth. Finally, after two cups of coffee and a pastry, Fabroni slid to the edge of the booth and heaved himself to his feet. A waiter was at his elbow immediately with a coat and umbrella.

"Looks like rain, Mr. Fabroni."

Fabroni took the items without thanks. Tony also noted he wasn't given a check and had made no attempt to pay for his meal.

As he followed Fabroni back to his estate, Tony made a call from his car phone.

"Mr. Costain, this is Tony. I finally have something to report." He related what he knew about Fabroni's trip to the restaurant.

"What restaurant?" Joel asked.

"A ritzy place called Alexander's."

"That's interesting. . . ."

"How come?"

"I just dined there myself the other night."

"You might have seen him then, without knowing it. He eats there every night."

"You're sure?"

"Got that from a bartender whom I assume is reliable. I couldn't ask too many questions for fear of burning the surveillance."

"Burning?"

"You know, blowing it."

"Do you think he's in for the night?"

"Probably. He's an old coot; I doubt he has much of a night life."

"Why don't you call it a night. This restaurant angle might be all I need."

"You're the boss. Call me if you need me again."

ᏮᏆᎥᎥᏆᎥᏓᏋ

Lena Westfall glanced at the tan Ford passing her as she approached her father's estate. She gave it no thought except to note that the vehicle was at least five years old and had several dings in its paint. Probably some tourist trying to get a glimpse of the rich and famous. The vehicle turned a corner and was out of sight as she slowed at the estate gate. She pressed in the proper code, and the gates opened for her. She had lived in this house several years before she married and left home. And she had returned for a short time two years ago after her very messy divorce from Travis Westfall, a wealthy Los Angeles real estate broker.

She parked in front of the huge neoclassical style house and strode purposefully up to the massive oak doors. A maid let her in and directed her to one of three drawing rooms where her father was having a brandy before he retired for the night.

"It's hardly eight o'clock and you're having a nightcap?" said Lena.

"When you get to be my age, the evenings will get shorter and shorter."

"You're hardly an old man. And you are more fit than many men your age."

Fabroni shrugged, absently swishing the brandy around in his glass. "Did you come here to rail at me about my habits, or do you have some higher purpose?"

"You'd do well not to be such a creature of habit."

"You know what they say about old dogs . . ." He sipped from his snifter, and for a brief moment his impassive features attained an appearance of pleasure as he savored the fine liquor.

"Well, Joel Costain is hardly an old dog, but he's almost as boring as you, Daddy Dear." Lena strode to the liquor cabinet and poured herself a brandy. "He has done absolutely nothing of interest. I was forced to dine with him and his boorish girlfriend. I'm almost certain he knows nothing about Charlie's business."

"I'm beginning to think my suspicions are unfounded."

"Then, why has Charlie been acting in the way he has, skulking around and staying away from his long lost son? Something is going on."

"Yet, why hasn't he approached me directly? It's possible Mitchell's death has scared him off."

"Perhaps he is just trying to get up his nerve," Lena said, sipping her brandy, thankful her father had expensive tastes. "Murder or blackmail isn't for the fainthearted," she added offhandedly.

"Charlie never had the killer instinct. The only way I was able to pull off framing him for that cop's murder was that Charlie always talked big, tried to act like a big shot. It was all talk, though."

"Well, it's a mistake to think Sullivan has backed off. You can't let down your guard."

"It's possible Mitchell was just blowing hot air. If Charlie really had something on me, why didn't he use it long ago?"

"You should have protected yourself from the beginning by having Charlie killed in prison."

"It's so heartening to have such a kindhearted daughter." Fabroni's lips twisted into a sarcastic smile. "Unlike you, my dear, I abhor unnecessary killing. Besides, I had no idea he had anything on me until his son turned up on my doorstep with his blackmail threats."

"I think you can rectify that mistake by stopping Charlie now."

"If I could find him."

"We know where his son is."

"Killing Mitchell didn't stop Sullivan."

"Don't you think you could draw Charlie out into the open if he thought his pitiful blind son was in danger? Mitchell's death was a fluke. We had no control, nor could we use it properly."

"I'll think about it."

Lena rolled her eyes. "Maybe you are getting old. How much thought did you put into killing that cop thirty-seven years ago?"

"I did what had to be done. He was a cop on the take who had suddenly developed a conscience. Unfortunately for me, I wasn't careful enough then—I acted rashly."

"Well, don't think too long, Daddy. I believe Charlie Sullivan represents more danger than you give him credit for."

The phone rang. In a moment a servant appeared announcing there was a call from someone saying only that he was an old friend. Father and daughter exchanged puzzled looks. Then Lena strode to the extension in the drawing room.

"Hello," Lena said.

"Sandy Fabroni, please."

"Whom may I say is calling?"

"That isn't important."

"I think differently." Lena glanced at her father and silently mouthed the words "Charlie Sullivan."

Fabroni stood, walked toward her, and reached for the phone. "I'll take it."

Lena shrugged and, saying no more, gave her father the phone. It was to her advantage to remain in the shadows of this affair as much as possible. If, for some reason, Sullivan did indeed have the means to implicate her father in illegal activities, she didn't want to go down with him. Family ties counted only so far.

⬥

Charlie had wondered all afternoon what he'd say to his old nemesis, the man who had betrayed him—the man he planned to kill.

"This is Sandy," Fabroni was saying into the receiver. His voice was much changed, aged and grainy, like Charlie's own voice.

"It's been a long time."

"Who is this?"

"I guess I shouldn't expect you to recognize my voice after all these years. Charlie Sullivan. I hope at least the name rings a bell."

"Yes, Charlie, it does. What do you want?"

"Can't I just want to renew an old friendship?"

"Seems to me we didn't separate as friends," said Fabroni, "but I'm willing to forget the past if you are."

"That's generous of you . . . old friend." Charlie could not keep the ire from his voice. "But you know what they say about the past, Sandy. Those who forget it are doomed to repeat it."

"Unless we've learned from it."

"What did you learn, Sandy? Is money not as important to you now? Don't you betray your partners anymore?"

"Come on, Charlie, that was a long time ago. I've changed. But, hey, I never betrayed you. It was just a matter of you being in the wrong place at the—"

"I've heard it all before. And maybe I wasn't in the wrong place, after all."

"What do you mean by that?"

A grim smile creased Charlie's weary expression. "Well, Sandy, I think it's about time you paid a little for what happened at Banducci's. Because I served your time in prison, you were able to make out pretty good for yourself. You could end up mayor of San Francisco. Maybe President of the United States someday. What's there to stop you?"

"Nothing," said Sandy. "This is America."

"But even Americans don't like their politicians to have been mixed up with crime—even crimes that happened thirty-seven years ago."

"You trying to blackmail me, Charlie? Because let me tell you right now, it didn't work when your son tried it, and it won't work now. Besides that, no one is going to listen to an old, broken-down ex-con, a cop killer."

"Yeah, you're right."

"So, leave me alone, Charlie, and I'll forget I ever spoke to you."

"Not gonna happen, Sandy. Like I said, it's time I received some benefits for time served. But don't worry, I'm not greedy. A hundred thousand should take care of things. Just a drop in the bucket for you."

Sandy grunted a humorless laugh. "I've no reason to give you a cent."

"I've got the reason, Sandy. I got it from that cop I supposedly killed. I'm surprised you didn't search him after you killed him, but I guess you were too anxious to get out of there so you could frame me. He had the goods on you, Sandy—some very incriminating stuff."

"If you got it, Charlie, why didn't you use it before this?"

"You framed me up too good. It would have taken more than that to get me off. It might have given you a motive for murder, but there were half a dozen other names in that cop's notebook who would have also had a motive. I had a motive, too, but unlike the rest of you, I also had opportunity, not to mention the fact that my prints were all over the murder weapon. No, it wouldn't have helped me to use it then. Probably would have just gotten my throat slit in prison. Believe me, I've given considerable thought to how I might destroy you with what I have. When I heard about you running for office, I thought it was a real missed opportunity for me. Then I got lucky for the first time in my life—I got cancer. It got me out."

"So, now you think you're going to destroy me?"

"No. I've lost my taste for blood." How easy the lie came. "I just want to spend my final days in ease, and to pass on something to my grandsons so at least they won't suffer as I have."

"How can I believe you have something on me?"

"I'm a dying man. I don't have time for games. You must have suspected something. Why else did you tear apart Costain's house? Why have you been following me?"

"I just wanted to keep tabs on you, that's all. Ransacking the house wasn't my idea—the guys I hired just got out of control."

"So, you want to deal with me, Sandy?"

"Maybe . . . for old time's sake."

"Okay, meet with me tomorrow night. Bring me the money and I'll give you the goods."

"I'll be there."

"Alone."

"I never go anywhere alone—"

"Too bad—I'm sure the *Chronicle* will gladly take the notebook off my hands—"

"All right!"

After giving him further details about the meeting, Charlie said, "See you then, old friend," and hung up. Then, perspiring, Charlie leaned against the pay phone enclosure. He pulled out his handkerchief and mopped his forehead.

Could he really pull this thing off? The conversation alone had exhausted him. He knew he could handle the blackmail, it was the other thing he was unsure about. Maybe he wouldn't have to do it—but, no, Sandy Fabroni was not a forgiving man. He'd not accept defeat gracefully. Charlie had to accept the fact that once he set this thing in motion there would be no turning back.

Forty-one

*I*rene glanced at her sister over the rim of her cup. Connie's expression was somewhere between a smirk and an enthusiastic glow. She had always made it clear she had no doubt Irene would find her spiritual way again. And she probably had the same intuition about Irene's romantic life, too.

"I'm afraid things are happening too fast," said Irene with her usual skepticism.

"Reenie . . . Reenie . . ." Connie smiled indulgently. "Can't you just once put the pedal to the metal?"

"Only when I drive." Irene sipped her tea, then set down her cup.

It was late afternoon the following day, and Connie had stopped by Irene's place after work, knowing Irene would also be finished at her job. The children were outside playing, and the two women were relaxing in the rare quiet. Connie had been dying to talk to her sister since hearing from Millie of Irene's comment about going to church. Irene felt a little guilty for not calling Connie immediately, but she had decided to take things slowly, both with Joel and with God. She wasn't going to trust her emotions, her feelings. She knew Connie would say just what she had about taking risks, and though Irene realized there was a time and a place for haste, she instinctively believed this wasn't it. Irene was going to be the skeptic, even the cynic, if she had to. She intended on confronting whatever happened with feet firmly planted on the ground. Not that it was entirely an easy resolve to follow. There were times, especially with Joel, when her emotions simply soared, and she wanted nothing more than to scorn caution and run, enraptured, into his beckoning arms. Sometimes she felt a need for him so intensely it was as if she had slipped into a dreamworld where perfect happiness was possible.

"What are you more afraid of, Joel or God?" Connie's question jarred Irene back to reality.

Her fear was as strong an emotion as love or need.

"Both, to some extent," Irene answered quietly, trying hard to put into words the tangle of her thoughts. "I guess it's easier to take it slowly with God. I do know He will always be there for me. He hasn't given up on me for all these years. And yet Joel was the one who helped me over that spiritual mountain. He gave me such a real and desirable example of persistence and trust. His life so clearly reveals a God who will make the rough places smooth, causing blind people to see in their hearts—seeing God face to face. I know you've been saying many of the same things to me, Connie, but I guess I needed a fresh voice."

"It was too easy for you to tune me out," said Connie with understanding.

"But why Joel? I keep asking myself over and over. Why Greg's brother? I know God uses strange instruments, but . . ." Irene completed her thought with a shake of her head. "Ah, well! God did use Joel—and in the process I fell in love."

"So, it's true, then. It gives me goose bumps to hear you say that." Connie's eyes were glowing.

"Me too." Irene wondered if she was glowing as much as her sister. Her heart was racing, at least, and her lip quivered. "But how can it be?"

"Just accept, Reenie!"

"Don't you think I want to! I'd give anything to be like you, Connie."

"Joel is a wonderful man—"

"So was—"

"Don't give me that 'So was Greg at first' argument. There's no comparison. Greg's self-centeredness, his phoniness, was always there. We were all able to look back and identify it in many specific instances. Our Christian naiveté made us a little blind. We wanted to be accepting, especially of a new Christian. I'm not saying we were entirely wrong, but Christians can be gullible at times. And Greg understood that and used it—used us. Joel is in a totally different class. Goodness, even Mom likes him!"

"She said something more to you?"

"Yeah, that he was handsome, rich, and very nice—and, if you didn't nab him, she was going to divorce Dad and grab him herself."

They burst out laughing. But Irene knew such words from her mother were high praise, indeed. Yet she wasn't looking for approval from others, was she? Maybe that's what she needed. If she heard enough affirmation from others, perhaps that would validate her own feelings and give her the courage to act on them.

"She didn't say anything about his handicap?" Irene asked.

"Don't tell me that's worrying you, too! If it's not one thing, Reenie, it's another. It was hardly an issue to Mom. It's obvious to anyone who's around him that *he* hasn't made it a focus—why should we? Irene, does it really bother you?"

"Not really. Maybe I'm just looking for excuses, a reason to run away." Irene paused, took a ragged sigh. "I'm afraid of making another mistake."

"Are you going to stop living, then?"

Connie always had the simple answers. But Irene really didn't want answers at all. She only wanted . . . Joel. Yes, she wanted him. She could no longer picture a life that did not include him. He occupied her mind and heart in ways only a loved one could. When she was with him she felt she was complete; when they were apart she knew a void. In the very core of her being she had to acknowledge that Joel was neither manipulating her nor deceiving her. His initial resemblance to Greg was even fading as Joel became more and more his own man.

Still she held back. Why?

She thought of the Scripture Joel was fond of—"Now we see as through a glass darkly, but then face to face." It was a verse with a multilevel message, the most obvious as it applied to Joel's vision and the promise that in eternity it would be twenty-twenty. But even to Joel that was not the Scripture's most heartening promise. The most important vision was spiritual and emotional. Coming to see God "face to face," with one's own feelings and motives laid bare, hiding nothing from Him, seeking to fully understand our innermost being. And Irene believed she didn't have to wait for eternity for this. It was an ongoing process she would constantly be growing toward.

God was—right now—bringing her nearer to that "face-to-face" reality. Each step she took toward God brought her closer. Suddenly Irene realized she didn't have to worry about her confusion. She was a lot less confused now than she had been a few days ago. Far, far less.

But she couldn't rush ahead. Of all her fears, the most ominous was that she would capitulate to the urgings of others. At least Joel wasn't pushing her—that would be her first clue to flee.

"I'm sorry," Connie went on to say. "I guess I'm not giving you any credit. It's just that I want so much for you to live 'happily ever after.' But I'm sure you're doing the right thing in taking it slowly. It's only been a couple weeks since you met Joel—it seems hard to believe, though, doesn't it? Even I feel connected to him in a special way. I know it's our faith, and I never felt that way with Greg. The only time I really talked to Joel was after Greg's funeral, and we never got into anything heavy, but I immediately felt a kinship with him. It's no wonder things progressed quickly between you two. There's no superficiality to wade through with him. The man is up front and real. You're the same way, Reenie, when you want to be."

"He met me that way, anyway—our situation was so intense there was no chance to put on a front."

"And it can only get better, don't you think?" Connie grinned. "If you can fall in love during a time like this, then imagine how it will be when there's smooth sailing. I remember when Norm and I ran into our first crisis—it was a few months after we got married. I can't remember anymore exactly what it was about, but it was a shock to our systems after all the idyllic months of dating. Well, you and Joel have gotten that out of the way early."

"I doubt it will be our last crisis."

"Definitely. But you know what you are getting into."

"Do you ever really know?"

"Eventually you build enough trust in a relationship so you can gauge the other's response. But then Norm has told me that just when he begins to think I'm getting predictable, I throw him a curve ball. Still, it's the trust that carries you through those times."

"Trust . . ." Irene paused, musing over that frightening, loaded word. "That's part of my problem. I want trust now. But it takes time for it to grow. Yet it takes some trust to allow it to grow. Oh, Connie. . . ! Sometimes I think I'm my own worst enemy."

Connie laid a comforting hand on her sister's arm. "Irene, do you want to hear something that may surprise you? You've said many times how you wished you could be more like me, more daring, easy-go-ing—you know, an all-around fun person. . . ." Her eyes twinkled playfully. "Well, here's the shock—there have been times when I wanted to be more like you. I've never said anything before, I guess I was too proud to admit it. I kind of liked having my big sister envy me for something. But your sensitivity, the depth with which you experience life isn't a bad thing. When we were kids, I secretly believed your walk with God was so much richer and fuller than mine because you could sit still long enough to think about spiritual things and actually understand them. True, your sensitivity got you into trouble occasionally, especially when it turned you against God for a time. But even that will only deepen the caliber of your spiritual experience. God has a place for each of us, even superficial, slightly flaky people like me. We are only at odds with ourselves if we try to squeeze into molds God never intended for us."

Irene's lips quirked into an affectionate smile. "Whoever said you were flaky? I do believe, sister dear, that you have been holding out on me." Both women chuckled. Then Irene said, "I guess what it boils down to is that I need to trust God—wow! It really feels good to say those words again. Christians can bandy about that 'Trust God' phrase so much it gets trite. But for now at least, it has a brand-new significance to me. I know what a void there was in my life when I wouldn't trust God. Now, I think even my confusion is more tolerable."

Irene knew she would always be the kind of person who searched, questioned, and worried. But now she had a faithful God to journey with her through those difficult times.

Forty-two

"This may not be on the front page," Arthur Eberhard stated firmly as he held up something before Joel's unseeing eyes, "but there is always the possibility of something like this blowing out of proportion. I suppose this is the first you've heard about the article in the *Chronicle*?"

Joel nodded, once again feeling like an errant schoolboy. "I guess I've been too busy to follow the news lately."

"Well, I'll summarize it for your benefit." Eberhard's fingers drummed on his desk, his tone reflecting impatience. "It tells of a prominent San Francisco attorney—naming you, Joel, and your firm—who turns out to be the son of a convicted cop killer who has recently been paroled from San Quentin after a thirty-plus year prison term. It gives a brief but no less lurid description of the old crime, then, in rather broad speculation, connects a more recent, and as yet unsolved, murder to those past events, if not to the prominent attorney himself."

"I thought you had spoken to the editor. . . ."

"I guess he couldn't pass this up even for friendship's sake."

"All I can say," Joel said calmly, "is that it boarders on libel."

"The reporter was too careful for that. Only the facts are given, and the reader is left to draw his own conclusions. It never even hints at the possibility of you being guilty of any crime. And I am certainly not worried about that. What really worries me, Joel, is that such material as this along with your actions of late could combine rather explosively—for you and for the firm."

"My actions. . . ?"

"How many appointments have you canceled this week alone? I've had several complaints. And our investigator has been so involved in your personal affairs, he's had little time for—"

"All right, Arthur, I get the point." Joel's sharp tone was aimed mostly at himself. Joel then recanted, moderating his voice. "I'm sorry, Arthur. I have been letting things go. It's not easy to admit, but . . ." Joel let a helpless shrug complete his sentence. "I'll call Jim immediately and release him. I'll—"

"Joel, perhaps it would be best for you to take a few days off, until all these personal distractions are cleared up. That would be better, don't you think, than having you only half here?"

"Of course."

"And as far as Jim goes . . . I hate to be a stickler—"

"You're being perfectly reasonable, Arthur. I should have hired someone else right from the beginning. I suppose it was just easier having a friend investigate these things. I didn't know what I would find. I still don't know everything that's going on. But from now on, I will deal with it in a way that won't affect the firm."

"No hard feelings, Joel?"

"Not at all." Joel hoped Arthur didn't notice the slight stiffness in his tone, but despite a sincere attempt, he couldn't quell all traces of his slightly bruised feelings. Maybe he'd had too vaulted a sense of his own importance to the firm, expecting more latitude.

Joel returned to his office and, before entering, instructed Linda to start weeding through his appointments for the next week—rescheduling what she could and shunting the rest off to other attorneys in the firm who had agreed to fill in. It wasn't easy, but he had to admit to himself that he couldn't handle it all. He'd tried and failed. He couldn't remember the last time he had taken time off work. He'd never considered himself to be a workaholic, yet as he now thought about it, he realized his work had filled a void in his life. And as dissatisfied as he was at times with his present work, it did bridge his personal emptiness—not spiritually or even emotionally, but a simple *physical* emptiness. His strong sense of independence prevented him from leaning heavily on friends or even family to fulfill him. It had been different with Ellen. They had shared a mutual need that had in no way impugned his independence. After her death, work had, in a way, stood in for that mutual need—but, of course, never really fulfilled it.

What surprised him most at the prospect of taking a week off was that for the first time since Ellen's death, he didn't mind the idea at all. His first thought was of spending time with Irene. When they were together, especially when the time didn't involve Charlie's mystery, Joel was hounded by a sense of guilt that he was stealing time with her away from more pressing, if not more important, matters.

She had once scolded him, telling him they weren't teenagers on a romantic romp. Perhaps their relationship did have to take second place, yet his feelings for her were too strong to be ignored altogether. He wanted to call her immediately. She had given him her work number, but it was almost three o'clock, and she usually went home at three-thirty. He could wait until then.

Besides, he had another matter to attend to that couldn't wait. He picked up his phone and dialed Jim Kincaid's cellular number.

"Jim, this is Joel," he said when the investigator answered. "I just had a little talk with Eberhard."

"It doesn't sound good," Jim said, obviously picking up on Joel's serious tone.

"He'd like to see you focus a bit more on firm matters." Joel chuckled dryly. "In fact, he'd like to see you focus *entirely* on firm matters."

"I was afraid that was coming."

"You don't need to worry that any of this will reflect on you."

"That was never an issue with me, Joel. Do you want me to get Tony Harper to take my place? He's pretty good."

"Okay, he'll have to do. Are you still following Charlie?"

"Yeah. And I was just about to give you a call. I should have called yesterday, but I got home late and Suzie had plans for the rest of the evening. Then this morning I had to drive to Sacramento to do some work for George Petri. Anyway, Charlie's back at his hotel now, and by the look of him when he got there yesterday, I'm not surprised he's still there. Tony said he left to get some breakfast then returned to his room. He was pretty wasted. But I ought to tell you that yesterday I saw him make a purchase in a back alley. I didn't see the actual transaction, but it's not too hard to speculate. I think he was buying drugs—didn't he mention that he'd lost his medication? The only other logical possibility is that he bought a weapon. Maybe that's reaching, but he also talked about being betrayed and—what were his words. . . ?"

"That he was going to 'take care' of the danger." Joel shook his head. "I was afraid he had revenge on his mind."

Was that really Charlie's intention? Joel didn't want to believe his father was a man of violence. Yet it might explain Charlie's peculiar activities lately, his reluctance to open up to Joel or spend time with him. In fact, now that Joel considered it, it seemed far more likely Charlie had indeed bought a gun. He was dying, he probably figured he had nothing to lose. Nothing but a son he didn't know and grandchildren he wouldn't live long enough to befriend. It answered a lot of questions, but it also raised just as many.

"Who could blame the man for wanting vengeance," Jim said, "if he was really betrayed?"

"Well, if that's what he plans to do, he'll have to contend with me first." Joel's tone was firm, perhaps even hinting a bit at anger. Charlie had no right to smash their relationship before it even had a chance to bud. Charlie Sullivan was simply not going to get off so easily. He was not going to flicker into Joel's life like a promise of sight, then disappear again into darkness. "Where are you, Jim?" Jim gave Joel the address of a hotel northeast of Golden Gate Park. "I'll be there in—well, as long as it takes me to get a cab."

Joel arrived in twenty minutes. Jim was watching for him and called out the moment he stepped out of the cab, reaching him before Joel had finished unfolding his cane.

"Charlie's still inside?" Joel asked anxiously.

"Unless he slipped out the back way, but it's pretty crude back there, and I doubt he'd attempt it unless he was desperate. I'm assuming he's crashed out in his room."

"Okay, I'll take it from here."

"I can stick around—"

"I'm afraid if you don't show your face at the office soon, Eberhard will have both our heads on a platter. This is nothing I can't handle on my own."

"I haven't been able to get ahold of Tony. He just left, and I told him I wouldn't need him for a while."

"Don't worry about it," Joel said with confidence that probably should have been concern, under the circumstances. "I just need to talk to Charlie. I'll probably be able to get him to come home with me."

"You think so? He's been pretty stubborn."

"I sensed before that he's tired of running and hiding. It won't take much to convince him to trust me."

"Okay, but you should at least have had the cab stick around."

"I don't need a nursemaid, Jim."

"Sorry." Still Jim hesitated, and it rankled Joel that even after all these years of their friendship, he didn't know any better. It was bad enough when strangers tried to help the "poor blind man," but to have a friend do so was almost demeaning. "Well . . . I'll be at the office, then, if you need me."

"You are officially off the case, Jim. Do what you have to do at the office then go home and spend some time with Suzie. Throw your cellular phone in the trash if you have to."

"Is that an order?" There was a smile in Jim's voice.

"You bet."

"Then, I'll try."

Jim turned and walked toward his car. Joel heard the door open, but again Jim paused. What was his problem? There was absolutely no danger at all involved in talking to a dying old man. And Joel was more than comfortable with getting around alone.

"I'll call you later," Joel said with pointed finality, then turned sharply. But he turned back as he heard the car door shut, a sheepish look on his face. "Ah . . . Jim, which way to the hotel?"

Joel heard the repressed chuckle in Jim's tone as he replied, "Directly across the street. Just follow your nose."

"Thanks." But as humbling as his question had been, Joel still waited until he heard Jim start the engine and drive away before he turned and faced the street, busy with rush hour traffic.

When the traffic sounds let up, he crossed, realizing for the hundredth time how he missed Ebony, but also thinking that it was good for him to be entirely on his own for a change. Joel's natural self-sufficient spirit made him constantly aware of the trap of becoming too dependent on anything outside himself. He thrust his cane out defiantly and did not flinch when he heard the sounds of screeching brakes. A horn blasted and a driver yelled at him.

On the opposite sidewalk, he continue to walk as if he'd been there a hundred times, though he doubted he'd ever been to this exact street before. It was about a mile from the park and in a slightly better area, but not by much. There were shops and apartment buildings in the neighborhood, and Joel heard the sounds of several pedestrians, bumping shoulders with someone as he attempted to stay in a straight line as Jim had directed.

Joel paused at what he hoped was the hotel door, feeling for the latch or knob, but before he was successful in finding it, the door swung open and someone barreled through, nearly knocking over an unsuspecting Joel.

"Hey, buddy!" the man yelled, or rather slurred in a thick, drunken tone, "You blind or somethin'? Watch out."

Joel kept his balance and took a breath to reply, but there was such a foul odor about the stranger that Joel nearly gagged and could get no immediate words out. The drunk continued on his way, oblivious. Shrugging, Joel hurried into the hotel before the door closed.

Inside the lobby, the stranger's scent seemed to linger, until Joel realized that was simply the general odor of the place—stale alcohol and cigarettes, the hint of urine, and a pervading scent of mold and age. Charlie shouldn't have to stay in places like this, and a strong urge to protect and care for the man, who was his father, nearly overwhelmed Joel. But Joel had a feeling Charlie was just as stubborn and independent as his son and would no more want a nursemaid than Joel would. Still, he was determined to do something for the man, if nothing else buy him a nice dinner. Joel resolved not to leave the hotel without Charlie.

"Is there anyone here?" Joel asked as he closed the door behind him. He had sensed immediately upon entering that he had stepped into a relatively small space. That sense became stronger as he spoke and listened to the sound of his voice reverberating against close walls.

"Yeah, over here."

Joel turned in the direction of the voice—a woman's—and, leading with his cane, came within a couple steps of what was probably a counter.

"You *are* blind," the woman said. "Pete never realized it, not that it would have mattered to him. He's the kind of guy who'd tell you it was okay to cross the street when there was an eighteen wheeler speeding toward you."

"Luckily, I'm blind and not stupid," Joel replied good-naturedly.

"Huh?" The woman paused a moment, and Joel heard her scratch her chin as she puzzled over his statement. Then, suddenly enlightened, she chuckled. "Yeah . . . I guess you could hear a truck coming."

"I hope so!" Joel said.

"Well, it still takes a lot of gumption to walk around these streets

like that—I mean, you know, blind and all. I gotta hand it to you.
Even people who can see take their lives in their hands every time they
step off a San Francisco curb.''

"Maybe it's an advantage to be blind.''

The woman laughed outright at this. Though Joel was anxious to
see Charlie, he realized it wasn't a waste of time to curry the desk
clerk's sympathy. Even in a hotel like this there were probably rules
about giving out a guest's room number.

"So, what can I do for you?'' the woman asked. "You obviously
don't want a room here, and you don't look like a cop. Maybe you're
a lawyer come to tell me I've just become heir to a fortune?''

"You are right about the lawyer part, but I'm sorry I have no inheritance to offer you. I'm looking for one of your guests, a man
named Charlie Sullivan. However, he may not be using that name.
He's in his late sixties, thinning gray hair, probably crew cut, about
five eleven, but kind of bent at the shoulders so he seems shorter. His
coloring is slightly ashen, and his breathing is probably labored most
of the time. He probably checked in yesterday.''

"Yeah, there was someone like that who checked in last night. His
name's Charlie, but a different last name—'' she paused, shuffling
through some papers. "Here it is. Says Cooper in my ledger.''

"What room might he be in?'' Joel asked casually.

The woman snorted and there was a wry grin in her voice. "Now,
I'm not supposed to give out that information. Our guests value their
privacy, you know.''

"It's important.''

"Is he the one who's getting the million-dollar inheritance?''

"Is that the only way you'd give me the number?''

"I probably wouldn't believe you, anyway.''

"I doubt you'd believe the truth either.''

"Try me.'' The counter creaked as she folded her arms and leaned
on it.

"He's my father.''

"That is a hoot. But, like you said, too crazy not to be true. You've
been separated for years and you've finally found him?''

"Something like that.''

"I'd like to help, really, I would. But what if he doesn't want to
be found. . . ?''

Joel casually took his wallet from his pocket, opened it, and withdrew a twenty which he laid on the counter. "I understand your position. But you don't have to give me his room number—it wouldn't help me anyway unless it was in Braille. Just a few brief directions . . ."

"I like that. Then—technically—I haven't done any wrong." She covered the money with her hand and slid it toward her. "You have to go to the third floor, then it's the second door to the right."

Joel smiled. "I really appreciate this."

"Sorry, there's no elevator."

"That's okay, just point me in the direction of the stairs."

Forty-three

*B*y the time he reached the top of the third flight of stairs, even Joel was winded. He once again felt great empathy for Charlie, who was forced to make this trek with lungs diseased with cancer. Joel was accosted with a sense of urgency to have this business over with soon so Charlie could spend his last days, and hopefully months, at ease. Joel didn't care how independent his father was, he was going to receive a few of the comforts of life, whether he liked it or not.

Joel found the second door to the right and knocked without a moment's hesitation. It was possible Charlie was asleep, and even if he was awake, it was likely he'd be spooked by an unexpected visitor.

"Charlie, it's me, Joel," Joel said, hoping his voice would allay rather than increase the man's fears. Joel knocked again, and when there was still no response, he said, "Charlie, please let me in. I have to talk to you."

Joel stood there for three minutes, his own fears rising. Maybe Charlie *had* bought drugs and was in a stupor from them. In despair he might even have taken his own life. Joel prayed fervently that that would not be what he was about to find on the other side of the door. Desperately, he tried the doorknob, but it was locked.

"Please open the door," Joel said. "I know I didn't keep my word. But—"

The floorboards inside creaked, then an inside latch scraped as it was slid open. Finally the knob turned. Joel could tell the door opened only a crack. He felt, even if he couldn't see, the eyes peering out at him through the small opening.

"You're okay!" Joel breathed with relief.

"What'd you want?" grated Charlie's voice, thick with sleep.

"Please let me in so we can talk."

"Why should I? I told you to leave me alone."

"And I told you to keep in touch," Joel returned with mild rebuke. "We both broke our promise. Did I wake you up?"

"I needed to wake up pretty soon anyway."

With relief, Joel heard the door swing open wider. He strode into the room before Charlie could change his mind.

"You want a chair?"

"Sure."

Charlie moved a chair into place and directed Joel to it. Charlie then sat on the edge of the bed, its old springs groaning with his weight. The two men faced each other.

"Well, what's so important that you had to break your word in order to see me?" Maybe it was Joel's imagination, but he thought he detected an undertone of affection beneath the gruff tenor of Charlie's voice.

"I just needed to know you are okay. We may be total strangers, Charlie, but you are my father, and I can't help caring about what happens to you."

"You're wasting your time."

"You were the one who found me." Joel thought about their first conversation and how futile it had been. He felt like this was going to be a repeat. "Listen, Charlie, you don't have to protect yourself with that hard-hearted routine. I'm not buying it. I'm your son. I'll bet you thought about both your sons a lot while you were in prison. I'll bet you wondered what it would have been like had things been different. Playing ball together or going camping—what other dreams did you have of being a father? Well, maybe we can't make those dreams come true, but you are still my father, and I am still your son. There's hope for us to have something, if we can let down our guard long enough."

"What about your adopted father? I doubt he'd want me muscling in on his territory."

"He'd never look upon it in that way."

"Do you love him?" Charlie asked suddenly, his voice soft and hesitant.

"Yes . . ."

"I don't expect you to ever love me like that."

"Maybe in time . . ."

After a brief silence, Charlie said, "I did think of my sons in prison.

Not a lot, though, because it would have driven me crazy if I had dwelled on it. When yours and Greg's birthdays would roll around, I'd try to imagine you at the various ages. Just before Greg's twenty-first birthday a kid was locked up with me who had also just turned twenty-one. He was an orphan, too, and for a while I kind of took the kid under my wing. I thought about my boys becoming men, and I worried a bit over what kind of men you might have turned into."

"I would have been in my last year of high school at that time," Joel said. "I was hardly a man, but I tried to act like one."

"I can imagine." Charlie's voice momentarily lightened, hinting at mild amusement. Then he grew somber again. "In my heart I was always a father. I cared about you, but like I said, I constantly had to let it go. It just wasn't healthy to love something so unattainable."

"But . . . you did love me?"

"Let me tell you something Betsy and I swore we'd never tell a soul. Greg was what you'd call an unplanned baby. In fact, Betsy and I weren't even married . . . you know—when we found out about him. We got married real quick, though, and were glad to do it. And we welcomed him, especially Betsy, who wanted nothing more in life than a home and family. Having kids in our financial position was nuts, but we both loved kids, and you were definitely planned, Joel. We were so excited to be having another baby. We didn't have two dimes to rub together, but we had love."

Charlie shook his head. "We were crazy, just kids ourselves, really. I was running numbers and collecting for a loan shark, and Sandy told me I had impressed the big boys. I was moving up and my family was going to start living right. I wanted to get Betsy out of that Haight Street dive. She was six months pregnant and had to trudge up and down three flights of stairs day in and day out. All I had to do to insure my future was help Sandy out on a job and he'd get me into the big time."

"Sandy. . . ?"

Charlie let out a frustrated sigh. "Never mind. These trips down memory lane aren't healthy."

Joel regretted breaking the spell of Charlie's rare openness. Maybe some other time he could hear Charlie talk about Joel's mother and the days when Charlie had been a young father and husband striving to keep his little family happily together. For now, however, it was necessary for Joel to focus strictly on that night when Charlie Sullivan's life had been destroyed. It was perhaps the only way to help the old man find peace at last.

"What does Sandy Fabroni have to do with all this?" Joel pressed.

"You ask too many questions."

"That's because you leave so many unanswered. What would be the harm in telling me? You already believe I couldn't possibly think less of you. So, why not reveal all? Don't you think I have a right to know how I lost my mother and father?"

Charlie rubbed a hand over his chin. Joel heard the scratch of his stubbly beard. "Maybe you're right. Pretty soon it won't matter anyway."

Joel wanted to know what that final statement meant, but he restrained his curiosity, fearing he might distract Charlie once more from revealing his mysterious story.

"Yes . . ." Joel prompted quietly.

Before continuing, Charlie fumbled around for something, then, after a brief clicking sound, Joel smelled cigarette smoke. "Sandy Fabroni and I grew up in the same Chicago neighborhood," Charlie began. "Sandy was like a big brother to me. I guess I kind of idolized him. He moved to California and a year or so later he wrote me and encouraged me to come west, too. Betsy had just had Greg and we were poor—the rats in our tenement lived better than us. We hitchhiked to California—with a baby, no less! We were insane. I don't know what made me so cocky, but I thought I could have anything I wanted."

As Charlie progressed with his account he did so haltingly, his breathing often heavy and labored between puffs on his cigarette.

"We got to sunny California flat broke. Sandy got me a job at Banducci's, nothing glamorous, just sweeping up, loading trucks. I started spending my little paychecks faster than I earned them, trying to live high, way beyond our means. Eventually we were in a lot of debt. That's when I asked Sandy to point me in the direction of some fast money. I knew he was working with the mob—I think the only one who didn't know was Banducci, but he was a gullible sap—" Charlie stopped short and croaked a dry, hard laugh. "I turned out to be a worse sap yet, but that was later. Sandy got me some free-lance work running numbers, collecting, whatever his boss had available. Betsy and I were able to move into a bigger place; the extra I made was just enough to get us into that flat on Haight Street—if you can believe it, that was a move up from where we were. It was still pretty crummy, but she did all she could to make it into a real home. That's all Betsy ever wanted—a house and kids like on TV. Mind you, 1950s television—*Father Knows Best* and *Donna Reed*, and such. And all I wanted to do was give that to her. . . ."

Charlie paused, taking several deep breaths. Joel sensed his difficulty was as much from rising emotion as it was from his illness. Joel said nothing, allowing Charlie to go at his own pace. In a moment, Charlie rose from the bed, went to a sink in the room, and from the sound of it, splashed water on his face then toweled the moisture off.

"You want a drink?" Charlie said. "All I got is water."

"No thanks."

The water ran again, and Charlie apparently filled a glass and drank. Joel wondered if the man wanted, and needed, something stronger. But then Charlie shuffled back to the bed and sat. He lit another cigarette.

"Maybe it's all excuses . . ." Charlie said. "We needed money. The debts piled up, Betsy was pregnant. I was up against it. Sandy told me the mob boss wanted to advance me in the organization. But they wanted to be sure I really had the stuff for it. Sandy said I could prove myself by pulling off a robbery at Banducci's. It was a payroll, only ten grand, but that was a lot of money to me. He said it was insured so no one was going to lose in the deal. It was so simple. I should have known I was being set up. But I was only twenty-five years old. I didn't know anything—although I thought I knew everything.

"That cop was on Sandy's payroll. You know, he looked the other way for all Sandy's shady deals. I'm not sure exactly why Sandy killed him. Probably the cop was getting greedy, maybe he had even developed a conscience and was threatening to turn Sandy in. I'm sure Sandy planned the whole thing. He very specifically told me to show up at the office at ten that night. I got there a few minutes early and didn't see any reason to wait. The place was deserted, what would a couple minutes matter? Sandy must have been in a hurry to leave after shooting the cop, especially when he heard me come, because he didn't even make sure the man was dead. When I arrived and found the body, the cop had enough life in him to give me a notebook and tell me to get his killer, get Sandy. The notebook was incriminating, but I never used it."

"Why? Surely it would have given Sandy a motive for murder."

"My prints were on the murder weapon. Sandy used a revolver he had loaned to me for some target practice. And I was caught at the scene. I managed to get away, but I was apprehended again the next day. But the two cops who responded to an anonymous call identified me as the man fleeing the scene. I even told the cops I had evidence that would link Sandy to the mob. But there was nothing to connect Sandy to the dead cop. And Sandy had an ironclad alibi. It wouldn't have done me any good to produce the notebook. If Sandy even knew I had it, I wouldn't have survived two minutes in prison."

"So, you kept quiet about it?"

"What else could I do? I had little hope of parole, not for killing a cop. It would bring me nothing but grief if I said anything. I was lucky the police who interrogated me never believed the story about the notebook, and so it never got out that I had it."

"But Fabroni found out about it eventually?"

"I suspect Greg opened that can of worms. The fool. Or maybe I was the fool for telling him about it. But I sized Greg up pretty quick after seeing him for the first time, and I knew he wouldn't give me the time of day unless there was something in it for him."

"Then it was Greg who tried to use the notebook to blackmail Fabroni?"

"And I'm sure that's what got Greg killed."

"But you weren't planning to blackmail Fabroni yourself?"

Charlie hesitated a long time before answering. "That's not important."

Joel shook his head. "Blackmail would never have been enough, would it?"

"No!" Charlie's voice rose, betraying his true anger for the first time. "Especially after he killed Greg! He would have—and still could—hurt you too, if he thought you were a threat to his lofty ambitions. Sandy Fabroni deserves anything he gets."

"From you?"

"Why not? It's my right! I spent thirty-seven years in prison for a crime I didn't commit—because of him. I lost my wife, my children. You're blind because of him. Greg is dead. Don't try to tell me revenge won't do any good, won't bring back my life. Don't even say it's only going to hurt me. I can't be hurt anymore—" Charlie's sudden agitation brought on a fit of coughing. When he spoke again, several minutes later, his voice was strained and thin. "I know you're a religious man, Joel, but even you ought to be able to see that this isn't just vengeance—it's justice!"

Part of Joel wanted to agree with Charlie. It was only right for a man like Sandy Fabroni to pay for all that he had done, and it was fairly certain no legal charges would ever be proven against him. An assassin's bullet might indeed be the only way for justice to be gained. Joel thought about what he had lost—his blindness was bad enough and the inevitable helplessness even he was bound to experience at times; but because of Sandy Fabroni, Joel would never know his mother and brother, and his father, too, would be dead before long. Hatred could easily burn within Joel, and even as he sat listening to Charlie's tragic tale, sparks of bitterness began to ignite in Joel's heart. Because of one man's sick and ruthless greed so much good had been destroyed.

Was Charlie so wrong? Who was Joel to blame him? Or to stop him?

But as Joel's heart began to pound with his growing ire, a Scripture exploded in his mind. Biblical words that had been used nearly to excess, until they were almost trite. Yet their truth was abiding. There was no way for Joel to deny it.

Vengeance is mine, says the Lord.

But Joel could never spout that to Charlie. Unless one really understood . . . unless one knew and loved the author of those words, they were difficult indeed to hear. Joel knew his Lord didn't hunger after vengeance or actively seek it. Vengeance was a destructive force, perhaps even a damning force. Only God could bear its devastating power. Charlie, or anyone else, would surely be broken by it. Joel could feel himself already breaking up a little inside by the tiny seed of hatred given a foothold. It made him sick to think what would happen to him, to his relationship with his God, if he succumbed fully to that emotion. God in His mercy was willing to take the burden of vengeance from man. The act of a truly loving God.

But what could he say to Charlie? What would the man hear? How could a man relinquish his hatred to God if he had no relationship with Him in the first place? How could he lay his revenge at God's feet if he had no personal basis on which to trust that God would deal with it in the best possible way?

"You know I'm right, don't you?" said Charlie, misreading Joel's silence.

"All I know, Charlie, is that if you kill Fabroni, I'm going to lose you again."

"Would you be able to forgive me?"

Joel didn't want to make it easier for Charlie, but he had to tell the truth. "Yes."

"I gotta do it, Joel."

"But I can't let you, Charlie."

"How are you going to stop me?" said Charlie. Was it a challenge or a plea?

Joel had no answer. Short of physical restraint, what *could* he do? He was younger than Charlie and more physically fit, but his disability was . . . just that. Even a sixty-two-year-old man could easily evade him if he tried hard enough.

"Just give it some time, okay?" urged Joel. "Let's have dinner together." Joel felt his wristwatch. "It's nearly six. You must be hungry. I know I am. Let's eat and talk some more. Later, if you still want to . . . well, you're right, I can't stop you."

"You can warn Fabroni."

"Doesn't he already know he's in some danger? He probably would figure a big man like him has little to fear from you."

"I don't have time for dinner," Charlie hedged Joel's logic.

"Are you planning to kill him tonight?"

"I'm glad we got to talk," Charlie said evasively. "It's good you know everything. Maybe you won't reproach me too much for what I gotta do."

Charlie jumped up and strode across the room.

"Don't leave, Charlie!"

But he hadn't gone toward the door. He had paused adjacent to the door and was opening a drawer.

"What are you getting?" Joel asked, also standing.

"Nothing."

Joel started toward Charlie, but he heard the old man quickly move away, this time in the direction of the door. Joel took another step but collided hard with a dresser.

"You okay?" Charlie was near the door and it sounded as if he was pulling on a coat.

"Please don't make this difficult." Joel said.

"You're the one who's making it hard. Give it up before you hurt yourself."

"Where are you going, Charlie?"

"I thought you had that figured out."

"What if I do warn Fabroni?" Joel wanted to keep Charlie talking so he could use his voice as a guide while Joel attempted to move slowly and he hoped, unnoticed, closer to the door.

"It'll be too late. Anyway, I still have the notebook, which Fabroni will do anything to get. I'm holding all the cards now."

"Don't kid yourself. You're going to walk into another trap."

"Do you think I expect to survive this night?"

"Charlie . . . please!" Desperation rose with the tears in Joel's eyes.

"I'm sorry, son."

"Then, put your arms around me before you go. I want to feel my father's embrace just once—"

"Why. . . ?"

"Can't you give me that, at least?"

For a moment Joel feared he had read his father wrong, that Charlie had hardened himself too much to be touched by Joel's entreaty. Then Charlie moved, not toward the door, but in Joel's direction. At first tentative, he lifted his arms, bending them somewhat awkwardly around Joel. When Joel returned the gesture, a deep emotional barrier seemed to be breached within the old man, and his arms tightened around his son with a remarkable strength and with a heart-wrenching desperation.

Joel thought he had at last broken through his father's stubborn determination to carry through with his violent intentions. All that was needed was the loving contact between father and son to convince Charlie that he'd be losing more than he'd ever gain with his revenge. Then Joel felt a hard object press against him, something wedged in Charlie's belt.

It was the gun Charlie had purchased yesterday in the alley.

Forty-four

As if Charlie remembered the weapon at the same moment Joel felt it, he loosened his grip on his son.

"I gotta go," he said.

"No!" Joel's hold on Charlie tightened, this time with more coercion than affection.

Charlie tried to shrug free gently, but Joel's hold was too strong for such a passive attempt.

"You can't stop something that has been destined to happen for three decades," Charlie said, struggling harder.

"You're a stubborn old coot!"

"And you're a chip off the old coot!"

They might have laughed if they weren't so desperate. Suddenly Charlie began to cough. His whole body contracted violently with convulsive hacking, and thinking it was his forceful hold that had brought on the attack, Joel loosened his arms. An instant later Charlie broke free and his coughing ceased.

Joel was surprised at the old man's craftiness, but he wasn't about to concede yet. He thrust out his hands again knowing Charlie was still within reach. He caught Charlie's jacket.

Charlie turned sharply, shaking loose Joel's hold, then, as Joel was catching his balance from this, he felt a hard blow against his chest. He could have held firm, but as he stepped back in another attempt to balance himself, he struck the chair he had been sitting on earlier and fell into it with such force that both he and the chair toppled over. On the way to the floor, Joel's head struck the corner of the bed's wooden footboard.

Momentarily stunned, he heard, as if from a great distance, the door open and close with a bang. Gripping the bed, Joel struggled to his knees, but his head swam, preventing him from further movement. With defeat, he dropped his head on the bed and groaned. Even if he moved that very instant, how would he ever find Charlie now? He should never have come alone. He should have made Jim wait. But he supposed cockiness was indeed a family trait.

Joel tried to move again. His head was throbbing, and when he touched the growing lump two inches above his left temple, he felt the moisture of fresh blood. But he had to keep moving. He may have lost Charlie for now, but he could not leave it at that. Charlie had left no doubt that he planned to kill Fabroni tonight.

Joel gained his feet and found he was quickly recovering from his injury, if not from his sense of helplessness. But he easily found his cane where he had laid it on the bed. That was something. Then, pausing a moment at the sink, he took a washcloth and tried to mop up the blood oozing from his head. Perhaps it didn't look as bad as it felt. Next, he had to get to a phone. No more misplaced confidence. He needed help if he was still going to stop Charlie.

The woman at the desk let Joel use her phone.

"So, he didn't want to be found," she said with a hint of a smirk in her tone.

"Guess not," Joel replied.

"You need something on that head."

"I need to make a call first."

Joel called Jim, but he wasn't in the office and didn't answer his cellular phone. He thought about calling Jim's home number but decided against it. He called Irene instead. He told her where he was, and he had no doubt she'd be there in thirty minutes as she promised, even from San Bruno, in the midst of rush hour. Then the clerk began cleaning Joel's head, giving him an ice pack to place over the makeshift bandage she had applied.

"I'm no expert," she said, "but it doesn't look like you need stitches."

"I'll take your word for it. I need to make a couple more calls."

"Be my guest."

Despite his previous lack of success in getting through to Fabroni, Joel called his residence but was told by a servant that he wasn't in. Then Joel recalled that Fabroni dined every evening at Alexander's. After the hotel clerk looked up the number for him, he called there.

"This is Joel Costain. It's very urgent that I speak with Mr. Fabroni."

"Just a moment."

The next voice Joel heard was a woman's, and it was familiar.

"Mr. Costain, may I help you?"

"Lena Westfall?" Joel asked, silently puzzling over why she should have answered.

"That's right."

"I was trying to reach Sandy Fabroni."

"I know. I can take a message."

"It's rather personal."

"I'm afraid, Joel, that I have practiced a little deception. You see, I am Mr. Fabroni's daughter."

"Really? Why the secret?"

She chuckled sheepishly. "I am a fiercely independent woman, and I have made it a practice not to ride on my father's coattails—I may have named my restaurant after him"—Joel suddenly realized that Fabroni's given name was Alessandro, the Italian form of Alexander—"but I pride myself on the fact that its success is entirely my doing. Now, would you like to tell me your message and I can give it to my father?"

"It would be better for me to speak personally to him."

"But he's not here."

"Do you know where he is?"

"Normally he would be here at this hour, but he left early this evening—"

"Where did he go?"

"I really don't know."

It seemed an odd coincidence that Fabroni's daughter had become Joel's client only days ago. Yet Joel saw no reason not to trust her—this was about her father's safety. Whatever her other motives, that must surely supercede all else.

"Well then, if you hear from him, you must warn him that his life may be in danger—"

"What's this? In danger? I don't understand."

"It's a long story, Lena, but there is a man named Charlie Sullivan, who has an old grudge against your father. He may try to harm him."

"Goodness! This is terrible."

"Is there any way you can reach your father?"

"I don't know . . . perhaps his car phone."

"If you find out anything, especially where your father might be, would you—" Joel realized that if he and Irene were out looking for Charlie, there would be no way for Lena to reach him. Joel would have been prepared with his portable phone, which he usually had with him—except now, when it mattered most. "I'm going to try to find Sullivan," Joel said. "I'll be in touch with you."

"But, Joel, is this Sullivan really a dangerous man?"

"He's old and physically sick. But I can't predict what he might do in his distraught state of mind."

"All right. I'll call my father as soon as you hang up."

⊙⥋⥋⥋⊙

Lena hung up the telephone and brought her slim, manicured fingers thoughtfully to her chin as she pondered all the ramifications of Costain's call. Of course it was no surprise to her that Sullivan was looking for blood. She had tried to impress that upon her father. But he was too distracted by his own sense of culpability in this whole affair to be rational. She had already decided that it was time to take the situation into her own far more objective hands.

Lena turned from the phone and walked into the dining room. It was a bit early for Alexander's dinner crowd. That's why her father chose the hour between six and seven for his nightly dinner ritual. Only three other tables were occupied, the conversation was soft, and the nightly musician, a rather talented pianist, would not begin playing until seven. She walked past the tables to the secluded booth in back.

"Hello, Daddy." She caught a whiff of pesto delicately seasoned with garlic; it was one of their standard entrees. "Nothing new tonight, Daddy? I thought for certain you'd try the Frittura Piccata. Hector is trying it for the first time tonight."

"I just had a hankering for pesto, but this is the first time I've had the grilled chicken breast. Quite good. Seasoned with restraint, yet with enough zest not to make me forget it."

"I'll pass that on to the chef. May I join you for a glass of wine?"

"I'd be disappointed if you didn't."

She slid into the booth, sitting opposite her father. A waiter was there in a moment with a glass which he filled with White Zinfandel.

She cradled the glass for a moment, gazing into the pink liquid as if she were actually hesitant or uncertain. In truth, she was nothing of the sort, but rather was simply priming herself for what she would say next. But she had a languid sip of the wine before speaking.

"So, Daddy, you are really going to meet with Sullivan?"

"Yes." He glanced at his wristwatch. "In less than an hour."

"Alone?"

"That's what he requested. But believe me, if I felt there was any danger, I would never go by myself. Charlie simply wants some recompense for the last thirty-seven years, and I don't blame him."

"He must be bitter."

"Of course he is, but Charlie was never the violent type. I remember telling him the mob boss was impressed by him, but that wasn't the truth. They were actually ready to fire him. He was the worst collector they ever had, giving second chances out like peanuts, sometimes even third chances. He acted more like Santa Claus than a mob enforcer."

"I still wish you'd let me go with you."

"That might spook him. It's best if it's just him and me. He's going to look at that briefcase full of money and feel like he finally got the better of me. A hundred grand means little to us, but to a man like Charlie who never had a cent, it's a fortune."

"What if he tries to bleed you for more?"

"I may feel sorry for the man, but I'm no pushover. If this"—he patted the briefcase beside him—"doesn't insure his silence . . . well, I'll deal with it."

Lena took a long swallow of her wine, savoring the light bouquet. "Okay, if you're sure. But come back here immediately afterward—I'll be terribly on edge."

Fabroni reached across the table and patted his daughter's hand. "A heart does beat inside you, after all."

She smiled. "For you, Daddy, always."

Lena finished her wine, then was called away by the *maître d'*. She wasn't troubled at all by the deception she was pulling over her father. He would thank her for it in the end. He might not realize it, but Charlie was indeed a very dangerous man, not only because of what she had learned from Joel—she probably agreed with her father that he didn't have the gumption to kill Fabroni, and even if he did, he probably didn't have the physical stamina to pull off such a deed. Nevertheless, Charlie was to be feared because of the notebook. Fabroni might think he and Charlie could make a simple transaction, a hundred thousand for the notebook, and that was that. But Lena, perhaps because she was devious herself, would never be able to trust Sullivan's word on the matter. There was nothing to prevent him from keeping part of the notebook. Her father, who had never seen it, would never be able to tell the difference. But even if Charlie merely made copies, they'd be damning enough. The merest hint of scandal would destroy Fabroni's chances at election to office.

Charlie Sullivan had to be eliminated. Of course, there were inherent risks in that. He might have left copies or part of the original with someone like his son with instructions to distribute it in the event of his untimely death. But that could be far more easily dealt with if Charlie wasn't present to give his side of the story.

Lena had been concerned with covering up Charlie's murder, but Costain's call would now all but exonerate her and her father. A crazed, vengeful killer was after Fabroni. Even Costain would have to testify that the man's murder was in self-defense. All she had to do was follow her father to where the meeting would take place and wait for the right moment. Lena's father might protest her plan now, but once Sullivan was dead he was sure to see the expediency of what she had done. A man with political ambitions simply had to be pragmatic.

Forty-five

The northbound traffic on the freeway was light compared to the bumper-to-bumper mess of Bay Area residents headed south out of San Francisco after a hard day's work. Irene accelerated to nearly seventy on the 280 freeway, weaving in and out when slower vehicles impeded her pace. She made good time until she exited on Nineteenth Street where she was met with the snarled downtown city traffic, made even more intense by rush hour. But she had grown up in this, learned to drive in it, and knew how to navigate it like a jungle native.

However, even Irene had some qualms about getting out in the early evening dusk in the neighborhood where the hotel was located. It wasn't far from where they had met Charlie before. The hotel was a fleabag with a half-illuminated neon sign that read "-otel Ha-gh"— Hotel Haight. She parked in an empty place three doors down, thankful that at that hour most of the shops on the street were closed.

She didn't see Joel in the lobby and her heart sank, fearing she had come to the wrong place. Then a woman's voice called out.

"Hey, you must be Joel's friend." She was around forty-five, slim, almost to excess, wearing heavy makeup and bleached blond hair.

"Yes, where is he?"

"Back in the office using the phone." The woman motioned for Irene to follow her. The door was slightly ajar. "Go on in. I have to get back up front." The woman left, and Irene pushed the door open the rest of the way.

Joel was just hanging up the phone. Irene noticed first the bandage on his head. "Joel, are you all right?"

He jumped up and took two quick strides toward her, almost as if he was about to embrace her. Then he stopped.

"I'm fine."

But she heard the despair in his tone and saw the need in his eyes, and her desire to allay that need, to comfort him, overcame her reticence. Letting impulse rule, Irene closed the gap between them and took him in her arms. She felt the immediate release of his tensions and unspoken worry as he returned the embrace, holding her tight.

"Irene, he's going to kill Fabroni," he said, his voice muted by her nearness. She didn't have to ask who he was talking about. "He got away from me, and now I'm afraid it's too late. Fabroni's gone, maybe to meet him."

"What can we do?" she said. It was easy to hold and comfort him, but beyond that she knew she was helpless.

Reluctantly, they released each other. But Irene realized that she, too, had needed that contact with him. She hadn't seen him since her conversation with Connie when she had first found the courage to voice the fact that she might indeed be in love with Joel. She'd longed to see him, to hold him like this, but at the same time she feared she would pull away from him, allowing Greg's insidious image to drive a wedge between them. But as she had held Joel just now, no ghosts came to haunt her. Joel was just Joel, his own man, the man for whom she cared deeply. The man she . . . loved.

Irene wanted to tell him these things right then, but this wasn't the time. She choked back the words as they rose to her lips. They had to think about Charlie Sullivan.

Joel paced aimlessly to the cluttered metal desk in the small office. He turned. "We've got to find him, and I think I've figured out where he might go."

"Should we call the police?"

"No," he said emphatically. "If they find him in possession of a gun, they'll send him back to prison, not to mention what they'd do about his other plans. But I'm almost certain if I can reach him in time, I can talk him out of it." He suddenly reached up and fingered the bandage on his head, then smiled ironically. "Well . . . I've got to try, at least. And he might not be very far from here. I've been thinking while I waited that a logical choice for what he is planning is the old house in Haight-Ashbury. It's deserted and in an area where suspicious activity would easily go unnoticed. Not to mention the poetic justice of making use of the place."

"You don't think it's too obvious?"

"I only came up with it a few minutes ago. But I think Charlie figured it would be over before anyone could tail him."

"Then we better not lose anymore time."

Joel grabbed his cane, then took Irene's arm, whispering as they exited the office, "Get us there on time, Lord!"

While they drove in the gathering darkness to Charlie's old house, Joel told Irene about his most recent encounter with his birth father, though he had time only for an abbreviated version because they arrived at their destination within ten minutes. The Victorian apartment house was dark and looked more deserted than ever. Were they too late?

Irene expressed her fears, but Joel said, "No . . . we can't be." And she tried to buy in to his confidence.

The house had an entirely different appearance now than it had during their earlier visit in broad daylight. Irene could well believe Charlie would choose this as the reckoning place for his long-desired revenge. Irene scanned the outside of the three-story structure and could see no sign of life. No lights burned inside, though, of course, the electricity was no doubt turned off. A couple of lights glowed from the windows of the house next door, and a young woman carrying a bag of groceries was trudging up the steps that led to the front door. It was the same student they had met before. She glanced at Joel and Irene as they got out of Irene's Toyota.

"Back again?" she said and paused, balancing her groceries on her knee.

"Have you noticed anyone else here today?" Joel asked.

"No, but I've been out shopping for the last hour or so."

"We just want to have another look inside."

"No business of mine." The woman scrutinized them, then continued to troop into her old building.

Irene fleetingly thought that it was such a shame for these old Victorians to fall apart. But Joel was nudging her with too much urgency to allow her time to solve the social problems of the city. She turned toward the open area between the two houses, and with her guiding but Joel definitely leading, they walked to the back as they had previously.

The door looked just as they had left it. Irene pulled at the plywood board over the door and it swung easily away. More easily than the other time, but that was no surprise for they had no doubt loosened the nails before. It didn't necessarily mean Charlie was here. A thief or vandal could have entered the house, if not now, then sometime since their previous visit.

Irene grasped the knob, but the door definitely needed a shove with much more force than before. She had to put her shoulder to it, but when she got it wide enough for them to fit through, she saw that the problem was a torn piece of linoleum that had curled up against the bottom of the door, catching it. It certainly had not been like that earlier. Though it could have easily warped and puckered on its own in the time since their last visit, she hoped and prayed it was an indication that Charlie was inside.

Even after her eyes adjusted to the darkness inside, Irene had to stumble and grope to get around. She wished she had brought a flashlight. In a way, Joel was far better off then she, making expert use of his cane, but in a new environment he did have some difficulty. Still, he stumbled no more than she. Irene, however, was able to spare them colliding with big objects, and after they had a look around the two ground floor flats, she led them to the back stairs, which creaked loudly as they ascended.

"Charlie," Joel called as they reached the second floor.

Joel gave Irene a despairing glance, shaking his head hopelessly. They both knew that if Charlie wasn't here they would waste too much time trying to find him anywhere else, if they could even come up with other possibilities.

"Come on, Charlie, be here," Joel said.

They walked through the rooms of the second floor flat, only giving them a brief inspection. Charlie had mentioned that Betsy had to climb three flights of stairs, so they assumed Charlie had lived on the third floor. Neither verbalized the fear, but as well as searching for Charlie, they were also making sure there were no corpses in the building. Peering through the rooms, Irene was feeling more and more confident that they had preceded Charlie to the house, if he had intended on coming here at all.

They started up to the third floor and Irene said, "If he's not here, should we wait?"

"We could be sitting here, and he could be . . . taking care of Fabroni someplace else entirely. Then again, he could show up ten minutes after we leave." Joel paused. "Let's stay here unless we can think of a better place he might be. It would be useless to chase all over the city . . . blindly, as it were."

"Maybe he won't go through with it."

"I only hope we're not . . ." but he stopped, unable to voice his fear.

Irene suddenly halted in their ascent of the stairs. Joel bumped into her. She offered him a quick apology then, facing him, added excitedly. "Joel, let's pray, right here . . . together."

"That's an excellent idea. I've been trying to silently, but it all gets lost in . . . I suppose in my anxiety." He reached out his hands and she grasped them. "I already feel better, not so alone. Would you like to pray?"

Irene realized she had never prayed out loud in front of Joel, and since she hadn't prayed aloud in years, she felt self-conscious. But would it bother him that she was still reticent about such things? Would he think less of her? Intuitively she knew the answer to her unspoken questions, but she couldn't help her introspection. Joel would just have to accept her as she was. And as she answered his question, she had no doubt he would.

"I'd rather you do it, Joel. But I am supporting you."

"That's all I need." He smiled, gave her hands a gentle squeeze, and continued in a natural, conversational tone. "Jesus, I've put this in Your hands many times, and I guess I have to do it again, or at least I have to remind myself that's where it is. You love Charlie, and whatever happens tonight, I believe it is Your will. We feel pretty helpless now but only when we take the eyes of our hearts off You. Help us to take the right steps and to make the right decisions." Joel sighed deeply as he finished. Irene felt, as she had in the hotel office, more tension fall away from him.

"Well, let's go," Joel said.

Hand in hand they continued up the steep, narrow flight. It again occurred to Irene what Joel had just told her in the car about his mother, six months pregnant, climbing up and down these stairs, probably balancing her four-year-old son on her hip. That hint of life she and Joel had felt when they first visited this house returned to Irene, even stronger now that she had a larger picture of the little Sullivan family who had lived here.

They were halfway up when Joel, who was behind Irene, tugged at her hand. "What's that?" he whispered, as if they were uninvited interlopers and feared being heard.

Irene shook her head. "I don't hear a thing."

"Listen."

They stood quietly for several seconds, then Irene heard it. Creaking floorboards. Someone was in the house.

"Charlie?"

"Come on." Joel turned and rushed back down the stairs, seemingly unconcerned that he was now leading Irene. But even in his haste, he didn't miss a step.

However, when they reached the bottom, he did stumble a bit because he had lost count of the steps. Irene was immediately at his elbow and took up the momentary lapse with ease.

"You'd think we'd been doing this together all our lives," he said offhandedly.

But Irene didn't get a chance to respond because the new arrival was coming up the section of stairs between the first and second floors, his visage just barely discernible in the dark shadows of the stairwell.

Forty-six

"What's this?" the man said.

Joel must have recognized the voice. "Fabroni?" he said. "What's going on?"

"You didn't get my message, then?"

"What message?"

"I left it with your daughter. She was to warn you not to meet with Charlie."

"I never got a message. But what business is it of yours? Is this some trap?"

"I know everything, Fabroni."

"You know Charlie Sullivan's side—the ravings of a bitter ex-con, a cop killer—"

"Then, why did you agree to meet with him?"

"That's a good question," came a new voice from the top of the third flight of stairs.

It was Charlie. Irene had a good view of him because of the glow from a kerosene lantern he was holding. But what captured her attention was the gun in his right hand, aimed down at her and the others. Charlie came down the steps toward them, the swaying lamp casting weird shadows on his sad, gray face.

"Don't try anything, Sandy," Charlie said. "This gun has a hair trigger, and though I'm not quite ready to kill you, I will if I have to." Then he said to Joel, "I'm glad you're okay. I shouldn't have left you in the room like that, but I figured in the long run it was best. I thought that would be the end of it. Why couldn't you leave it alone, Joel?"

"You know the answer to that, Charlie."

"Well, don't think it changes anything. I've had a long time to think about this; it's not a snap decision."

Charlie reached the landing, and still keeping his weapon trained on Fabroni, he set the lantern on one of the steps immediately behind him and turned up the wick. They were now all on the small landing between the second and third floors. Fabroni was at the top of the flight of stairs that led down to the first floor; Charlie stood at the foot of the stairs leading up. The two lifelong adversaries were less than six feet apart. Joel and Irene were in the middle of the landing, which had but one window in it, covered by a tattered old shade. Irene had the sense that they were like stalking animals, poised and waiting for . . . she was uncertain what they might be waiting for but couldn't believe whatever it was would be welcomed.

"Costain, stop him," Fabroni said desperately. "He won't shoot you. Get that gun from him."

"I won't kill you, Joel, but I can temporarily incapacitate you or Irene if I have to." Charlie's tone was deadly serious, his expression hard as steel. "I wasn't a killer thirty-seven years ago, but you don't know what serving three and a half decades of hard time does to a man."

"I refuse to believe that," said Joel.

"I truly wish it could have been different. I wish you didn't have to be here for this—"

"Charlie!" Irene said suddenly. "If you do this, you'll never meet your grandchildren."

"It's too late for that. I've got to do this. There *has* to be justice."

"Listen here," said Fabroni. "I've got money." He moved his hand, and for the first time Irene noticed he was holding a briefcase. "A hundred thousand dollars, Charlie, just like you requested. It's all free and clear, too. You could live your last days quite well on that, and you could leave your grandchildren set up for life."

"What's to stop me from killing you and taking the money any- way?" Charlie sneered. "Put the briefcase down and kick it to the woman. It still won't make us even, not for all you've done, but I am a practical man."

Fabroni did as he was told. The leather case scraped across the bare floor, and when it reached Irene, she just stared blankly at it. She fleet- ingly thought about what that kind of money could do for her chil- dren—a nice house to live in, college, security. But were any of those things worth what taking this money would cost?

"I'd like to see what that kind of money looks like," Charlie said. "Go ahead," he told Irene. "Open it up."

Irene picked up the case, unfastened the clasps, and lifted the lid. Neat piles of hundred dollar bills greeted her.

"I kept my word to you, Charlie," Fabroni said, his tone disintegrating into a whine.

"And I'm going to keep mine." Charlie raised his weapon until it was aimed at Fabroni's heart.

"Charlie, no!" Joel cried as if he had seen his father's movement, probably sensing that the dreaded moment had arrived.

Irene had closed the briefcase and was gripping it with white knuckles as she stared intently, helplessly, at the scene transpiring before her. It seemed to be rushing with unstoppable force toward what must seemingly be its inevitable conclusion. Her heart was thudding, and even when Charlie seemed to hesitate with Joel's cry, she couldn't see how this could end any way but tragically.

Then something stirred on the steps. Until now no one noticed the entrance of a new arrival.

⚬⚬⚬

Her plan was ruined now. There were too many witnesses, and Lena Westfall was herself too pragmatic and practical to consider covering up one murder by committing two others, especially when one would be of a prominent lawyer.

When she had reached the top of the stairs and saw Charlie holding his .22 on her father, she had the presence of mind to tuck her pistol, a powerful nine millimeter semiautomatic, into the belt of her stylish Dior pantsuit, the jacket neatly obscuring the weapon. This was accomplished before anyone had even noted her arrival. She was uncertain what her next move would be, but she was going to be prepared.

"Lena! What are you doing here?" asked Fabroni.

"Who's this?" Charlie asked before she had a chance to answer her father's question.

"My daughter," said Fabroni.

Lena heard the fear in her father's voice—but couldn't he at least have had the presence of mind not to reveal her identity? Sullivan might kill her just to make a clean sweep of the family.

"All right . . . Miss Fabroni," said Charlie, "you move over there with the other two." She could tell from Sullivan's tone that her arrival had unsettled him. Maybe she could use that. But for the time being, she obeyed Sullivan's order and stood next to Irene.

"Charlie," Joel said. "Things are getting out of control. It would be foolish to go through with this now."

"It's now or never."

Lena had no reason not to believe Sullivan. His hand was shaking slightly as he gripped his pistol, but a man confused and afraid was often the most dangerous kind. She had to move soon if ever. Maybe she couldn't eliminate Charlie now—there would always be another time for that—but at least she could keep him from killing her father. And there might also be a chance of recovering Charlie's notebook. For even if she saved her father, that notebook could still effectively destroy him.

Slowly, while all eyes were focused on Sandy and Sullivan, Lena reached behind her and slipped the pistol away from her belt. It was then an easy matter—too easy, really—to make her next move. She grabbed Irene, not knowing why, or what good it would do, but the woman was close at hand and would give Lena some leverage because of her relationship with Joel. Hopefully Joel's distress at knowing his lover had a gun pointed at her head would be enough to convince Sullivan to give up.

Lena was a strong woman, five inches taller than Irene. If that wasn't enough, her weapon effectively discouraged any thought of escape.

"Irene!" Joel called upon hearing the woman's startled gasp.

"She's all right," Lena said, "—unless I have to use this weapon I'm holding to her head." Then, to Charlie, "Sorry to crash your little party, Sullivan. But it's my show now, and my first request is for you to drop that little peashooter you're holding." When Charlie hesitated, she added, "I mean what I say. You've spoiled my plans, and I'm pretty upset, at the moment, so don't toy with me."

"What plans?" Charlie asked, slowly lowering the gun.

"I was going to kill you, Mr. Sullivan, hopefully before you got to my father. I didn't expect there to be such a big reception committee here to greet me. I still think I might get away with it though—my word against theirs. But I could just content myself with getting my hands on that notebook of yours. How does that sound? Give me the notebook, and you and your son and his girlfriend all can leave with your lives."

"And if I don't?"

"Don't push me, Sullivan."

"You might have gotten away with killing me," said Charlie, "but there's no way you'll harm us all."

"You don't think I could make it look like the poor, bitter, demented ex-con went on a shooting spree? You underestimate me."

"Charlie, give her the notebook," urged Joel.

"I don't have it with me."

"I'm losing my patience," Lena snapped. Then, "Daddy!" she screamed as Sandy dove toward Charlie.

As Charlie fell backward under the sudden attack, he knocked over the lamp.

An instant later the small place went black.

ᏩᎥᎵᎪᎧ

Irene surprised herself by reacting quickly to the sudden darkness. She thrust her elbow backward into her captor's ribs, and while Lena was off-balance from the sudden blow, Irene wrenched herself from the woman's grasp. But Irene must have delivered more force than she had thought herself capable, for Lena dropped her gun—at least a sharp thud on the floor indicated that to be the case. However, so much was happening at once that Irene didn't want to take any risks. If Lena was still wielding that dangerous-looking weapon, she thought it best to get as far away from her as possible. With Charlie and Fabroni tussling by the flight of stairs leading to the third floor, the stairs that led down were clear.

But she had to find Joel first.

"Joel!"

That was a mistake. Lena quickly located her from the sound of her voice and caught Irene again. Did she have the gun? Irene struggled, praying she didn't. But the woman's hold was strong. After a few moments, Irene's eyes readjusted to the darkness, and she caught a glimmer of the weapon lying on the floor.

And to her astonishment, Joel was reaching for it!

Did he know what he was doing? But even if he did, what good would it do for him to have the gun? She was learning never to underestimate him, so instead of questioning his actions, she did what she could to help him. She kept talking.

"Joel, we're here . . . Lena has me. . . ."

But Lena, perhaps sensing Irene's motive, tried to work her hand over Irene's mouth. In her struggle, all Irene could manage to say was an occasional "Joel." She hoped that would be enough.

Then, as Joel's fingers wrapped around the weapon, another sound shattered the already chaotic scene.

A gunshot!

It couldn't have been Joel; he'd hardly touched Lena's gun, much less had a chance to fire it. But Irene had nearly forgotten about the two old men struggling together. A cry she couldn't immediately identify followed the gunshot.

Was this day going to end in tragedy, after all? How could she have hoped differently with these desperate people wielding guns and hatred with equal venom?

Oh, God, don't let it be! Irene prayed with silent fervor.

Forty-seven

*T*he blast of Charlie's gun dashed Joel's hopes of stopping this melee before anyone was hurt. He heard a sharp cry of pain from where the old men had been struggling. He wanted to believe it was Fabroni's voice, but even Joel could not be certain.

Joel's hand closed on the cold metal of Lena's pistol, and he jumped to his feet in the next instant.

"I want this to stop—now!" Joel fired the pistol in the air for emphasis.

But the first shot from Charlie's pistol had already shocked the group into stillness. Joel's shot impressed a different kind of silence into the group. He imagined they were all gaping with wide-eyed fear at the blind man wildly firing the pistol. But he was in greater control than they might guess.

"Irene, are you all right?" he asked, forcing calm into his voice.

"Yes."

"Charlie?" He asked with more trepidation.

"He shot me!" That was Fabroni. And Joel felt no guilt for his own relief at the man's words.

"Charlie, kick your gun to me," Joel ordered. When there was no sound of response, he said sharply, his voice shaking with tension and fear, "Charlie, you still can't be thinking of going through with this." Nothing.

Joel fired his gun again, this time not in the air but straight ahead. Several gasps followed. "I'm going to keep firing, Charlie, until I hear that gun." He squeezed the trigger of Lena's nine millimeter pistol. "I hope no one gets hurt, but—"

Charlie's gun scraped across the floor, stopping as it tapped against Joel's toe. Joel gently released the trigger then asked Irene to get the gun. But while she was doing that, something new assailed his senses. He'd had a hint of it before but had thought it was simply the odor of gun powder. It was stronger now and was accompanied by a sound like crumpling paper.

"Irene, where's the lantern?" he asked with new urgency.

"It fell over—" she paused a moment. "It's not here! It must have rolled down the stairs."

"We have to get out of here," Joel said.

∽⊙ⅢⅢ◎∾

As Irene looked about for the lantern, she, too, could now smell smoke. It was drifting up the stairwell. As she glanced down the stairs, flames greeted her. The lantern must have rolled down there when Charlie knocked it over. The closed area and the draft in the stairwell was acting like a fan for the growing fire. Irene paused only a moment before rejoining Joel.

"Charlie, is there another way out of here?" Joel was saying.

"The front stairs. They're in bad shape but that'd be the only way out."

"Okay, lead the way."

Lena helped her father, who appeared to be wounded in the thigh. Irene took up the rear as Charlie opened one of the doors that led from the landing to the second-floor apartment. Glancing back just before they hurried into the room, Irene saw the fire had fully engulfed the stairwell and flames were spreading quickly into the landing where they had just been.

The room they passed through was empty except for a couple pieces of broken-down furniture. Irene closed each door behind her in what was probably a futile attempt to slow the fire. The old timbers of the already-condemned house acted like a tinder box, inviting instant combustion. She thanked God a dozen times during their hasty evacuation that there was another exit.

There was one moment of mild panic as the group encountered the front door—locked with a deadbolt and boarded up. Firing Lena's pistol at the rotten wood surrounding the lock loosened it enough so that by putting their shoulders to it, the rotten wood of the doorjamb finally gave way. Another shove and the outer plywood barrier also broke free.

Approaching sirens greeted them as they exited into the fresh night air. But these heralded police cars, two of them, not fire trucks. The vehicles screeched to a stop and four officers jumped out.

"Hank, call the fire department," one of the officers said before facing the group.

Fabroni accosted the man before he could take another breath. "I've been shot!" He wagged a finger in the general direction of Charlie, but exactly who he meant wasn't easily discernible since Joel and Irene were standing close by. "That man did it. I want him arrested!"

"We had a report of gunfire," said the officer.

Joel nudged Irene and asked her to take him to the officer. "The shooting was accidental," Joel said. "They were scuffling and the weapon went off."

"He was holding us hostage," Lena put in.

"You'll all get your two cents in soon enough," said the officer. Then he turned his attention to Fabroni. "How serious are you injured?"

"I don't know. I might be bleeding to death."

Another officer announced that he had called an ambulance. He also produced a blanket which he laid on the sidewalk, and he helped Fabroni to lie down.

The first policeman said, "All right, who's who here? Gimme your names." He pulled out a notebook and began writing as everyone identified themselves. He was also assured there was no one left in the burning house.

Fabroni had to add, "Sullivan is an ex-con—on parole, and he had a firearm in his possession."

"That true?"

Charlie held up his arms as another officer searched him. Joel had already turned over the two weapons.

As each participant gave a report of the events of the evening, two fire trucks arrived on the scene. The house was pretty far gone by then, and the main emphasis of the fire fighters was to save the neighboring buildings. Irene observed the flames licking up through the house with a heaviness, almost as if this had been her home, where her memories had been stored. Joel had turned his face, too, toward the burning building. Irene wondered if he was thinking about the fleeting quality of memories. He had barely been able to grasp a part of the life that had been denied him, when even that had suddenly gone . . . *up in smoke.*

It hadn't been a great life, yet Irene knew what it was like to listen to her parents talk of things that happened when she was a child and even before she had been born. She cherished those stories because they were part of her parents, who they were. It was her history. Joel had so little of his father, Charlie. It had meant so much to be in the house where his mother and father once lived.

"I feel a little sick inside knowing it's gone," Joel said, "but it was bound to crumble eventually." He inclined his head toward where Charlie was having an intense discussion with the police officer. "I've got to make sure I don't lose him, too."

"What will you do?"

"I think he needs a good lawyer."

"Will some money help?"

"What. . . ?"

She gently thumped the briefcase she had been holding since escaping the house. "I nearly tripped over it when I was looking for the lantern," she explained. "Everyone else seems to have forgotten about it."

"They won't for long. I think you ought to find a nice safe place for it."

Irene strolled casually to her car parked close by, took her keys from her pocket, opened the car, deposited the briefcase into the backseat, and relocked it. She would sort out moral issues later. For now, it seemed that Charlie clearly deserved some compensation from Fabroni. If they were plagued by conscience later, they could just give Fabroni the stupid notebook. Nothing would clear Charlie's name for the murder of the cop thirty-seven years ago, not even the incriminating notebook. Better to get rid of it before it caused any further tragedy.

When Irene returned to Joel's side, he had joined Charlie in the discussion with the policeman.

"A detective is on his way here now," said the officer. "But, Sullivan, from all I've heard, it appears as if we're gonna have to take you into custody. You, Mr. Costain, ought to round up a good lawyer for your father."

"I'm looking at the best lawyer I could get," said Charlie.

"I'm not a criminal attorney, Charlie," said Joel.

"You're the only lawyer I'll trust."

Joel shook his head. "But—"

Fabroni broke in, "It doesn't matter who you have for a lawyer." He yelled as he was being carried on a stretcher to the ambulance, "I'm going to have your hide for this! I was going to show you some mercy, but look how you repay me!"

Fabroni quieted only after he was loaded into the vehicle and it drove away.

When the officer who was talking to Charlie went to take care of other business, Joel said quietly to Charlie, "I don't think we have to worry about Fabroni's threats—not as long as we have that notebook."

Charlie shook his head then nodded toward the burning building. "It's in there—in the house."

"I thought you said—"

"I was bluffing."

"I think that's for the best," said Irene. "I don't know if any of us would be safe with it around."

"Yeah," said Charlie, "but how are we going to convince Fabroni that it no longer exists?"

"I can deal with Fabroni," said Joel confidently. "And if you do decide to use me as your attorney, Charlie, one thing I'll guarantee is that you're not going to spend another minute in jail."

Joel was good for his promise. Charlie did not spend that night, nor any other in jail. Nor did he spend another night in any of the fleabag hotels he had been frequenting. Charlie Sullivan spent his last days in more comfort than he had ever known in his life.

Forty-eight

Millie Lorenzo was in her element with a houseful of holiday guests. She'd had Ray buy the biggest Christmas tree he could find, and it dominated the living room where everyone was now starting to gather for gift opening. Irene paused at the door of the living room to take in the scene. All of Connie's family was there, and their brother from Los Angeles had come up with his family. But there were new additions also—Walt and Adrianne Costain were there, and so was Charlie.

Tears welled in Irene's eyes as she watched Charlie, seated on the sofa between Mark and Adam, looking at their baseball cards. He had lost more weight in the last month-and-a-half since the night of the fire in Haight-Ashbury, and he looked rather withered and pale. He didn't have much time left and probably should have already been admitted to a hospital, but he had wanted to spend one Christmas with his family. She knew he was in constant pain, but one could hardly tell from the grin on his face as he talked to the boys. Irene tried not to think of the thirty-seven holidays he'd spent in a bleak prison. She just tried to focus on the joy of this particular one—the one he'd remember most.

By now he was great friends with his grandsons, having spent as much of the last weeks as possible with them. Thanks to Joel he had lived every minute of that a free man. He'd had to answer to parole violations but was given six months' probation and placed in Joel's custody. No other charges were pressed against Charlie. Joel had convinced Fabroni that was one can of worms he might greatly regret opening. Irene wasn't entirely certain how he had done it without the notebook—but he had been successful. It did seem unfair that, for all Fabroni's crimes, he was still a free man. But nothing could be proven against him.

Regardless, on this delightful Christmas day, Irene felt no compulsion for vengeance. It hadn't worked when Charlie tried it, and there were too many good things ahead for all of them to risk spoiling it with bitterness.

"I love this house!" came Joel's voice; Irene hadn't even heard him approach. "It was made for a blind man with all its rich fragrances. Pine, of course, yeast and spaghetti sauce and anise—I never thought I could enjoy anise so much, not only smelling it but tasting it in your mother's cookies."

"Yes . . . that, to me, is almost as much a part of Christmas as pine."

"Guess who came by a couple minutes ago?"

"I haven't a clue."

"Jim Kincaid."

"Oh! You should have invited him in."

"He was on his way to his in-laws' for the day. But he did deliver a little Christmas gift for us." '

"He shouldn't have. I didn't even think to get him something."

"You couldn't have topped his gift."

Joel held up a white box, the type a wallet might come in. Irene took it and lifted the lid. Inside was a small book, or what was left of a book. It was quite charred but still somewhat intact. In fact, as Irene carefully fingered it, lifting the blackened cover, she saw a few pages were still there.

"Joel, it's not—?"

He nodded. "It was recovered from the ruins of the house. Apparently it was hidden in some loose bricks of a fireplace, protected from the heaviest effects of the fire. Jim tells me some pages are still legible."

"Yes, I believe he's right. Do you think it can still be used against Fabroni?" Irene handed back the box, which Joel slipped into the pocket of his brown tweed coat.

"We'll never know," he said. "I'm going to send it to him. After all, he did pay a hundred thousand dollars for it. Besides, Mr. Alessandro Fabroni is going to have a lot more to worry about in the days to come than this notebook."

"Really?"

"Jim had another, even better, Christmas gift for us. Detective Reiley couldn't reach me so he called Jim this morning. It seems they arrested a suspect in Greg's murder—a man who has turned out to be quite talkative. Since he's going down, he intends on taking everyone else with him. His name is Lenny Wilcox, and he can produce some pretty solid proof that Fabroni hired him to follow Greg."

"So, the police can arrest him for the murder?"

"I doubt that, but if we're lucky, he could be charged with accessory after the fact. But even his part in covering up the crime and impeding a police investigation will keep him in legal hot water for some time. At least he lost this past election, and I doubt he'll ever try a bid for public office again."

"Charlie will be glad to hear that."

"I don't know. . . ." Irene glanced up at Joel and saw a twinkle in his eyes she hadn't noticed before. "I haven't had a chance to tell you," he went on, "but Charlie and I had a great conversation this morning before we came here. That's why I wasn't home when the police tried to call. We went to the cemetery where my birth mother is buried."

"Oh, Joel . . ." Irene said with sympathy.

"No, it was really a marvelous experience. Charlie told me some more things about her, and I'm convinced she was a Christian. Charlie said she was always trying to get him to go to church with her. But he was too macho for 'sissy' religion, as he called it back then. Now he can see how wrong he was, but still thinks he's too far gone for God to want him."

"I know the feeling," Irene said.

"Later, he mentioned something about how he'd soon be with his Betsy. Then he stumbled over his words and his tone went hollow, stricken when he realized that might not be the case. I didn't say a word, Irene—I didn't have to. Everything began clicking in his mind—I could almost hear the gears working."

"Joel, did he. . . ?"

"Not quite, but I know he will before he dies. His heart is open toward spiritual things and tender toward God."

"And I thought that joy I saw on his face was just because it's Christmas."

"For Charlie, it truly is Christmas—Christ's advent in his heart and life."

"What a present!" Irene said, and before she realized it she had placed her arm around Joel and hugged him close.

Nothing felt more natural. But in the last several weeks, Charlie wasn't the only one finding his way in life. Irene, too, was gaining an inner peace, with herself and with the past. The fears that had held her in bondage for so long were being replaced with trust. As she became more and more confident in God's abiding presence and in the fact that He had *always* been there, she was learning to step out with assurance . . . with faith. She thought about the Christmas gift she had under the tree for Joel. She knew everyone was going to think it a peculiar gift for a blind man, but Joel would understand and be moved by it. Irene had completed her first painting—a portrait of Joel from a photograph she had taken of him about a month ago when they had gone hiking through the woods in Santa Cruz. It was impressionistic in style, set against a background of redwoods. She thought the most striking feature of the painting was Joel's eyes in which there was a faint reflection of the majestic trees. It was her way of expressing that Joel's vision was more acute, more profound than many who could actually see such trees.

Irene glanced at him now—his face was turned in Charlie's direction and he was smiling. She had no doubts at all about her future. God had cleared the dark images in the mirror of her life, and through the crystal-clear glass, He had let her see Joel. A thrill coursed through her as she considered the Scripture in Corinthians: "For now we see through a glass, darkly, but then face to face." God, in His goodness, had allowed Irene to have a glimpse of His truth and love now, without having to wait for Eternity. She truly understood what that Scripture meant to Joel.

"I can't remember being happier," Irene murmured.

He inclined his head toward her and grinned. Then he took her hand. "Come with me a minute."

He led the way, his cane in one hand, Irene in his other hand and slightly behind, giving occasional directions. They entered the kitchen and headed toward the back door.

"Where are you two going?" asked Millie. "I'm having a hard enough time getting everyone into the living room. The kids are chomping at the bit to open their presents."

"I'm . . . ah . . . just going to show Joel the camellias," said Irene.

"The camellias? Can't that wait? The kids—" Millie stopped suddenly, a glint appearing in her canny eyes. "The camellias, you say. . . ? Well . . . don't take too long." She gave Irene a wink.

"Just a few minutes," said Joel, his hand on the doorknob.

Outside, the afternoon air was crisp but not cold enough for coats. Irene was comfortable in the bulky green sweater she was wearing with a black and white checkered wool skirt.

"So, are you interested in seeing Daddy's early blooming camellias?" Irene asked.

"Even if I could see, I wouldn't be interested right now," he said. "I have something else on my mind."

"Oh. . . ?"

"How long have we known each other, Irene?"

"Two and a half months. But it seems as if it's been longer. . . ."

"Still, you've been wise in insisting we take our time to get to know each other. There's been so much going on, so much transition. I've never held your reticence against you."

"I know. I've appreciated your patience."

"You may want to wait even longer when I tell you what my plans are for the future. You see, working on Charlie's defense has convinced me of where I belong in the legal profession. I don't know if I'll be a great criminal defense attorney, but that's what I have to do. I plan to open my own practice as soon as I can work out all the details."

"That's wonderful, Joel! And you will be great!"

"I can believe it with someone like you to support me."

"That's what I want . . ." she murmured so softly she wondered if he heard.

He put his hand into his pocket and withdrew an even smaller box than the one holding the notebook. Irene's heart gave a leap, or was it more a flutter of her old fear? The velvet box could hold only one thing.

"This is a Christmas gift I wanted to give you in private. It doesn't have to be a big deal if you don't want it to be." He opened the lid. The ring inside had a beautiful amethyst stone surrounded by small diamonds. When Irene gasped, Joel said, "You once said your favorite color was purple."

She nodded. She realized he couldn't see the movement of her head, but the lump in her throat made it impossible for her to do more. Joel smiled as if he sensed the reason for her silence.

"It's not an engagement ring," he said. "But perhaps it can be an engaged-to-be-engaged ring."

"You mean we're going steady?" Levity was the only way she could manage speech at all. She knew she'd cry if she really expressed what was welling up inside her.

"Gee whiz . . . I guess so," he countered lightly. Then he added more earnestly, "I'll wait as long as you want, Irene. If only I know you want—"

She put her fingers to his lips. "You don't have to say more, Joel. You must have noticed I've grown up lately, letting go of so much junk that was holding me down."

"I know. That's what gave me the boldness to go this far."

She took the ring from the box. "Would you. . . ?"

"With pleasure!"

Irene placed the ring between his fingers, and he had no problem finding the hand she held out to him. She could not restrain her tears as he slipped it on her right ring finger.

"It's beautiful!" she said. "Beautiful enough to be an *engagement* ring."

There were tears in his eyes also as he pulled her to him in his tender, loving arms. "Not as beautiful as you!" he replied in a husky, emotional voice. "I know now what it's like to touch an unseen angel."

Irene glanced at the ring, now sparkling in the sunlight, as he held her. Yes, it truly did belong there, as she knew she belonged at Joel's side.

Other Books by Judith Pella

LONE STAR LEGACY

Frontier Lady
Stoner's Crossing
Warrior's Song

THE RUSSIANS

The Crown and the Crucible*
A House Divided*
Travail and Triumph*
Heirs of the Motherland
Dawning of Deliverance
White Nights, Red Morning

THE STONEWYCKE TRILOGY*

The Heather Hills of Stonewycke
Flight from Stonewycke
Lady of Stonewycke

THE STONEWYCKE LEGACY*

Stranger at Stonewycke
Shadows over Stonewycke
Treasure of Stonewycke

THE HIGHLAND COLLECTION*

Jamie MacLeod: Highland Lass
Robbie Taggart: Highland Sailor

THE JOURNALS OF CORRIE BELLE HOLLISTER

My Father's World*
Daughter of Grace*
On the Trail of the Truth†
A Place in the Sun†
Into the Long Dark Night†
Land of the Brave and the Free†

*with Michael Phillips   †by Michael Phillips